THE GIRL WHO COULDN'T GET OUT

The Salazar Redwood Forest Thrillers
Book 2

LAUREN STREET

STERLING & STONE

ONE

Dina
_____

FIVE YEARS AGO...

THE EXCITEMENT of getting on the red-eye bus from Seattle, Washington to Rush, California — even after her best friend Tiff had pulled out at the last second — had faded around the four-hour mark. Now, all Dina could think about was the gnawing pit in her stomach, identifiable as hunger because of how loudly it growled, and how uncomfortable the bus seats were. She'd tried to catch some sleep during the longest stretches of highway between the more frequent stops just outside Seattle, but it was patchy sleep at best, and she just couldn't get comfortable.

Thinking of Tiff and home, Dina pulled her cell phone from her mostly full backpack for the first time since boarding the bus and turned it on.

She'd turned off her phone to save its battery life. Clearly, that had been a huge mistake.

The second she powered it on again, the home screen flashed with one incoming notification after another, over and over and over again.

The first message was from Tiff with a timestamp of just after Dina had boarded the bus last night: *I'm so sorry, Dina. I feel awful about not being able to come with you. And I wouldn't be a good friend if I didn't say this. I don't think you should go on your own. Call me?*

A few minutes later: *You can't go alone. How will you know where to go? Or what if something happens? Two heads are always better than one, right? Mine won't be there, and I'm not saying you can't do it on your own, but I'm worried.*

Then: *Okay, I'm kind of freaking out. Did you just leave because you're pissed at me? Call me back.*

Tiff wasn't the only one blowing up her phone. Her mother's texts made the gnawing in her stomach worse.

- *I know Tiff isn't going with you. This is a bad idea.*
- *You think you know what you're doing, but you're young and the rest of the world is so much bigger than you. Don't start making the same mistakes I did.*
- *I know I'm not the best mother in the world, honey. I should have done so many things differently. I should have worked harder on being better for you and your sister. I'm doing the best I can. Please don't shut me out like rhis. No reason 2 keep punishng me. This won't play out th way u want I promise I've lived so much longer than you and Ia know more bout the world than u ever possibly could.*
- *Fine then if this is how u want 2 handle it go ahead. I'm don tryng 2 shelter u from the worstof liufe. Go by urself 2 a city u don't know, surrounded by ntgbu strangers 2 dig ursef a deepr hole with DRUGS and*

watch when I'm nt there 2 help pull u out. U want 2 be aadult? Frm now on, your on ur own.

THERE WERE MORE, but that was the last comprehensible one.

It was amazing how quickly her mom's "concern" spiraled into total abandonment, and Dina had no doubt that the angrier the text, the less sober she'd been. She checked her missed calls and saw three voicemails. One was six minutes and twenty-four seconds long. Dina didn't need to listen to know they'd be drunken rambling.

It was better to keep her gaze forward, keep moving one step after the other, and not let her mom's issues weigh her down.

That was, after all, one of the main reasons she'd decided to leave last night, even without Tiff. She'd had to — for her own sanity and survival.

Angela had stopped reaching out to her daughter at just after one o'clock in the morning, which counted as an early night for her.

Dina didn't want anything to do with her mom right now. The least she could do, though, was respond with an update. One brief message to reassure her mom — and maybe herself — that she could do this.

EVERYTHING'S FINE, *mom. I'm safe. Still on the bus, but we're only a few hours out from Rush. I won't have any problem meeting good people out here, and I know how to take care of myself. I can do this. I don't want you to keep worrying about me. Just take care of yourself. I love you.*

· · ·

3

HER THUMB HOVERED over the send button for a few seconds too long, and Dina almost deleted the whole thing. But then she forced herself to send it anyway. If nothing else, it would show her mom that she was still alive and still capable of communication, even if she had no intention of calling back today, or tomorrow, or maybe even the next few days. Not until she'd gotten settled in Rush with a new trimming job and had racked up enough positive experiences to support her case for independence.

A case she shouldn't have even had to make in the first place, but it was what it was.

After a few deep, steady breaths to help calm herself, Dina closed her eyes as she leaned back against the frayed, poorly padded seat cushion and promised herself that she wouldn't let her mom get to her while she was out here. If she focused more on worrying about Angela than she did on paying attention to her work, even trimming, she wouldn't make as much money as the full potential this kind of job offered.

Assuming what Tiff had told her about trimming work was true, anyway.

She hoped so. She needed the money to kickstart her college career. She couldn't rely on her mother for help. With anything.

When she opened her eyes again, she felt a little better. As she looked up across the aisle, she caught the gaze of another young woman sitting on the other side of the bus, two rows up. This girl was smiling right at Dina, shamelessly, as if she didn't know that staring from across the bus, even one they'd both slept in overnight, wasn't normally considered polite.

The other girl's smile was infectious, though — broad and gleaming, surrounded by dimples and a splatter of freckles, her heart-shaped face framed by an unruly and yet somehow still stylish halo of untamed honey-blonde curls that fell down below her shoulders.

Dina decided.

After a quick glance up the aisle at the driver, whom she hadn't seen pay attention to anyone or anything else but the road this whole time, Dina left her backpack and her carry-on suitcase on her seat, shimmied around them, then she darted across the aisle to take the empty seat directly behind the new friend she hoped to meet.

"Hey," the girl said, twisting around in her seat to peer back at Dina, both hands gripping the outside of the seat cushion. All but two of her ten fingers were covered in multiple rings, and Dina thought she caught a glimpse of some kind of tattoo in vibrant pinks and purples on the underside of the girl's wrist. "This is one long-ass bus ride, huh?"

Dina's smile widened. "Tell me about it. You've been here overnight too, right?"

"Yep. Straight out of Portland. But I'm pretty sure you were already here when I hopped on."

"I got on in Seattle."

"Nice." The girl looked Dina up and down, as much as was possible with an entire seat between them, then cocked her head. "First time on a red eye?"

Dina rolled her eyes and huffed out a laugh. "Am I that obvious?"

"Just a little. Mostly judging by the fact that you look like shit right now, so I'm guessing you didn't get any sleep. I didn't either, my first time. You get used to it after a while."

"You do this kinda thing all the time?" Dina asked.

"Overnights on buses?" The other girl ran her fingers

through her tangled mane and gave up halfway through when her fingers snagged. The motion was as natural as if she'd run her fingers all the way through, so apparently that was as far as she ever got. "I mean, it's not like I have a thing for buses specifically. But yeah, I've made this route at least a dozen times by now. From Portland to Rush, anyway."

"Rush, California?" Dina pointed toward the front of the bus, which didn't really translate to the fact that she was referring to the highway sign for Rush she'd seen not too long ago.

The other girl didn't have any trouble catching on. "The one and only. I've tried Grass Valley and Nevada City a few times. Went to Truckee once, but it got way too cold there. Rush is my favorite. It just felt like it fit, you know?"

"I don't know, actually." Dina shrugged. "This is pretty much my first time out of Seattle."

"For real?" With a widening grin, the other girl climbed up onto her knees so she wasn't twisting so far for their conversation. "That's so rad, dude! What are you going to Rush for?"

Dina took a deep breath, didn't quite know how to start, then finally blurted, "Trim season, actually. I heard it was pretty great in Rush, so I figured I'd come check it out. You know, for the money and everything. Not for, like, anything else…"

For a moment, the other girl stared at her without a word, her grin unchanging and her wide blue-green eyes occasionally glinting in the flashes of early-morning sunlight streaming through the thick pine trees lining both sides of the highway. Then she nodded like everything was right with the world. "You couldn't have picked a better town for the job. Trust me, I know almost all of them."

6

"You going to Rush to trim too?" Dina asked.

The other girl barked out a laugh and rose on her knees, spreading her arms as she looked herself up and down. "You mean you couldn't tell my profession just by looking at me?"

"Hey, I'm not trying to judge, here," Dina replied. "And honestly, I wouldn't know how to tell, anyway."

"Don't worry. After this season's over, you'll know exactly what to look for. Trust me." Then the girl she sat back on her heels again and extended her many-ringed hand toward Dina. "Call me Shell."

Dina hadn't seen anyone make such an awkward handshake around a bus seat look so completely normal and natural, not to mention friendly. Then again, this was the first time she was shaking hands with a stranger on a bus. Shell's fingers were surprisingly cool.

"I'm Dina."

"Nice to meet you, Dina. And welcome to the life. Best one available, if you ask me."

"How long have you been doing this?"

Shell tilted her head and squinted across the bus aisle. "Five years. Took me some bouncing around to figure out that Rush was the best spot if you wanna make some real money doing this thing. Three years ago, I met my boyfriend. He's from there, a townie through and through. I go to Rush to build up my cash stacks, and spend time with him all fall and through the winter. The rest of the year, I use the money I made to travel. I get to do whatever I want, whenever I want. There's always a spot waiting for me when I get back."

"Sounds like a lot of fun..." Dina said it more like a question, and Shell stopped laughing.

"I mean, it's definitely not for everybody. I'm guessing you're doing this just to try it out. Get a feel for what it's like to work with the plants, spend your time outside, maybe even puff a little."

Dina shook her head. "I don't smoke. Anything."

"Hey, no judgement here." Shell shrugged. "I mean, obviously, you're not looking for a full-time salaried position with benefits and everything if you're going to Rush for trim season. But you might change your mind about it. Or if not, at least you're walking away at the end of the season with a whole stack of cash you don't have to pay any taxes on. No paper trail, you know?"

"Huh." Dina tilted her head. "Never thought of it that way."

Shell wiggled her eyebrows. "There's a lot you don't think about your first time around."

"Hey, uh … I'm not trying to make this weird, but since we're going to the same place, would you mind just kinda showing me the ropes? Once we get there."

"You mean, like, take you under my wing?" Shell flapped her elbow like a wing, still wearing that goofy and yet somehow unfailingly brilliant grin. "Make you my padawan?"

"Your *what*?"

The other girl laughed. "Never mind. Point is, don't worry. I got you, Dina. Do you already have a farm in mind?"

"A farm?" Great. Now Dina just sounded like a broken record repeating everything as a question.

"As in pot farm? Come on, Dina. You do realize you're coming out to California to trim *marijuana plants*, right? And not, like, hedges or beards or some shit."

Dina couldn't help but laugh at that and shook her head. "No, I know what I'm going to trim. I just didn't know it would be on a farm. Like, they're technically called farms, is that it?"

"Oh boy. You really *are* brand-new to this, aren't you? This is gonna be fun!"

Shell waved Dina forward, the rows of beaded bracelets and thin silver bangles clanking and jingling on her wrist. "Come on up here, my young apprentice. Might as well sit next to me now that we're officially friends."

Dina couldn't decide if she wanted to act serious about this or keep laughing like Shell. She pointed across the aisle to her old seat. "Let me just grab my stuff."

"Nah, leave it there, it's fine." Shell waved it all off again. "If anyone tries to take your shit, what are they gonna do? Jump out of a moving bus?"

With another shrug, Dina did as she was told. Shell had already scooted over to the window, holding her enormous duffel bag, which looked like it was made out of an old rug, upright between her knees. She leaned back against the corner of the window in her seat so she could face Dina as much as possible. "So. Tell me about yourself."

They chatted, never letting the conversation dive much deeper than the surface. Mostly that was Dina's doing. Shell seemed like an open book, but Dina didn't want to talk about the deep shit.

At least, not right now.

The conversation turned to the various farms in Rush and their owners, what the work as a trimmer entailed, where all the best spots were for camping or good coffee or stocking up on cheap toiletries when they inevitably ran out.

"It's not, like, the best work in the world," Shell explained. "I mean, yeah, we get to be outside, we can play music, talk if we want — if we can talk and pay attention to details at the same time. Lunch is free on days we're actually working, which is super nice. And most of the time, there's plenty of shade. If we're not taking everything into the trees, Rip usually sets up a few giant outdoor event tents so we're not baking in the sun all day, you know?"

"Rip?" Dina asked.

"Oh, yeah." Shell tossed her hair over one shoulder, but it immediately flopped forward again the second she turned her head. "Rip's the best guy to work for, trust me. He can be a real hard-ass sometimes, which, you know, makes sense. It's his livelihood after all, and he's a stickler for details, which is also good, because you wanna be on your game. But he also pays the best. Like, by a lot. I honestly had no idea why anyone was trimming on any other farm until, you know, I met the guy and realized how serious he was about his business and who he hires. But he's definitely the best."

"I don't have to, like, have an interview or anything, do I?" Dina asked, mostly serious. That hadn't seemed like a requirement for something like this, and she was completely unprepared for anything that remotely resembled the traditional definition of professional.

Shell barked out a loud, shrill laugh that ended with a startling snort and didn't for a second look embarrassed. "No way, dude! There's no interview for this. Not the kind you're thinking of anyway. You just have to tell him a little about yourself. See if you're a good fit with the farm and everyone else, then you're in. Don't worry, I'll put in a good word for you the second we get there. You won't have any problem, though. I can already tell."

"Okay, cool." Dina nodded slowly, mulling over the surprising intricacies of trying to enter this brand-new world she knew less than nothing about. "Thanks."

"Wait…" With a crooked smirk, Shell looked at Dina from the corner of her eye, then flashed a sidelong glance across the bus aisle toward Dina's backpack and wheeled carry-on. "Don't tell me you packed, like, an actual *business* suit or some shit for this."

With wide eyes, Dina gaped at her new friend. Then both girls burst out laughing as the bus slowed and pulled onto the exit ramp for the town of Rush, California.

Who Guards C—

turn on. Don't let me see you like this. At least let me turn off some of the—

With a soft groan, Dhiraj opened her face mask gingerly, both with hers. For her fingers at the sleeve, she shoved a hand behind onto the examination the arm of Keith Collision.

TWO

Sam
_____

Sam Salazar thoroughly enjoyed her sleep when she could get it. It had been a long time since she'd slept through the night without some kind of nightmare, though in the last few months they'd come a little less often. Not by much, but enough to make a difference. That was enough for Sam.

Except this morning, her newfound ability to sleep was cut short by some other asshole in Birdsong Park screaming his head off for no reason at all.

That asshole sounded a lot like the trailer park's owner and, by default, her friend. So Sam grabbed the pillow beside her with a groan and pressed it over her head to drown out the noise.

Syc Fox, on the other hand, had different plans.

She couldn't make out the words, but his incessant shouting was enough to convey all the necessary emotion. Whatever his deal was, the guy was already having one hell of a morning.

Just as Syc's angry shouts died down and she felt herself drifting back off into the blissful nothingness of unconscious slumber, a new sound ripped her right back out of it again.

Almost like squealing tires, but not quite.

Almost like some creature begging for something.

But Sam didn't have any pets.

That was technically true, but it didn't change the fact that Syc's dog, aptly named Dog, was in her trailer this morning, right where he'd settled down for the night. Or that whining was coming from him.

With another groan, Sam rolled away from the rear window of the trailer where the twin-sized bed had been squeezed into place and flopped one arm over the other side of the mattress as she tried to open her eyes.

"Are you serious right now?" When her vision cleared, she found Dog sitting back on his haunches two feet from the bed. "You can't just wait, like, another hour? Maybe an hour and a half?"

Dog's only reply was to whine again, this one more desperate sounding than the last. The next thing she knew, Sam's hand was being unceremoniously slobbered on as Dog lapped at her palm. Even when she pulled away, he didn't give up his unwanted kisses. Then he whined again, as he took a surprisingly gentle swipe at the side of her mattress with a massive paw.

"All right, all right," Sam grumbled. "Just give me a second."

She fumbled with the sheets, didn't quite manage to untangle herself from them the first time, then hopped around in a groggy state of half consciousness before she found her hoodie on one side of the tiny space that counted as the trailer's bedroom and her sneakers all the way on the other side next to the door. It didn't help that Dog, in his over-excited canine wisdom, kept inserting himself between her legs and directly underfoot. She almost stepped on him several times, then almost ate it in her own trailer just to avoid falling all over him before she reached the door.

"Okay, yeah. I get it. We're going," she told him and tugged on the trailer's door three times before remembering she'd actually bothered to lock it last night.

A new habit for Sam. Recent events had convinced her that safety and security were now, in fact, real issues for her in Birdsong Park, and she didn't have anything to lose by using whatever locks came with her new home.

Except potentially a decent smell in the trailer, if she took longer to open the damn door than Dog's bladder could handle.

When she finally did, Dog went rushing out ahead of her with a yelp, skidding across the browning grass on which most of the trailers at Birdsong Park were parked. Before Sam had even fully stepped outside, Dog had disappeared to take care of business, and Sam found herself in the unique position of having a front-row seat to someone else's business.

Syc's, to be more specific.

While Sam shuffled slowly away from her trailer, pulling the sides of her hoodie closer around herself and folding her arms against the chill, Syc stormed across the small but plentifully open "yard" between his trailer and hers. The man's face had already contorted into a scowl of utter disgust, and in his excitement, he seemed to have developed something of a limp. That didn't stop him from hobbling her way, and it certainly didn't slow him down any.

Sam gazed around the park, taking in the familiar sights of the few trailers and campers scattered across the open wilderness, most of them rundown and empty. She didn't see anything out of the ordinary here other than Syc stomping toward her like he'd just caught *her* dog soiling his front lawn off-leash. Except Dog was *his*, so that didn't even make sense.

Something rustled against her sneaker with her next step, and she looked down to see a bouquet of a dozen pink roses lying there in the grass.

Frowning, she picked them up, searched them for a card or some sign of where they'd come from, but found none.

Then Syc reached her, and she ran out of time to investigate the bouquet. Despite having been so unceremoniously ripped from sleep — and really, any form of waking up was unceremonious these days — Sam attempted to put her best foot forward. Which also meant she attempted a smile at the park owner and tilted the bouquet toward him. "You didn't happen to drop a bundle of pink roses in front of my trailer by accident, did you?"

Syc snorted, barely sparing a second glance at the flowers. "The hell would I do with a bouquet?"

Sam shrugged. "Just thought I'd ask. Everything okay this morning?"

"The hell it is." Syc thrust a hand toward her and shook a thin stack of papers in her direction. "That little twat thinks he can come in here and threaten me? *Me*. He's grown way too big for his pull-ups, Sam, I tell you what."

"Who?"

"Fuckin' Mr. Mayor," Syc spat and shook the papers at her one more time.

Not needing another prompt, Sam stuck the roses in the crook of one arm, then accepted the mystery papers from Syc to take a look for herself. "Little Pete brought you these? All the way out here at … hell, what time is it, anyway?"

"Time to kick that spoiled son of a bitch's ass," Syc fumed. "Like he owns the whole goddamn town."

"Well, his dad does own most of it," Sam mused.

He snorted and turned to stand beside her, folding his arms as he searched the open space of the park. "Like I give a shit about any of all that. And no, Prince Pete Wilder didn't come down here himself. Couldn't pay that man-child to dirty his fancy shoes in a place like Birdsong Park. He sent over a damn messenger boy to do his dirty work for him, 'cause he can't grow the balls to look me in the eye."

"Sounds about right," Sam murmured, still trying to blink the rest of the sleep out of her eyes.

"The little shit just served me this morning. Says he's gonna shut down the park for illegal zoning if I don't fix everything on that list right there. It's total bullshit."

She didn't have to read anything to instantly feel guilty for what the man was forced to deal with now. As far as she could tell, Syc had spent his entire existence here in Birdsong Park, sticking to his own business and staying well away from everyone else's. Now he was being served with Little Pete's fuck-you because of Sam's involvement in Rush's small-town politics.

Because she just couldn't help herself.

If she hadn't gone with her gut so often instead of using her head the way she'd been trained, she never would have pulled so much focus toward herself. More importantly, she never would have pulled Syc into the spotlight simply by association.

This ridiculous show of so-called power on Little Pete's part was an attempt by Rush's newest mayor to get revenge on the outsider who had stuck her nose in so many places it didn't belong.

Nothing she had discovered before his mayoral appointment had made a difference anyway.

Beth was gone now, no matter how hard Sam had tried to help the woman before the end. And Little Pete had gotten away with everything, not even a wrist-slap. Worse than that, he'd been handed the mayorship for his troubles.

She'd tried not to dwell on it since, which was fairly easy to do provided his name didn't come up in early-morning conversation or she didn't see his smug, self-satisfied smile leering at her from a table in the Back Bar. Today just didn't happen to be one of those days.

"He won't get away with this," she murmured, forcing herself to focus harder on the words in front of her.

"Yeah, well..." Syc sniffed and sucked on his lower lip as he waited for her to read over the paperwork.

When she finally got her brain working, Sam made quick work of reading the so-called zoning infractions. All the paperwork looked undeniably official, which almost made her think things were really about to change around Birdsong Park, and not for the better. But then she flipped to the very back page, scanned the information, and clicked her tongue. "Well, no one's ever said your bullshit meter's broken, huh?"

"Meaning what?" Syc growled.

She tilted the last page his way and flicked it with a finger, which somehow was still possible even with a bouquet in the crook of her arm. "Everything in this is definitely official, for the most part. But it doesn't have a signature."

"And?"

"And whoever served these to you this morning is either a complete idiot or doesn't take their job seriously. The order of intent, or whatever the official name is, isn't valid without the signature of the person serving you. So this could be an extra bit of toilet paper, for all the good it does. You want me to take care of it?"

Syc blinked at her, his eyes slowly widening, then snatched the papers out of her hands. "Nah, I've got it handled."

He marched toward the firepit almost exactly halfway between Sam's new trailer and his own and produced a lighter from one pocket, flicked the striker for a nice healthy flame, then held it against the official but useless legal documents to set them ablaze. The papers caught instantly, and he chucked them into the firepit with a grunt before returning the lighter to his pocket. Staring at the flaming paper quickly curling into black crispy strips and delicate white ash, Syc reached down for the can of lighter fluid he kept just beyond the outer border of the pit and sprayed a good-sized stream of it onto the flames.

The small fire roared to life, blasting extra heat across the small yard between their trailers. Sam blinked and leaned back a little.

Adding lighter fluid to three pieces of burning paper was probably going a little overboard, but she didn't comment on it. Syc could do whatever the hell he wanted with legal documents, valid or not.

After giving him a bit more space to gaze into the flames and let his emotions burn right along with the documents, Sam joined him. They stood there together in silence as every last bit of legal document burnt to a crisp and shriveled away.

"I'll be damned if I ever let this park go down, Sam," he grumbled. "The folks calling Birdsong Park their home aren't gonna lose that home. Not on my watch. Little Pete can just fuck right off."

Sam let out a worn, tired-sounding chuckle. "That's the spirit."

His only response was another non-committal grunt, and when the conversation didn't pick up from there, Sam figured she might as well get her day started. She was up already, awake and halfway dressed — though flannel pajama pants and a hoodie with hair that looked like she'd just tumbled out of a bush didn't necessarily count as getting ready for work.

"Well," she said, breaking the silence, "if you need any help sorting through this, just let me know."

"Uh-huh." Syc didn't take his eyes off the pile of ash in the firepit, even after the flames had burnt down to embers now and had almost stopped smoking. "You know what? Maybe you *can* help."

"Oh yeah?"

"Yeah." Syc sniffed again but didn't turn around to look at her. "If you know anyone with decent prices for contracted hits, Sam, don't get rid of the number just yet."

"Ha. Trust me, I hang onto useful stuff like that. It's always good to know people."

Syc was the kind of man who would continue to decline any and all offers of help. But Sam was the kind of person who would willingly give it anyway.

She just hoped for Syc's sake it wouldn't come to that. This trailer park, despite being rundown and mostly empty, had become her home too. She enjoyed the silence and the fresh air. She enjoyed being surrounded on nearly all sides by the giant redwoods looming over the place. She enjoyed the remote location, not despite how long it took her to drive into the main parts of town but because of it.

If she had to, she would fight to protect this place, just like she would fight to protect anything else she cared about. Even when so many things she cared about had already been lost to her along the way.

Only once she'd stepped back inside her trailer did she

remember the bouquet of pink roses nestled in the crook of her arm. Her place was a little lacking in flower vases, but she made do with an empty coffee tin she hadn't gotten around to throwing away. She washed out the few specks of coffee grounds left inside, filled the can with water, and stuck the bouquet inside before setting the makeshift vase down on her tiny kitchen table that was little bigger than a stool.

Sam had never been the kind of woman to fall head over heels for a dozen roses, no matter the color, but she couldn't deny they were beautiful. At least she'd have *something* nice to look at when she got home from work tonight.

Stepping back to take a look at the flowers on the table gave her another opportunity to scan the rest of her home, which was more than enough to fit her whole life into at this point. An entire life that could be pared down to what did and did not exist inside this trailer.

Honestly, she preferred her old Airstream to the Deville, though she wasn't going to complain when Syc had let her fix this place up for free after the Airstream was completely destroyed, all thanks to Little Pete himself. Plus one curious little bear cub that had gotten itself shoved into a trailer, then shoved right back out of it again when Mama Bear came calling.

The Deville was quite a bit smaller than the Airstream, and it definitely didn't have all the same comforts of home to which Sam had grown accustomed, even in Birdsong Park. But it was simple, relatively insulated, and covered most of the basics; anything the Deville didn't have, she could get from the park's shared facilities. Most importantly, the thing was free, and she had Syc to thank for that.

Seeing as the Deville also happened to already have been set up right next to Syc's personal trailer, Sam could also thank him for the relatively close proximity to those shared facilities, like the community showers.

Which was exactly where she meant to go next. Not that she had to thank the guy for his logistical planning in their current setup. Syc already knew how grateful she was for everything he had done to make her feel welcome and at home here. It hadn't been all that much in the scheme of things, but it was more than most people in Rush had offered her over the last two and a half years of Sam calling this town her home and its people her people.

More or less.

She gathered up her shower supplies, a towel, and a change of clothes, bundled them all up in her arms, and headed toward the showers conveniently located on the other side of Syc's trailer.

Twenty minutes later, Sam had to pass by the firepit on the way back for the second time, catching a clear view of the pile of ash left behind by Syc's one and only response to Little Pete's threats. Knowing Syc, if he hadn't already lit up inside the trailer, the man would soon be parking it in a lawn chair on the browning grass in front of his home for a nice long toke in the crisp air to calm his nerves.

Somehow, Sam didn't think burning a stack of official documents made invalid by a single missing signature would be enough to stop Little Pete. Not now that the new Mayor of Rush had turned his vengeful eye and all the governmental power it held onto Sam and Birdsong Park.

Once she was dressed and ready to head out, all she had left was to lock up. It actually surprised her that she even thought about using a lock at all with the Deville — something she hadn't bothered to consider with the Airstream. Not that a simple lock on the rather flimsy trailer door would do much to keep someone out if they really wanted to get in, but it was something.

Plus, the fact that her new lodgings were right next to his own trailer made this new arrangement feel a hell of a lot safer. If there was ever a repeat break-in, whoever was dumb enough to try it would make enough noise for Syc to hear. And the park's owner took a lot less kindly to break-ins and trespassers than even Sam did.

The only farewell she got before loading into her Jeep came from Dog, in a series of happy barks and wagging tail as he leapt around her vehicle and panted like he hadn't seen her in years.

"Yeah, yeah, all right," she murmured as she climbed behind the wheel. "I'll be back, I always come back." Then she raised her voice a little, in case Syc was still paying attention from inside his trailer. "Don't worry, Dog. When I'm home again, you can come hang out with me, and we'll pretend it's always been that way."

Dog barked one more time as if in agreement, then leapt out of the way before Sam pulled the door shut behind her and started the engine.

THE DRIVE into Rush was as uneventful as every other day she'd made it, except for one minor difference when Sam rolled past the Kalamack Club on her way in.

This morning, a woman of indeterminate age wearing jeans and a wool sweater stood outside the club, holding up a handmade sign with both hands. The sign was white poster board instead of cardboard, which instantly caught Sam's attention as she slowly rolled past. The urgent words scrawled across that white poster board were even more out of place here.

The old picket sign's bold, blocky letters spelled out one short, incredibly simple message: *Justice for Dina.'*

What was that about?

Though Sam had called Rush home long enough to get a decent feel for the inner workings of the townspeople — good ol' boys, townies, trippers, hippies, seasonal migrant workers like trimmers, and the small community of immigrants — she certainly hadn't met every single person rolling in and out of Rush over the last two years. That was impossible when seasonal workers came in droves from all over the country and even across international borders during trim season. But anyone who was convinced that holding a picket-style sign outside the Kalamack Club would be a useful way to spend their time couldn't have been a new or even temporary addition to the town.

Still, Sam couldn't recall having met or heard of someone named Dina or anything happening to a woman that might have prompted a demonstration like this. Even a one-person demonstration.

It wasn't enough of a mystery to make her change her plans, though. Plenty of people in Rush had their own secrets, mysteries, and haunted pasts that came back to bite them, just like in any other town. If Sam hadn't already known this firsthand, she definitely would have figured it out after having gotten herself so uncharacteristically involved in the personal issues of Rush's residents, like Beth Garrick or Little Pete Wilder, who clearly had an issue with anyone's nose getting stuck in his business.

THREE

Sam

ROLLING up to the Community Center on the outskirts of town felt just like every other time Sam had made the exact same drive for the exact same reason.

Here she was, showing up for yet another meeting and hoping this one wasn't any worse than the last one she remembered.

She hadn't been back since falling off her own short-lived wagon and nearly throwing herself off the deep end — literally — the night she came face to face with a terrified, frantic Beth Garrick on the Miller Bridge.

That was what she'd first thought of Beth that night, terrified and frantic, though Sam had been through at least one bottle of liquor before making her way to the bridge and trying to satisfy her craving for self-flagellation and punishment for all her own personal mistakes. She'd thought it remarkably unfortunate then, but luckily for Sam, she didn't get to play God with who lived and who died.

Including herself.

She would have made a shitty God, anyway.

She didn't exactly make a great recovering addict, either.

In the back of her mind, the other *other* little voice in her head that still knew a thing or two about how to live life like a real human being had told her getting back into a meeting was probably the best thing for her after her last faceplant off the wagon. After Beth's death, though, Sam couldn't bring herself to step back through these doors right away.

Basically, it all boiled down to one bullshit excuse after another. She was too busy. Chris had given her more shifts at the Redwood to *keep* her busy. She'd promised Dog to be up and about and ready to let him out of her trailer at a certain time of day and couldn't let the canine down. She was too exhausted from work, too exhausted from all the personal shit that had floated up to the surface after Beth's charred corpse. It took too much of Sam's available time, energy, and mental strength to just focus on not picking up the bottle.

And driving out to a meeting full of recovering addicts and alcoholics just to hear about how hard it was for them to not pick up a bottle or a handful of pills or a needle was more likely to throw her off the rails again.

Sam had given herself all these excuses and more as to why hitting up a Twelve-Step meeting just wasn't the right idea at the right time. But she hadn't even stopped to consider the real reason she'd waited so long to return until she stepped through the double doors of the meeting room inside the Community Center and the smell of cheap coffee — brewed twice as strong to make up for its shitty taste — blasted her in the face.

The meeting was already two minutes in.

As Sam headed to her seat, Meredith quickly finished up the opening statements and reading, like she'd been doing for the entire two years and change that Sam had lived here.

She didn't look Sam's way once.

That added a small but relatively negligible amount of discomfort to her arrival and the fact that she hadn't made it on time to her first meeting in months. That was also frowned upon, especially for newcomers or those who had started using again before remembering why they'd stopped in the first place.

Meredith was slumped much farther back in her seat than usual, her gaze trained on the surface of the cheap wooden table in front of her. She'd already slid some pamphlet or booklet across the table to the man sitting beside her.

Without skipping a beat, he dutifully continued with the opening reading that was supposed to set the tone for the remaining forty-seven to fifty minutes afterward.

Then it hit Sam like an empty booze bottle over the head.

She'd taken so long to come back to these meetings because a part of her had known this was exactly what she'd feel when she got her ass back into one of these seats.

The awkwardness of being a part of something that had once been whole but no longer was. And no one had noticed that wholeness until it was gone forever.

The guilt she'd managed to keep at bay through a slight increase in her daily cigarette habit, working more shifts than normal, and spending as much time as possible at Birdsong Park with Dog and Syc and the redwoods.

The cringy, gut-squirming, skin-crawling, logic-defying malaise that overcame her now at the sight of one particular empty seat around the circle of NA members' chairs.

There had always been more chairs than there were participants at these meetings. Just in case. But one specific chair had always been occupied by the same person, and today, it was empty.

It would always be empty, because the person who had filled it — the person who belonged there and who had occupied that space despite all the judgmental bullshit the people of Rush and the people of this NA meeting threw at her — was gone forever.

Beth was dead.

Sam couldn't have been the only person here who recognized that truth and had chosen to pick any other seat but the one that had always been Beth's. Whether that was conscious or unconscious for the rest of these recovering alcoholics and addicts was anyone's guess. But now Sam knew why she'd stayed away for so long.

Sam might have been the only person in the entire town who had treated Beth Garrick like a real person and not like the town lunatic. The one who had tried to help Beth at all. But she hadn't managed to save Beth, even after solving the mystery the rest of Rush hadn't given two shits about in the first place. All of Sam's efforts had been for nothing.

Sam knew it. So did everyone else in this room.

Which meant that every time someone glanced her way, Sam felt the weight of their judgment and the biting sting of their disapproval behind it. Worse yet, she could feel their pity, which made for one giant, fucked-up mixture of serious discomfort.

She forced herself to sit through the entire hour, which felt like ten. The hard plastic chair with its swooping bucket for a seat was slanted at the worst possible angle, making first one of her hips ache, then the crook of her neck on the opposite side, then the middle of her back. She shifted left and right, shoving both hands into the side pockets of her hoodie and slumping back in the chair almost as deeply as Meredith had in hers.

Something had definitely changed in this group. It could have been Beth's death that had broken them into so many scattered pieces. It probably had quite a lot to do with the fact that every person sitting here remembered all too vividly how often they had shifted impatiently in their seats every time Beth started talking about having seen her dead sister.

No one had believed her then. Now, everyone knew it was all true.

Sam was the first one out of her seat before the meeting's last words were uttered.

No one said a word to her, or approached her, or even looked her in the eye as they broke from the meeting to put the chairs away and gather around the table of shitty coffee and powdered creamer they called the "refreshments" table.

Sam didn't actually want any coffee — not this kind, anyway — but she poured herself a cup anyway. While everyone else avoided her, Sam waited for a chance to approach Meredith alone, just to check in, maybe even confirm that Sam wasn't losing her mind since she'd broken her last streak of consecutive clean time months ago.

You never could fall off the wagon too many times for a Twelve-Step program to take you back. That was both the beauty of it and, for some people, the worst part.

Finally, as Meredith headed across the room after cleaning up, Sam got the closer look she'd been waiting for.

The woman's cheeks were sunken, and her eyes were puffy, red-rimmed, with a pink-tinted hue to the whites — one hell of a haunted look that just didn't fit with Sam's view of the woman.

It could have meant anything. Meredith could have spent the majority of her morning sobbing into a pillow before pulling herself together just enough to run this meeting today. She could have been going through something personal she didn't want to talk about. She could have been mourning Beth still. Maybe even for the same reasons Sam found herself mourning Beth from time to time.

Or Meredith could have been hitting the bottle again, adding at least ten visible years to her outward appearance.

If Sam could see it, that meant everyone else here could see it too. The only person from whom an addict could truly hide their darkest secrets and basest shortcomings was their self.

Sam knew that just as well as anyone else here.

After that split second of eye contact, Meredith picked up the pace and disappeared through the double doors.

"Morning, Sam."

She spun to the side and found Hector Aguilo beside her, his kind smile standing out from among all the other somber frowns and morose scowls that had dominated the meeting.

"Hey, Hector," she replied. "How's it going?"

"Same old shit. One day at a time, right? Good to see you back in here, though."

"You might be the only one."

"Yeah, well, what everybody else thinks of you is none of your goddamn business, is it?"

A soft chuckle escaped him, and Sam responded with the last dying flutter of a smile. Then Hector pointed absently toward the refreshments table. "Hey, are you wanting any of this coffee or the fixins?"

Sam looked down at the to-go cup of black shit in her hand and shook her head. "Nah, I got mine right here."

"Then you won't mind if I start cleaning up."

She stepped away from the table, jerked her chin up at Hector in a wordless farewell, and pushed her way through the meeting room's double doors.

Maybe not everyone blamed her for Beth's death. Then again, Hector had probably only said hi because she'd been standing in the way of his coffee duty.

FOUR

Dina

FIVE YEARS AGO...

DINA HAD EXPECTED her first trip beyond Seattle to feel like entering a different world the second she stepped off the bus. Though Rush was a small, rural mountain town, it didn't feel nearly as foreign as she'd imagined.

She and Shell walked side by side down the sidewalk, toting their own personal luggage. The older girl pointed out a series of personal landmarks, including her favorite cafe, the best place for movie rentals, where never to let herself be caught dead at any time of day or night. Eventually, they stopped in front of a building separated from the majority of the buildings along the main strip.

Shell opened the front door to reveal the darkened entrance beyond and nodded inside. "Come on. This is the best spot, I promise."

Dina looked up at the slightly faded sign above the door marking it as the Redwood Rings Grill and Pub. Despite how much fun she'd already had without barely even having gotten started, the sign itself made her grimace. "I don't know … is this an actual *bar*-bar?"

"Yeah, it's a *bar*-bar," Shell replied cheerily. "Come on. We'll go grab a seat and a drink and just relax for a bit."

"I don't drink."

"Why? Because you're nineteen?" Shell chuckled. "You don't have to worry about that here, trust me. No one's gonna ID you."

"No, I mean, even if I was twenty-one, I still wouldn't drink. I just … don't." She tried not to make it sound as weird as it felt to say but quickly realized she'd been worrying about it all for nothing.

Shell's only response was to shrug it all off and haul the Redwood Rings' front doors open even wider before standing aside and gesturing with her free hand toward the bar's innards. "Okay, great. You don't have to drink alcohol, but I'm pretty sure everybody needs liquids of some kind. I'm not trying to get you drunk this early in the day, dude. We're here to meet up with the others. That's it."

Dina finally tore her gaze away from the sign over the door to frown at her new friend. "The others?"

"The other *trimmers*." Shell laughed, stretched her hand out, and grabbed Dina's wrist before the younger girl could back away or change her mind. "Come on, it's not gonna kill you to step inside, and you're not gonna get the kinda job you want if you're just standing out here all day. Let's go."

She hauled Dina after her through the door, which swung silently closed behind them, and it took Dina's vision all of five seconds to adjust to the bar's low interior lighting.

The place was mostly empty. Dina was surprised it was even open at this hour, but maybe it just happened to be that kind of bar. Not like she had any real idea what kinds of bars there were out there. Her mom never went to bars. Angela rarely left the house these days. And Dina honestly couldn't remember the last time she'd seen her mom out and about, or socializing with anyone, or entirely sober for that matter. But she followed Shell all the way to the back just the same.

She hadn't noticed the group of young people also around her age, none of them older than twenty-seven, until she and Shell had almost reached them. Then a loud, excited shout echoed through the mostly empty bar, puncturing the mid-morning silence that still lingered even through the low-key, mellow rock music Dina thought she could hear playing over the speakers.

"Well, holy shit. Look who finally made it." The five other young people sitting at the table all turned around to look at Dina and Shell's direction, and the guy who'd shouted at them spread his arms where he sat and grinned. "We were almost starting to think you wouldn't show up, dude."

"Yeah, and Phil was this close to convincing Matt he should just give up on you altogether," said the young woman sitting beside him. The whole table laughed.

"I'll have you know," a second guy with a long, dark-brown ponytail added, "that I specifically stopped listening to anything that came out of his mouth, like, half an hour ago."

"Uh-huh," Shell said as she and Dina approached the table. "And that's why I love you. Because your brain is big enough to keep you out of all the wrong kinds of trouble."

The guy with the ponytail stood from the table and opened up his arms. Shell dropped her duffel, ran toward him with open arms, and jumped halfway up onto him before planting an enormous, noisy, almost uncomfortably too-long kiss on him.

Uncomfortably long for Dina, anyway, because now realized she was definitely intruding on a private moment. So she switched her gaze to the other young people.

Phil caught her looking them all over and flashed her a winning smile before wiggling his eyebrows at her. "Some crazy shit right here, yeah?"

"Did you just get off the bus?" one of the three other girls asked her.

"She was with me the entire ride," Shell said, standing beside Matt now that they'd disentangled themselves from each other. "And believe it or not, we only started talking to each other, like, this morning."

"Where you from?" someone else asked.

Dina smiled. "Seattle."

Phil raised his eyebrows at her again. "City girl coming to try out the trimming season for the first time, huh? Look at that!"

"Go easy on her, Phil," Shell told him. "Dina's awesome, and I'm gonna show her around. So the rest of you assholes can forget about playing any jokes on her or trying to make her earn her keep or whatever the hell you've been doing to newbies lately."

Then Shell made the introductions all around, with plenty of good-natured jokes and smiles and laughter. Then Dina followed it all up with a friendly, "Nice to meet you guys. I'm glad I finally made it."

"Spoken like a girl who just spent way too long on a public bus," one of the other girls replied. "And who now needs a strong-as-fuck drink. Right?"

"Yeah, well, Dina doesn't drink," Shell cut in. "So all of you can keep minding your own fucking business. And we'll go grab something at the bar." She made a face at him, then turned and nodded for Dina to join her. "Come on, let's go."

"I'll come with you," Matt said, before flipping Phil the middle finger, and making everyone else at the table crack up all over again.

As Dina hurried with Shell to the bar, and laughter rang out from the back table, Shell looked over her shoulder at the other girl and flashed that same winning smile. "They're all really great. They're just, you know, a little lacking when it comes to people skills. Mostly Phil, actually."

"No, really?" Dina quipped with a smirk. "I couldn't tell."

Shell stopped, turned all the way around to stare at her in disbelief, then burst out laughing. "That was sarcasm. Yeah, you're gonna have no problem fitting in here. I promise."

They all made small talk at the bar while the bartender made them their drinks, including Dina's Coke. At least, she'd ordered a Coke, but the guy had told her Pepsi was all they had, so she'd ordered that instead. Then when she tried to pull out her wallet to pay, Matt put a hand on her arm and shook his head.

"Don't worry about it," he told her.

Dina paused, glancing at her wallet. "Don't tell me Rush is the kind of place where people don't have to pay for a soda."

"Not *our* people." Shell nodded at the bartender and started to turn away to head back to the table with her drink in hand. "Put it on Rip's tab, huh?"

The bartender still said nothing, but he clearly wasn't going to put up a fight about three drinks going unpaid for, even on a slow day like this.

After handing everyone their drinks, the group couldn't have had more than five minutes to drink them before Phil jumped awkwardly in his chair to a round of surprised laughter from the others, then pulled his cell out of his back pocket to check the new message. "Ah, shit. He's here. Time to roll."

Everyone immediately stood from the table. Chairs screeched, scraping against the hardwood floors and groaning beneath the unexpected assault. Then all the duffels, backpacks, and other luggage were hauled up off the ground and onto shoulders or in hands. Dina realized she was the only one who had packed anything in a roller carry-on, but it was too late to switch bags now.

The group filed across the bar's main room, engaged in their own quiet and more private conversations, and Dina turned to Shell. "Who's here?"

"Rip." Shell winked at her. "Trust me, D, you're gonna fucking love it."

But when she stepped outside and saw where the rest of the group was headed, she felt the first tingling itches in her mind of her mother's warning voice returning with full force.

Apparently, her new employer Rip drove a white, slightly dented painter's van complete with a lack of windows in the rear doors and heavy, almost opaque tints in all the windows.

This isn't a carpool. It's a fucking kidnapper van.

The snap-second judgment didn't keep her from bringing up the end of the line and hauling her carry-on after her. The wheels rumbled and thumped across the uneven asphalt of the bar's parking lot that looked like it hadn't seen maintenance repairs in years, drowning out all the other conversation around her because the carry-on also made her the slowest of the bunch.

Someone had already opened the van's rear doors, and half the group had disappeared into the back. Shell stood beside those doors, grinning at Dina and waiting patiently for their newest co-worker to get with it. "Are you coming or what?"

"Yeah, I'm coming. I just — this stupid—"

Matt popped out of the van with an easy, friendly smile. Seeing him standing beside the vehicle finally made it clear just how tall he was. He reached her with a little jog, bent down to pick up her entire suitcase, and slung it over his shoulder. "Don't wanna miss the ride out, D. I think it's pretty hard to find another one."

"Thanks," she said, but he was already most of the way back toward the van.

Then he disappeared inside with her luggage, and Dina put on another burst of speed so she wouldn't keep everyone waiting.

Apparently, here in Rush, it looked like she'd just have to get used to being called D. Because two people using the nickname for her in as many minutes felt like something that was going to stick.

Not that she minded, really. Dina had left her life behind her for the adventure of the unknown and of carving her own path, even if the next step took her in a slightly different direction than the medical degree that had been her main end goal for so long.

Dina Copely could be left behind in Seattle. Maybe it was time for D to show up now and learn how to live a little.

FIVE

Sam

SAM'S DAY immediately kicked up a notch on the excitement scale when she drove past the Kalamack Club after the meeting. Given the caliber and status of the club's exclusive member list, she normally didn't see a police cruiser parked out front of the main entrance, and the sight was enough to instantly grab Sam's attention.

She slowed down and parked her Jeep just ahead of the lot's entrance. She didn't have to wait long before the details of such an unexpected event revealed themselves.

Oh, this *is gonna be good…*

If a police cruiser at the Kalamack Club was an unexpected surprise any day, seeing Chief Colton standing on that porch was even better.

The man was already deeply engaged with a woman standing on the club's front stoop. Sam had never seen her before, but that didn't really mean anything this time of year. Even more interesting, this woman didn't seem to understand the way social interactions in Rush worked. Or that the Kalamack Club was off limits to non-members and anyone who didn't possess a certain economic value easily determined by the number of zeros in their bank account.

The woman also clearly didn't grasp the gravity of her situation, including a verbal confrontation with Rush's Chief of Police.

It only got better from there.

The woman on the porch argued with Colton, her hands flying animatedly in all directions as the chief's hands went to his utility belt — not quite over the grip of his service weapon, but close. Sam noticed one of the thick, opulent curtains on a front window of the club rustle slightly. The face behind that swept-aside curtain was definitely familiar.

Sam couldn't remember her name, but the blonde receptionist who had so smugly prevented Sam away from entering the Kalamack Club months ago was the same woman peeking out through those curtains now. Based off the very few incredibly short interactions Sam had had with her, she figured this blonde was the one who'd also called the cops on the naive woman who didn't fully understand where she was or how things worked around here.

Naturally, Miss Snooty-Nosed Leggy Receptionist would find her dose of morning pleasure in watching someone else's pain from her very own front-row seat on the other side of that window.

The woman on the front porch shouted something, her voice muffled by distance and the glass of the Jeep's windows. Then the argument switched from a potentially heated verbal exchange to the woman's face and chest pressed up against the siding of the club's entrance beside the door, her hands twisted behind her back as Colton secured a pair of handcuffs around her wrists.

Whatever the woman had been trying to argue with him about, it clearly was no longer her priority. In fact, while Colton spun her around to guide her somewhat roughly down the steps of the front porch toward his cruiser, the woman kept her mouth firmly clamped shut.

Even from where she'd parked her Jeep, Sam clearly made out the terror and disbelief on the woman's face. Knowing this town and the way it was run, both by civil servants and the people who technically owned the majority of Rush, Sam bet the woman would spend twelve hours in county lockup — twenty-four at the most, if Colton was feeling curmudgeonly today and wanted to teach her a lesson — after which she'd be let loose again with a stern warning not to stick her nose in other people's business and to absolutely stay away from the Kalamack Club for the duration of her time here.

Whether or not the woman chose to heed the warning was a different matter entirely and none of Sam's business.

Sam did, however, glean an unexpected amount of joy when Colton finished folding the woman into the back seat of his cruiser, closed the door, and looked up at Sam's Jeep. Their gazes met, she lifted a hand for a half-hearted wave, then she flashed the chief a brilliant grin reserved only for moments when a smile like that meant "eat shit" and nothing remotely friendly.

Whether or not he knew this, Colton merely scowled back at her, offering no sign whatsoever of neighborly, small-town friendliness - not so much as a wave or even a nod.

Then he marched around the front of his cruiser and disappeared behind the wheel.

And that was Sam's cue to just keep driving.

~

BY THE TIME she finally stepped into work, the Redwood Rings had already opened its doors to its late-morning regulars: Christian, Eddie, and Levi were there as usual, bent over their drinks at the bar in relative silence while they started up their drinking for the day. Each of them looked up at her when she crossed the dining room toward the back, offering nods and waves.

Christian flashed her a brilliant grin and winked.

Sam flipped him the bird without slowing down.

The guys' echoing laughter followed her through the swinging doors into the kitchen.

There was a certain comfort in knowing she could walk through these doors, head through the kitchen to the office in the back to drop off her personal effects, and expect the fast-paced monotony of serving drinks all day to the same faces sitting nearly at the same exact chairs or bar stools.

Routine was important. Sam had had that drilled into her early on in her career as a U.S. Army MP. Routine was something she had tried to maintain on a regular basis, even before moving to Rush. Even after having lost everything that had previously defined her life. Even when that routine was as simple and bareboned as waking up to the whines of a dog she didn't even own, hitting up a meeting, and driving straight to work.

That comfort disappeared the second Sam walked through the kitchen and came face to face with Chris moving purposefully through the swinging double doors from the front.

He probably tried to keep a straight face in an attempt to maintain the whole tough-love-from-a-boss facade, but the corner of his mouth still flickered into an undeniable smile.

Sam honestly would have preferred a grimace of

disdain coming from him, had it been genuine. With Chris, it never was.

"You're late," he said as he stepped around the line and stopped at the dishwasher to grab a rack of freshly washed glasses.

"I have no idea what you're talking about," Sam replied as she joined him on the other side of the sinks to slide the next rack of dirty glasses into the dishwasher. She pulled down on the steel bar to close the contraption, setting off the loud, swishing roar of the steaming pressure wash all their dishes endured. Then she looked at Chris and spread her arms. "I get here at the same time every day."

Already on his way toward the doors into the front pub, Chris paused, raised an eyebrow at her, and almost rolled his eyes. "Just because you show up late every day doesn't change the time your shift starts."

"Then maybe you should change the shift times."

"Nice try." He continued through the double doors leading behind the bar, then disappeared.

Sam glanced behind her at the doors into the Back Bar. Normally, she would have headed straight through them to start her shift behind the bar. But something felt different today.

Maybe it was the weirdness of the first NA meeting she'd been to in months this morning. Maybe it was knowing that newcomers to Rush were still being given the red-carpet treatment, even in places like the Kalamack Club's front porch, complete with the cold weight of hand-cuffs and the hard back seat of a police cruiser.

Or maybe she just wasn't ready to peek her head through the door into the Back Bar and face whatever assholes had decided to stop in for a little late-morning-cocktail pick-me-up.

More often than not, those assholes turned out to be the same ones nearly every day. That didn't change the odd, empty, not-quite-steady feeling in her gut that pushed Sam to hurry through the doors into the front instead of manning her station in the back.

Chris had already gotten through emptying out half of the freshly cleaned glasses by the time she joined him behind the bar. She fumbled for something to say before he had a chance to notice she'd followed him up here just to not be completely alone for a few more minutes.

"Did you leave flowers outside my trailer?" she blurted. It was a total non sequitur and the first thing that burst out of her mouth.

With a chuckle, Chris turned toward her and cocked his head. "Definitely wasn't me."

"As in you know that for a fact, or are you just trying to be cute?"

"As in I'm pretty sure I'd remember if I ever brought you flowers, Sam. I'd have to work up a shitload of courage just to do something insane like that. Even to just leave them right outside your front door. That's not the kinda trauma a guy forgets right away."

Sam snorted, shook her head, and approached the glasses rack to continue unloading them while Chris turned off the bar sink now that the bucket of soapy water for their ration of daily bar rags was full. "Yeah, I guess I should give you credit for being a little smarter than that."

"Just a little. What kind?"

"What?" She paused mid-stretch toward the back counter beneath the liquor shelf where they stacked the clean glasses.

"Didn't think it was a complicated question." Chris wrang a rag out over the bucket, then wiped at the bar top in front of him. "Were they white roses? Red roses?

Yellow? A dozen? Half dozen? They come in all colors and numbers, Sam."

"Jesus," she muttered, clinking down the next clean glass a bit harder than she'd intended. "They're pink."

"Huh."

"What's that supposed to mean?"

"Just huh." He laughed again when she scowled at him. "I find it interesting, all right? Pink roses... Not exactly what I would've chosen to give you. *If* I ever chose to give you flowers, which I definitely would not."

"And what exactly would you have chosen in this hypothetical situation I'm only letting draw out this long because we don't have more than three customers right now?"

"Well, judging by the look you're giving me, I'd say a bouquet of something dead. Partially rotten. Or maybe even a pile of ashes that used to be flowers, just to save you the trouble of burning them later anyway."

Sam let him have that one, served up on a platter with a short-lived smirk as she grabbed the last two glasses off the rack. "Smart man."

"So," Chris continued. "Two dozen pink roses. Just left on the doorstep of your trailer, huh?"

"I never said it was two dozen," Sam corrected sharply.

"Fine, then. A dozen pink roses." When she didn't correct him a second time, he nodded like he'd just solved all the mysteries of the universe and tossed the rag back into the bucket of soapy water before hauling the empty glass rack off the counter. "Sounds like you've got yourself a secret admirer, Sam."

"Bullshit," she said. "The last thing I'm ever gonna have is an admirer, and the last thing I want is anything to do with secrets."

"Duly noted," he said.

44

"Here, you stay. I'll take that back." Sam reached toward the drink rack in his hand, but Chris pulled away from her. Whether it was playfulness or something less superficial, she couldn't entirely tell.

"Actually, *you* stay," he said. "You're still working the front today."

"Oh yeah?" Sam spread her arms. "And you're gonna work the Back Bar?"

"Nina's already got it covered."

"Nina." She clicked her tongue and figured she had a fifty-fifty shot at getting him to break beneath the next five seconds of deadpan stare she fixed on him. "Is she suddenly the best bartender we've got on staff now, or did I miss something?"

Chris turned his head away to gaze at her from the corner of his eye. Another smile failing to parade around as a fake scowl flashed across his face. "I can't tell whether or not that's rhetorical."

Of course he played it safe. That was Chris Nelson in a nutshell. One safe, soft-spoken, diligently loyal nutshell wrapped up in a smile that could get Evel Knievel his daily dose of adrenaline.

"Come on, Chris," she tried again. "It's been long enough, and I took a peek in the back when I came in. The Petes aren't even here. You don't have to keep handing it off to Nina."

"Nina actually shows up for her shifts on time. Not her own personal version of on time, either. The version plastered all over the schedule on the office door."

"So *that's* the kinda details we're getting hung up on now, is that it?"

"*You're* clearly not."

How easily he smiled when the joke was at her expense.

It felt like she still had room to push just a little harder. "How about I pop back there and talk to Nina about it myself?"

"Not today, Sam."

"Oh, I see. You know, I'm starting to get the feeling she's got something on you. Some kinda blackmail. What dirt could that walking billboard photo in a bartender's apron have possibly pulled up on you to get herself such a cushy deal?"

Chris's easygoing smile didn't so much die as disappear altogether without a trace of its former existence. "Not funny."

"So there *is* dirt to be had on you in the first place." Sam snorted. "Never thought I'd see the day."

Chris headed toward the kitchen doors again, the empty glass rack swinging at his side. "The front. That's all you're getting today."

"And when exactly are you gonna let me work the back again, boss?" she called after him.

"When I'm sure I can trust you to behave," he replied over his shoulder.

The kitchen doors swung back together behind him.

Sam pressed her lips together so hard, the next thought that scurried through her mind was a memory of some random adult from her childhood warning her not to make faces or she'd end up getting stuck that way for life.

Sam was stuck, all right. It just had nothing to do with her face.

Whether or not it was for life, though, still remained to be seen.

SIX

Sam
___

SHE DIDN'T HAVE MUCH MORE time to ruminate on the level of stuckness her life had or hadn't reached. The Redwood Rings quickly filled up with the usual rush of tourists thinking they'd found a hidden gem within the streets of the small town.

Working the front, her face always got tired from her repeatedly botched attempts to look somewhat pleasant for the groups of random lunch crowds with their floppy sunhats and stripes of zinc oxide on their cheeks and noses to keep off the worst of the sun's damage at such high altitudes. Whether or not these tables noticed how uncomfortable their bartender and single server was with the simple act of not scowling — and they could forget about exchanging pleasantries altogether — Sam didn't give a shit; this was her job.

These tables brought in a steady paycheck. The tips were decent on the best of days, and it gave her something to do. Routine.

Once the first early lunch rush died down and the place settled into that brief half hour or so of calm before the next wave hit, Sam put an order through to the cook for her shift meal, entering a note into the system that printed on the kitchen's tickets: *'Surprise me.'*

Jackson pounded on the kitchen bell, and Sam instantly took off to grab the single plate resting on the line.

"What's on the menu today?" she asked, reaching for the plate.

Their line cook scrubbed superficially at the flattop and didn't once look up at her. "Surprise."

"It always is." She took her lunch back to the bar and hopped up on one of the stools to eat.

She hadn't gotten through a quarter of the wrap dripping with Southwestern-flavored ranch around something that was either leftover pork chop from yesterday or grilled chicken — she couldn't tell — when Chris emerged from the kitchen with his own plated shift meal in hand.

He took a seat on the bar stool next to hers and without a word proceeded to maneuver the enormous burger on his plate into both hands. With said burger raised halfway to his mouth, Chris paused, his gaze settling on Sam's plate and his mouth gaping open. He abruptly shut it. "What are you eating?"

"Jackson's surprise of the day." She slid her plate along the bar in his direction. "You tell me."

He eyed her meal for a moment, then shook his head and went back to his burger. "No, I'm good."

They ate in the comfortable, non-expectant silence Sam preferred over every other type of interaction. This was the carrot on a stick Chris used when he wanted to hang out with her outside of work, alone, privately, with the added bonus of 'we don't have to talk' thrown into the mix just to sweeten the deal. Who knew that could make this shift meal feel more like a date than a break between the lunch rushes? And that wasn't what Sam wanted right now — they'd already mixed too much business and pleasure as it was — and she had to break the silence.

"Hey," she said after swallowing another bite. "Have you heard anything about that woman down at the Kalamack Club this morning?"

"What woman?"

"Some out-of-towner. I saw her this morning on the front porch with a picket sign. Colton didn't look like his usual chipper self either when he dealt with *that* peaceful protest by putting her in cuffs."

Chris stared at her a moment, his burger once more poised on its way to his mouth. He almost took another bite, then sighed heavily instead and dumped the burger back onto his plate. "Come on, Sam. You gotta give it a rest."

"I'll take that as a no," she said. "You haven't heard anything."

"You can take that however you like. But this next thing I'm about to say, I really hope you take seriously as the strong advice it's supposed to be. If it has to do with the Kalamack Club, your best bet is to stay out of it. I don't care what it is."

"Stay out of anything that has to do with the Kalamack Club, huh?" Sam crammed another massive bite of her mystery-surprise wrap into her mouth and added through a garbled mouthful, "Or do you actually mean stay away from anything that has to do with Pete Wilder? Big *or* Little."

"Is there a difference?"

She slurped down another refreshing gulp of Pepsi and shrugged. "I mean, one of them's old and growing fat and happy with the spoils of all his shady business over the last few decades. And the other one's just a slimy bastard with a lecherous smile who can't take a hint and thinks being mayor makes him Emperor of the Universe."

"Not between Big Pete and Little Pete," Chris clarified. "I'm talking about the Kalamack Club and the Wilders, Sam, and I'm pretty sure you know that."

"Well, it wouldn't kill you to be a little more specific when you're trying to make a point."

Sliding his partially eaten burger away from him across the bar, Chris swiveled on the bar stool to face her more directly. "And that is exactly why I'm keeping you out of the Back Bar."

That didn't fully compute for Sam, but if she argued, he'd probably come up with some smartass explanation for why her simple curiosity was now included on the list of reasons he'd taken it upon himself to teach her a lesson about patience and personal boundaries.

So she changed tactics.

"You know, it's interesting that you bring up the mayor," she continued.

Chris scowled at his burger. "No, that was you."

"Because this morning, Syc got a Wilder-shaped wrench thrown in his gears. You hear anything about the mayor trying to shut down the trailer park?"

That made Chris look up at her again, his expression twisting into a concerned frown as he realized what she was saying. "Birdsong Park? No. I had no idea. What for?"

"Zoning infractions. Syc got served the intent papers this morning. Could be an empty threat or Little Pete's shitty attempt at a major flex. But if you don't know about it, that means the mayor hasn't decided to make it a public town issue yet. Feels like a small win."

Chris opened his mouth to say something else a second before the front doors opened and a brand-new group of tourists surged inside, hot and tired and ready for their drinks with a side of lunch — or appetizers at the very least — to get them through their day.

"Hey, folks," Chris called, greeting them with the kind of warm, inviting smile Sam still couldn't force herself to drum up for anyone. "Go ahead and take a seat wherever you like. We'll be right with you."

Sam didn't give him time to weasel anything else out of her before she snatched up a handful of rolled silverware from the basket on the bar and completed it with enough menus for her newest table. "Feel free to finish your lunch. I've got this."

~

WHEN HER SHIFT was finally over, Sam couldn't wait to get out and get back home as quickly as possible. Even if she'd plastered a giant neon sign to her forehead that said, 'All I want is to lock myself up in my tiny trailer and daydream about the cold beers I can't have, so don't talk to me,' Chris probably still would have approached her anyway. Like he did now.

"You heading home?" he asked.

Sam glanced at the giant keyring where he kept all his keys, personal and business, and pursed her lips. "It'll be kinda hard for me to leave after you've already locked up for the night."

He ignored her quip with as much grace as he ignored the majority of Sam's bristly nature and nodded toward the doors. Before they walked that way together, he said, "That was me asking if you had any plans tonight."

"Just to go home."

"Want some company?"

Sam stepped through the front doors and stood silently by while he locked up behind them. Then she waited for

Chris to look at her again so she could justify to herself that she wasn't giving him any reason not to take no for an answer tonight. "Having enough room for company in the Airstream was a tall order on its own," she said. "My new place is probably half the size."

Chris double-checked the lock on the front door with a quick tug. Then he jingled his keys as they headed toward the parking lot with only their two cars occupying it now. "You could come over to my place instead... We can think about the beers you can't have all you want there. The only difference is you'll have someone to talk to about it. Or not talk to about it, if that's better. Or to distract you from thinking about it at all."

Sam sighed and shook her head as she pulled her Jeep keys out of her pocket. "Not tonight, Chris."

"You sure?" Chris gently asked a split second before she realized he'd walked her all the way to her Jeep without making it obvious that he was walking her to her Jeep.

Smooth. But not smooth enough. Not tonight.

Sam had gone through one too many changes in difficult emotions today, and she wasn't sure she had it in her to deal with the sense of peace and calm and momentary rightness that overwhelmed her every time she hung out with Chris outside of work for 'company'. Comfort and safety were rare enough in this world, and if she let herself get used to it, she'd end up trading one vice for who knew how many more. Chris didn't deserve to be relegated to such simple terms. She knew for a fact she didn't deserve him anyway.

"I'm sure," she said. "I'm honestly just wiped for the day, you know? Dealing with all those *tourists* in the front really just wears me to shit."

"Nice try. Not putting you on the Back Bar. Yet."

"I never said anything about the Back Bar."

"All right, another time, then. If you change your mind, you know how to get ahold of me."

"Yeah. I know where you live too."

"I'm sure that's supposed to creep me out when you say it like that," he called over his shoulder as he walked away back toward the building, because the guy lived right above his own business. "But somehow, it doesn't quite have the intended effect."

"Just give it some time."

With a laugh, he shook his head, waved good night, and headed toward the back of the Redwood Rings, where he would reenter the building and finish locking up from the inside.

He waited, however, for Sam to pull out of the parking lot before he disappeared.

SEVEN

SEVEN

Sam

The lack of shouting outside her trailer first thing the next morning felt like a good sign, with the extra bonus of no whining from Dog from his spot on the floor.

He jerked his head up the second she rolled over to face him.

"So you *do* know how to sleep in when Syc's not outside screaming the sky down. Sorry you gotta deal with that asshole when I'm not here, buddy."

Dog stood and elongated from snout to tail in one massive canine stretch, followed by an equally massive yawn that ended in a cheery squeak.

Sam chuckled. "Yeah, good morning."

She might have even said she was in a good mood today, for no apparent reason. With a gentle smile, she scratched behind Dog's ears with one hand and unlocked her trailer door with the other while her furry friend, who preferred to spend his nights lying at the foot of her bed and not his owner's, sat and patiently waited for his first outing of the day.

The door squealed open. Dog shoved it the rest of the

way with a nudge of his snout before he leapt from the doorstep, avoiding the stairs altogether, and zipped around the yard to tend to his morning business.

Sam let out a sleepy sigh as she watched him disappear around the corner. Then her gaze dropped to the unexpected offering lying right there in the browning grass in front of the last metal step down to the ground. Dog had completely missed it, which she couldn't blame him for. Something like this wouldn't mean shit to an animal. Or to anyone else, really.

But it just pissed Sam off.

"What the hell?"

She looked up to scan the area of the park visible from her front door. No sign of anyone who wasn't supposed to be there. No sign of anyone who *was* supposed to be there, either, which meant she could forget about asking if Syc had seen anyone new roaming around Birdsong Park.

Because another bouquet of small, plump, bright-pink roses was once more waiting for her in the grass that might as well have counted as her doorstep.

Leaving them there, Sam turned, slammed the door shut, and went to gather her things for a trip to the park's showers.

On her way out, she glanced at the empty coffee-grounds tin now acting as a vase for the first bouquet. Those roses had really bloomed nicely in the last twenty-four hours, all of them more than halfway open now from the tight buds they'd been yesterday.

So she wasn't losing her mind, at least. Those roses were here, and a whole new dozen of them were outside her trailer.

Again.

She purposely did not look at that second bouquet again when she left her trailer for the showers.

ON THE WAY back to her trailer twenty minutes later, freshly showered and dressed, Sam found Syc and Dog sitting in their usual places by the fire pit. Syc wasn't smoking anything this morning, but he didn't look particularly happy, either. Not that he ever really did.

Dog, on the other hand, leapt up again and trotted toward her, his tail wagging as he greeted his favorite human with a happy whine.

Syc tilted his head in her direction and called, "Sounds like someone forgot to feed someone else this morning."

"I wonder who *that* could've been. Seeing as one of us doesn't even technically have a dog anymore. I'm pretty sure this one adopted himself on my behalf just to get away from you."

"So you *did* feed him?" Syc asked.

Sam shot him a deadpan stare, but he'd already returned his attention to the fire pit, which didn't have any fire in it this morning. "Shit. No. Come on, Dog."

Dog followed her dutifully, trotting along and wagging his tail and licking his muzzle in anticipation of breakfast. Sam paused in front of her trailer door, stared at the roses she wasn't going to pick up a second time, then pointed at them and scowled at Dog. "It's a good thing I haven't been paying you for your services. You're a shit guard dog. Just so you know."

He sat, gazing up at her with wide, glistening eyes as his tail whacked back and forth across the grass.

"Yeah, that's what I thought."

Sam let him into her trailer, which was now apparently Dog's favorite and only place to eat, though she couldn't remember exactly when his dog food had been moved in with the rest of her things. Or his bowl.

It wasn't as much of a mystery as whoever had left her another goddamn bouquet of roses in front of her trailer. But at least feeding Dog was normal.

While he ate, she gathered her things for a morning of quick errands. The second she let him out again, Dog bounded away from her across the trailer park's open spaces as if he'd never needed her at all. Then Sam locked up, headed down the stairs, and stopped yet again with the second bouquet of roses still lying there at her feet. "Damnit."

She stooped to pick them up, handling them much more roughly than the first batch, because one bouquet of a dozen pink roses was a nice surprise. Maybe even a somewhat sweet gesture, depending on who had left them there and why.

But two in just as many days was a pain in her ass.

First of all, whoever had been leaving these knew that she'd seen and taken the first one, and then they'd thought it was a good idea to leave her another.

Like Sam Salazar was the kind of woman who would lose her head over a few dozen flowers and think it was cute to get the same surprise in the exact spot every morning.

It wasn't.

She slung the roses roughly under her arm and headed for her Jeep.

"Are you sure you didn't see anyone creeping around the trailer?" she called to Syc.

His head swiveled toward her, then he shrugged. "I'm getting up there in years, Sam, but I'm not that old."

"Could've fooled me."

"If I was gonna do something nice for you, it sure as shit wouldn't be pink roses. Oh, wait. I already *did* something nice for you."

He wasn't wrong. Letting her stay in his park for free could have been a big deal. Letting her take over the Deville after her Airstream had literally been ripped to shreds was just another scoop on the Syc's goodwill sundae.

As Sam reached her Jeep and climbed behind the wheel, she tossed the second bouquet over her shoulder into the back seat. She forced herself not to look at it as she cranked the engine and headed out of the park.

On the schedule for today was a trip to the pharmacy for Beth's aunt, Ruthie Garrick, picking up her next supply of insulin, a package of fresh syringes, and groceries. Sam was the only one in the old woman's life now that Beth was gone. She had a feeling Ruthie wouldn't last even a month if Sam wasn't willing to perform these simple yet vital errands for her.

In the grocery store's parking lot, Sam loaded everything into the back seat of her Jeep, got behind the wheel, and pulled out a cigarette before she'd even thought about starting the engine. But she paused with the smoke resting loosely between her lips and both hands cupped around the lighter poised in front of it.

Somehow, her attention had returned to the now slightly battered bouquet of pink roses, which she'd unintentionally glimpsed while loading the groceries up into the back.

Sam sighed.

This smoke break would have to wait.

She tossed the unlit cigarette and lighter into the little pocket in the center console, then snatched up the bouquet and slammed the driver's-side door behind her before storming back into the store.

Ironic how the first and only time she'd ever walked up to the floral section of any store was to damn near interrogate whoever worked there and get to the bottom of this second bouquet she'd never wanted.

The young woman behind the counter looked friendly enough. "Good morning, how can I help you?"

Two seconds later, her smile dropped.

Because Sam practically slammed the bouquet down on the counter between them. "I need to know where this came from."

"Um, okay…" The store employee slowly looked down at the bouquet, tilted her head, and reached out to touch the wrapping around the long stems for all of three seconds before she pulled her hand back as if the roses were a can of venomous snakes. "Well, you came to the right place. These definitely came from us."

"Great. Now I need to know who sent them."

The young woman's smile flickered like a dying lightbulb. "I'm sorry. It's against our policy to share customers' personal information. That includes people who purchased flowers or made their orders through us and those individuals scheduled to receive flower deliveries."

"And if I'm the person receiving the deliveries?" Sam asked, well aware the young woman didn't deserve her brusqueness. But two days of mystery roses by some anonymous creep pretending to be some brilliant gift-giver had really gotten on her nerves.

"I still can't give you that information," the young woman said, sounding more uncertain by the second. "I'm sorry. It's against—"

"Against policy. Yeah. I get it." Sam folded her arms. "What *can* you tell me about these flowers?"

"Probably not a whole lot. Though these aren't the kind of flowers we get all the time, so… let me take a look, if you don't mind waiting while I check the computer."

Sam stepped back to give the young woman plenty of

space, even with the entire checkout counter between them.

She didn't like surprises or mysteries that involved her personal life — let alone the patch of grass in front of her trailer door.

Something was going on here, she could feel it.

It didn't take the young woman long to find the information and return to Sam.

"Okay," she said with a stern nod. "This is what I *can* tell you. The flowers definitely originated from this store, like I said, but no one came in to order them. It was an online transaction, so we really don't even have much information about the person in the first place. Even if that was something I could give you."

Frowning, Sam stared at the crinkled cellophane wrapping around the bottom of the bouquet, which boasted several tears from all its recent mistreatment. "Is there anything in that online order about why they wanted *these* flowers to send to me specifically? Something left in the notes section?"

"I'm sorry," the florist said, matching the sentiment with a strained smile that perfectly echoed her words. "There wasn't anything like that left on the order form we received in our inbox. Whoever placed the order *did* make it very clear that these were to be Sophy's Roses and nothing else."

Sam nearly choked on her next breath.

"What did you just say?" she asked, hating the way she sounded now that her mouth had gone suddenly dry, but there was nothing she could do about it.

Of course, the woman on the other side of the counter remained completely oblivious. "Sophy's Roses. We don't normally sell them, so we had to get them shipped in on special order just to fill the one we received. Our system shows the order was picked up the day before yesterday, right before closing. So I'm guessing this is the second bouquet—"

"That would match the records you *do* have, yeah," Sam murmured. She'd completely lost her ability to filter her words or even the tone in which she delivered them, and now, she just sounded pissed.

The florist took that and ran with it in a completely different direction. "This order was for seven bouquets of these Sophy's Roses. Supposedly one a day, if they follow the same schedule that's already been set with pickups."

"Seven days of this shit?" Sam asked, pointing at the bouquet. "Cancel it."

"I'm sorry?" The florist's voice trembled a little at the end of her nervous laugh, and she failed to hide a quick glance over Sam's shoulder toward something else behind her. Probably looking for another store employee to come save her from this unexpected encounter with a woman who wanted to cancel seven days' worth of rare, special-order roses.

"I said what I said," Sam added. "Cancel them. I don't want them. Hell, go ahead and sell 'em to someone else, for all I care."

"Ma'am, I can't resell these flowers. They've already been paid for."

"I don't give a shit if they've already been paid for," Sam said, her voice rising in volume and now completely out of her control. "Cancel the goddamn order!"

The florist's eyes widened, and she blinked quickly without saying a word.

Sam recognized how shitty she was being and took a step back with a sigh. "I'm sorry. I know you're just doing your job. But please, do whatever you can to make sure they don't get delivered to the address on that online order, okay? You couldn't possibly know anything about this from where you're standing, but at this point, me getting any more of those things counts as harassment."

"Ma'am, I promise you we're not trying to harass—"

"Can I help you, ma'am?"

Sam spun around and found a tall, broad-shouldered man in his mid- to late thirties almost looming over her from behind as he peeled dirty plastic gloves off his hands, though the hairnet and full-length apron stained with watery rust-red splotches remained.

This grocery store didn't have the resources for a full-time security staff, which generally wasn't a thing for any of the grocery stores Sam had used, but apparently this guy from the meat department would do just as well in a pinch.

Sam now realized the young, startled florist had been making eyes at him the whole time, over Sam's shoulder, in a wordless plea for help.

"It looked like there might've been an issue over here," he added. "Is there an issue, ma'am?"

"No problem," Sam replied, forcing herself not to grit her teeth so the statement would sound even a little genuine. "I'm just hoping this young woman understands I *don't* want any more flower deliveries."

The young woman she licked her lips and nodded. "I understand, ma'am. I promise I will do whatever I can to help you with this issue."

"Great." The big guy stepped forward to try looming over Sam from the side now. "Anything else?"

"Nope. That's all I needed."

Then Sam started to walk away.

"Oh, ma'am," the florist said. "Don't forget your flowers."

It was all Sam could do not to growl as she spun

around again. She stopped short when the deli guy with the hairnet extended the mashed bouquet toward her and raised his eyebrows.

"Right," Sam hissed. "Don't wanna forget the fucking roses."

She snatched them out of his hand, then marched toward the store's entrance.

EIGHT

Sam

ONCE SHE GOT behind the wheel, Sam couldn't bring herself to do anything else.

"Whoever placed the order did make it very clear that these were to be Sophy's Roses and nothing else."

Roses named after her daughter.

Whoever had sent the roses had wanted to hurt her and had known the one thing that would do the most damage.

The list of people who'd want to hurt Sam Salazar wasn't short, even when she narrowed it down to people in the town of Rush alone. Starting, of course, with the Petes.

Little Pete Wilder clearly had it out for her in more ways than one.

But Sam didn't think Little Pete was capable of coming up with something like this all on his own.

No, something this private and personally backhanded felt much more like the kind of low level to which Big Pete Wilder would stoop in order to make a point.

But Sam didn't talk about Sophie as a general rule. She'd mentioned her daughter once, maybe twice, during her first few NA meetings in Rush, but that was it. Chris knew too. And Syc. That was it.

When she imagined who would be at the center of the Venn Diagram connecting people who wanted to hurt her and people who knew the intimate details of her past — like the name of her daughter — only one person immediately sprang to mind.

When he did, Sam practically had no choice. She had to know.

Pulling out her phone, she searched for the number she hadn't had reason to call in years. Honestly, she'd barely thought of Ian in years, and when she did, it was only with pure rage, the debilitating sting of betrayal, and the agony of everything he symbolized for her now. He was the one man she had decided to trust after so many years of not trusting anyone.

The one man whom she never should have let herself trust in the first place, because Sophie's father was the one who had let Sam's sweet little girl slip right through his fingers forever.

RIGHTEOUS FURY. Uncontrollable rage. Debilitating grief that never really went away but, when combined with the other two, merely intensified.

It didn't matter what she felt anyway. Sam just needed an answer.

She stabbed his number still saved in her phone and bashed her cell against her ear with a grimace. The phone rang four times, and she cursed the bastard for not answering until the line finally clicked and a woman's voice came through.

"Hello?"

"I need to talk to Ian," Sam said. "Is he with you?"

"Who is this?"

"You can tell him it's Sam. Then give him the phone."

The phone rustled, followed by hushed, slightly muffled voices. Someone cleared their throat before the line went deathly silent.

She waited for him to say something first. If Ian was behind the flowers, he would know exactly why she was calling, and he'd probably be smiling to himself right now, thinking the whole thing was so fucking cute no matter how much it hurt her.

"Sam?" he finally asked, sounding completely lost from the start.

Either he really didn't know what this call was about, or he'd seriously improved his lying-asshole persona.

"Sam?" Ian asked again, then sighed. "Okay, I know you're there, and you're not hanging up. What I can't figure out is why you're calling me."

The sound of his voice made her ball her fists, though one of them had a cell phone in it, and she had to force herself not to squeeze it so tightly that she broke the damn thing in half. With all the rage trembling through her now, it wouldn't have surprised her if she crushed it to pieces with her bare hand.

"I just need a straight answer," she said evenly. "No bullshit, Ian. Have you been sending me roses?"

Coming from anyone else, the long pause on the other end of the line would have signified complete disbelief or shock. From Ian, though, it could have been anything.

He'd managed to get her to trust him with Sophie's life, which had been the worst mistake of Sam's. Who knew what else he was capable of?

"That's definitely not even close to anything I expected you to say," Ian replied slowly. "What's—"

"Just answer the question."

"I…" A sharp, tense chuckle escaped him, followed by an audible swallow. "Sam, I'm not sending you anything, let alone roses. I don't even know where you live these days."

It wouldn't have been all that hard to figure out if he'd put any amount of effort into it, but Ian had already proven he wasn't the kind of person who put any amount of effort into anything. Even his responsibilities as a father, which had lasted all of a week before neither of them had a daughter to be responsible for in the first place.

"You still haven't answered the question," Sam seethed.

"No, Sam. I haven't been sending you flowers. That's not something that's ever occurred to me, honestly, but it's nice to talk to you. It's been … a long time. How are you?"

Sam jerked the phone away from her ear, glared at the screen with his name stamped across it above the green call-in-progress symbol, then stabbed her finger down on the red circle to hang up on him.

Her cell bounced on the passenger seat beside her, rejected just like the second bouquet of flowers, and she was much happier to see a phone there instead of more goddamn Sophy's Roses.

Ian had sounded genuinely surprised by her call and maybe even genuinely glad to hear from her, which was beyond her comprehension. Sam could have gone the rest of her life without speaking to him or seeing his face or thinking about him in any way, let alone remembering that he existed. But that wasn't one of those problems she could just wish away and let time take care of the rest.

Those types of problems had run out for Sam a long time ago, along with her ability to let things go.

With no other immediate names popping to mind for who else could possibly be the asshole trying to send her this kind of messed-up message, Sam grabbed her keys in the ignition, cranked on the Jeep's engine, and pulled out of the grocery store parking lot.

She probably would have gone straight home then, but she wasn't finished with her errands.

Dropping off Ruthie's insulin was a whole hell of a lot more important than Sam's discomfort right now.

A matter of life and death, actually.

AFTER DELIVERING the old woman's groceries and prescriptions — and having to remind Ruthie who she was several times while the old woman had tried to convince her that Beth wasn't actually dead because an actual body hadn't been found or placed in the casket at the woman's funeral — Sam briefly stopped back home to drop off the food she'd bought for herself. Then she jumped back into the Jeep and took off to the Redwood Rings for her shift.

Fortunately, there were no more screaming Sycs storming across the park, no more roses waiting for her in front of her trailer, and no more deeply concerning distractions. When she drove past the Kalamack Club one more time on her way into town, there was also no sign of either Chief Colton or the strange woman from out of town who'd been holding up a picket sign with the name Dina scrawled across it.

When she finally stepped through the front doors of the Redwood Rings' front pub and officially started her shift — after her prerequisite fifteen to twenty minutes of tardiness — she found herself studying Chris from the corner of her eye every chance she got without having a single thing to say to him in the process.

She'd asked him point-blank if he'd sent her that first bouquet, which he denied easily and with a rational explanation for it that had passed Sam's own personal version of the Rorschach Test.

Still, she'd mentioned Sophie to him once, in a moment of weakness, when all her armor had been stripped off and tossed onto the floor of his apartment for the momentary safety and security that spending intimate time with him afforded.

Now, having done that felt particularly dangerous, because he was one of the few people in the entire world who knew pretty much all of her secrets.

The question now was more complicated than Sam wanted to admit, but she had to.

Could she truly trust Chris the way she wanted to, the way she hadn't trusted anyone in so long because the last time she had, she'd lost the only precious, innocent, truly wonderful thing in her life and there was no getting Sophie back?

After everything they'd been through and the copious amounts of her bullshit Chris had put up with over the last few years, he'd given her no reason not to trust him.

As Sam poured two more foaming beers from the tap, he turned toward her and flashed her a crooked smile before he took off through the swinging doors into the kitchen.

No way did that look like the smile of someone who was trying to seriously fuck with her, and why would he want to in the first place?

Sure, Sam didn't exactly take him up on every one of his offers to hang out together or spend the night together or do any other number of things they had done together over the last several months, with any variation of her physical and emotional armor on or off. But Chris seemed to care about Sam despite her heavy baggage and the number of thorns in which she covered herself.

Far more even than those found on a bouquet of a dozen roses.

No, Sam decided she *could* trust him. Men like Chris were few and far between, which didn't make things any easier with him. She didn't think he would willingly hurt her with something like these damn Sophy's Roses, because that was the only reasonable explanation for why someone had been delivering them.

To cut Sam to the bone quickly and deeply and maybe even leave her there to bleed out on the grass right outside her trailer, if she wasn't careful.

That couldn't be Chris. Right?

NINE

Sam

It DIDN'T TAKE MORE than an hour through her shift at the Redwood for Chris to pick up on how upset Sam was or that there was clearly something else going on she hadn't previously mentioned. He kept giving her those looks across the bar, across the room, or across the kitchen — complete with that crooked smile but now also with raised eyebrows and a look of both uncomfortably piercing compassion and the kind of silently-asked question Sam couldn't interpret as anything but, *"Are you sure you're okay?"*

She wasn't sure of anything beyond the fact that she just wanted to get through this shift and call it a night. But Chris had other plans.

He usually did.

When the Redwood Rings reached its first real lull in the late afternoon, he sidled toward her behind the front bar. "Hey."

"I've been here for hours already," she said, shooting him a sidling glance. "And you said hi when I got here."

"Oh, so I only get an allotment of one greeting per day, huh? Is that how it's gonna be now?"

"You do if you don't wanna start some serious shit with me," she quipped.

"Sam, just looking at you starts serious shit with you," he said through a chuckle. "I'm pretty sure I'm past the point of being turned away by that now, don't you think?"

"So you're saying you've built up an immunity to me."

"Something like that. So what's up?"

Sam stared across the empty bar in the front pub and shook her head. "It's just not a good time."

"Looks like a great time to me." He gestured around the empty room. "There's literally nothing else to do."

"Wow. That's a surprise coming from my *boss*."

"Well, you know, I've gotta bring *some* perks to the job. Otherwise, you'll walk right through those doors without a second thought the minute something better shows up."

"Oh, *that's* what you're afraid of me doing."

He shrugged. "Not really. But I do know there's something on your mind today. And I'm a little worried about what it might do to you if you keep bottling it up like that."

"Jesus." She slapped the damp rag in her hand down on the counter behind the bar, because she'd finished wiping the bar clean five minutes ago. "Am I really that much of an open book?"

"Depends on who's reading." Chris flashed her that crooked smile again. "I mean, today, I'm pretty sure that's me. So yeah."

"Great. Just what I always wanted."

He was starting to break down her defenses again, just like he'd done so many times before, simply from his doggedness and stubborn inability to take no for an answer. He certainly didn't back down easily, which was what made it so hard for Sam to keep telling him no. So she lowered the rest of her prickly-thorn defenses to tell Chris exactly what was going on with the Sophy's Roses. He already knew about the first bouquet from yesterday, but the deepening frown darkening his expression more and more as she explained what was going on only reconfirmed for Sam that this was a serious issue.

She wasn't just being overly emotional or way too sensitive and blowing the whole thing out of proportion.

Not like that was something she ever did anyway. But hey, there was always a chance it might start someday.

Just like there was always a chance she would fall right back into a bottle of booze or pills, which therefore made it that much more important for her to always remember that possibility still existed.

Once an addict, always an addict.

Once an Army MP turned to mush by motherhood, always somehow still broken and twisted up inside.

When she finished, he drew a deep breath and let it out in a slow, thoughtful sigh.

"That's heavy," he said.

Sam snorted. "No shit."

"Have any idea who it might be?" he asked.

"I bet I could give you two guesses and you'd get both of them right on the first try."

"The Petes?"

"Yeah. I thought of that." Sam gulped down almost half her Pepsi and fought back the belch immediately bubbling right back up again in its wake. She puffed out her cheeks and thumped a fist against her chest, which seemed to keep most of it down where it belonged for now. "I also thought it might've been Ian."

"Ian? As in…"

"The asshole who gave me the best thing in my life and took it away just as easily?" she muttered. "Yeah. As in *that* Ian. I actually called him."

Chris sucked in a pained breath through his teeth and wrinkled his nose. "Ouch."

"Trust me, it was more painful for me than it was for him, and that wasn't anywhere close to what I was going for. He didn't do it."

"You sure?"

"He was never a good actor, Chris." She looked up to meet his gaze for the first time since starting this conversation. "Or even a decent liar."

"Fair enough. Anyone else on your list?"

Sam shrugged. "Not for the moment, no. Which is even more frustrating because the only two names I haven't marked off the list are the two names I want to mark off the most but probably shouldn't. You know, staying in my own lane and all that." It was definitely a crack at all the times Chris had basically told her the same thing whenever Sam's frustration and fiery indignation got the better of her.

Like the time she'd gotten both of them into a fistfight with Big Pete Wilder over a whole bunch of nothing, as it turned out.

Chris clearly caught on to her attempt at a joke, but he didn't find it funny. At least this time, he also didn't find the need to tell her that.

Instead, he just studied her face before gently asking, "Was *I* ever on that list?"

"No, Chris," she lied right to his face. For the first time in a long time, lying to anyone's face like this didn't immediately fill her with squirming, roiling guilt. "Your answer was way too perfect yesterday when I asked if it was you."

"Well, I'm glad it was convincing enough, at least." His attempt at a smile flickered, then they stood there behind the bar in a mutual silence that wasn't quite awkward but definitely carried the weight of something more than what had been said between them. Then Chris shook his head. "Tell you what. I'll handle the rest of this up here in the front. Why don't you go take the Back Bar today, huh? Get your mind off all these uppity tourists. Give it another shot. We'll see how it goes."

She wanted to laugh in his face, but he was dead serious.

"For real? You're giving me the Back Bar for the rest of the day as … what? A consolation pity-prize?"

"I mean, that's not exactly what I had in mind, but if that's how you wanna see it…"

The front door to the pub opened with a little jingle of the bell hanging above it, and Sam glanced that way.

It was just second nature at this point to see who in their right mind was heading into their place of business in the middle of the traditional after-lunch rush. Sam was on the verge of taking Chris up on his unexpected offer before she realized exactly who had stepped through those doors.

It was the woman. The stranger from out of town who'd been standing outside the Kalamack Club with her picket sign before she'd been escorted right into the back of Chief Colton's squad car.

So she *was* free. For today, at least. And she'd decided to make the Redwood Rings her next stop.

"You know what, Chris?" Sam said. "I'm gonna stay up front today."

"All right, well then you better get back — wait, what?"

She grabbed a roll of silverware and a menu from the end of the bar, offered Chris a dismissive nod, and hurried into the dining room, trying not to look too eager as she approached the woman who'd taken a seat at a corner table by the front windows.

"Hey, there." Sam stopped a few feet away from the

table because the woman sitting there now looked particularly skittish up close.

Or maybe that was just because Sam already knew the kind of night this woman had spent, and it sure as hell hadn't been in a cozy hotel room or Airbnb.

The woman looked up at her with wide, doleful eyes, which instantly made Sam think of a basset hound just waking up from the world's longest nap. "Hi..."

Sam set down the menu and silverware, then backed up again smiled. She hoped to make the woman feel comfortable enough that she might open up to her lunch server for the day. "What can I get for you?"

The woman scanned the menu, flipped it over for her gaze to dart all around the opposite side but not land on anything, and looked up at the bar. "Do you happen to have orange juice?"

Sam raised her eyebrows. "Just orange juice?"

"If you have it."

"Yeah, we've got it."

"Then I'll do half orange juice, half club soda, if you've got that," the woman added. "Otherwise, just the orange juice."

This was a new one.

Even the tourists didn't come into the Redwood Rings for orange juice when it didn't include champagne or vodka and cranberry to go with it. But who was Sam to judge? She never drank anything stronger than the Pepsi here herself.

"Orange juice and soda," she said with a nod. "You got it. You wanna eat here too, or is it just the OJ?"

The woman slid the menu away from her across the table and attempted a more genuine smile. "I'm definitely hungry. What would you recommend here?"

Sam couldn't help it. She snorted and nodded through

the front windows. "If you want my recommendation, you should probably go to the place across the street."

It was supposed to be a joke. Sam thought it was funny, but the woman at the table flinched at the words, clenching her eyes shut for a moment before letting out the kind of sigh that sounded more like it was coming from someone on their death bed instead of a potential customer.

"Thank you for the suggestion," she said, surprising Sam by scooting back noisily in her chair and rising to her feet. "Forget the orange juice, then. I'll get out of your hair."

Without another word, the woman brushed past Sam, shouldering her small handbag and booking it out the front doors of the Redwood like she was being chased.

"Shit," Sam whispered.

She glanced over her shoulder, but the bar was empty. Chris had gone elsewhere, probably to take over in the Back Bar because she'd refused him. And now she'd just driven off the one woman she actually wanted to speak to today.

The mystery of this newcomer to Rush — and her picket signs screaming out for *Justice for Dina* that had apparently been enough to get her thrown behind bars for a little lesson in how to not step on the wrong toes in a town like this — was just too good to pass up.

Fine. Sam had fucked it up, and now she had to go clean up the pieces and try to put them back together.

Hoping no one came through those kitchen doors in the next two minutes, Sam darted across the dining room, pushed open the Redwood's front doors, and quickly spun to the left where she'd last seen the woman standing out on the sidewalk. Now, the stranger looked even more lost than she had when ordering an orange juice and club soda.

"Ma'am?" Sam called after her.

The woman looked practically accosted when she saw it was her server of twenty seconds chasing her out of the bar.

"I'm not interested in any more of your recommendations, thank you," she said stiffly. "I've taken your first to heart, and that's all I have the energy for now."

"No more recommendations," Sam said. "That was petty of me. I get that." She glanced through the front windows of the Redwood, though it wasn't like she'd be able to see if anyone had come to the front since she'd stepped out. But trying to make amends now still felt like a priority, especially with a completely empty dining room and bar behind her. "I came out here to apologize, actually. Sometimes, I try to make jokes. And they don't always land very well. That's on me."

The woman turned her nose up to Sam and eyed her sidelong. "Not always? Would you call that a fifty-fifty split?"

Sam huffed out a laugh, though she wasn't entirely sure the woman was yanking her chain, either. "Okay, you got me. Most of the time my jokes don't land. And I'm sorry, you don't have to come back inside if you don't want to, but I didn't wanna let you leave without apologizing to you first. And if you'd like to come back inside and get some lunch, I'm happy to serve you."

After studying her a moment longer, the woman finally said, "Well I accept your apology. But I'm not coming back inside." The woman glanced up at the marquee above the pub's front doors. "Not because of you. I shouldn't have stepped into this establishment in the first place, you know? Not good for my sobriety."

If Sam had tried to hide her surprise at that small confession, she would have failed anyway. "Well, that's something I absolutely understand."

The woman turned her nose up at Sam one more time, let out a non-committal hum of either acknowledgement or dismissal, then spun around and marched right off the sidewalk toward the Redwood Rings' parking lot, where she got into a maroon Honda Accord.

With a sigh, Sam returned to her actual job inside the bar.

～

AT THE END of her shift, Sam didn't even give Chris the opportunity to ask if she wanted to hang out tonight. He'd picked up on the fact that she didn't want to do much of anything with anyone, especially after their conversation about the Sophy's Roses and her asshole mystery admirer. The only attention he paid her was a nod and a wave as Sam headed out the door, calling after her, "Don't worry about it, I'll lock up on my own."

"I wasn't worried at all," she said over her shoulder without stopping.

But she didn't expect to find an extra car in the parking lot this late at night. Chris's vehicle was still there, as was Jackson's, and another vehicle parked a few spaces down from Sam's Jeep.

A maroon Honda Accord.

That didn't make sense.

Had the woman seriously been sitting there behind the wheel of her own car for hours without moving?

Slowing on her way to her Jeep, she couldn't stop looking over her shoulder at the picket-sign lady. It was already dark out. Both bars had closed up for the night, or were almost closed, and there was no one else out here.

When the woman met Sam's gaze through the windshield, she winced and instantly looked away.

The alarm bells in Sam's mind flared up instantly.

Sam was in a particularly unique position to recognize the look of an addict of any substance warring with herself over what she thought she wanted and what she knew she could never have again. It was the same look Sam had seen so many times in the mirror before making the incredibly difficult decision to keep what she thought she wanted far out of her own reach so she wouldn't keep fucking everything up with another tumble off the wagon.

Did this woman look like she wanted to be left alone right now for another four hours or more in the parking lot outside the Redwood Rings? Absolutely.

Should she be left alone?

Instead of continuing toward her Jeep, Sam veered toward the woman's car instead.

The woman jumped when Sam knocked on her window, then she looked completely baffled by the fact that anyone would be standing outside her car at this time of night.

After several seconds of scowling back at Sam under the dim yellow light from the street lamps flooding the Redwoods' parking lot, she rolled down her manual window with crank after sharp, agitated crank of the lever. "Can I help you?"

"No, I'm all good," Sam said, not sure if she should laugh or feel slightly offended by the instant bite in the woman's words. "But I saw you out here, and it doesn't look like you've moved much since our last conversation earlier today. So I thought I'd come by to see if you're all right."

The woman glowered at her. Then, without warning, her lower lip trembled, and she heaved a massive sigh. "No, I'm not all right. I meant to go find somewhere else in town to have a late lunch, but as it turns out, somebody thought it would be fun to slash my tires."

"You don't say." Blinking slowly, Sam took three steps away from the vehicle, and all it took after that was a quick glance at the front and rear tires on the driver's side to confirm the woman's claims. "Have you at least called the police to tell them what happened? Maybe ask for some help?"

The woman wrinkled her nose and avoided Sam's gaze after that. "I don't think I'd still be sitting here if I had."

"Why didn't you?"

"Because I got myself into a little bit of … trouble yesterday with the local police. The officer who so graciously let me spend the night in a holding cell told me to leave town as soon as possible and never come back."

Sam nodded. "Maybe I can help."

TEN

Dina

FIVE YEARS AGO...

AFTER TWO WEEKS of working as a trimmer on Rip's farm, Dina wasn't so sure she was cut out for this work after all. Even Tiff's descriptions of what trim season was like fell far short of the harsh realities, in Dina's opinion.

The workdays were incredibly long — twelve hours from damn near sunrise to slightly after sunset, where the workers gathered under the outdoor tents strung with lights that switched on once the sun went down, so they could see to finish their work for the day. And it was grueling work.

After two weeks of twelve-hour days of continuously grasping and gripping and squeezing her pair of tiny garden shears, Dina's right hand was cramping.

This morning, even after a good night's sleep, the cramping and the shaking were even worse. All her fingers trembled as she tried to stretch out some of the stiffness before climbing out of her bunk and getting dressed for the day, but there wasn't much improvement.

What if she didn't recover, even with rest? A surgeon wasn't going to become a surgeon with even one of her hands permanently damaged by this kind of repetitive-motion stress day in and day out.

Maybe Dina truly just wasn't cut out for this at all.

All day, as she struggled to find a grip that hurt less, she couldn't stop worrying about whether she was destroying the career she was working to pay for. So, when Shell invited her to come back into town with their group of friends to party on a Friday night and blow off a little steam, Dina figured she might as well.

Taking herself too seriously up here at this job wouldn't do her any favors, and more than anything, she just wanted to forget about her hand.

At least for a little while.

DINA HADN'T BEEN BACK to the Redwood Rings since her first day in Rush, but she hadn't exactly felt like she'd been missing anything.

According to everyone else, this was the place to be on a Friday night when they had a little bit of time to kill, some cash to burn, and a hell of a lot more steam to let off.

Unlike her first day in Rush, however, the pub was packed when Dina and her new friends stepped through the front doors. Music played through the loudspeakers, something she thought might have been close to modern country, but she couldn't be sure. Bodies packed the spaces around tables, and it was hard to find a table where their entire group could fit — even harder to get one of the two bartenders' attention.

Shell dragged Dina toward the bar, elbowing her way

through the crowd, then shouting out the entire group's order in one rapid-fire breath.

Despite being asked multiple times, Dina still refrained from drinking anything but Pepsi.

Would she have liked to unwind a little, maybe even settle what was left of the stiff pain in her hand? Definitely. But she'd seen way too much letting loose in her life, all of it with her mother at the center of such demonstrations. Honestly, she'd rather just get blazed out of her mind whenever one of the other trimmers inevitably lit up a joint — which they would — than start drinking now. Or ever.

Eventually, Dina forgot about trying to hide the tremor in her hand as she lifted her red plastic cup of Pepsi to take another sip.

"Whoa, D," Amanda said, her eyes widening as she stared at the trembling drink with ice clinking all over the place inside it. "Are you *sure* you don't want a drink?"

Everyone else found that particularly funny.

Dina immediately set her Pepsi back down on the table. "That's got nothing to do with it. I'm just feeling the work a little, I guess. Did anyone else's hands start doing this your first season?"

The others all looked at each other, exchanging glances of confusion or amusement or a mix of both.

Then Shell shook her head and shrugged. "Not really, no. That hand kinda looks serious, though. You okay?"

"Yeah, I'm fine. Maybe I just need more hand strength or something. I'm not sure if I should keep trimming the same way or maybe try to switch it up, but … I don't know."

"You want me to take a look at it?" Matt asked. "I mean, I'm not a doctor yet, but I *will* be. Eventually."

Dina shook her head. "No, thanks. I'm good. I think I probably just need to give it a break, you know?"

She grabbed her drink with her left hand instead now and tried to act casual beneath the undeniable awkwardness of lifting anything to her mouth with her left hand.

As the night wore on, the bar got louder and louder, and her friends kept drinking. She finished her second Pepsi and got up on her own for a refill.

It didn't look like anyone noticed her temporary escape as Dina maneuvered her way through the bar. Where the entire dining area had been jam-packed with customers two hours ago, now there was more than enough room for Dina to get to the bar. But when she got there, the bartender didn't even bother to ask for a drink order this time. When Dina set her empty Pepsi cup down on the counter, he set down a brand-new red plastic cup with Pepsi on ice in front of her, then went to the next customer without a word. He didn't look at her either — for the hundredth or so time tonight.

Well, I guess I'm only halfway invisible, then...

She was just about to pick her drink up off the bar and head back toward her friends when a man sidled up to her. Despite there being plenty of room, he'd decided to ignore the concept of personal space.

She almost made a face at the fresh burst of cologne and semi-sweet aftershave wafting off him and mixing with the easily identifiable scent of booze on the guy.

"Having a good night?" the man asked. He sounded friendly enough despite the cloying smell and how close he stood.

Having no real experience being approached by men in bars, she made the mistake of turning toward him. "Sorry, were you talking to me?"

He flashed her a brilliant grin, and she found it almost

impossible not to stare at the abnormally white sheen of his perfectly straight teeth within that smile. He might have been decent-looking — no, he definitely was — but the smell of alcohol on him overpowered whatever good looks he might have had. Besides, he had to be in his late sixties, at least. If he was hitting on her right now, just the massive age gap between them grossed her out.

"Yeah, actually," he said. "You look a little lost, honestly."

"I don't normally go to bars."

"I picked up on that," he said without taking his eyes off her. Then he shifted sideways, bent over the bar to prop his forearm on it as he swirled a glass around in his hand.

Dina leaned away from him, then took an awkward step in the opposite direction, hoping it wasn't ruder than she wanted to be to anyone, even a creepy guy who could've been her grandpa.

"I'm sorry." The man chuckled, which made him sound even friendlier as he shook his head and bashfully glanced down at his drink. "I came at this the wrong way. I promise I'm not trying to make you uncomfortable."

"No, you're not. It's fine." Instantly, she wanted to kick herself for saying something so stupid. It wasn't fine. He was definitely being creepy, looming over her like that, and she really wished she knew how to get herself out of this conversation.

"The thing is," he continued, "I couldn't help but over-hear some of your conversation earlier when you were talking to your friends." He gestured toward the back corner of the bar where Dina's friends still huddled around that three-top pushed against the wall. None of them looked her way or even glanced at the bar, and she was pretty sure no one had even noticed she'd left.

Great.

"I wasn't eavesdropping. I was just sitting down at the next table over and got an earful of your conversation."

"Right." Dina sipped at her Pepsi. "Sorry if they're too loud."

A deeper laugh burst from his open-mouthed smile, and Dina almost found herself smiling back at the sound of it. Almost.

He was friendly enough, but something about the guy made her pause, like he was the human embodiment of a déjà vu moment, a photograph that just didn't look quite right. There was something about him that begged further scrutiny.

"Don't apologize, sweetheart," the man said when he finally stopped laughing. "If you're interested, I know a place right here in town where you can earn way better money than you ever could out at Rip's farm. Even if your hand keeps giving you problems."

Dina instantly whipped her right hand back toward herself as if she'd just touched a hot stove, then awkwardly wiped her palm on the leg of her jeans before settling for folding her arms onto the bar.

Even if he'd meant well, this was definitely still creepy. No matter how many times the guy said he wasn't trying to be.

And yet, the idea of making more money than what she'd expected to make at Rip's, which was out of reach with her hand slowing her down, definitely caught her interest. She should have walked away right then and there and wished the guy goodnight, but she didn't. "What kind of work?"

"Nothing too strenuous," he said with a casual shrug. "Just a little—"

"There you are, D!" Shell shouted a second before

appearing at Dina's side. She linked her arm through Dina's, effectively breaking the younger girl's folded arms, and jostled her a little. "You just disappeared. I thought maybe you'd left on your own to walk home or something."

"Are you kidding?" Dina snorted. "I wouldn't get back 'til sunrise if I walked."

"Well, good thing you didn't try it, then."

The man at the bar waited patiently until he found an opportunity to reinsert himself. "Is this a friend of yours?"

Dina opened her mouth to answer, but Shell gripped her arm even tighter and said, "You don't have to keep talking to this guy, okay? Let's go back to the table—"

"Excuse me," the man interrupted, leaning away from the bar now as if he meant to step between the girls and their direct path back to their friends. His smile remained friendly, but the icy sheen behind his eyes matched the sharper undertone in his voice.

Dina recognized that subtle transformation, because she'd witnessed it herself more times than she could count in her own mother. The deeper Angela got into her bottle or two and the longer into the night, the less point there was in trying to reason with her.

Her instant gut reaction was to grab her Pepsi cup with her left hand and tighten her linked arm within Shell's.

"And now the conversation's over," Shell replied. Her smile had turned bitter, sarcasm dripping from her voice. "You got your drink, right, D?"

"Yeah, but I—"

Shell yanked her away from the bar so hard, Dina almost tripped and splashed Pepsi everywhere. Somehow, she managed to catch her footing as Shell dragged her back toward their table.

"Just think about it, huh?" the man said, turning to

watch as Dina stumbled away after Shell. "If you change your mind, I'm here almost every night."

Shell whirled on the guy and practically hissed at him, "She's not looking for any work."

The man caught Dina's gaze and dipped his head, his smile once more tame and friendly. "It's legitimate work, sweetheart. Nothing dirty or unsavory about it. And you'd be well-suited to the job. Kind of a perfect fit, if you ask me. Just think about it."

"She doesn't need to think about it," Shell snapped. "The answer's no."

She tugged Dina after her again until they were back at the table in the back corner.

The conversation had come to a complete stop, and all the other trimmers stared at either Dina or Shell or the man at the bar.

"What was that about?" Matt asked.

"Just another douchebag thinking he owns everything and everyone who steps foot in this town," Shell said with a grimace. "Good thing I was there to pull you away, D. You don't wanna get involved with someone like that. Trust me."

"Who is he?" Dina almost turned around again to look back at the man in question, then thought better of it.

"Was he bothering you?" Phil asked.

"Not really," Dina said. "I guess he overheard us talking about my hand, so he offered some other kind of work in town that apparently pays better than Rip's—"

She was cut off by a resounding collective groan from the group.

"That's Pete Wilder," Matt said.

"He's bad news, D. Don't get mixed up with him over anything, okay? Believe me, you're much safer sticking with us."

"Matt knows what he's talking about," Shell added in a playfully lilting voice before she poked Dina in the ribs to make her jump.

Everyone else laughed, including Dina as she slapped her friend's hand away, but she couldn't help wonder why everyone was afraid of Pete Wilder.

~

AS THE NIGHT WORE ON, Dina's friends just kept drinking, and Dina's boredom levels just kept growing. Until, with a laugh, she remembered the half-smoked joint in the pocket of her hoodie.

She borrowed a lighter and stepped outside, strolling around the side of the building, which effectively blocked both the chilly breeze and the view of anyone in the parking lot.

Which meant she now had just the right amount of privacy.

The half-smoked joint was still perfectly shaped, its rolled-up paper end a little stinky and crisped with flakes of burnt plant material, but that didn't matter. Dina stuck it in her mouth, lit the end, and puffed. She got a few decent mouthfuls of smoke, but somehow that didn't quite seem like enough, so she lit it again and took the kind of drag she'd learned how to take in the last two weeks of working at Rip's farm.

She coughed once, then the sound of footsteps scuffling across the sidewalk toward her made her suck in a giant breath and hold it, as if that could somehow make her invisible.

Unfortunately, holding her breath even after getting herself particularly high in under five minutes did not make Dina invisible. She wasn't sure what to do next when

Pete appeared around the corner of the building, saw her, and flashed her that same overly friendly grin.

"Oh," he said as he took in the sight of her puffed-out cheeks holding her breath and both hands thrust once again into the pockets of her canvas jacket. No doubt he could also smell what she'd been up to, which Dina imagined was the biggest giveaway of all. "So that's why you don't drink, huh?"

"I don't—" Another coughing fit overtook her, but she cleared her throat and tried again. "I don't know what you're talking about."

"Yeah, okay." He slid his hands into the pockets of his slacks and meandered toward her, his smile unchanging. "Where's your guard dog?"

Dina squinted up at him in the semi-darkness broken by the bar's dim exterior lighting. Then a giggle escaped her, and she immediately clapped her mouth shut, pressing her lips together while she mulled over where the hell that giggle had come from. "You're talking about Shell. She's back inside with everyone else."

"And you're out here, huh?"

Dina nodded. "Just to get some fresh air."

Pete looked her up and down with a raised eyebrow. "Right. Listen, I was serious about having a better job for you. It's fairly easy work compared to all that trimming bullshit up at the farm. What are you pulling out there right now? Twelve, thirteen-hour days? This won't be more than two-third that per shift, and you can double your take-home pay in less than half the time. It's a win-win. But you look like the kinda girl who's smart enough to figure that out on her own."

"Well thanks." Gone was her previous discomfort. Dina started to think maybe those sensations stemmed from being around the trimmers and not Pete.

She stayed where she was, leaning back against the brick wall behind her, not moving when Pete loomed closer.

He removed one hand from the pocket of his slacks, then flicked his fingers out toward her in a nifty little trick that produced a business card between them. "Pete Wilder."

"Yeah, I know," Dina stared at the offered business card and realized it was actually for her to take, so she took it. "I'm Dina."

"Nice to meet you, Dina. When you're ready to earn some real money and give yourself the kinda big break you deserve, you should give me a call. Anytime."

"Okay."

He looked her up and down one more time, his smile flickering, then he turned and walked back around the side of the building with that slow, echoing shuffle of his loafers that Dina only now realized were particularly shiny for anyone in a town like Rush.

She'd all but forgotten the rest of the joint still in her other hand. By the time she did remember it, though, it had already gone out. She'd probably already had enough for the night anyway.

The business card contained only the man's name and a cell number, the writing embossed into cardstock thicker than she'd known business cards could be.

On her way back into the pub, she passed a trashcan topped with an ashtray for smokers, and she almost tossed Pete's business card into the bin.

Something stopped her from opening her hand.

Instead, Dina slipped that card into the pocket of her jacket, which no longer carried any joints — smoked or unsmoked — and walked back into the bar.

None of her friends asked her about her brief hiatus

from their group revelry once she rejoined them, and she didn't mention the second conversation with Pete.

Once they were all safely back at Rip's Farm and everyone had gone to bed, Dina found herself lying on her bunk with that same business card in her hands, trailing her aching fingers over the depressions stamped into the thick cardstock that spelled out Pete Wilder's name.

The more she thought about his surprisingly convenient offer, the more appealing it sounded.

ELEVEN

Sam

THE PICKET-SIGN LADY hadn't wanted to call the police about her slashed tires, but Sam had no such reservations.

The woman had begrudgingly introduced herself as Angela Copely when the officer — not Chief Colton, which Sam would have found hilarious — arrived on site.

Sam ended up staying for the entirety of Angela's interaction with the man, as well as the first stages of the preliminary investigation.

Chris was more than willing to cooperate with the officer's line of questioning and wanting to take a look inside the bar. For what, Sam had no idea, but she figured this officer must really be a rookie if he was pulling out all the stops like this. Unfortunately, Chris did not keep working security cameras anywhere around his business' parking lot, so there was no security footage to scour.

"Well then," the officer told them, flipping through multiple pages of his lined notebook, his deep frown making him look clueless. Sam imagined he'd been going for contemplative. "If that's all we got so far tonight, there's not much more I can do for you, ma'am. There's no suspect, no evidence, and no leads to follow at the moment. The best I can do is recommend you get a ride home tonight and find a good mechanic in the morning."

Somehow, Sam doubted the guy was at the top of the department's list for the first officer on duty to send out to anyone's aid. Which was probably why he'd been selected to respond to *her* call.

"Thanks for the help," Angela murmured as she glared after the squad car as the officer veered out of the parking lot and disappeared down the dark street.

"That was a whole lot of nothing, huh?" Sam added.

"You don't sound surprised," Angela said.

Sam shrugged and scratched the side of her head. "Not really. The majority of police interactions I've had since moving here have been completely useless at best. For the most part."

Angela gaped at her. "Then why did you keep encouraging me to stay and wait for the police?"

"Just so you had all your bases covered. Now you can say you *did* file a report, that you've gone through all the proper legal channels to try to help yourself out, and that you weren't deliberately or willfully ignoring the strong suggestion you received this morning to get out of town and stay out of town. You literally have no other option now. And *that* means Colton doesn't have a leg to stand on. For now, anyway."

That bit of information did not visibly reassure Angela. But then, she'd had one hell of a last twenty-four hours in Rush, and it didn't look like the next twenty-four would be much of an improvement.

"Hold on just a second." Chris lifted a hand in the air like someone was about to call on him. "What's all this about Chief Colton and warnings to leave town?"

Angela sighed. "I don't think I've been completely

honest about my situation here. I came to Rush because my—"

"Don't worry about explanations right now," Sam interrupted. "You don't have anything to be sorry for, and you don't owe us a thing."

"I would beg to differ," Angela said with a tense laugh. "The two of you have been so incredibly helpful through this whole disaster, and I haven't exactly been forthcoming—"

"Like I said, Angela," Sam repeated before placing a gentle hand on the woman's shoulder in solidarity, "you've had a hell of a last twenty-four hours. I think the best thing is to get back to wherever you've been staying, maybe take a nice warm shower, and settle in for the night. There's always a fresh perspective in the morning, you know?"

"What about my car?"

"Friend of mine owns a garage in town," Chris said. "I'll have him come by in the morning. He can tow your car to his shop, and I bet he won't have any trouble finding a decent price on a set of new tires."

"I really, really appreciate all this," Angela said. "From both of you. Your willingness to help me like this... I'm a complete stranger."

"Not anymore, you aren't," Sam said.

Angela's uncertain smile wavered, then a moment of awkward silence filled the space between all three of them in the cold night air before Chris finally decided to break it.

"Excuse us for just a second," he told Angela. "If you don't mind."

"Not at all," she replied too quickly as she clutched her plain brown leather purse against her chest. "It's not like I'm going anywhere, anyway."

Sam went with Chris willingly enough when he nodded

for her to join him. Once they were sufficiently out of earshot, he fixed her with a skeptically raised eyebrow. "What are you doing?"

"Helping a woman who's clearly down on her luck right now," Sam replied casually. "Is there something particularly concerning about that?"

"You can't tell me you don't already know who she is," he murmured.

"Well, sure I do. She's a tourist who became the victim of an anonymous tire-slashing incident tonight."

Chris shot Angela a quick glance over his shoulder, then folded his arms as he faced Sam again. "If *I've* already heard it, I'd be surprised as hell that you haven't. This is the woman who was protesting outside the Kalamack Club yesterday."

"Really?" Sam didn't particularly try to feign ignorance, so her adopted cluelessness sounded exactly as fake as it was.

His brow furrowed even more. "The one you said you saw Chief Colton putting in cuffs the other day."

"Huh. Small world."

She knew full well she wasn't fooling him with the act, but she also didn't want to drag him into the conversation she fully intended to start with Angela later tonight. Something told her the other woman would be a lot more likely to talk when she felt safe around another woman, possibly even around another addict, if the topic ever came up again. Chris was neither of those.

"So I'll ask you again," he said. "What are you doing?"

She flashed him a brilliant smile, which probably wasn't the best move because Chris already knew that a smile like that on Sam's face only meant she was full of shit and trying to hide it. She did it anyway.

"I'm just being neighborly," she said. "And from the

looks of it, Angela could use something like a neighbor right about now, don't you think?"

"Neighborly." He cocked his head. "Sam, the only neighbors you ever even talk to are Syc and his dog."

"That's because Syc and Dog are the only neighbors I enjoy. Mostly Dog, though, if I'm being perfectly honest…"

"Oh, yeah? And *this* woman feels like she'd make a good neighbor?"

"Look, she's had a hard time of it, she's not from around here, she doesn't know what she's doing," Sam said. "I'm offering some help. I didn't think you'd have a problem with that."

"I wouldn't if I didn't think your definition of *being neighborly* didn't directly translate to interfering in someone else's business because you think Pete Wilder's involved somehow and you have a serious vendetta against him."

She scoffed. "Well don't ask me to define neighborly, I guess."

"You need to be careful, Sam. The last time you dug into someone else's business and it led you anywhere close to the Wilders, that was way too close for comfort, and we both know it. It's not gonna turn out any differently this time if you can't drop this weird obsession and just let it go."

"Obsession." Sam folded her arms and nodded slowly, as if she were actually considering the wisdom of his words — had she thought there was any. "Well, I'll keep that in mind, Chris, thank you. And while I keep it in mind, I'm still gonna help this woman however I can, since we're here. Or would you rather I tell her, 'Sorry, I can't talk to you anymore, or do anything for you, or even look at you, because maybe the mayor of Rush is somehow involved in the hellacious twenty-four hours you've had here in this town, and I would rather cover my own ass than extend a helping hand'? I mean, if that's what you're telling me, if that's what you really think, I'll go ahead and say it right to her face. Right now. She's waiting."

"Don't … do that." With another heavy sigh, Chris gazed up at the dark sky studded with stars around them — stars that were much brighter up here in Rush but still somewhat dampened by the ambient light of a town that, for its small size, still required a significant amount of illumination even at night. "That's not what I'm trying to say, either, and you know exactly what I'm talking about. Be nice. Be neighborly. That's all great. Just…you know. Be careful, yeah?"

"You got it, boss," she told him with a wink.

It wasn't meant to piss him off or make him laugh but somehow she managed to elicit both reactions in him simultaneously. Which meant that his frustration with her wasn't nearly as poignant as it could have been and his laugh was coated with an agitated bitterness bordering on exasperation.

"Great," he grumbled.

"So, would you like to be neighborly *with* me, or…"

Chris rolled his eyes, puffed out another sigh, and walked right past her on his way back toward Angela. "Ms. Copely?"

The woman turned toward them both with wide eyes, looking like she'd never seen either of them before. "Please, call me Angela. We're all on a first-name basis at this point, aren't we?"

"One hundred percent," Sam chimed in as she joined them.

"Why don't you come inside for a bit?" Chris suggested. "I can get you a water, coffee, or something else if you want, and I'll call a cab for you. You're welcome to wait at the bar 'til it gets here."

"That's very kind of you," Angela said. "I don't want to put anyone out, though. It's my own fault I've fallen into this situation."

"Don't beat yourself up too much," Sam said. "Any one of us could've gotten our tires slashed tonight."

"Yeah, but I'm the one who did."

"Just another run of shitty luck, if you ask me. Forget the cab. I'll drive you back to your hotel."

"Sam," Chris started, the exasperation once more perfectly clear in his voice.

"It's not a big deal," she said playfully. "And no one will have to wait. My Jeep's right over there."

"No, no, that's really okay," Angela protested. "I'm happy to wait for a cab."

"I know *I* wouldn't mind a little company and friendly conversation for a bit," Sam added, hoping her smile looked as inviting as she tried to make it feel. "I've been working all day. And I promise I'm a much better conversationalist when I'm not standing in front of a table ready to take orders. It's no problem."

Angela responded with a flickering smile, as if she wanted to laugh at Sam's mention of their first interaction but wasn't sure if that would be entirely appropriate. Then she swallowed thickly, her smile flickered a little brighter, and she finally nodded. "Okay. I guess I don't need anything if my car's getting towed out of here in the morning, right?"

"First thing," Chris said with a nod. "Sam'll give you the number for the garage. You shouldn't have any problem finding it tomorrow."

"Thank you." For the first time today, Angela genuinely seemed grateful and a little relieved.

"We'd better get a move on, then," Sam said and nodded toward her Jeep one more time.

Angela practically jumped to attention again, as if she'd forgotten she'd accepted a ride back to her hotel.

Sam nodded at Chris before taking off across the parking lot. "See you tomorrow."

"Uh-huh," he replied, his arms still folded. "Don't be late."

She snorted and walked to her car.

TWELVE

Sam

ONCE THEY WERE on the road, the first few minutes of their drive together toward Angela's hotel passed in complete silence. Sam hoped the woman would try to strike up some kind of conversation, because the only thing Sam could think of right now was blurting out a whole bunch of questions about what the woman had been doing with her picket signs on the front porch of the Kalamack Club and exactly who Dina was.

Just as her patience reached its last leg, Angela finally spoke up.

"Listen, I know you and I got off to a rocky start, and you have no real reason to be this kind to me. I want you to know that this isn't normally who I am."

Sam shot her a quick sidelong look but had to focus her gaze on the road again before she shrugged. "I don't see anything wrong with this situation at all."

"I just want to make it clear that I'm not some vagabond rolling through town after town and breaking all the rules, you know? I'm not a criminal. It's just, everything happened so fast…"

"I get it," Sam said. "I didn't for a second think you were a criminal, Angela, so don't worry about it. You came to Rush for a reason, and you still haven't found what you came here for. Something tells me you don't give up, even when you run into a little more trouble than expected. It's actually pretty admirable."

Angela sucked in a sharp breath and stiffened further in the passenger seat. "How do you know I came to this town looking for something?"

Well, if Sam hadn't been sure before, she sure as shit was now. Angela sure didn't have much of a poker face.

"All right," Sam said. "I guess it's time for a little confession of my own."

Angela blinked and shot Sam a curious look from the corner of her eye. "I'm sorry?"

"Yeah, me too, I guess." Sam readjusted her grip on the steering wheel. "For not having said anything about it right away. I did see what happened to you in front of the Kalamack Club yesterday morning."

"You saw all that?" Angela whispered.

Sam nodded. "From the minute Colton's boot came down on the top step of that porch to your head disappearing inside the back of his squad car. Got a good look at the blonde receptionist peeking out the front window too. I always knew she was a bit of a Peeping Tom. Or … Peeping Tina."

"Oh my god…" Angela leaned forward over her lap and buried her face in both hands. "This is so embarrassing."

"What? Being arrested?" Sam snorted. "Hey, it happens to the best of us. And in this town, the best of us aren't always the people you'd think."

"It doesn't happen to *me*," Angela replied, her voice

muffled between her hands. "I've never been arrested before."

"Well, now you can stick it in your tool belt of experiences to grow stronger from, right?" That felt like a pitifully poor attempt at reassurance. "What I meant to say was that it could be worse."

"How?" Angela finally removed her hands from her face, but she still sat doubled over, the seatbelt straining across her chest and shoulder.

"Well, for one, you could've committed an actual crime."

"He told me I was being arrested for trespassing on private property. I thought that *was* a crime."

"Technically," Sam said with a shrug. "But it's non-violent. It doesn't disturb the peace, for the most part. The only peace it does disturb belongs to the people who deserve it and then some. Colton could've kept you longer, or he could've cut your brakes instead of slashing your tires."

Slowly, Angela sat upright in her seat again and gaped at Sam. "You think the *police* slashed my tires?"

"What?" Sam did a double take before turning off the main road in the direction of Angela's hotel. "No, that's not what I'm saying at all—"

"I mean, I knew *something* was off about this place, but I didn't for a second think it extended as far as corrupt police endangering innocent citizens and visitors just to stop somebody from asking questions…"

"A lot of people in this town have done a lot of things to stop others from asking questions. A set of slashed tires doesn't even scratch the surface." The words just spilled out of Sam with absolutely no filter.

You gotta start slow with this one, Sam. There's something else going on here that doesn't quite add up.

Something told Sam the various pieces of Angela Copely's life hadn't added up for quite some time, long before the woman ever decided to come to Rush.

When she pulled into the hotel parking lot lit by the wan yellow-orange light from of the street lamps, it was hard not to notice the constant low buzz and unending flicker coming from another lamp on the far western side of the property. It made a fine introduction as to exactly what type of establishment Angela's hotel really was. Not Rush's finest in hospitality.

Sam turned off the engine and sat there in silence with Angela. "This is you, right?"

"Oh. Yes. My hotel."

"Step one. We're in the right place."

"Right." Angela fiddled with her purse in her lap, slowly unbuckled her seatbelt, then reached for the passenger-side door handle. She paused before her fingers ever touched the metal, then let out another massive sigh and dropped her hand into her lap again.

"Something else on your mind, Angela?"

Angela nodded once. "You know, after everything that's happened in the last two days, I don't really want to be alone right now. That's not something I'm used to feeling, let alone saying it out loud to anyone."

"Nothing wrong with it," Sam said.

"Maybe for *you*. My older daughter offered to come with me on this trip to help me look for Dina, because two sets of eyes are always better than one, right? But it didn't seem necessary at the time. Maybe even a burden. But now, I'm starting to think telling her no might've been a bad idea."

Sam studied the woman's profile.

"I know what that feels like too," she finally said. "It's

still hard for *me* to ask for a little company, or accept it when it's offered."

Angela let out a bitter laugh and didn't look at her.

"My plans for the night after I got off work consisted of sitting around a firepit in a lawn chair and probably chain-smoking, so if you want someone to talk to, Angela, I'm free."

Angela finally managed to look Sam in the eye and bit her lower lip. "I'd like that, actually. Thank you."

"Don't mention it." Sam opened the driver's-side door before nodding up ahead toward the hotel. "I can't vouch for the rooms or the beds or the room service. I do know this place has a twenty-four-hour cafe attached to what we all pretend is a lobby. They make a decent cup of coffee, and I'm pretty sure they have orange juice and soda water too, if you'd rather go with that."

With a nod, Angela opened her own door and slipped out.

~

COFFEE WAS the only thing Sam felt like drinking anyway, though she ordered two waters for the table just in case. There was no telling how long she and Angela were going to be here, and the further they could get with fewer distractions, the better.

Angela focused intently on doctoring up her mug of twenty-four-hour hotel-diner sludge. The woman's spoon clinked over and over against the inside of her glass as she stirred, and her hands shook during the first half of raising that ceramic mug to her lips for her first slurp. She didn't seem to taste her creation, but put it right back down again.

Only two other patrons joined them tonight at nearly

midnight. One sat at the counter, nursing his own coffee. The other guy had an oversized trucker hat pulled down low over his face and stared at a sad-looking plate of soggy bread that was probably supposed to be French toast. Sam recognized neither of them. But they weren't paying attention to her, so she didn't care.

Finally, Angela relinquished her hold on the mug to dig through her purse. It took her a bit, but she eventually found what she was looking for and settled it into her lap to stare at it a moment longer. When she lifted it above the table and extended it slowly toward Sam, she'd lost her ability to make eye contact again. "This is probably the most recent picture I have of Dina."

Sam gingerly took the photo.

The young woman in the picture could have been Angela herself twenty-five, maybe thirty years ago, from her thick, straight, dark-chestnut hair to eyes more gray than blue. Sam didn't need more than a few seconds to look over the image before handing it back.

"This is your daughter." It wasn't a question.

"My youngest." Angela nodded. "She came to this town for what was supposed to be only a few months of work." She spat the last word out as if it had already spoiled long before she chose to use it. "A few weeks after she left home, I stopped hearing from her altogether. That was five years ago."

Five years ago.

That length of time still baffled Sam whenever she stopped to truly consider it.

Five years ago, she'd been happy. Loving on Sophie. So naively certain that nothing else in her life would ever be more important or bring her as much joy as those healthy pink cheeks and the soft, chubby little fingers laced through her own.

She'd been right about the joy part. But five years ago, Sam couldn't have possibly known that losing that joy would trigger the most devastating grief and ongoing self-loathing she could have possibly imagined.

The look on Angela's face told her that now wasn't the time to question why it had taken the woman five years to come looking for her allegedly missing daughter. If there had ever been a chance in hell of Sam finding Sophie again, she would have walked across the entire country on foot, without stopping, to get to her that much faster.

Instead, Sam held her tongue and swallowed, pushing thoughts of Sophie aside.

"That's a long time," she said instead.

"It is." Angela wrapped both hands around her coffee mug again and stared down into the cup of caffeinated half-and-half tinted slightly darker than the freckles dotting the backs of her hands. "Have you seen her around town? By any chance?"

"No, I haven't. I'm sorry."

"Well, it was worth a shot."

"To be fair, though," Sam added, "I've only been here a little over two years, so I'm probably not the best person to ask when it comes to recognizing people's faces. Do you think she's still here?"

"I hope so." Disappointment coated Angela's face like a mask meant to hide whatever other emotions also existed.

Disappointment, though, was good enough for now. The woman still cared, even if she'd taken five years to finally act on it.

But Sam could work with that.

"Why don't you tell me about her?" she suggested.

When the dullness of Angela's eyes lit up again, Sam knew she'd pushed the right buttons in the right order.

With a nod, she raised a hand in the air to flag down their waitress and asked, "Do you like pie?"

If Angela had been hesitant to accept help from strangers, she certainly didn't share the same reservations when it came to talking about her daughter. Before their slices of pie even made it to the table, Sam had learned more than enough about Dina to be able to fill in some of the larger blanks on her own. Though she would keep that part of this woman's personal puzzle to herself until she actually had proof and could verify her initial assumptions.

She learned that Dina had chosen to take a gap year after graduating high school, that she had been accepted into medical school in Washington, and that the school had also accepted her deferment for that gap year so she could enroll and begin her college career the fall after she left Seattle for Rush. Apparently, Dina had planned to become a surgeon, and she'd come here to earn her tuition by trimming marijuana plants for a single season.

Dina had sent her mother a handful of text messages in the first month she was gone, though they'd been short on specifics.

"Then her texts just stopped," Angela continued, staring into her freshly refilled coffee cup again. "At first, I thought maybe she was just sick of me begging her to come home. She was already making the kinds of life decisions she was well within her rights to make as a legal adult. Maybe she wanted to cut ties with her mother to make it easier.

"I had convinced myself she wouldn't text me back or answer any of my calls to get back at me. Maybe even make me feel a fraction of the pain and worry and ... I don't know, emotional turmoil I inflicted on both my daughters over the course of their lives."

Sam tilted her head. "Why would she want to hurt you

like that? Dina sounds like an incredibly smart girl, the way you've described her. There are so many other ways a teenage girl can lash out at her mom that stay a hell of a lot closer to home and don't require nearly so much effort to achieve."

"You talk like you know from personal experience," Angela said.

Sam had to give the woman credit for turning the tables on her like that.

"I don't talk about much of anything that doesn't come from personal experience," she replied. "Otherwise, what's the point of putting any stake in it?"

"Fair enough." Angela cut off a rather large bite of what was left of her pie but didn't lift the fork from her plate just yet. "At the time, I was so wrapped up in my own shit that I thought *everything* was all about me, and I didn't even know it. Or maybe I did know it and just wasn't capable of looking it in the face. Either way, I still blame myself for that."

Sam offered a nod of understanding. "You weren't sober five years ago when Dina decided to catch that bus to Rush, were you?"

"I did tell you walking into a bar was bad for my sobriety, didn't I? What about you? How long do you have under your belt?"

"Not as long as I used to have," Sam finally replied. "It's been a few months this time around. When I fell off the last time, it didn't last very long. But I guess that doesn't matter in the scheme of things."

"No," Angela said gently. "It doesn't. Not really."

"So, Dina came all the way out here to make some money for college and get away from a tumultuous home life all in one fell swoop, huh?"

"Pretty much. It took me a long time to admit that her

radio silence for months *wasn't* still part of some personal vendetta against me. I wasn't even able to fully acknowledge my own fears that something could have happened to her until I'd been sober for a while. I realize it probably looks like too little, too late, but I have to find out what happened to my daughter. Even if it took me five years to get here."

"I understand." Sam pushed the last bits of pie around her plate, then asked, "What did the police say? I'm assuming you went to them first when you got here."

"They all claimed there wasn't anything they could do for me. One of the officers made it a point to tell me that Dina was seen leaving town sometime in March that year, and that nothing about her alleged disappearance falls under the umbrella of a missing person."

"I hope you filed a report, anyway," Sam said.

"He made it abundantly clear I *couldn't* file a report. Not if she wasn't officially considered missing. He even told me," Angela continued, "and I'm quoting, here, 'I wouldn't waste my time, if I were you. If your daughter was already an adult and just never came home, I suggest taking that as a sign that she just never wanted to.'"

The woman pressed her lips tightly together and stared fervently at Sam. Though she kept her cool, the visible anger and frustration rising inside her, coupled with a mother's fear of discovering the worst possible scenario was actually true, made Angela look like a pressure cooker.

"Well, that officer should've kept his fucking mouth shut," Sam replied.

Surprisingly, that made the corner of Angela's mouth twitch with the briefest hint of a smile. So at least the woman didn't completely lack a sense of humor.

"If this town were any bigger," Sam continued, "I'd suggest filing a missing persons report at a different precinct still within the city's limits. But the only other thing out here is the County Sheriff, and the likelihood of the county filing a legitimate missing persons report when the Rush PD already denied the possibility of it are slim to none. Closer to none, honestly."

"Well, thanks for saving me the trouble of trying *that*, I guess," Angela said. "Sounds like you know more about police procedures and missing persons cases than the average small-town bar waitress."

Sam's smile was as close as she could get to remembering the past and better times with anything resembling fondness. "Probably because I do. But there's something else I've been wondering. If Dina was working on a pot farm outside Rush, why were you picketing in front of the Kalamack Club?"

Angela's face paled considerably, and she swallowed before lowering her gaze to the crumby, sticky-filling mess smeared around her plate.

There was definitely something else the woman wasn't saying. Sam was determined to wait here for as long as it took for Angela to spill.

THIRTEEN

Sam

WHEN IT SEEMED Angela had finished explaining every detail she could think to remember, Sam still had to follow up with one more line of questioning to be sure she had all the facts.

"Just so I've gotten all this straight, Dina came out here five years ago by herself to trim on a farm outside Rush for the season. But she ended up changing her plans and taking on a different job at the Kalamack Club instead. I'm assuming because it paid better."

"That's what she told me." Angela nodded, then reached for her purse to fish around for her phone. "I never really got the chance to talk to her about it in detail." The woman scrolled through the messages she had apparently kept on her phone for the last five years, then turned the device over to Sam. "Here."

Sam read through the text messages as well to confirm that yes, Dina had described the Kalamack Club through rose-tinted glasses and with far more excitement and admiration than Sam would have given the place credit for.

Though both sides of the text conversation were visible and still on Angela's phone, Sam made a point to neither linger on the snappy, not-quite-motherly responses from Angela five years ago, nor did she mention them.

That wasn't the point.

"I always just assumed this place was more like a dance club or something," Angela added, nervously folding her hands on the table beside her almost empty pie plate. "That she was serving drinks behind a bar or cocktail waitressing. It didn't even enter my mind that this might have been a gentleman's club."

"Gentleman's club?" Sam looked quickly up from the woman's phone before returning it to her.

Angela shrugged. "Or whatever it is they do there. Believe me, I tried getting more information from the receptionist just inside the front door. When I wouldn't leave, she called the police."

"Yeah, I've met the blonde. She's something else." Sam sat back against the booth's thin cushion. "Were you at least able to confirm with someone at the club that Dina had worked there?"

"That was all the receptionist would say. That yes, Dina worked there through the winter and into early spring, and that she left toward the end of March."

"Not very helpful, either, then. Angela, can I ask when you finally decided to get sober? Something tells me it wasn't last month."

"No." The woman swallowed, but her answers had become a lot more forthcoming in the last several hours than they'd been in the beginning. "No, I'm coming up on two years, actually. I know that still seems like a really long time to go without speaking to my daughter. It wasn't that we didn't talk anymore because of my drinking. Well, not specifically because I was drinking. Just because of who I was when I did drink. Which was more often than not."

"I understand."

"I'd like to think I would have come out here sooner if things had been even a little different," Angela continued. "But unfortunately, I inherited a certain astoundingly high level of stubbornness, which I know I passed on to both my daughters. Much more with Dina, for sure. I thought *that* was what had kept us from speaking for so long."

Sam nodded for the woman to continue, but Angela paused and resorted to staring into her coffee mug again, which had now been empty for the last half hour.

There's some other part to that equation, though, isn't there?

So, Sam finally had to ask.

"And what about the circumstances might have been different?"

Angela sighed and seemed to shrink into herself at the memory, but at least she'd loosened up with her story. "We had a huge fight. And I mean *huge*. It felt like it anyway. There was the one time I think we spoke over the phone since she'd left on that stupid bus, and it … well, it didn't go well, to say the least. I was far beyond anything resembling sobriety, and Dina was finished with me. I'm sure at that point she realized how much of my bullshit she'd been forced to put up with her entire life, especially once she got away and got a taste of what life could actually be like when her mother wasn't embedded into every single part of it and dragging her down.

"My other daughter actually had to come stay with me for a while after that, and then Dina and I didn't reach out to each other at all. This is honestly a little embarrassing after we've been sitting here this whole time talking about it, but when I drove into Rush four days ago, I could so easily imagine Dina still living here, still working at that club, whatever it is. I imagined her in a little apartment on her own, or maybe, I don't know, renting a mother-in-law suite somewhere off a rustic cottage. The stupid things you think of when you've never been to a place and hope your child has done well for themselves, you know?"

"Makes sense," Sam said. "So you hadn't spoken to her for almost five years, but you thought you knew where she was and sort of where she worked because she hadn't come home and she hadn't told you she was going anywhere else."

Angela blinked furiously and swallowed as she lowered her gaze to the table again. "Exactly."

"All right. The police don't consider her a missing person because one of her friends at Rip's Farm remembers Dina saying she was going home."

"That's what I was told, yes. That she was seen going home. Which I'd heard nothing about until just a few days ago."

"And she doesn't still work at the Kalamack Club, obviously. What do you think might have happened to her?"

"Oh, I don't have the foggiest," Angela said, then paused again. "I mean, I've considered several possibilities, ninety-nine percent of which I know would lead me into a tailspin of devastation and self-loathing and ... pure terror. I do prefer not to dwell on worst-case scenarios, which is something of a new practice for me. But beyond that, I really couldn't say.

"Since I've been here and spoken to a number of people, the police, the receptionist of that club, getting my tires slashed right after twenty-four hours behind bars... Call me crazy, but I can't shake the feeling that something terrible happened to my daughter at that new job of hers, whatever she was doing at that club, and that those involved are lying to me about all of it just to cover their tracks, hoping that I'm as naive and stupid as I look and that I'll just take their word for it and go away. But I won't go away, Sam. That's not something I can stomach. It wouldn't have been something I could stomach back when I wasn't nearly as strong as I am now, and I'm not just *going home* without getting some real answers first."

Sam nodded again, part of her attention diverted from what felt like the final bit of Angela's confession, because something else in the cafe had caught her attention now.

Most specifically, their single waitress working there through the overnight shift. The woman had been decently friendly when they'd gotten to their table. She'd brought consistent coffee refills and made sure it was hot every time, if not entirely fresh. The pie was palatable, or at least the closest it was going to get to real food, which Sam was more than used to.

But now their waitress seemed to be busying herself with wiping tables that hadn't seen any customers the whole time they'd been here, taking her job duties just a little too seriously for such a dead night and parking herself just a little too close to her only two customers right now at one of the nearby tables.

"I would expect nothing less," Sam said slowly, "of a mother who only wants what's best for her daughter. Even if she eventually realizes she was wrong."

Sam hadn't been staring at the waitress by any means, but her gaze reverted suddenly to Angela when a short, strangled croak arose from the other side of the table.

Angela had clamped a hand over her mouth, probably to keep back the rest of the strange noises threatening to break out again. But her eyes swam with tears now, glistening in the cafe's low light as her cheeks and nose took on an unnaturally rosy hue Sam associated with only two things.

Drinking or crying.

Sometimes it was even both.

"Angela, are you all right? I didn't mean to—"

"Thank you," the woman whispered from behind her hand, then finally dropped it and nodded. "Thank you so much."

"For what?"

"For what you just said. Acknowledging what I'm trying to do, my intentions, if not necessarily my actions or the decisions I've made along with them. You seem to have a knack for knowing exactly what I'm thinking and going through. I can't be the only person who gets to experience how nice that is on the receiving end."

Sam almost told the woman that Angela was probably the only person in Sam Salazar's life who would agree with that sentiment. But she didn't.

Angela wasn't wrong. Sam had just found herself sharing a lot more in common with this woman than most people who crossed her path on a regular basis. Maybe that was the point.

"You're welcome," she said and left it at that.

After another quick glance at the waitress, who walked slowly away from them now, as if she'd be paid more for taking the maximum amount of time on any one task, Sam drained the rest of her water and nodded. "It's way later than I thought. We should both turn in for the night. Take another stab at this with fresh eyes in the morning."

"Oh, sure." Angela reached for her purse again. "I'll grab the bill. Just give me a moment—"

"Not a chance," Sam interrupted. "I got it." She stuck her hand in the air and had barely called out for the waitress before the woman was already on her way toward them with a plastic smile.

"Anything else I can get for you?"

"Just the check, thanks."

And the name of whoever told you to spy on this woman from out of town every chance you get.

~

ON THE WAY HOME, Sam slowed almost instinctually now as she drove past the Kalamack Club toward Birdsong Park. Most of the time, she didn't even think about it anymore when she did it, but tonight was different. No more women from out of town picketing the place on the front porch tonight, no. But as the Jeep slowed, Sam could have sworn she caught a flicker of light moving around inside the clubhouse.

She glanced at the clock on her dashboard — 2:07 a.m. — then frowned back up at the front of the club.

The place had already shut down hours ago, and even Big Pete didn't love the place so much that he'd stay this long after hours. She doubted the man allowed his own employees to do the same.

She almost pulled the Jeep to a complete stop but decided against it when she didn't see any other light or movement again through the two stories of windows lining the front of the clubhouse.

It could have been all in her head too. Maybe. She'd just spent the last few hours drilling Angela about her daughter and trying to put some of the pieces together for herself, fueled by nothing but countless cups of diner coffee and a piece of cherry pie that now felt like it had halfway turned to cement in her gut.

It could have been a trick of the light from somewhere

else. A street lamp out here, a reflection off any number of things inside the Jeep, maybe even a flash of headlights from some passing car she hadn't noticed until it was already gone.

That was always possible.

Sam didn't quite care enough to look into it any further than that.

FOURTEEN

Laila

When Laila approached the front gates of the Kalamack Club the next morning, she couldn't help but slow her vehicle for extra time to scope the place out first. Part of her had been worried about having to deal with that picket-sign nonsense again, but she quickly found herself more relieved than on edge.

No one stood outside the clubhouse. The parking lot was completely empty, and there was no sign of anyone around.

Her routine was the same every morning. Park in her spot behind the building, then she was out of the car, her purse over her shoulder with jingling keys in hand to unlock the back door of the clubhouse and make her way through the quiet, empty building to her quiet, neatly organized desk inside the front door.

Halfway down the back hallway toward the reception desk in the front, she stopped at an enormous mirror wreathed in a gilded frame etched with all types of curious shapes and took a quick look at her own reflection.

Her makeup looked good. The bags under her eyes from the weekend had disappeared.

Thank god for night cream.

When she ran a hand through her hair, she caught a glimpse of the discoloration along her scalp. At first, she thought it might have been something in her hair until she realized for the hundredth time what she kept forgetting recently.

She was in serious need of a touch-up fairly soon. Her roots were looking darker than ever.

Or maybe she was just overthinking things.

Running a hand through the rest of her brilliantly blonde hair one more time, Laila squinted at her darker roots in the mirror, then clicked her tongue and turned away.

Her large tote purse went down at the very far edge of her desk when she reached the reception area. Then Laila booted up the desktop computer no one ever used but her, turned on the lights at the front of the clubhouse's entry-way, and instantly stepped away when the overhead light revealed what had been waiting for her the whole time in what she considered her private workspace.

Just beneath the recently added banner celebrating the Kalamack Club's 75th Anniversary coming up in a few days and crossing slightly over it in the process was an enormous message scrawled across the wall in bright-red paint that almost didn't even look real on its own.

"Let Dina Go."

She stared at the message that definitely hadn't been there yesterday when she'd locked up and let out a frustrated groan. "Here we go."

Laila snatched up her purse again, tugged it angrily over her shoulder, and stormed down the back hallway again toward the rear of the clubhouse before bursting through the back door and huffing halfway back to her car. As soon as her heels clicked down on the asphalt of the side parking lot, she had her cell phone out and her 911 call already placed.

Once dispatch informed her an officer was on the way to the clubhouse, Laila ended the call and instantly made another, which was drastically more important in the scheme of things.

"Mr. Wilder," she said when he answered, "I'm sorry to bother you this early, but there's been a break-in at the club. Yes. No, I've already called the police. They're sending someone now. Yep, I'll be sure to—"

Laila was so used to cutting herself off every time her employer turned away from her or hung up on her or closed the door in her face when she was talking, it hardly registered at this point.

~

TWENTY MINUTES LATER, Chief Colton once again stood in front of the Kalamack Club. Laila led him into the clubhouse to point out exactly where she'd found the message.

"I'd call that vandalism, Chief, wouldn't you?"

Colton raised an eyebrow at her before taking a single step toward the wall and studying the sloppily scrawled message. Without a word, he slowly perused what constituted her daily office during club hours, moving finally toward the front wall to visually inspect each of the four large windows that could be seen from the club's front parking lot. "Someone said there was a break-in."

"Yes," Laila replied. "That someone was me."

"Uh-huh," he said, slowly turning around to face her. "And where's the break-in?"

She gawked at him for a moment, then gestured one more time at the literal writing on the wall with a sharp toss of her hand. "Right there, Chief. The sign of a break-in. Words don't get painted on walls in a building like this unless someone breaks in to put them there."

"Well, that's easy to assume. I'm talking about actual signs of breaking and entering, though. Forced entry or something else."

"What do you mean something else?"

"I don't know, Laila. You tell me."

She scoffed. "How am I supposed to know? I just walked into the building this morning to start my day, and this was already here."

"Did you lock up last night?"

"I lock up every night." She fixed him with a deadpan stare. "And you already know that."

"Well, the front door doesn't show any signs of forced entry, and the windows all look perfectly intact. If you can't tell me where this alleged intruder was supposed to have broken into the building in the first place, I can't investigate a B-and-E, because at that point, it wouldn't exist."

Laila stepped aside. "What are you talking about?"

The chief did not look amused by this little game of his, nor did he seem willing to explain the less commonly understood subtleties of the way the Rush PD investigated any kind of criminal activity around here. He did open his mouth again, looking like he was about to get to something else fairly important, but the front door of the Kalamack Club squealed open before banging heavily against the interior wall.

Laila recognized the sound of those pounding footsteps even before the shouting started.

"What the hell's going on here?" Big Pete Wilder appeared almost instantly around the corner, red-faced and fuming as he stormed toward Laila and Colton. "Why am I getting a call about this first thing in the morning? And why are the two of you just standing there? I expected the perpetrator to have been apprehended by now, and instead, I'm standing here staring at the two of you, neither of whom look like you have anything to say. I'm starting to think you're as useless as you are clueless!"

"I only just arrived on the scene, Pete," Colton started.

"I don't give a flying fuck what you just did," Pete boomed. "I care about how quickly you fix this. What happened?"

Laila tried only once to chime in with her version of events, but she was cut off by the chief and quickly recognized her employer also didn't care about her version of anything. Big Pete Wilder cared about results, and that was as far as it went.

"Well then, find the idiot who broke onto private property, *my* private property, and defaced it with this … whatever the hell this is."

"That's exactly what I plan to do," Colton replied calmly, though his face had reddened and he wore a perpetual scowl now to keep himself from mouthing off at the one man who owned the vast majority of this town, even as the vast majority of this town was well aware that they'd been owned for quite some time. "I'd like to take a look at your security footage, if you don't mind."

"It won't show you a damn thing, Ralph," Pete growled. "The only cameras we have are outside in the parking lot. Doesn't exactly inspire confidence for our members if we've got security cameras recording everything that happens on this side of that front door."

"Well then, I'd like to take a look at those, just the same." Colton nodded at Laila. "I'd like you to go back through what you remember when you got here. See if there are any details you left out."

"I already told you everything I know," Laila said. "There's nothing more to remember. I left the club last night after locking up because I was the last to leave, just like I've been the last to leave pretty much every night since I started working here. It's been long enough for me to have proven myself. In case you were hoping to try and pin something like this on me."

"It's never crossed my mind," Colton replied blandly.

She certainly could have done without all the extra sarcasm, but Laila wasn't the one in charge here.

Pete didn't seem all that bothered by it, though he grumbled something incoherent and nodded for Colton to follow him through the narrow door in the back of the front room Laila used as her office.

She stayed behind her desk, glaring at the message painted across the wall while Pete and Colton went over what security footage the club did have from last night and this morning, taken from the cameras mounted out in the parking lot. There wasn't much to find. No one had exited or entered the premises after the footage of Laila pulling her car around the side of the clubhouse before disappearing from the video's view and leaving the Kalamack Club's property altogether. Between then and the time she showed up this morning, there had been no other activity.

"Do we have any possible suspects who could turn out to be this unexpected vandal?" Colton asked afterward.

"The out-of-towner," Laila blurted. "The woman who was here the other day with her stupid picket sign asking all those questions about her daughter."

Both Colton and Big Pete looked at her with matching gazes of renewed interest slightly dampened by suspicion.

Laila glanced back and forth between them and added,

"The woman you arrested right there on the front porch, Chief."

Then she tossed a hand one more time in the direction of the red paint message on the wall.

Colton's frown deepened. "And she came to mind because…"

"Because she was here asking about her daughter first," Laila reiterated. "The daughter she hasn't seen or heard from in years. Are you seriously not following? Okay, listen. The woman's daughter's name is Dina, right? Look right there. 'Let Dina Go.' It's so obvious it's almost funny. It was that woman with the picket sign, I'm telling you. No one else would've used that name in something like this. Not here."

The corners of Colton's mouth turned down in consideration.

"Then it's settled," Pete grumbled and thrust a finger toward Colton's face. "I want that woman found. I want her arrested. Yes, *again*. For *these* crimes. And I want to press charges to the fullest extent of the law. She can't do this."

"I'll go talk to her first," Colton replied, his expression a blank mask, though one hand clenched briefly into a fist before he stretched it wide open again. "I'll question her about it, see if she has any alibis, and we'll get to the bottom of it."

"Be sure you do," Pete warned. "Because if you can't do your job, Colton, I can fill it faster than you can blink with someone better suited to get results. Don't act like you earned your last promotion on your own merit alone."

Laila stepped back behind her desk, expecting some kind of uglier confrontation between the men now that Big Pete's temper had flared up as quickly as it always did and he was already threatening people's jobs at almost 7:00 a.m.

She was admittedly impressed, however, when Colton somehow managed not to take the bait.

Instead, the Chief of Police approached the wall with the graffitied message sprawling across it, pulled his cell phone from the pocket of his uniform pants, and proceeded to snap several photographs of the evidence from a series of different angles without a word.

"What can either of you tell me about this Dina person?" he asked when he'd finished.

"There's nothing to tell," Pete said. "Find the woman who did this and get it handled."

With that, the man stormed off out of the front reception area, his footsteps pounding heavily up the long staircase behind Laila's desk. Even when he'd reached the second story, his footsteps continued clomping above their heads, the floorboards creaking beneath his agitated weight.

"Laila!"

She couldn't pretend she couldn't hear him down here, but she didn't have to offer a response.

"I want that shit cleaned up before the start of business today!" A door slammed immediately behind his command with final emphasis, then even the sound of Big Pete's angry pacing in his second-story office cut out as well.

Laila shot the chief a brief glance, then rolled her eyes.

"I'm gonna take a look around," he said, gesturing toward the remainder of the clubhouse's ground floor.

"Be my guest."

When Colton returned from his initial inspection, he specifically pulled her aside again to answer a series of questions.

To Laila, they seemed like nothing more than a variation of the same questions he'd first asked her before Big Pete had come storming in. She responded to each bit of interrogation with a straight face and gave him the exact same answers.

"And yes," she finished, "I've known about that window in the lounge area for months now. I've already advised Mr. Wilder of the situation, but apparently, he just hasn't gotten around to fixing it yet."

"I strongly recommend that gets taken care of first," Colton said with a stern nod.

"Of course." She dipped her head, trying not to sound bitter and completely exasperated. She didn't try that hard, though. "I'll get on it right away, Chief. Thank you so much for your time."

Whether or not he picked up on her attitude, the man didn't show it. He merely nodded at her again, took another sweeping glance around what could be seen from here of the lounge area and then the entirety of the front entryway, including Laila's desk. Then with both thumbs hooked over the top of his utility belt, the police chief moseyed back on through the front door of the Kalamack's clubhouse, leaving Laila with ample time to get to work following her employer's barked orders to clean up the mess.

She found a spare apron in the back utility closet and covered herself up before going into the kitchen at the far back of the clubhouse for a bucket of warm, soapy water and the roughest sponge she could find. She also opened a new box of wire scrub brushes just in case.

For fifteen minutes straight, Laila scrubbed at the bright-red graffiti paint covering the wall. First with only one hand because the job hadn't seemed that difficult, then with both hands because the paint just wasn't coming off.

Even when she brought a plastic bottle of dish soap and sprayed strips of it on the wall itself before adding more water and sponge and wire brush to the message of vandalism scrawled right there beside her desk for everyone to see.

It was as stubborn as the person who'd put it there.

And because Laila really didn't have the time to play maintenance, repair, and housemaid right before the club opened to members for the day, she picked up the phone and called the hardware store in the center of town. No one could blame the receptionist at the Kalamack Club for not being able to take care of this particular situation. But if someone else in Rush whose profession literally centered around improving homes and walls and even terrible paint jobs, this had to be a piece of cake.

If it wasn't, Laila would still be off the hook.

FIFTEEN

Sam

_____

SAM GROANED as she rolled over in bed the next morning. Technically, it still felt like the night before, because technically, she hadn't gone to bed until after 3:30 a.m.

Her head pounded, the Deville spun around her nonstop, and her stomach lurched with every movement.

Jesus Christ, what did she drink last night?

Her eyes flew open at the thought, because she hadn't had anything to drink besides coffee and water.

She hadn't really had any sleep, either. Not last night, not the two nights before, nor the several weeks before that. The logical result was that she felt like shit just the same.

She had to force herself out of bed to head for the Deville's tiny bathroom, dizzy and stumbling around before the rest of her fatigue cleared. After that, she remembered Dog hadn't come inside with her last night. Probably because he'd already relented to spending a night with Syc due to his actual favorite human having stayed up too late.

Thinking about Dog led her to sweeping her gaze across the trailer one more time, where it landed squarely on the empty tin can meant for coffee grounds and now repurposed into the closest thing to a vase she'd ever owned.

Holding the first bouquet of those damned Sophy's Roses like a dozen unfurling practical jokes all laughing in her face.

And there were supposed to be seven of them.

Suddenly wide awake, Sam stormed across her trailer and barreled through the door.

The early-morning air before sunrise was crisp and cool, carrying with it the slightest bit of dampness because Rush was just far enough north to get cold and just far enough south to never see snow.

But she didn't feel any of it, because when she looked down into the dry grass at the base of the Deville's steps, her morning only got worse.

One more goddamn bouquet of the same dozen Sophy's Roses lying right there in the grass right where the last two had been.

Which meant either she'd been too pissed off to see it the first time, or someone had snuck up to her trailer in the last five minutes and left them there while she was busy trying to wake the hell up.

"Motherfucker," she growled and turned to scan the trailer park.

That was when she saw the cyclist pedaling right by on the road — wearing a black-and-white-checkered hoodie and moving suspiciously slowly for someone who liked to take their morning bike rides before the sun came up.

"Hey!" Sam shouted.

The guy just kept pedaling along. Fifteen seconds later, he was out of sight down the road. If Sam had had more sleep, or had bothered to put on her shoes, or wasn't a little concerned about waking up Syc and Dog, she would have kept shouting, and she would have pursued the checkered hoodie on foot.

Instead, she tore back into her trailer, slamming and stomping and tossing things about as she got ready for the day. She decided taking the necessary time for a shower would only make her angrier instead of its normally opposite and soothing effect.

Dressed and with all her things gathered in less than ten minutes, Sam barreled back out of her trailer. Now she cursed herself for her new habit of locking the door because it meant she had to stop and take even more time to continue that habit, but she did. At the bottom of the Deville's front steps, her heel came down directly onto the center of the third bouquet of Sophy's Roses, crushing them with a somewhat satisfying snap before she finally relented to stooping and picking them up.

There was only one place she needed to be today. And if they weren't open by the time her road rage carried her in the Jeep all the way to the parking lot, she'd wait.

THE SUN HAD BARELY BEEN UP for five minutes, and Sam's Jeep screeched to a halt in the parking lot of the grocery store. She did have to wait a whole three minutes for the automatic front doors to be unlocked because the store hadn't quite opened yet, and of course no one was going to willingly let her in before store hours. When those doors finally opened with a hiss and rumble across their worn tracks, Sam narrowly avoided running right into them because she walked faster than they operated.

She walked just as fast all the way across the store, ignoring the two different employees who offered her smiles and tired-sounding good mornings before recognizing the look of a pissed-off customer who just didn't have the time, energy, or self-awareness to pretend like she wasn't here for blood.

All things considered, it was kind of a miracle that no one else attempted to intercept her before Sam finally made it to the floral section of the store and its checkout counter. At the back of the section, even the young woman Sam had spoken to yesterday about the ridiculous special order of these roses some anonymous asshat had requested online greeted her with a brilliantly flashing smile before recognizing Sam.

She also recognized yet another bouquet of crushed roses clenched in her hand.

Sam didn't slow down in front of the counter until she was almost directly on top of it, then she chucked the roses down with a wet-sounding slap and a rustle of leaves and cellophane wrapper.

"I said no more flowers."

"Good morning," the young woman replied, her smile tightening. "How can I help you?"

"You can help me," Sam growled, "by listening to me the first time and canceling the goddamn order like I said."

"I'm sorry, ma'am. These flowers have already been purchased and paid for in their entirety. There *is* no order to cancel."

"Then cancel the fucking guy who's been delivering them to my home!"

"Well, I'm sorry, ma'am, but I'm afraid that's also not possible. We're not the ones delivering the flowers."

"Fine." Sam rolled her shoulders back and dipped her head before waving toward the general space behind the counter. "And because they're already bought and paid for and they keep ending up in front of my door, why don't you just bring them all out here right now? I'll take the rest of them. And then we can avoid any repeats of this entire situation, which I'm sure neither of us is particularly enjoying right now."

The young woman was impressively calm for having a five-foot-five, pissed-off Latina woman in her forties practically screaming in her face. Even that screaming apparently didn't change her answers. "I'm sorry for any confusion or inconvenience this is causing you, ma'am—"

"And *I* said the same thing the last time we talked. This is harassment. And I want it to stop."

"If I could help you, I would," the girl said. "But unfortunately, the rest of that order of these particular roses isn't here. We haven't been delivering them. They were picked up the day before you came in the first time. And it's out of our hands. There's nothing I can do."

Sam blinked at her. "Why the hell didn't you tell me that yesterday?"

"You didn't ask yesterday," the young woman said, as if that was the most obvious thing in the world. "But have you thought about contacting the police?"

Sam barked out a purely bitter laugh that echoed around the entire grocery store, shook her head, then spun around with the intention of marching right back out of the store again before one more thought occurred to her. So she ended up spinning in a complete circle all the way back toward the florist and pointing at the young woman. "You know what? I'm being harassed. The flowers aren't helping. They're unwanted. Someone's stalking me. And I demand to see your shop's video footage over the last several days, including the day you say this order was picked up by whoever's apparently delivering these flowers. Right now. Go ahead. I'll wait."

"Ma'am?" The young woman said, lowering her voice. "I'm going to tell you this one more time before I call the police first and have them remove you from the store, which is well within my rights because I work here. It is against my employer's policy to divulge any personal information about customers or recipients of our products. Nor can I hand over video surveillance footage or any company information at all simply because someone showed up and didn't leave it. Now, if you came back here with a warrant, that's a completely different story. But until then, I'm sorry. There's nothing more I can do to help you."

Sam bit her lower lip to keep her mouth shut.

It sounded like somebody had shopped around for a bit of legal advice and maybe even some coaching for how to deal with the shittiest of all customers.

Sam should have demanded surveillance yesterday. Now, she was out of options.

She slapped a hand down on the counter and whirled away from the young woman to finally stomp back toward the front of the store.

"Oh, ma'am," the young woman called after her. "Don't forget your flowers."

"Are you fucking kidding me?"

She didn't stop or slow on her way back through the store's front doors. But then she had to stop, because someone shouted somewhere behind her and Sam couldn't keep ignoring the man after the third time he had shouted, "ma'am."

She finally whirled on him and snarled, "I don't want the fucking flowers!"

The man stopped short halfway toward her in the parking lot, blinking with wide eyes. Then he lifted both hands in concession and offered a sheepish smile. "Hey, judging by how big of a deal you're making out of the whole thing, I don't blame you."

She noticed the distinct lack of Sophy's Roses bouquet

136

in his hand and realized this was the same clerk from yesterday, from the deli department. Today, he looked a little friendlier, maybe even sympathetic to her plight if that was what she was calling this bullshit.

"What do you want?" she asked him.

"I probably should have said something yesterday. Claire's kind of a tight ass. You know, stickler for the rules. Even though I'm pretty sure they wouldn't be all that strongly enforced if she learned how to loosen up a little."

"So you're going to sneak me back into the store and let me watch surveillance footage from the last four days?" Sam asked.

The broad-shouldered young man chewed on the inside of his cheek. "I can't actually do that either. But I do remember the guy who showed up a few days ago to pick up those roses you don't want. He made almost as big of a scene with getting them out of the store as you did with bringing them back."

"Good to know I'm not the only one who leaves an impression."

"Yeah, well at least you can hold a decent conversation," he said. "So far. The guy who picked up those roses, though? He didn't even thank me for helping him get them all the way out here."

"Did you happen to get his name?"

"No. But he wore a black hoodie that was way too big on him. And he was on a bike, which made it even more of a pain in the ass to help him get those flowers into the stupid homemade basket set up he'd tied to the back. It was a nightmare."

"Black hoodie, huh?" she thought, noting a detail that might be useful later.

There was always a little bit of disparity in the truth versus what people said they remembered after the fact. It could have been a black-and-white checkered hoodie. The fact that the guy wearing said hoodie came along with a bicycle made Sam pretty damn confident that she'd actually glimpsed the flower delivery guy early this morning.

Probably should've gone after him barefoot anyway.

"Thank you," she told the clerk. "You've been more helpful two minutes after chasing me out of the store than that florist girl… You said her name was Claire?"

He nodded. "You're not gonna try to get her fired, are you?"

"Only if I find out that *she's* the one who's been leaving these flowers on my doorstep."

At first, he looked terrified by the thought. Then he realized Sam was kidding and let out a nervous laugh. "Gotcha."

She didn't bother to tell him it was mostly not a joke.

She did, however, save her number in his phone and tell him to reach out if he thought of anything else about the delivery cyclist in a baggy hoodie that might be useful for her to know.

As soon as she started the Jeep's engine, Sam rolled down the windows and pulled out her smokes, getting ready to light another one for the road. But then her cell phone buzzed in the front passenger seat beside her, and she glanced sideways at the screen.

It was Angela.

"Ah, shit," she muttered, then returned her attention to the cigarette hanging loosely between her lips and cupped a hand around the end with her lighter ready in the other.

Her phone kept buzzing, and when it stopped, presumably going straight to voicemail, Sam thought she was in the clear for all of half a second. But Angela called again.

With a sigh, Sam tossed everything into the center

console again, snatched up her phone, and figured she might as well answer.

"Angela. Everything okay?"

"Sam, hi. I'm so sorry to bother you, but I didn't know who else to call. They're here. I didn't do anything, but they just showed up… They're at my hotel. Right outside my room, and they're basically screaming at me to open up, and I don't know—"

"Whoa, whoa, hold on. Angela, slow down a second. Start over. *Who's* outside your hotel room?"

"The police. They're banging on the door. They know I'm in here, obviously. I'm sure they can hear me as much as I can hear them. And they're saying I'm wanted for breaking and entering into some place last night. I … I really need you to get here, Sam. They'll listen to you."

Yeah, maybe…

"All right, hang tight." Sam glanced at her watch. "I'll be there in three minutes. Just don't say anything until then, yeah?"

Earlier this morning, she hadn't thought she would be driving anywhere as quickly or in as much haste as she'd driven to the grocery store to kick someone's ass about the stupid flowers. But now Sam had an even better reason to hurry, and it wasn't road rage fueling her down the frontage road toward Angela's hotel.

It was disbelief and surprise and indignation.

At least Angela had had the presence of mind to call anyone at all before trying to deal with the police on her own, and fortunately for her, she'd had Sam's number.

Sam was at the hotel in three minutes exactly, just as she'd promised. By the time she jogged through the front doors, though Angela was already out of her room, her hands in cuffs behind her back yet again as Chief Colton and one of his junior officers escorted the woman down the hall toward the joke of a lobby.

Or maybe Colton just had a thing for Angela and didn't quite know how to tell her.

Sam held back a snort and headed straight for them.

"Sam!" Angela practically sagged in relief at the sight of her, then tried shooting multiple wide-eyed glances over her shoulder at the chief of police with one hand on her cuffed wrists and the other centered along her upper back. "Sam, tell him. Please. Tell him I was with you all night last night. He won't listen to me."

"What's this about, Chief?" Sam stopped in the center of the narrow hallway, which for the first time was actually appreciated because it meant two uniformed officers and a wrongfully arrested citizen couldn't just blow their way past her to continue to the squad cars. They had to stop if they didn't want some kind of physical altercation.

"None of your business, Salazar," Colton replied blandly. "And I highly recommend you step aside, or I'll have to charge you with interfering with a criminal investigation."

"Criminal investigation, huh?" Sam folded her arms and tilted her head. "And here I was this whole time thinking there was nothing criminal whatsoever about sitting in a twenty-four-hour cafe for a cup of coffee and a slice of pie. If that's part of town law, Chief, your department should probably post it on a big-ass sign somewhere. It's not the kind of thing regular people just automatically assume, you know?"

"We're not having this conversation. Step aside."

"Not until I hear straight from you what you've arrested this woman for." Technically, the man didn't have any obligation whatsoever to inform her of the charges against someone else, but Colton knew her well enough by now to know she wouldn't back down until she got what she wanted.

Apparently, he wanted to get Angela out of this hotel and into his car badly enough, and he was willing to play her game.

"Breaking and entering," he said. "Last night, this woman broke into the Kalamack Club after hours and vandalized club property, so I'm taking her in."

"Around what time was this break-in?" Sam asked.

Colton scrunched up his face in agitation. His junior officer, however, didn't know Sam quite as well and therefore took his authority as a Rush Police Officer seriously enough to open his mouth. "The club closes at ten. So, between the hours of ten and five o'clock this morning, when the club's front receptionist showed up and found the vandalism on site."

"With signs of forced entry too?" Sam asked.

The junior officer opened his mouth, paused, and shot Colton a quick look.

The chief blinked slowly and sighed. "Come on. I'm doing my job, and it's probably about time you focus on yours, too. Whatever that is."

"Well, right now," Sam retorted, "I'm making it my job to help you do yours, because it sounds like you can use all the help you can get, Chief. Angela and I were together all night last night, from, let's see... When did I get off work? About ten o'clock. Maybe ten thirty. All the way up to nearly two in the morning."

Colton raised an eyebrow and said flatly, "Is that right?"

"Yeah, we were talking." She nodded toward the hotel's attached cafe. "Right over there, actually. Twenty-four-hour place with a decent cup of coffee. Pie's not too bad, either. You should try it sometime."

The chief almost rolled his eyes. "Is there anyone who can corroborate this?"

"Our waitress," Angela added quickly. "She was there the whole time we were."

"Yes, she was," Sam said. "And I'm willing to bet a fine establishment like this one keeps their security cameras rolling twenty-four-seven, seeing as that's when they're open. Middle of the night like that, I'd want to keep my cameras on too, just in case. Did you check that footage, Chief?"

He didn't acknowledge her question, which was obviously meant to stoke the already smoldering embers of the enormous trash fire this would become for Rush's Chief of Police wrongly arresting, charging, and locking up an out-of-towner without having covered all his bases first.

He nodded at his junior officer to go look into the security footage, then scowled at Sam. "If anything you just told me doesn't check out on that footage, we're gonna have a lot bigger problems than you blocking me in this hallway. You understand?"

"Absolutely, Chief." Sam topped the whole thing off with a flickering smile they both knew did not mean she was more than happy to help. Not him anyway.

"What does that mean?" Angela asked, her voice shaking as her entire body still trembled from the shock of being put in cuffs twice in three days.

"It means you're not going anywhere until we hear about that video footage of you and I in the cafe last night," Sam told her. "Any chance you wanna loosen up those cuffs while we wait, Chief?"

"Not on your life. Come on." He firmly but gently guided Angela along with him past Sam standing in the hallway and out to the empty, sprawling lobby of the hotel that had all of two chairs in it, on opposite sides of the room. He directed Angela to sit in one of them, without removing the cuffs, and stood beside her chair while he waited for his rookie partner of the day to return.

Sam took a shot at reassuring Angela that everything was going to be fine, but she didn't get very far.

"Uh-uh," Colton said, wagging a finger at her and shaking his head. "You stay right where you are. I'm not in the mood to deal with any more of your shit today, Salazar, and you're not talking to my suspect until I have confirmation one way or the other. If you're bullshitting me, though—"

"If I'm bullshitting you, Chief, you might as well cuff me too and charge both of us for the same thing."

He glowered at her and said nothing.

When the junior officer returned from the cafe, his buoyant eagerness to do as his chief instructed had deflated into grim-faced acceptance.

With a warning glare in Sam's direction, Colton stepped away from Angela in the chair, thumbs hooked through his uniform belt once again, and joined his junior officer on the other side of the lobby for a remarkably quick conversation in low tones. Sam couldn't hear what they were saying, but she didn't have to.

She met Angela's gaze from across the room and winked at the woman before offering a reassuring nod.

Angela still just looked mortified.

Finally, Colton returned, stooped to grab Angela's upper arm and pull her out of the chair, then told her to turn around. Without any further explanation, he undid the cuffs before returning them to his belt.

Angela responded like a deer caught in headlights and didn't even turn around to look at him, focused instead on rubbing her wrist in dumbfounded shock and staring at the old, patterned carpeting of the hotel lobby.

"Looks like you can check another suspect off your list, Chief," Sam said.

Colton turned toward her with his never-ending glower. "Not today, Salazar. I'm not doing this shit today."

"You don't have to. I just wanna commend you for your excellent police work this morning. And I figure, now that we've got this whole 'pinning the break-in on the wrong innocent person' situation out of the way, I might have something that can help with your continued investigation."

The man visibly struggled between ignoring her to carry on with his day and taking the bait, which Sam knew he eventually would, and she wasn't disappointed.

"Talk," he finally said. "Quickly."

"Sure. I did drive past the Kalamack Club late last night. On my way home from the very same cafe your partner just walked out of. He can confirm that if necessary. I know I was on that footage as well."

"Listen, if you're just blowing smoke…"

"No, no, I *did* see something in the club just a little after two o'clock, like I said. There was a light on inside. Moved around a bit somewhere on the ground floor. I saw it through the windows, and then it went off again. Didn't see anything else after that, though. It could've been a trick of the light something, sure, but knowing there was a break-in and vandalism at the exact same time… I mean, I wouldn't be surprised if that was your perp right there."

Colton stared at her, his tongue poking against the inside of one cheek in aggravation.

"Thanks for your testimony, then," he said. "Would I be correct in assuming you're willing to come down to the station to make a statement? Sounds like you know the drill by now."

"You just tell me when, Chief," Sam replied with a

shrug and a small smile. "Though any statement I give is gonna be exactly what you just heard. Sorry I couldn't be more helpful, but that's all I know."

"Uh-huh," he said, then he turned back toward Angela, who was still frozen stiff facing the wall. "Ma'am."

She jumped and spun around toward him.

"There's no possibility of you having been in two places at once, so I'm letting you go. And this is the last time you get a warning from me and not another twenty-four hours behind bars. Minimum. Understand?"

Angela slowly nodded.

"The best thing for you right now," he continued, "is to climb into whatever car you drove into Rush, turn it around, and drive back to wherever it is you came from. You've caused too much of a ruckus in this town already. There's nothing more for you to find here and no one else to help you. Go home. Then we can all rest easy knowing this is behind us, yeah?"

Angela didn't say anything.

"And you." Colton pointed at Sam. "Stop interfering with every goddamn thing that has nothing to do with you. You're not law enforcement. You don't have a say in what happens around here. And I'm tired of seeing your face pop up everywhere I don't want to see it."

Sam wanted to tell him to eat shit and die if, of course, that was okay with his boss, but she didn't.

After how many times she'd struck out trying to help Beth with her personal problems months ago, there was no way in hell Sam was going to give up trying to help one more woman no one else wanted to listen to.

Beyond that, it just felt really damn good to be right and on the winning side about something as important as this.

To both of them.

SIXTEEN

Sam

_____

THE FIRST PLACE Sam wanted to go after leaving the hotel was straight to the Redwood Rings, and only because she knew the place was a hub of information.

Angela remained silent during their drive to the pub. That silence continued when Sam pulled the Jeep into the bar's parking lot, which was practically empty.

The woman's first words after her close encounter with repeat incarceration were, "My car's gone."

"Yeah," Sam said. "Ernie from the garage picked it up this morning and towed it to his shop, remember? I left his number for you last night."

"Oh…" Angela nodded vacantly and didn't seem capable of much more mental processing at the moment.

Knowing what she knew of the woman, Sam couldn't blame her.

Inside the bar, they were immediately greeted by Chris, which consisted of a concerned frown and a rare hustle in his step while he dropped a damp rag onto the bar in passing and hurried to intercept them inside the front doors.

"Sam, what's going on? And don't tell me you felt like coming into work several hours early for your shift today."

She thought it might have been his attempt at a joke, but based on the way he kept frowning in concern at Angela, even Chris's attempts at lightheartedness fell short from time to time.

"Please tell me you're all right," he said, looking back and forth between the women.

"We're totally fine," she said.

"All thanks to Sam," Angela added, finally pulling out of her stupor enough to at least attempt putting Chris at ease.

It didn't work as well as the woman probably expected it to.

"Please tell me you didn't do something totally stupid," he said, staring at Sam with wide eyes. "I don't know how many times I've had to tell you to be careful, and now I'm getting a strong feeling you just did something that goes way over the line—"

"It's actually the complete opposite," Angela interrupted.

Now it was Chris's turn to look entirely stunned.

"Did I just hear that right?" he asked.

"I was this close to being wrongly arrested and charged with a crime I can promise you I didn't commit," Angela said. "Sam stepped in to help. I'd be behind bars right now if she hadn't been so brave."

That confession just made Chris frown.

Sam pressed her lips together and waited for a better response to come to her. She definitely wouldn't have called her intervention on Angela's behalf *brave*. More along the lines of stupid and reckless, which were both exactly the kinds of adjectives Chris had used on numerous occasions.

She shrugged at Chris instead.

Angela smoothed her dark hair away from her face with both hands and nodded as she let out a heavy sigh. "I hope it's not too much, but I am incredibly thirsty right now. Do you think we could—"

"How about a Pepsi," Sam suggested. "On ice."

Angela nodded, but before Sam could hurry off to fulfill that order, Chris set a hand on her shoulder to stop her and shook his head. "I'll take care of it. You two take a seat. We've got a few things to talk about, and you both look like you've been through it."

When he returned with their drinks, Sam dove immediately into explaining everything she and Angela had been through since they'd left him in the parking lot last night.

Chris listened intently, then spread his arms and leaned back in his seat. "Okay. So what are you doing *here*? I mean, besides the Pepsis, how can I help you?"

Sam bit back a smartass retort. "I figured it was a good idea for us to head here right away and see if you'd heard or seen anything in the last couple days that might have involved a number of things that can seriously help Angela."

"As in potentially overhearing some drunk in here bragging about how he planned to vandalize the Kalamack Club?" Chris asked with a raised eyebrow. "Or maybe you wanna know if I've heard anybody talk about how much certain town officials and persons of interest around here deserve to be brought to justice for one reason or another? Not that that would excuse breaking and entering or vandalism of private property, but just to be clear, is that the kind of thing you're looking for?"

Sam wasn't going to take the bait. She was already on a roll with helping Angela out of multiple potentially dangerous situations, and now that had become her sole focus. Chris didn't want her getting involved, but it wasn't his call to make.

"Actually," she said, "I was thinking—"

"Hold that thought just a second, Sam," Chris interrupted, then cleared his throat. "Angela?"

She looked up at him, her shocked stare blank and glassy.

"I got a call from Ernie right before you two showed up. He towed your vehicle hours ago this morning, took a look, and had a few updates to pass along."

"And those can't wait until she's ready to pick up her car?" Sam asked.

"They seemed important enough to pass along now," he said. "Seeing as we were already on the topic of dangerous situations, right?"

"Oh no..." Angela shrank into herself even more. "What happened to my car?"

"It's a bit more than just the tires, actually," Chris said. "He's got a new set of four on order, and they should get here in the next day or two. That's the good news. The not-so-great news is your engine's missing its spark plugs too."

"No shit," Sam murmured.

Angela frowned. "Why? What does that mean?"

"Well, spark plugs don't just fall out," Chris said. "Which means someone had to remove them on purpose. Ernie ordered more of those too, so he's also waiting for those to come in. But if you ask me, suddenly disappearing spark plugs probably means someone's got it out for you."

"I already got that impression with the slashed tires," she said.

"That could've been anyone, honestly," Chris added, rubbing his hairless chin in thought. "But with missing spark plugs? Yeah, my guess is you poked the wrong bear in this town, and someone's trying to send a message."

"Someone?" Sam asked. "Or the bear?"

There were multiple bears in Rush that could be poked. Sam knew that all too well. But only one of them immediately came to mind.

It took a little longer than it probably should have for the information and the implications of it to sink in, but then Angela's face grew incredibly pale. She swallowed thickly, then gulped down enough ice-cold Pepsi to bring some color back into her cheeks before letting out a heavy sigh. "That sounds like things just got a lot more complicated for me."

"That's one way of putting it," Chris said.

"Complicated or not," Sam said, "we'll get to the bottom of this." She ignored the warning look Chris gave her, which she had been ignoring ever since he'd started sending those looks her way. There was no doubt in her mind that someone related to the disappearance of Angela's youngest daughter had gotten wise to the woman's presence in town and her ceaseless determination to get to the bottom of what had happened to Dina. Missing spark plugs were a sure sign of that and couldn't be ignored.

Sam quickly filled Chris in on the rest of the details Angela had given her the night before in the cafe.

"What I really want to know now," she said when she'd finished, "is what exactly goes on at the Kalamack Club these days. You know, the stuff that isn't town business. I mean, I know I'm not involved enough in Rush's affairs to even care about politics, and everybody already knows about the meetings and fundraisers and whatever else they hold in there. But Dina wouldn't have taken a job just for politics and fundraisers, right?"

"Absolutely not," Angela said. "She was never interested in politics or government work. And she would've mentioned it to me in her texts if that was what she'd gotten involved in. Like I said, I thought it was a gentleman's club or something."

Chris scrunched up his face in a comical effort not to laugh. Fortunately, Angela didn't seem to notice.

"It's close enough," Christian from a ways down the bar said, then turned back toward their table with a crooked smile.

Sam looked across the bar at Christian and the other guys, wondering if they'd really been there the whole time.

"My guess is sex orgies," he added.

Sam rolled her eyes. "Because there's any other kind?"

"No, no, that ain't it," Levi said, pointing at Christian. "That's where all the town bigwigs do their devil worship. Didn't you know?"

"Oh my god," Angela said.

"God ain't got nothing to do with it at the Kalamack Club," Levi quipped.

Sam leaned slightly toward Angela and muttered, "Ignore them."

"Y'all let your imaginations get the better of you every damn time," Eddie added on his way back from the men's restroom, wiping his still-dripping hands on the legs of his jeans. "The only thing those folks get up to in that club is boring business talks, and that's it. They just want us to think there's all kinds of exciting stuff happening behind the scenes, but that's as far as it goes."

"But if it was *sex orgies*," Christian added, "you'd be the first to sign up for a new membership, wouldn't you, Ed?"

All three locals burst out laughing, their guffaws and wheezing chuckles filling the otherwise silent and empty bar.

Despite the hilarity of watching all three of them crack up like that, Sam was also painfully aware of the renewed horror taking up residence on Angela's face. She shook her head and called out to the guys, "You're all so full of shit, it's a miracle you can even see anything else."

That got them going all over again.

"Don't encourage them, Sam," Chris muttered, leaning back in his chair again. "They'll get over it eventually."

"Well, then we need to find the right person to ask about this. Someone who knows what actually goes on there but who wouldn't have a problem talking about it. To us specifically. Do we know anyone like that?"

"Sure we do," Eddie said, spinning all the way around on his bar stool to face her table after having just sat down.

"Let it go, Ed," Chris chided. "Now's not the time."

"No, I'm serious. I know exactly the kind of man you're looking for. Y'all should go talk to Greg."

"Greg?" Sam asked, looking back and forth between the chortling bar patrons and Chris. "Who's Greg?"

"The doctor," Christian added, nodding sagely. "At least, I *think* he's still a doctor. Can't be all too sure about that now, though. He was planning on taking over the Reginald Jones practice some years ago, but that ended up falling through. Some folks think the other doctors didn't want him there or maybe even the other patients, but all those plans changed around the time Greg was kicked out of that hoity-toity club in the first place."

Sam almost grinned now that she'd put together where this was going. "You mean someone can actually get kicked out? I'm talking about membership and everything, not just physically."

"Oh yes, ma'am," Christian added. "It's only happened just the once, as far as I can tell, and that was

Dr. Greg kicked out physically and lost his membership, and no one who ain't part of that fancy place knows exactly why."

"But the whole town turned against him just like that," Eddie added as he reached for a bowl of peanuts lying almost out of his reach on the bar. "Whole damn town turned their back on him, and ol' Greg didn't have much of anywhere left to go after that. So he moved on out to the sticks."

"Which sticks, exactly?" Sam asked.

All three men fell silent as they thought about the answer.

"I don't know," Christian finally said. "Somewhere out in the boonies but still close enough to Rush that he actually technically still lives here."

"Right up off the highway a bit past that farm," Levi said, snapping his fingers in an attempt to jog his memory. "Oh, what's that place out there? *Way* out there. Big old pot farm with all those security guards and the fancy gates and shit."

"Rip's farm?" Chris asked, his curiosity clearly piqued now as well.

Levi pointed at him. "That's the one. Last I heard, Dr. Greg had cleared out of his big old fancy doctor house in town and moved all the way up out there. Some tiny little property of his own. The cabin. Just him and himself. It's right past the turnoff to Rip's farm up there. Can't miss it."

"Well, you *can*..." Eddie interjected. "But it's a lot harder to miss if you're actually looking for it."

"True."

"And no one knows why he was kicked out of the Kalamack Club," Sam reiterated.

"Probably broke the rules," Levi said.

"And those rules would be?"

"Kind of like that movie." Levi grinned. "You know, the real good one with all the fighting. Where the guy ended up being crazy and, like, two people at the same time."

"*Fight Club*?" Christian asked.

"Uh-huh. Yep, that's the one."

"And everybody knows the first rule of Fight Club," Eddie chimed in.

All three of them cracked up laughing again, howling and slapping the top of the bar. Eddie nearly fell off his stool.

Chris just stared at them before eventually letting out a heavy sigh and shaking his head.

Sam would have joined him in that, but the wheels in her mind had already started turning, and they weren't going to stop until she acted on them.

"Angela, how do you feel about going on a little road trip?" she asked. "Not a long one. Just a few hours there and a few hours back, give or take."

"You know you do have work later today, right?" Chris reminded her.

"Are you expecting the place to fill up much more than this?"

He pursed his lips at her but didn't say anything else.

"You don't have to get all bent out of shape about it," she told him. "Think of it as a chance to save a few bucks on the off-season, right? If I don't work a shift, you don't have to pay me."

"Yeah, but then I have to work *your* shift," he said.

"Well, you won't have to pay yourself either, will you?"

He scowled at her, then huffed out a laugh and ran a hand through his hair. "Jesus, I know it's pointless to argue with you. You've already made up your mind."

"And you learn quick." Sam pointed at him, then pushed herself out of her chair. "If we're gonna do this, we should get going now. It's still early enough we can be back in town by dinner, if everything goes according to plan."

Angela started to get up as well, then her eyes widened, and she settled herself stiffly back down again. "And if things *don't* go according to plan?"

"Well, I can't imagine it getting much worse than us not being back by dinner," Sam said. "What I mean is, it's not a dangerous drive. Don't worry about it. At the very least, we can get a much better idea of the kind of work Dina was doing at the club when she was there, and if we're lucky, that might come with a few clues as to how we can track her down."

Angela finally stood from the table and collected her purse again.

"Okay, listen up," Sam called to the guys sitting at the bar. "Can anyone give me clear, simple directions to this Dr. Greg's place out in the sticks?"

"You don't need directions, Sam," Levi said. "I already told you where it is."

"Just keep going right on down the road past Rip's farm," Eli added. "You can't miss the place. Just a little turn right off the road and you're good to go."

"I'm going to hold you to that, then," Sam said as she pointed at the guys.

Christian started laughing as he shook his head and smacked a hand down on the bar. "If you can't find it, girl, don't come storming on back here and telling us it's *our* fault."

Sam nodded at Chris on her way out while Angela stood from the table to follow her. "I'll try not to take too long."

"Yeah, and I'll try not to call you in case I need help behind the bar." Chris snorted and, despite having just released her from her duties as an employee of the Redwood Rings for the day, he couldn't help but smile.

Sam and Angela had just gotten on their way out of the Redwoods parking lot when Sam's phone rang.

"Syc," she answered, surprised to get a call from him. "Is everything okay?"

Her landlord grumbled something unintelligible before he finally said, "Yeah, I just thought you should know I got served another stack of bullshit paperwork this morning. And this time it was signed. In all places."

"Sounds a lot more official this time. What are you gonna do?"

"What am I gonna do? Hell, I already did it. Burned the fucking things just like last time."

"Little Pete's not gonna be happy when he hears about that," Sam said. "You know that, right?"

"Won't be happy? Of course he's not happy. He's the one who delivered them to my face, and I'm the one who got the satisfaction of seeing his when he watched me throw them in the fire. And in case you were wondering, it felt damn good."

Then he hung up.

Sam chuckled in surprise before she dropped her phone into the center console to return her focus to the road.

"Who was that?" Angela asked.

"A friend," Sam said. "And my landlord. It's a fun situation."

"Everything okay?"

"For right now, sure. Things might not be so okay for him in a few days."

"Do we need to help him?" The amount of concern in

Angela's voice made Sam do a double take at the woman sitting in her passenger seat.

"Help him? No, Syc wasn't calling for help. I think he just wanted to rub a minor victory in my face before it blows up in his."

~

SAM KNEW her way up to Rip's farm simply because it was a straight shot up the highway with practically nothing else between Rush and the man's sprawling property that contained at least a hundred acres.

After almost two hours of driving, they finally saw signs of an occupied, well-kept property. Then they came upon the front gates, which were impossible to miss from the road.

The two enormous wrought-iron gates on wheels and a mechanized system were mounted between stone pillars at either side of the driveway branching off the frontage road. Multiple cameras were mounted along both the gate posts and the equally tall rock wall extending in either direction around the farm. The guy had serious security concerns, which made sense when Rip had made a reputation for himself as one of the most prolific and profitable marijuana growers in this part of the state, maybe even the surrounding northwestern part of the country.

"This is Rip's farm," Sam said, nodding toward the grounds between the gates and what little of it they could see through the wrought iron bars. She slowed the Jeep to a crawl and gauged Angela's reaction.

The woman's face was practically plastered to the passenger-side window. She took in all the details of her daughter's last known whereabouts, according to anyone else in Rush.

"This is where she worked?" Angela asked.

"For the first couple weeks, at least. As far as we know, right? But now you can see it's a decent-looking place. Clean. Organized. Well-protected, with plenty surveillance."

Angela turned slowly away from the window to raise an eyebrow at Sam. "Is that supposed to make me feel better?"

"You know, I thought it might until you just looked at me like that. Sorry."

Shaking her head, Angela sighed. "I wish she'd never come to this stupid town. I wish she'd never left home."

Sam fully empathized with the woman's pain. She knew there was nothing she could do, but she also knew that if wishing over and over for all the things she'd wanted in her life since losing her Sophie actually worked, everything would have been different.

And no amount of wishing actually worked.

SEVENTEEN

Laila

LAILA TRIED to focus on work, but she couldn't think of anything but the sound of Big Pete screaming upstairs.

The words were muffled and accompanied by lots of stomping footsteps from the second floor above her. Probably while Pete dished out an earful to David about the vandalism issue from last night.

The commotion made Xavier — the only employee Rush's single hardware store ever sent out to handle work orders for the Kalamack Club — pause his scrubbing of the bright-red paint on the wall to meet Laila's gaze. She shook her head, shrugged, and figured it was best not to say anything else about the acrid, choking, sour, stinking chemical Xavier now applied to the dried crimson paint job.

While Big Pete finished throwing his fit upstairs, Laila walked toward the closest window and had to jiggle it back and forth a few times before she could get it open just to air out the stink.

As soon as her nose stopped burning from the fumes,

the club's front door opened again, and in strode Hank Topping.

"What the hell's going on in here?" he asked, whipping off his sunglasses and gazing all over the place as if he'd never stepped foot in the club before. "Looks like something from one of those crime-scene shows my wife's always talking about."

"Good morning, Mr. Topping," Laila said, turning from the window to approach him and putting on her best last-minute smile. "I'm so sorry. Unfortunately, the club is closed today for some last-minute deep-cleaning and repairs. We open again first thing in the morning, regular hours."

"Goddamn it!" Big Pete's pounding footsteps crashed down the winding staircase toward the first floor behind Laila's desk. "What is that smell? And who the hell's here? We're closed. How hard is it for everyone to understand that?" He burst through the back staircase entrance and stopped beside Laila's desk when he saw Xavier scrubbing chemicals on the wall and Hank Topping standing closer to the front door. "Who called the cleaners in here?"

"I did," Laila piped in, her grin maybe even frozen on her face for the rest of her life.

Pete's clear, glistening eyes blazing with fury settled directly onto her face. "I didn't tell you to call in the damn cleaners. I told you to clean that shit off the walls. *You*, not Pablo over there," he said, gesturing toward Xavier without even looking at the man.

To his credit, Xavier just kept scrubbing and pretended not to hear a thing.

"I did everything I could on my own," Laila continued. "But that paint wasn't coming off. And the club doesn't stock the kind of cleaning supplies this needs. So I called the hardware store to see if they could do it for us. Also, Chief Colton was adamant this morning about getting that window fixed in the front room. You know, the one that doesn't close."

With a grunt, Big Pete stormed across the front room and nodded at Mr. Topping. "Get out of here, Hank."

"But it's a club, Pete," Hank replied with a crooked smile, spreading his arms. "And I'm a paying member."

"Sure, you pay your dues. But I own the damn place. And when I say we're closed, we're closed. See you tomorrow."

It looked like the other man was about ready to jump Pete Wilder for speaking to him like that in front of two employees. Instead, the man smiled, dipped his head, and spun around to hit the door.

As soon as the front door shut again, Big Pete whirled around to settle his anger on Laila again. As usual.

"Someone was in here last night," he said, stabbing a finger at the floor in front of him as his voice wavered on a growl. "Vandalizing my property and putting up some stupid sign like that. Someone's responsible for it. I depend on you to make sure this place is locked up tight at the end of the day, Laila. So, you're gonna explain to me how some idiot managed to get in here when I'm supposed to have one of the best damn receptionists in the area working for me."

"Well, to start," she said, maintaining her smile that had now grown particularly bitter, "getting that window in the front room fixed would alleviate a significant portion of our uncertainty."

Big Pete clicked his tongue and rolled his eyes as he spun away from her, though he didn't leave. Instead, he paced slowly across the front room, and Laila grabbed her clipboard with the daily opening and closing duties checklist from the bottom left-hand drawer of her desk where she always kept it.

"I'll have you know," she added, "all this is *not* a result of me slacking on the job, Pete. Look at this. My list every single night before I leave at ten o'clock six days a week. Here, it's right here for you to see. Close and lock all the doors. Close and lock all the windows. Check that every single room is empty with lights turned off before closing those doors. Turn off all the lights on the premises, except the light on the front porch and in the front hallway. Set the security alarm. Walk out the back door. Drive out of the parking lot. I follow this to a T in the exact same order every single night. This wasn't an oversight on my part, I can assure you."

By the time she finished her diatribe, Laila realized she had most likely overstepped her bounds with her employer. Big Pete Wilder did not take kindly to anyone talking back to him, least of all a woman and certainly not a woman in his employ.

Instead of exploding again, however, he glared at her, stabbed a finger in her face, and growled, "It's a good thing you're so pretty, or I'd send you packing. I *pay* you to look pretty and handle things for this club's members here in the front, not to explain every second of the day to me like I'm a goddamn toddler." Then he swung his finger toward the writing on the wall. "Get it fixed. I don't have time for this shit."

After that, he stormed past her again and disappeared up the back stairs.

With a sigh, Laila headed through the clubhouse and into the back kitchen to make herself a cup of tea. And to grab a little space to clear her head and settle her nerves before she settled back down at her desk to do her job the way Big Pete wanted.

Xavier was still working on the wall when she returned, but she didn't say anything to him. She merely sat at her desk, carefully sipped her still piping-hot chamomile, and glanced at the phone. Then her gaze slid to the small necklace on a delicate, thin silver chain resting on her desk beside the phone.

The pendant hanging from it might have been sterling silver, though it was just tarnished enough to make Laila suspect it was a cheap knockoff. The pendant itself was shaped as a capital letter D with a few embellishments of flowery vines etched around the perimeter of the letter. No other adornment.

It didn't look like the most expensive piece of jewelry or the most valuable. But it wasn't hers. It obviously belonged to one of the members or their wives or girlfriends or daughters or whoever else they brought into this place, and someone would be looking for it.

The lobby was completely empty, so Laila headed upstairs to ask the usual suspects for personal items that got left behind or picked up in the building.

She'd expected only a short, brief conversation with David to ask if he recognized the piece of jewelry, but instead, she found the clubhouse's manager slumped forward in his office chair behind his desk, his face bright red and his eyes rimmed with an even angrier hue. His eyes were glassy as he glared at the surface of his desk.

Now that Laila was here, she couldn't very well turn around and pretend she hadn't appeared in the open doorway of his office.

She cleared her throat and knocked on the door. "Hey there," she said cheerily.

David grunted, wiped quickly at the corner of his eye with the back of a hand, then sat up straight in his office chair and nodded at her. "What do you need, Laila?"

Big Pete really must have laid into the guy hard if it had made David this upset.

"I found this necklace downstairs," she said, dangling the inexpensive silver chain from one finger and holding it up toward him. "It's just a big silver D on a chain, but I figured I'd ask around the employees first. It was just sitting on my desk. Your name starts with a D, and I don't think anyone else's around here does, so I thought it might be yours."

David leaned forward over his desk and squinted at the piece of jewelry, then shook his head. "It's not mine. I have no idea where that came from. Anything else?"

"No, that's it. Thanks."

She left the man to his solitude then, which the man clearly needed, and took the necklace back to her desk.

Whoever it belonged to would obviously want it back. She draped the thin silver chain around one of the push pins in the bulletin board beside her desk and let it hang there in full view.

If this belonged to any of the members or their family, someone would see it, and then she could get it back to its owner.

Before she could pick up her cup of tea to enjoy more than the first sip, the club's front door opened again with another little jingle of the bell, and Dr. Reginald Jones stepped inside.

"Well, would you look at this," he said, widening his eyes at the graffiti on the wall that still hadn't come off before he flashed a brilliant grin at Laila. "That's not something you see every day, is it? You got something to say about this, darlin'?"

Laila stood and approached him with the same smile she offered everyone else. "Good morning, Doc. We're working on cleaning and maintenance today, unfortunately.

It was an unscheduled closure. And we'll be open again for normal hours first thing tomorrow morning like usual, but today, the club's closed, sorry to say."

"Well, figures. Guess I'll just come back tomorrow."

He was a lot easier to turn away than Mr. Topper, but then Laila remembered the additional small task she had pinned on herself and called after him. "Oh, Dr. Jones?"

He stopped at the front door and peered over his shoulder.

"I found a necklace here in the front room this morning. Sterling silver, capital letter D on a silver chain. Doesn't belong to you or your wife by any chance, does it?"

The man's eyes narrowed slightly, and his chuckle came out in a way that sounded a whole lot like Dr. Reginald Jones didn't buy a whole lot of women's jewelry in the first place. And if he did, it wasn't for his wife. "Definitely doesn't belong to me."

"Any chance you might know who it *does* belong to if you? Maybe you've seen someone else wearing it around."

"I'd love to help, but I got no idea. Good luck."

Though his words were friendly enough, his face had paled in those few seconds of conversation, his smile unusually tight, and a thick vein had stood out along his temple.

If Laila hadn't known better, she would have said Dr. Jones was suddenly in a very big hurry to get the hell away from the Kalamack Club.

Or away from *her*.

With that, he walked right out of the clubhouse and Laila was left alone once more with the diligently working Xavier and the stink of his weird chemical still filling her workspace despite the open windows.

At least now she could finally enjoy a little bit of her

tea and hope the rest of the day started to calm down from here on out.

She'd barely touched the teacup to her lips when the phone on her desk rang again.

"Kalamack Club, this is Laila. How may I help you? Yes, hi, Mr. Potter. Good morning. Yes, you heard right, unfortunately. The club is closed today. Yes, absolutely, I do understand. Yes, Mr. Potter, thank you. I'm absolutely aware that the club has always remained open, even during the great strike of '76."

EIGHTEEN

Sam

TWENTY MINUTES past the front gates of Rip's Farm, Sam couldn't keep ignoring the feeling that she'd gone a little too far, and she had to turn around.

Once they'd driven another fifteen minutes back the way they'd come, Angela nearly leapt out of her seat and looked like she was trying to claw the passenger-side door open when she pointed out the window. "There! Right there. Look! There's a road, I think. It's overgrown quite a bit, but it *is* a road, isn't it?"

Sure enough, it was.

Sam took them down the incredibly long driveway and kept the Jeep at a slow crawl so she and Angela could scan the surrounding landscape in search of a cottage or an outbuilding or some sign that someone lived here.

Just when she was beginning to think they had taken the wrong turn, they took a surprisingly steep bend in the road, then they found themselves entering a small clearing in the woods, complete with a decent-sized cottage at the back, two outbuilding sheds that looked hand-built by someone who didn't entirely know what he was doing with mountain-home construction, and a large SUV that seemed remarkably out of place in the middle of nowhere.

To the side of the SUV and just in front of the cabin stood a man in jeans and a black t-shirt, throwing his arms back for a mighty swing before he brought the axe head down on the block of wood laid out on a tree stump.

"Looks like we found something," Sam said.

"Is that supposed to be the doctor?" Angela asked.

"We're about to find out."

When Sam rolled the Jeep to a stop, tires crunching across the gravel and dirt and small pebbles in the road, the man stopped chopping wood and stepped to the side before hefting the axe handle up over one shoulder. Then he stared brazenly at the Jeep's two occupants, silently daring them to come any closer.

At least that was what it looked like to Sam, and she was always up for a good challenge.

"I don't know about this," Angela said, wiping her palms on the legs of her pants. "Maybe we should go back, huh? Look somewhere else, like in a phone book or something."

"We're already here, Angela," Sam said. "If a person in Rush doesn't want to be found by anyone else in Rush, we sure as hell aren't going to find their name, number, and address in a phone book."

She shut off the engine but left the keys in the ignition before stepping out.

When she was close enough to not have to shout across the clearing, Sam nodded at the man with the axe and called out, "Morning. Are you Greg?"

"What do you want?" he asked, looking back and forth between her and the Jeep.

Sam almost smiled when she heard a door opening and

shutting behind her. At least Angela was willing to do what it took to find her answers.

"Actually," Sam said as she approached even closer, "we were hoping to talk to you about the Kalamack Club."

The man was already back in mid-swing as she spoke. The axe thumped down onto another piece of wood. Both halves instantly toppled onto the ground, the cut visibly clean and almost perfect. But when the axe head remained embedded in the tree stump, the man didn't bother to pull it out again.

Instead he looked up at Sam in surprise. "Kalamack Club, huh? You two wanna come inside for a bit? It's a little more comfortable, and I could use another cup of coffee."

"Sounds good."

He nodded for them to follow as he turned back and opened the front door of his cabin.

The place was small but cozy. Though it lacked any touch of homeyness in either decor or color, it did contain all the requisite comforts of a man living as far away from civilization as he was willing to get all on his own without needing anything, for the most part. Two couches, a coffee table, a sideboard, an old warped dry bar in the main room. No TV, but the far wall contained large bookshelves stuffed with all kinds of books, and the fireplace in the back had been thoroughly cleaned out. The kitchen was just a series of cabinets mounted on the wall with two tables pushed together as a counter, and they looked hand-made as well.

If Sam had to guess, there was only one bedroom off the narrow hallway in the back. A bathroom was probably pushing it. She wouldn't have been surprised to find an outhouse or some modern equivalent behind the cabin. She didn't think they'd gotten nearly far enough in their conversation yet for her to ask if this place had running water.

"Can I get either of you something to drink?" Dr. Greg asked as he busied himself in the small kitchen to presumably make himself that cup of coffee.

"Just a water, please," Angela said.

"Sure thing. Take a seat."

When he came back with a fresh steaming tin mug of coffee in one hand and a glass of water for Angela in the other, he sat opposite the women on the other couch and took a slow, slurping sip. "So. What did you wanna know, exactly?"

"We heard you're a doctor," Sam began.

He snorted. "And I guess people still aren't telling the whole story of things down in town, are they? I *used* to be a doctor. Retired now."

Angela swallowed her water. "You look a little young to be retired."

"Normally, I'd take that as a compliment. But my circumstances might be considered a little different. I still consult from time to time online. It keeps the mind sharp. Keeps me relatively in the game, if I'm ever needed for emergencies now and then. But for the most part, yeah, I'm retired. Left the practice right in the middle of town, believe it or not, but something tells me you two already knew that part."

"We might've heard a thing or two," Sam said.

"Uh-huh. That's not something I'm generally fond of discussing with anyone these days. So I'd love to hear it from you first — why you came all the way out here to talk to me about the Kalamack Club."

"Yes," Angela said, leaning eagerly forward toward the edge of the couch as she nursed her glass of water in both hands. "We heard you were a good person to speak to first who might know something. Anything at all. I'm trying to find out what happened to my daughter Dina. Dina Copely. Do you know her?"

Dr. Greg slurped his coffee one more time, then stood and returned to the kitchen to putter around there before he even started answering. "I do remember Dina, yeah. Lovely girl. Great smile. She was always kind. Had a decent sense of humor too, which is hard to come by in a town like this where you're either in on the joke or the joke's on you. She did well with the members at the club, I remember that much."

The sound of silverware and pots and something being chopped on a wooden cutting board came from the kitchen. Sam turned slightly around in the couch to look across the room at him and frowned. It didn't really seem like the best time to start cutting up a bunch of ingredients for cabin-in-the-mountains stew, but okay.

"She made quite a name for herself as the fresh young face working for Pete Wilder at the Kalamack," Greg continued. "It seemed like everyone there was in love with her."

"Do you remember anything happening to her?" Angela asked. "Did she get in trouble or upset someone or start some kind of argument or get involved with anyone?"

"No, it was never anything like that." He shook his head, though he didn't look up from his work. "Not that I know of. Then again, I'm probably the last person you'd want to ask about any of this. I wasn't all that involved in club business before I retired, but I do remember the girl. There's not much more I can tell you."

"Did you ever talk to her?" Sam asked.

Letting Angela steer the conversation toward panic was one thing. The woman needed to ask what she needed to ask and get it out of the way, but that wasn't going to get them the kind of answers they needed. Angela didn't understand that. Sam sure did.

Greg stopped chopping for a second, then picked right back up again as if nothing had happened. "A few times. Mostly it was just in passing. 'Good morning, good night, see you next week,' that kinda thing. She'd been working at the club for a while and seemed fairly happy, but I don't know. I couldn't help the feeling that a girl like her was too good for a place like that. I tried once to encourage her to leave, you know? Find a different job somewhere else. I figured she could do so much better in a place that wasn't so … biased, more or less."

"That place being the Kalamack Club, right?" Sam clarified. When the man nodded, she continued, "We heard you got kicked out. Stripped of your membership. Told never to come back. It was kind of a big deal, according to everyone else in town."

Apparently done with his chopping, Greg slid all the various items on his cutting board into a large pot set out on one of the tables, scraping off the stragglers with the edge of his knife. "Then you heard correctly. I didn't agree with some of the club's policies, and I guess they didn't like coming up against any differences of opinion."

"Doesn't really seem like a good enough reason to kick someone out of a lifelong club membership altogether, thought, does it?"

Dr. Greg stopped what he was doing and looked up to fix her with a knowing stare. "You don't need much of a reason for anything if you're Pete Wilder. Something tells me you already know that too."

"Sure I do. I just don't quite understand why you'd join a club like that in the first place if you didn't like the way Big Pete was running it."

"I didn't *join up*." Greg grabbed the pot, took it to the

small sink at the back of the kitchen, and when the sound of running water filled the cottage, that answered Sam's question about the plumbing. "My spot in the club was passed down to me. Belonged to my father. And when he died, I inherited a cushy little seat along with everything else. But honestly, it's probably not the best idea to be discussing any of the club's business with anyone, especially now that I'm off the member list."

"Why not?" Sam asked. "That seems to me like the perfect time to start talking about it out in the open."

Greg shook his head. "No, you've got that backwards. And I'm really not trying to start up any more trouble. I had plenty enough of that when they kicked me out. Moving out here was supposed to get me far enough away from it that it wouldn't be an issue anymore, but here you are."

"Do you have any idea what specifically what Dina's job duties were while she worked at the club?" Sam asked.

He grabbed a wooden spoon from a piece of crockery on the back counter and got busy stirring the oddly simple veggie soup he'd just put together. "Like I said, I only spoke to her a few times. And I'm not all that interested in speaking with anyone else much these days, either. Is that all the questions you have? Because I've got a lot of work to do around here, and there are only so many hours in the day."

Sam stood from the couch and slowly perused the main room of the cabin. There were no pictures here, no personal touches, nothing to imply that Dr. Greg actually enjoyed his time up here. He clearly didn't have a family, or he would have brought them along too, but he also didn't feel a particular attachment to this place. Otherwise he probably would have put a little more effort into making it feel like home.

Either that, or he didn't plan on staying out here much longer.

"Anything you can tell us, Doc, would be incredibly helpful," she added. "Dina was last seen working at the Kalamack Club, and then she hasn't been seen since. That was five years ago. We're just trying to figure out what happened, track her down, help her out if she's gotten herself into trouble. For a young woman everyone in town seemed to like, there sure aren't a lot of people willing to talk about her."

"Again, I didn't know her that well. Not much I can help you out with beyond that." After tapping the wooden spoon against the edge of the pot a few times, he set it down, turned, and gazed out the large window along the far wall set beside the door. The frown darkening his face grew more and more worrisome by the second before he asked, "Did you tell anyone in town you were coming all the way up here to talk to me?"

"Not at all," Sam said. "We're looking for Dina. Trust me, you're not the center of our conversations these days."

He looked sharply at her and swallowed. "I think it's time for you two to leave."

"That's fine." Sam motioned for Angela to get up. "If there's anything at all you remember about Dina and you think you might be able to help us—"

"Listen," Greg interrupted. "I'm sorry, okay? I really am, but I just can't think of anything. I didn't know much of anything in the first place, and you staying here to keep asking me the same question fifty different ways is just a waste of your time. Sorry you came all the way out here for a whole lot of nothing, but I can't do anything else for you now. Please, I'm asking you to leave my property. And don't come back."

The urgency in his voice and the concern in the tight,

bitter lines around his mouth told Sam he was absolutely serious and terrified all while trying incredibly hard not to let it show.

He tried to get away from the Kalamack and Big Pete all the way up here, and he's still so scared of the guy. He won't even talk about these things in the privacy of his own home. Looks like Big Pete's got a longer reach than I thought.

"Thank you for your time, Doctor," Angela said with a nod as both women headed for the door.

"Just Greg," he corrected her at the last minute. "No one calls me Doctor anymore, and I'd really prefer to just be Greg now. If it's all the same to you."

"Understood."

The second the women stepped back over the threshold, Dr. Greg practically slammed the door shut behind them, followed by two quick, heavy thunks of deadbolts turning.

"Well, that was useless," Angela said as they hurried down the dirt drive back toward the Jeep.

Sam almost looked over her shoulder at the cabin one more time, then decided against it. "I wouldn't be so sure."

NINETEEN

Sam

WHEN SAM and Angela passed by the front gates of Rip's farm one more time, Sam slowed the Jeep and scanned as much of the premises as she could see from the side of those large gates.

"Maybe we should drive on up in there," she suggested. "Strike up some conversation with the employees and staff and whoever else is on site today. Ask if anybody remembers Dina when she worked here. A lot of these trimmers keep coming back year after year. I bet there are even some who were here five years ago with your daughter."

"I don't know," Angela said nervously. "That's a lot of people. The chances of any of them knowing her ... maybe we should just go back into town and look for a better idea."

"I get your concerns, totally," Sam said. She fixed another pointed look at the farm security gates. "But town's almost another two-hour drive from here, and we've already come all the way out this way. Might as well make the most of it on the same trip, right?"

"Fine," Angela relented.

Sam pulled the Jeep up to the large wrought-iron front gates where they came into full center focus of at least three different security cameras with an intercom mounted on a post right outside any vehicle's driver's-side window. She rolled down her window and pushed the call button before a sharp buzz crackled over the speaker, followed by a tinny male voice.

"State your business here."

"This is Sam Salazar. I work at the Redwood Rings down in town. And I'm here to talk to Rip about a former employee of his, if he's available and has the time."

Another buzz sounded, followed by a long pause.

"Why are you telling him all that?" Angela asked.

"This guy gets all kinds of people up on his farm," Sam said. "Most of them are seasonal workers and trimmers, yeah. But some are random folks coming into town looking for work. I imagine some are probably screwing around trying to play spy for some of the other pot farmers up here. If he knows where I'm coming from and where I work, that gives him a chance to vet me pretty damn quickly before he lets us through. I'm not technically an outsider anymore, but who knows? This Rip guy just might be curious enough to wanna see why we'd bother driving up to his gates in the first place."

The box buzzed again, and the tinny voice returned. "Please drive slowly through the gates and follow the road to the left up to the main lodge. You can't miss it."

"Thank you very much," she called happily at the box, then dropped back into her seat and rolled her eyes as the wrought-iron gates slowly rolled away from each other on their enormous wheels.

When they passed through the gates, Sam noticed the three men converging around the back of her Jeep far before Angela did. Up ahead, another man sprawled out in a lawn chair stood and stepped into the middle of the road Sam had been told to follow. He motioned for her to stop and explained that no vehicles were allowed beyond this point, so Sam and Angela would have to follow him on foot.

They obliged, of course, though Angela was particularly concerned about the fact that they were now being escorted by four large men, each of them carrying rifles and walkie-talkies mounted to their persons while they made the rest of the trek on foot.

"They didn't tell us we would have an armed escort," she whispered harshly to Sam.

"Lucky for us," Sam muttered back, "that just means we're well protected."

The men surrounded them all the way up the road to the main lodge itself, where they were then handed off into the loose custody of two more men inside the door. Both of these had personal firearms strapped to their waists, which was a step down in intimidation levels from the enormous precision rifles.

They were told they were being directed to Rip's office, but then the armed men took them all the way through the back of the main lodge, out through a door on the other side, and right up to nothing but a simple trailer parked out in the open grass behind it all.

"That's his office?" Sam asked, fighting back a laugh.

Their escorts simply nodded, refusing to make any conversation, then stopped at the front door to the parked trailer. One of them knocked, then opened the door and left it open before gesturing for both women to step inside.

Rip's so-called office was as bare-boned as one would expected from a temporary building like this all the way out here. Inside that trailer, sitting at a simple folding banquet table with a cheap spinning office chair behind it, was the man they were looking for.

She hoped.

"You Rip?" Sam asked with a nod.

"I'm guessing you're the one who wants to know," he said, then sat up a little straighter in his chair. "You work at the Redwood, don't you?"

She spread her arms and smiled. "You caught me."

If this Rip guy remembered Sam from the bar, he'd most likely heard his fair share about her from Pete himself, meaning he probably already didn't like her. At least he wasn't throwing her out of his office the second he put two and two together.

"We're actually here to ask a few questions about one of your former employees," Sam said.

"Dina Copely," Angela added. "My daughter."

Rip's eyebrows shot straight up. "Dina, huh? That was a long time ago. Couple years, if I remember."

"That's right," Angela said. "So, you do remember her?"

"Girl who thought she had to prepare for some kind of interview or something before she could officially be brought on." Rip chuckled. "She didn't last long though. Got too worried about her hands after a couple weeks of hard work with the scissors."

He mimed a cutting motion as if he held a pair of scissors in his hand already.

Angela let out a weak laugh. "That's definitely my daughter."

"Yeah, you know what? I didn't hold it against her for leaving." Rip placed a pair of reading glasses back up onto the bridge of his nose to look over some other bit of paperwork on his makeshift desk. "Probably made the best call for herself. The kid was aspirational, you know. Didn't quite belong in a place like this. Hell, I'm not gonna turn away a hard worker, but she left for better things, and that's fine by me."

"Do you have any idea where she went after leaving the farm?" Sam asked.

"Nah, I don't keep my nose in the business of every trimmer comes through here," he said. "But she had a few friends. Not a whole lot of them I know personally. You know how it is in a place like this. People are in and out every season, but I do know someone who probably knows more than I do. Hold on just a minute." He picked up the phone on his banquet-table-desk, dialed a number, and didn't wait very long before speaking into it. "Yeah, hey, Bud. Will you go find Jordan for me? Bring him around my office. Got a couple people here asking questions he's way better suited to answer than I am. Yep. Thanks."

He hung up, then responded to both women's confused frowns before either of them had a chance to ask the question. "Jordan liked Dina. I mean, enough that it was noticeable."

"Did they like each other?"

"Looked like a decent friendship, from what I heard. I remember that much. Maybe he's got more information about her."

Sam and Angela both thanked him, then left the trailer to wait outside with the security men who hadn't budged. About five minutes later, a much smaller man walked up the hillside with another armed man beside him. The two were talking, maybe even joking around a little, and Sam wondered just what kind of work this Jordan kid did if he could be called up by the boss of the farm, escorted up by an armed guard, and still have enough comfort and confidence to crack jokes with all of them along the way.

He looked somewhere in his late twenties or early thirties, with long scraggly hair shining greasily in the sun. The rest of him was just as badly in need of a shower, dirt caked onto the backs of his hands and under his fingernails, streaking up his arms. His neck and face weren't much better off, but he greeted the women with a broad smile and was friendly enough. "How can I help you ladies?"

"We're here to ask a few questions about an old farm employee from about five years ago," Sam said. "Dina Copely. Rip told us the two of you were friends."

"I mean, sure, we were friendly," he said, then ran a hand through his stringy hair.

"What do you mean by that, exactly?" Angela asked.

Sam put a hand on the other woman's shoulder to steady her. If Angela went all Mama Bear now, their chances of finding any useful information decreased significantly.

Jordan didn't seem to notice and shrugged. "We talked sometimes. You know, I'm here all year round, so I don't ever go anywhere. And she wasn't like most of the others. She didn't go into town to party or anything on the weekends. Maybe once, but then she was mostly here, even at night. Sometimes she'd sit around wherever I was working until I finished up the odd jobs Rip put me on. And yeah, you know, maybe I even liked her a little bit more than that, but nothing ever happened."

"Did Dina tell you about the job she'd taken at the Kalamack Club?" Angela asked.

"Yeah, she mentioned it." He shot her a confused look. "Right before she left for good, I told her it didn't seem like that great of a job. You know, there were better places in town to do something different if she didn't like trimming. But the Kalamack Club? I don't know. The people who go there are ... they're not the kinda people

I'd wanna spend time around, if you know what I mean."

"Perfectly," Angela muttered.

"Yeah, I got a little worried about her, I guess. When she left. Didn't really hear from her after that, though. I just kinda figured she'd found other friends. It happens."

"Wanna go for a walk?" Sam suggested. No one had any immediate reservations about the prospect, so the three of them headed across the field. Apparently, Jordan was enough of a trusted employee at Rip's Farm for the armed security men guarding Rip's office to feel comfortable letting the two visiting women out of sight with him.

"You said you liked her," Sam continued. "As in…"

"As in I *liked* her." He shrugged. "Sure. Maybe more than a little."

"And you never heard from her again after she left the farm to go work at the Kalamack Club?"

Jordan slowed his step a bit, then sighed. "All right, fine. No, I didn't just forget about her just like that. I tried to visit her a few times, actually. She told me she went to go work at the Kalamack Club, gave me the first week of her schedule, and when I had some time off, I went to town. Wanted to visit her, you know? See how she was doing, make sure everything was okay, that she was safe, I guess."

"You didn't think she'd be safe working at the club?" Sam asked.

He shot her an incredulous look. "There are a lot of places where people aren't anywhere near as safe as they think they are. I don't like that place. I don't like town very much either, and that's why I'm up here all year. Got my little cabin on the farm and everything, just right up that way."

Sam nodded. "All right, then. You said you tried to visit her."

"Yeah, went right up to the club and everything, but they turned me away more than once. Wouldn't let me in. Said it was for members only."

"It's infuriating," Angela added.

"Uh-huh. I didn't give up so easy, though. I kept trying a few times, then heard from Dina that she was gonna come meet me after work one day. She never showed up, so I tried again, you know? To catch her on a lunch break at the club or something, but whoever she was working under, her manager or boss or whatever, they wouldn't let her out."

"What do you mean wouldn't let her out?" Sam asked.

"I mean, like, literally, wouldn't let her step through the doors just to come talk to me," he said. "It was super weird, and I couldn't get ahold of her for a while after that. Then whenever we texted, she just said she was super busy, the club had her working a whole bunch of hours, and she just couldn't get away. But we still tried to see each other sometimes."

"Did she ever talk to you about what kinds of things went on in the club?" Angela asked. "What they talked about or discussed? What the members did there on a regular basis?"

"Hey, man, your guess is as good as mine. From what I can figure, they probably all just sit around in a circle to bitch about all their rich-people problems, you know? Doesn't seem all that fun to me."

"Yeah, that makes two of us," Sam muttered.

"Did you hear anything from Dina after that?" Angela asked. "Any word that she might have wanted to leave Rush or come back home? That she was done working there?"

"No, nothing like that." Jordan shook his head again and now just looked sad. "I kept trying to call her for a while, but that never got me anywhere. She didn't text me back either, so eventually I stopped, you know? I figured maybe she just didn't want to talk to me anymore. I mean, I hoped she wasn't just trying to be nice to get me off her back, but I don't know what happened to her after that. Hey, if you find her, though, I'd really love to talk to her again. Just to say hi. I mean, she's a really cool person, and we had a good time hanging out. Maybe you could let me know?"

"Yeah, we could probably do that," Sam said, without looking to Angela first. She couldn't make any promises, of course, but there was no harm in saying they could try, mostly because they also had no idea whether their search would turn anything up about Dina's current whereabouts.

"What about any other friends here on the farm?" Sam asked "Did Dina spend more of her time with anybody else than the others? Outside of working hours, nights, weekends, besides you?"

Jordan considered it for a moment, then nodded. "Yeah, this girl Shell. Crazy chick, actually. Not in a bad way, just not as chill as Dina. They were together a lot, at least in the beginning when everybody first showed up here, you know? I'm pretty sure Dina and Shell bunked in the same employee cabin way down at the end of the field out there."

"Any clue what her last name is?"

"Ah, shit. No. Sorry," he said with a chuckle. "Most people's last names just kinda disappear in the wind. Shell trimmed up here for years, though. I'm pretty sure she married her boyfriend, so her last name wouldn't be the same anyway. He lives in Rush. They got married a few years ago. Never got any of her contact info, though. Sorry."

"No problem. Thanks for your time, Jordan."

Apparently, the farm's security didn't think it necessary to escort the women all the way back around the main lodge or up to Sam's Jeep again. They were allowed to walk across the property on their own, climb back into Sam's Jeep, and head calmly and without incident back through the wrought-iron gates before quickly getting back to the road.

Sam's guess was that Rip figured neither one of them were much of a threat after having met them. The man hadn't seemed worried at all about anyone stopping by to ask questions about Dina, and he'd even offered up one of his full-time employees to help them out, though Sam declined.

Still, she walked away from the visit with the distinct impression that whatever had happened to Dina, if anything, it hadn't happened there.

But now that mention of this Shell person had come into play, that felt like the next logical place to look.

AFTER THEIR LITTLE ROAD TRIP, Angela asked just to be dropped back off at her hotel again, seeing as her car wasn't ready yet and she had nowhere else to go.

Sam was more than happy to oblige.

She pulled up along the side of Angela's hotel and the other woman paused before getting out. "Thank you, Sam. Thank you so much for everything. All your help. It's been more than I ever expected I'd get here from anyone."

Sam almost shrugged the whole thing off, not quite wanting to sit through some unnecessarily gushy moment with a woman she'd just met. Admittedly, though, they had formed something of a connection, however casual and on the surface for now.

"You're welcome," Sam told her with a curt nod. "And just so you know, I had a daughter. I know what it feels like to worry about her. If my girl had gone missing, I'd hope someone else would've chosen to help me out in any way they could so I could find her. So, you know, I get it."

Angela's excited smile died as she studied Sam's expression. Fortunately, though, she said nothing more about it but merely got out of the Jeep, thanked Sam one more time, and headed into the hotel, her spirits much higher now that she was so excited about finding this Shell woman.

Sam just didn't have the heart to tell her she thought it was false hope. That wasn't her job anyway, and she hadn't promised to keep Angela from getting too excited.

Only to help her find out what had happened to her daughter, and that was where Sam had decided to draw the line.

TWENTY

Laila

THAT EVENING, Laila made a specific point out of carrying her closing checklist on the clipboard with her literally everywhere she went, just in case Big Pete brought it up again. She followed the checklist to the letter just like every other night.

After finishing her rounds on the second floor, she came back downstairs to do the same thing on the first and ran into David on his way out. "Getting out of here?"

"Yep. Finally. You're almost done here too, yeah?"

"Won't take me much longer at all. I'll just be a few more minutes double-checking that everything's closed up."

"All right. See you tomorrow, then. Hopefully it's a hell of a better day than today was." David turned around and headed for the club's front door.

"Don't you need to wait?" Laila asked, stepping after him.

He frowned at her. "Wait for what?"

"The woman." Laila stuck a thumb over her shoulder in the direction of the stairs. "The woman wearing all white. She was headed up right before I went to handle all the other closing that's not in your office. I thought you were expecting her."

The club's manager stared blankly at Laila before huffing out an uncertain laugh. "Good one. Have a good night, Laila. Maybe you should get some sleep too."

"It wasn't a joke, David," she said, hurrying toward him before he could get out the front door and dismiss her entirely. "I watched a woman head upstairs. You're the only other person here besides me, so I thought she was here to see you. Seemed the only reasonable explanation."

"Sure, maybe," he said, squinting at her. "But there was no one upstairs. You already turned off all the lights. I hit mine in my office on the way out. The place is empty."

As if their conversation had been overheard, a light flickered on upstairs at that exact moment, spilling down the stairwell and illuminating a small patch of hardwood floor right in front of Laila's feet when she spun around for a better look.

"You sure about that?" she asked.

"Well, if there's somebody up there, you need to go tell them to leave," he said.

"Why do I have to do it? She was here to see *you*."

"I wasn't expecting anyone."

"Well…" Laila frowned at the lit staircase and wrang her hands. "It's only ever you and me left here at the end of the night, and I always lock up after you because you're out of here in such a hurry. Can't you just…"

David heaved a massive sigh behind her. "Can't I just what?"

"Can you please just come upstairs with me? If whoever's here isn't supposed to be here and they're not actually speaking to you, then, you know … they could be here for anything. And I would feel much more comfortable if I didn't go up there to deal with them alone. Turning away disgruntled members and dealing with their meltdowns is one thing, but this is after hours. It's late, it's dark, it's..."

"I get it, I get it. Fine. I'll come with you. We'll kick them together, whoever it is. You don't have to keep explaining it."

"Thank you." Laila dipped her head toward him, then gestured toward the partially lit staircase for David to lead the way.

On her way after him, she fished her cell phone out of her purse just in case she had to make a quick call to get this unknown woman in white out of the Kalamack Club for closing. She kept her hand wrapped firmly around her cell phone as David took the lead by a few feet up the stairs. They walked together side by side down the hallway when they reached the second floor, peering into each individual room one by one.

In five minutes, they'd searched the entirety of the clubhouse's second story and didn't find signs of anyone up here.

"Huh." Laila readjusted the strap of her purse over her shoulder and looked around the hallway again. "I guess I must've just been seeing things or something."

David shook his head. "Next time, you should probably figure that out *before* you start talking about random people heading up to my office, all right? Neither one of us needs to deal with that headache."

"You know what? You're not the only one who had a crappy day at work. Give me a little slack."

The man opened his mouth to argue with her — an argument he wouldn't have won anyway because Laila was well versed in inserting her own personal experience into nearly everything and somehow removing herself entirely from the majority of the blame, no matter the situation.

He didn't get the chance.

Before he said anything, another light in one of the second-story rooms behind them flicked on, spilling beneath the door and out into the hallway.

They both turned to stare at that new sliver of light.

"You've gotta be kidding me," Laila whispered.

"Well? Go check it out."

Rolling her eyes, she made her way back down the hallway toward the room with the newly illuminated light. It just so happened to be one of the guest rooms laid out in the clubhouse's second story, which was an odd place for the lights to be on now, anyway. None of the guests or members were staying here at the moment. No one had reserved the room.

She reached for the doorknob, almost knocked out of habit, then reminded herself that no one was supposed to be here, so they had automatically given up the right to be courteously made aware of someone on the other side of the door.

Instead, she briskly twisted the knob open, pushed the door in, and searched the room.

"Excuse me, but I have to remind you that—"

There was no one there. This bedroom was entirely empty.

"Laila?" David asked behind her?

She shook her head and looked at him over her shoulder. "There's no one in here."

"Huh. You know, maybe it's a short in the wiring or something. This place has gone way longer than it should've without the right kinda maintenance. I wonder if—"

He stopped too when another light on the opposite end of the hall flicked on.

They stared at each other, then Laila slapped off the

light in this first bedroom, firmly pulled the door shut behind her, and headed after David toward the newly lit bedroom.

Just before they reached it, the light shut off again, casting the entire hallway into much deeper darkness. David practically leapt at the door, and it was amazing that he didn't rip the doorknob right out of its setting before shoving it open.

In one swift movement, he stepped into the room, pivoted toward the wall, and slapped up the light switch right there inside the door. The entire room blazed with brilliant light again, the overhead bulbs working just like they were supposed to.

"See?" he said, gazing at the ceiling and squinting at the lights. "I'm telling you, there's something faulty with the wiring."

"Oh my god!" Laila gasped and clapped a hand over her mouth, while the other one almost dropped her cell phone but somehow managed to hang onto it.

David followed the direction of her wide-eyed gaze, and then he froze too,

Scrawled across the left-hand wall in the same deep, crimson-red paint as downstairs was the same simple message: *'Let Dina Go!'*

"No," Laila whispered. "No!"

She spun away from the room and barreled down the hallway, her heels thumping against the carpeted floors and wobbling dangerously beneath her ankles that threatened to roll at every step. But she wasn't slowing down. She took the stairs as fast as she could, barely holding herself back from jumping them two at a time because that only increased the likelihood of twisting an ankle or breaking a heel or falling and snapping her neck on the stairs.

"Laila!" David shouted behind her.

"No, no, no, no, no..." She made it to the first floor and only then realized she still tightly clenched her cell phone. So she stopped and tried to dial 911 before realizing that couldn't have possibly been the right number to call. Could it?

"Laila, what are you doing?" David asked as he finally reached the bottom of the staircase.

"I'm calling the police."

"About some flickering lights?"

"This isn't just flickering lights, David," she almost shrieked. "This is more vandalism. More criminal activity on private property. And whoever it is, I want them out of here!"

"Hey, hold on a second." He stepped toward her, placed a gentle hand on her shoulder, and got her to momentarily look up from her cell phone. Only then did she realize her hands were shaking. "It's definitely a good idea to call the police. But maybe take a few deep breaths first, huh? We're not in any immediate danger. This is just someone playing a joke on us. If you call the police and start ranting to them about it, chances are pretty good they're not going to come out here and try to help. They're going to tell you the same thing I'm telling you right now. Just to take a breath and think about this rationally, huh?"

"Rationally? You think I'm not thinking rationally right now? Me. I'm telling you, David, I saw a woman upstairs. A woman wearing all white. And she has to be the one responsible for this."

"Okay, so we tell the police that she's still here, but if you call them in this state..."

"They'll think I'm crazy," she muttered, then instantly turned off the screen of her phone and abandoned her attempt to call the police. "I'm not crazy, David."

"Hey, I never said you were." He lifted both hands in

concession and slowly shook his head. "I know you're freaked out, okay? That's what whoever's doing this wants us to be right now. They want us to react. There's a rational explanation for it."

"Then how come we didn't find anyone in those bedrooms? The second we headed that way, the lights turned off again. Those windows don't open either, David. I know. I've checked for myself. They were bolted shut decades ago, and they can't open again. If someone was up there trying to play a joke on us, tell me how they just got away at the last second if they couldn't get out the windows, huh?"

"I don't know."

"You know what I think this is?" Laila spun around and pointed animatedly at the staircase. "I think this is something bigger than even the police can handle, okay? I saw what I saw. That woman in white upstairs. And if she isn't a real person we can see when the lights are *on*, she's … I mean, she has to be a ghost, then, right?"

He snorted and rolled his eyes. "Oh, come on."

"I'm serious," Laila snapped. "It could be a ghost. Or maybe it's this Dina person I keep hearing about. Oh my god, that makes so much sense."

"What?" David gaped after her as she hurried across the ground floor toward her desk. "Nothing you just said makes sense, Laila."

"It does when we take the necklace into consideration." She headed toward the corkboard against the wall beside her desk. "It's right over here. A capital letter D. This could be D for Dina, right? Something happened, and there's some kind of ghost issue now. The necklace could belong to Dina. That's the name scrawled all over these messages that keep popping up. She's what all this is about."

"Well then, let's see it," he said.

With a sigh, she went to the corkboard beside her desk and froze. "Wait, what?"

"I said let's see it."

"It's … where is it?" Laila stepped back to scan the floor by the wall and even bent to look under her desk. "It's gone."

"The necklace?"

"Yes, the necklace, David. That's what I've been talking about. It was right here. I hung it up on this pin right here, and now it's gone. I promise you I wasn't just imagining it."

"No, I know you weren't," he said. "You came and showed it to me in my office earlier this morning."

"You never bothered to look up at it in the first place, though."

"Are you trying to prove that this necklace was real, or are you just trying to…" His words trailed off into nothingness as he gaped at something around the area of her shirt collar.

Laila scoffed. "We're in the middle of a conversation here, and you can't stop staring at my chest? Seriously?"

"Your name tag." David's eyebrows flickered together, then he pointed at the name tag Laila pinned to her shirt every single morning before work.

"And? I wear a name tag. So do you. What about it?"

His lips worked soundlessly for a moment before he finally managed to get out the words. "Why does yours say Dina?"

"What? Don't be ridiculous. My name tag says…" She couldn't finish that sentence, though, because when she looked down at the name tag pinned to her shirt, expecting to find the exact same name tag she always pinned there every morning with her first name scrawled across it in golden letters, that was not in any way what she found.

With an ear-splitting shriek, Laila finally did lose her grip on her phone, which flew from her hand and clattered across the floor away from her. She fumbled desperately with the pin-on name tag resting just below her shirt's collar, because it did, in fact, now have the name Dina stamped across it instead of Laila.

Her fingers trembled as she finally worked open the clasp that held the pin in place, ripped the entire name tag from her shirt, and chucked it across the room. "What the hell is happening?"

~

TWENTY MINUTES LATER, Chief Colton stood in the front room of the Kalamack Club after hours with both Laila and David.

They recounted everything that had happened with the lights, finding no one upstairs, then the missing necklace Laila had found that morning, and then the name tag she'd pinned on herself upon arriving at work that had the name Dina instead of her name. The whole time, Colton listened to their tale, but his frown darkened with each passing second.

"And why would you put on a name tag that says Dina?" he asked.

Laila scoffed. "Well, I didn't do it on *purpose*. It's part of my routine. Every single morning, I do the same thing. I open up the club, I make sure the security alarm gets turned off, I turn on the lights, I come here to my desk, I open the top middle drawer, pull out my name tag, and pin it on. I always put it in the same place every single day, so why would I read my own name on it first?"

"Well, clearly to keep from identifying yourself as someone else," Colton replied, gesturing now toward the name tag in question, which sat precariously at the edge of Laila's desk.

Just then, the front door of the clubhouse burst open, and in stormed Big Pete yet again, this time with his wife Elaine on his arm. Neither of them looked happy to be there.

"What the hell is going on?" Pete growled. "We were just heading out on our way to dinner, and I get some ridiculous call about more vandalism and all this other damn ... I can't even wrap my head around *what* this is, but somebody better start explaining real soon."

"I swear I'm not making any of this up, Pete," Laila said, hating the way her voice shook as she met her employer's gaze. "I swore I saw somebody here, okay? A woman wearing all white, and she was upstairs. That's who I thought was turning the lights on and off, but there was no one up there, and now all this with the necklace and the name tag..." She swallowed, wringing her hands. "Honestly, I'm starting to think this place is haunted or something. I've never experienced anything so downright creepy."

"Haunted." Pete snorted and turned away from all of them. "Don't be stupid, woman. This is the last thing I need right now. Some bullshit rumor about ghosts floating around here. You know, I must've been giving you way too much credit this whole time. I thought you were smarter than this."

"Wait a minute, Peter," Elaine said. "I wouldn't be so quick to dismiss this whole thing."

He stopped and slowly turned around to gape at his wife.

She nodded slowly, then met Laila's gaze with a surprising amount of sympathy. "I've always had my suspicions about this place. Which is why I don't often come here anymore. I don't think you're crazy, Laila. I've had the same sort of experiences. Nothing as drastic as this, no, but I've always felt there was some kind of spirit in this house. It doesn't matter if it's been repurposed into a clubhouse or not. That spirit is very clearly still here."

For a moment, no one else said anything until Big Pete barked out a bitter laugh. "Jesus Christ. Get two women together in the same room, and they come up with all kinds of ridiculous ideas. What the hell is wrong with you two?"

Neither of them paid him much attention now that they'd found someone else who shared their suspicions about this place.

Laila nodded fervently. "I couldn't agree more. I think I saw some kind of spirit in here tonight, and you know what? It might even be this Dina girl. It makes sense. The name tag. The necklace..."

"It could literally be anything!" Pete boomed. "And the two of you are making a whole lot of noise about something that doesn't even make sense. There's no such thing as ghosts."

Elaine turned toward her husband, her lips firmly pressed together. "Well, dear, you are absolutely allowed to form your own opinion about these things. You will anyway, no matter what. But I for one very much believe in spirits. This poor young woman is obviously in shock over what she's seen tonight, so if you're not going to do anything to help her, I will. Come on, dear." She held her hand out toward Laila, who took it gratefully before the women walked toward the clubhouse's front door, arm in arm. "I want to hear everything about what you've seen and heard in this old house. Don't leave anything out. We'll get to the bottom of this. Believe me."

Pete's wife opened the front door and led the club's

receptionist outside for some fresh air. Then the door shut behind them and blocked out everything else the women said to each other, their voices muffled through the walls as they began their unplanned evening stroll around the front of the Kalamack Club property.

Inside, Pete, David, and Chief Colton all looked at each other in silence. When Pete turned his scowl on to the chief of police, Colton lifted both hands in concession and shook his head. "Don't look at *me*, Pete. I don't do ghost calls."

TWENTY-ONE

Sam

_____

SAM HADN'T EXPECTED Chris to go out of his way to do anything nice for her after she got back from her impromptu road trip with Angela. She'd still shown up relatively on time for her shift. Or she *would* have been on time if her shift had started two hours later.

At first, she thought he was joking when he put her on the Back Bar for the rest of the evening, but then he told her he needed the help, he had plenty of open tables already in the front, and he trusted her to be able to handle one busy night in the Back Bar while he was otherwise preoccupied.

"Just don't keep showing up hours late and expecting to get everything you want," he said as a final warning before she headed into the back.

So far tonight, her shift had boasted a fortunate lack of complete assholes. She'd only been catcalled twice by someone whose name she hadn't bothered to learn, but the scowls she'd sent the guy's way seemed to shut him up quickly enough before he eventually left with his buddies.

Sam was just thinking about how grateful she was that

nothing worth stoking her temper had happened tonight, and that maybe she'd get her permanent placement in the Back Bar returned to her after proving to Chris that she could actually handle it.

But then the Back Bar's entrance banged violently open, and in blustered Big Pete Wilder, his face already deep crimson and his eyes wide with rage.

The noise in the bar died down instantly as everyone turned to see what the issue was, including Sam, who was halfway through making a new drink order for another table when Pete found her and barreled straight back toward the bar, seething.

And she hadn't even served him a drink yet.

"You!" he shouted, stabbing a finger in her direction as he just kept coming.

Sam calmly continued with her drink order and made a point of not looking him in the eye. "Well, hey there. I'll be with you in just a second as soon as I finish whipping up this drink."

"I know what you're doing," he snarled before slapping both hands down on the bar. "You've had it out for me since you got here, and now you've taken it too far, you little bitch. I know what you're trying to do. You think you can tear everything apart right before the club's seventy-fifth anniversary? Make everyone freak the hell out and rethink what they're doing? You keep your dirty little nose out of my club and out of my fucking business, or so help me—"

The swinging doors from the kitchen banged against the wall as Chris hurried into the Back Bar. "What's going on here?"

Sam shot him a completely baffled look and shrugged.

"I'll tell you what's going on," Big Pete growled. "This

nosey little shit keeps trying to screw with me, and I swear to Christ it's for the last time."

Chris frowned at Sam. "What did you do?"

She couldn't help but bark out a laugh. "I didn't do anything. Honest."

"You lying little bitch," Big Pete bellowed and started for the end of the bar, apparently meaning to cross over that line between bartenders and customers so he could more easily get at Sam without a giant slab of wood between them.

"Whoa, whoa, whoa." Chris quickly stepped around Sam to intercept Big Pete and held up a hand. "Hey, calm down, Pete."

"Don't tell me what to do! I own this town and everything in it. If I want to get behind this bar, I'll goddamn get behind the bar!"

"No, you won't!" Chris shouted. Somehow his open palm ended up pressed flatly against Big Pete's broad, barrel-shaped chest. Both men froze and looked down at Chris's hand before he immediately removed it. "Listen, if you're upset, that's fine. That's your business. But don't bring it back here into my bar."

"I'm just here for *her*," Big Pete snarled.

"Well, I'm telling you right now, whatever it is you think she did, it wasn't Sam. She's been working all afternoon because she was scheduled to work all afternoon, and she's been here working her shift. So, you're wrong, Pete. If you need to take it out on somebody, you came to the wrong place."

"You trying to cover for her now?"

"Cover for what?" Chris asked.

"This dirty cunt vandalized my club," Pete roared, pointing another fat finger in Sam's face. "Spray-painting signs all over the walls. Breaking in—"

"Now hold on just a second," Chris interceded again. "Sam hasn't been anywhere near the Kalamack Club. She's not trying to get up in your business."

Big Pete laughed again, the sound of it drowning out all other noise in the Back Bar, which had gone eerily silent so everyone could watch the action unfold. "Seems like she's gotten pretty damn good at lying to you too, Nelson. I know for a fact your little señorita's been snooping around my members. She was up at Dr. Greg's place earlier today, and then she skipped right on down to my clubhouse to play a little fun with my employees. And now my own wife won't shut the hell up about ghosts all because of this dirty little—"

"That's enough," Chris interrupted, standing firm against the giant of Rush, who towered over him by a few inches and had a good fifty pounds on him at least. It wasn't all muscle, but a decent portion of it was.

Both Chris and Sam already knew what happened when either or both of them tried to get physically involved with Big Pete. That didn't seem to matter to Chris now, though.

He took one more step toward Pete and dipped his head in warning. "There are a lot of people in here right now," he said calmly, "so I'd make sure that whatever you do next is something you actually want to do with a whole bunch of witnesses who could all tell pretty much the same version of the story afterward."

Pete snarled again before his gaze darted toward Sam. "You stay the fuck out of my club."

"I've never been past the front door," Sam said. "You know, whatever happens inside your club is your business, but I can tell you right now, I'm not the one who broke in. So I would very much appreciate being taken off your suspect list, all right? It wasn't me."

"You'll say anything to cover your own ass," he growled.

"Well, you're not wrong. But I'm pretty partial to the truth too, and that's exactly what you're getting right now."

For the next few seconds, it seemed like Big Pete was too far gone to his own fury to listen to reason or hold himself back. Then he slammed the side of a fist onto the bar again, making several glasses rattle against each other.

Without another word, he whirled away from the bar, stormed across the room again, and barreled through the front door like he was being chased out. Or it would have seemed that way if everyone here didn't already know that no one and nothing chased Big Pete Wilder anywhere.

The door swung shut behind him, and the Back Bar continued its stunned silence for a moment longer.

Chris turned towards Sam. "Are you okay?"

"Not like getting yelled at right up in my face is anything new. I'm fine."

After eyeing the rest of the Back Bar for a moment, which slowly but steadily picked up the noise again as the other conversations at the various tables continued — not without a number of odd looks thrown toward the bar owner and its current bartender — Chris stepped toward Sam and lowered his voice. "Well now I gotta ask just to be sure. All this break-in business … you don't have anything to do with it, right?"

Sam finished making her current drink order for the most recent table and didn't look at him. "Yeah. I'm sure I had nothing to do with it, Chris. But if you don't believe me, I can also tell you I was with Angela all afternoon." She finally looked up at him with a scathing glare. "You know, in case you wanna double-check my alibi."

Then she collected all the freshly made drinks and headed out from behind the bar to deliver them.

~

SAM CONTINUED the rest of her shift like any other night. Fortunately, Big Pete didn't feel the need to make another appearance in the Back Bar for more unwarranted accusations. Sam remembered her promise to Angela that she'd ask Chris about this Shell woman who was a trimmer with Dina up at Rip's Farm. But now she didn't feel like talking to Chris at all, so she had to improvise on that one a little.

When the Back Bar slowed down a bit, Sam took the opportunity for a small break and slipped into the pub up front because Nina was working up there tonight. The woman had been working here almost just as long as anyone else. Asking her about Rush's locals was probably just as useful as asking Chris.

"Shell?" Nina repeated as she dumped out bussed drinks into the sink behind the front bar. "I mean, I know a Michelle Jones. Shell. Michelle. Is that who you're talking about?"

"I don't know," Sam said. "I've never met her, but I just heard the name Shell thrown around. Apparently, this girl worked at Rip's for a while."

"Oh, yeah," Nina said. "Then that's her. Michelle. You know, actually, I can't remember what her maiden name is. Isn't that funny?" Nina giggled at her own statement, which wasn't even a joke. "She *married* a Jones, though. Reginald Jones's son. The doctor."

"Does this son have a first name?" Sam asked.

Nina didn't skip a beat before laughing again. "Of course he does. I honestly can't remember what that is either. Just one of those days, I guess."

Here was this tall, good-looking young woman talking about days where she couldn't remember things to Sam, who was almost twice her age. "Well, what does Dr. Jones' son do?"

"Oh! Yeah, I remember. He was going to medical school to become a doctor. Turns out he wasn't smart enough or something like that, so he's not actually a doctor now. Took a job at the lumber mill instead. Kind of an embarrassment for Dr. Jones himself, you know? But Michelle still married him, so it couldn't have been all that bad."

A burst of laughter distracted Sam from whatever else she might have been able to pull out of Nina before the other woman finished cleaning up behind the bar. The next second, Nina was off again to help other customers in the front, and Sam's attention had been completely diverted to Levi, Christian, and Eddie, all of whom sat together at the bar now, yukking it up about something all three of them clearly thought was hilarious.

"What did you guys get yourselves into now?" Sam asked as she sidled toward them down the bar.

"Oh, you know…" Levi said. "Just sharing the newest gossip in town. Surprised you haven't heard, Sam."

"Enlighten me," she said.

"There's been *hauntings*," Eddie added with a grin. "Of the ghost variety."

"I didn't know there was any other kind," Sam said with a crooked smile.

"Not here, there ain't."

"Down at the Kalamack Club, too," Eddie added, wiggling his eyebrows. "Guess the place really does have a whole bunch of ghosts, huh?"

They started laughing all over again, cracking up every time they tried to meet each other's gazes.

Sam smiled along, but they'd definitely caught her attention. "Has this kinda thing happened before?"

"Oh, sure," Christian said. "Of course, depends on what this kinda thing *is*. But now that they've got some kinda eyewitness down there, Elaine Wilder's having a fucking heyday with this one."

Eddie snorted into his drink, which got them all going again.

Sam played along, pretending to laugh. "Elaine as in Big Pete's wife?"

"That's the one," Christian added.

"What's going on down there?" she asked. "I heard there was a break-in and some vandalism, but this is the first I'm hearing about ghosts."

"Of course it is," Levi said. "No one's gonna talk about ghosts out in the open. Except for Elaine."

"Uh-huh. Next thing we know, she's gonna be holding a séance down there while Big Pete has a damn heart attack over the whole thing."

"Well, at least she'll be able to talk to him right away…"

They all burst out laughing again, hooting and hollering and making a giant ruckus in the front bar — enough that several tourists sitting at their own tables turned to frown in the guys' direction.

Shaking her head and chuckling right along with them, Sam figured it was best to get back to her actual work in the Back Bar. But she didn't dismiss their jokes entirely.

So, instead of writing the whole thing off as a case of breaking and entering, Big Pete's wife believed in ghosts and thought the Kalamack Club was haunted, huh? The story just kept getting better and better, didn't it?

Sam stayed through her shift and all the way up until closing for the night, partially because she wanted to make it up to Chris in whatever way she could for being so late to this shift, even though he'd let her pick up the Back Bar again a lot sooner than she'd expected. Nina had since gone home at the end of her shift, so it was just Sam and Chris by the time both bars closed, all the patrons were gone, and the cooks had already closed up the kitchen.

Sam waited for him just outside the office in the back while he counted up the drawer and handled the final details of closing for the night. They hadn't said anything else to each other since Big Pete's wild bustle into and right back out of the Back Bar. They didn't say anything now either until Chris had completely finished settling out the drawers and turning everything off in the office. Then he stood and walked out to find Sam waiting there for him.

"You know you can leave when your shift's over, right?" he told her.

"Yeah, I know. Just figured it was better if I stuck around for a bit. You know, kinda dangerous to let someone close up all by themselves without a buddy."

With a snort, Chris closed the office door, locked it, then turned toward her. "Listen, Sam. About earlier, when I asked if you'd had anything to do with the break-ins at the club…"

"Yeah, that was a fun conversation."

"I'm sorry," he said with a genuinely sheepish shrug. "I didn't mean to imply that I actually thought you were involved in anything like that or that you wouldn't automatically tell me the truth, you know? I just…"

"I get it," she said, trying to wave the whole thing off. "Trust me. It makes sense. You wanna make sure none of your employees are rolling around town tagging walls inside the private clubs of men who like to think they run the place."

"Actually, I wanna make sure that *you're* safe. That's all that was about, and I know it came across as me being overly suspicious. That's not even a little what I wanted. So, I'm sorry."

"Careful. If you keep apologizing like that, I might get the wrong idea that you actually care."

He laughed it off, because Chris was just the kind of guy who could handle laughing off something like that without taking it personally, especially when it came from Sam. For whatever reason, he was still capable of putting up with her. And right now, she found that more endearing than she had in a while.

"You got any plans tonight?" she asked. "I mean, after closing."

He smiled at her. "You trying to ask me if I'm busy?"

"More or less. If you're not, I figured you could come on back to Birdsong Park with me. Have some tea."

"Tea?"

"Or whatever. Hot water, if that's what you prefer. Hang out for a bit. See what happens."

His bright smile returned as he searched her face. "We could stay here too, you know. Not that I'm not a fan of the Deville or anything, but there's a lot more room upstairs. And all the furniture's … bigger."

Yeah. Like the bed.

He didn't have to say that out loud.

"Tempting," Sam said. "But I still wanna get back to my place tonight. And now you're standing in the way of me having my cake and eating it too."

He laughed. "Oh, is *that* what we're calling it now?"

"Honestly, Chris, I'm trying to multitask here."

"Oh yeah? How so?"

"I'm still getting those damn flowers in front of my house every morning. And I'm this close to catching the asshole who keeps dropping them off. I wanna be there the next time he tries it so I can actually catch him in the act and interrogate the shit out of him."

"Oh, I see what this is…" They walked out the front door together. Chris switched off the lights, then he pulled the front door shut behind him and locked up. "You just want an overnight bodyguard, is that it?"

"Hey, if you don't wanna come, it's cool." Sam shrugged. "I'll just ask Syc to hang out instead."

"Syc?" Chris stared after her as she headed across the parking lot toward her Jeep, then sighed and hurried in her wake. "Well, okay, don't be so quick to throw me right out the window."

"Doesn't sound like you're all that interested, though."

He somehow managed to leap in front of her and block her from opening the driver's-side door of her Jeep, fixing her with a crooked smile. "No, I didn't say that. And I'm definitely interested."

"Well then, am I gonna be able to call you my bodyguard for the night or what?"

They stared at each other, standing inches apart. Then Chris laughed and removed his hand from against her door. "You got me. I'll follow you."

SAM MIGHT HAVE PUT on just a little more speed than usual on her way back out of town, knowing Chris was behind her in his own car.

When they reached the property line of the Kalamack Club, though, she couldn't help but slow down just to check the front porch and downstairs windows like normal. Not that she expected to find anything useful, but it had now become a habit to give the place a once-over whenever she passed.

Tonight, she found way more than she expected when a light popped on upstairs, spilling out through the curtains of the second-story window. The second Sam saw it, she pulled her Jeep to a stop just in front of the entrance to the club's parking lot and watched a bit longer in case she saw more movement or got a good glimpse of who would be up there at this hour, way past the club's closing time.

She jumped when a brisk knock sounded on her front passenger-side window.

It was Chris.

Sam rolled down the window and managed to hold back a smile. "Can I help you?"

He didn't look all that amused. "Hey, did you see that light come on upstairs?"

"Uh-huh."

"You want me to call the cops?" He turned around to look over his shoulder at the same upstairs window in the clubhouse, but the light had gone off again. "Maybe we should—"

"Hell no, are you kidding?" Sam snorted. "If someone wants to break into this place, let them break in. Hell, they can rob the clubhouse blind, and I'm not gonna lift a finger to stop them."

Chris raised an eyebrow at her. "What happened to being neighborly?"

"Come on, Chris. Pete Wilder is *not* my neighbor."

He got back into his car, and she waited for him to flash his lights at her from behind before she pulled back onto the road to make the rest of the drive to the trailer park. Just before the turn-off onto the park property, Sam slowed even more than usual when she noticed the half-dozen city barricades set off to either side of the park's entrance.

Looks like someone's finally gonna put some maintenance work into this damn road. Took 'em long enough.

TWENTY-TWO

Dina

———

FIVE YEARS AGO...

DINA STOOD behind the front desk in the reception area of the Kalamack Club and checked the time. Nine in the morning. She probably had just enough time to ask the cooks nicely if they could make her breakfast before she grabbed another cup of coffee, but then Pete Wilder emerged from the hallway leading toward the main sitting area just inside the front room, wearing slacks and a long sleeve button-up shirt beneath a brightly colored sports jacket. He was already grinning even before he turned the corner and approached her at the desk, his hands clasped behind his back.

"Good morning, Mr. Wilder." Dina greeted him with a giant smile of her own. Since she'd started working this desk at the Kalamack Club, she'd started to feel more and more like herself when she smiled easily and with confidence, knowing she was part of something bigger and that the work she put into it was paying off. Plus, Mr. Wilder had been good to her, and she wanted to take full advantage of every opportunity to show him that.

"Enough of this Mr. Wilder crap," he said as he approached the other side of her desk. "I told you from the beginning, sweetheart, you call me Pete and that's that."

"Of course," she said. "Can I help you with anything this morning?"

He chuckled as he looked her up and down, as if he thought it was the cutest thing in the world that an employee would ask what *he* needed, all without lifting a finger of his own. "Don't need a thing. How are you doing? Now that you've had a chance to settle into the new job."

"I'm definitely very happy with the job," she said, still smiling. "So much better than trimming on a farm, believe me."

"Oh, I have no doubt," he said, laughing right along with her. "Looks to me like you've taken to this place like a duck to water, sweetheart. Clients already love you. The members have been seeking me out the last few days, telling me what a joy it is to see your smiling face up here first thing when they step inside."

"I'm glad it's all working out," Dina said.

"Uh-huh." He removed his hands from behind his back to reveal a small, simple flat box with a silver bow tied around the top. He handed it toward her and said, "Your first Sunday brunch is coming up. So I got you a little something."

At first, Dina thought it might have been a joke. But the eagerness behind her new employer's eyes made her smile grow even wider as she accepted the box.

"Go ahead and open it," he said.

She tugged on the end of the silver ribbon before lightly prying off the top of the box. With no one else in the club right now, it didn't seem inappropriate for her to pull the garment out and hold it up to take a good look.

A black velvet gown ending just below the knee with a plunging neckline and a delicate cut to the thin — but not too thin — straps over the shoulders.

"Wow," she breathed.

"You're going to wear that on Sunday," he said. "That's when all the members come by for brunch. They bring their wives with them. Everybody has a grand old time, and we like our daily hospitality staff to join in on the fun whenever possible. That includes you now, sweetheart. You've proven you've got what it takes. This is how I say thank you."

"Thank *you*, Mr. Wilder." She gently folded the dress back into the box. When Pete raised an eyebrow at her, Dina couldn't help but laugh. "Thank you, Pete."

"Don't mention it. And don't forget. Sunday brunch." As he turned away from her, pointing at the box, he shot her a quick wink and walked right out of the Kalamack Club to go home for the evening.

Dina eyed the dress a moment longer, then finished tucking it gently back into the box, tied up the ribbon as close as she could get to what it had looked like before, and set it on the floor beside her purse.

It was an unexpected gift, but she wasn't going to turn it down. Absolutely not. She'd thought she'd had an amazing opportunity by coming out to Rush for the trim season and working on Rip's farm. But this, working here at the Kalamack Club for Pete Wilder, had already exceeded her expectations for the kind of opportunities her time in Rush might afford. And it just so happened to come with a gorgeous new dress she wouldn't necessarily have picked out for herself, most likely because she never could have afforded it.

After another long but not nearly as grueling day, Dina waited for all the other employees and staff of the clubhouse to head out for the night before she finished her closing duties. Because she hadn't had anywhere else to stay after leaving Rip's farm, Pete had offered one of the unused guest rooms on the second story to use as her own living accommodations for the duration of her employment here. Even the bedrooms were extravagantly nicer and plusher than anything the employee cabins at Rip's farm had provided.

It almost made this whole thing feel like a dream. Sure, Dina was working, but she wasn't killing herself for that work. She was, in fact, making far more money than she would have at Rip's. Her first paycheck had proven that. She didn't have to pay rent on the bedroom she stayed in upstairs. And everyone here at the club was just so nice.

For the first time, probably ever, Dina had started to feel like she was part of a family, like she belonged somewhere, like she was wanted. And the Kalamack Club had started to feel more like home than the house in which she'd lived her entire life.

Once the clubhouse was all shut down and locked up for the night, Dina grabbed the box with a little black dress in it, as well as her purse, and headed up the back staircase toward the second story.

Her bedroom was the third room on the left. Easy to find, quick to get to, and with a decent view of the front parking lot of the clubhouse as well as a bit of the valley on the other side of the road before it gave way to the thick tree line of one of many forests in and around Rush and the surrounding areas.

Dina had to try on the dress first just to see how it looked and took a moment to admire herself in the full-length standing mirror mounted on an antique swiveling frame. She ended up looking at herself in that mirror a lot longer than she'd intended.

She looked good.

And apparently, Pete Wilder was incredibly skilled at guessing the perfect dress size.

A gentle alarm beeped on her phone, and she went to the low dresser beside the bedroom door to grab it.

The new incoming text made her smile.

WHERE ARE YOU?

THE NUMBER SAVED in her phone was under the name Home, though of course it wasn't Home. Wherever Home had been for Dina, it certainly hadn't had its own attached cell phone for texting, and all of Dina's family, which amounted to her mother and older sister, were saved in her contacts list under their own names.

No, this was her way of being cautious because she had to be.

Mr. Wilder had made it perfectly clear the day he'd hired her that there was a strict no-exceptions policy against any of the staff dating, having intimate relations with, or fraternizing with any of the club members or clientele. Nothing more than what was perfectly normal and natural over the course of the club's business hours, as long as it fell under the category of her duties and responsibilities.

Dina hadn't exactly been following that rule to a T, which was why the text came from Home instead.

Just in case.

Glancing at herself one more time in the mirror, Dina grinned as she typed up a reply.

• • •

STILL AT WORK. *And Pete just gifted me this fantastic dress earlier today. Black velvet.*

SHE ONLY HAD to wait a few seconds before the instant reply hit her screen.

I WOULD LOVE *to see you in it.*

WHY DON'T *you come on by and take a look for yourself? I'm wearing it right now. And I just finished closing up, so there's no one else here.*

WHERE AM *I supposed to find you?*

UPSTAIRS BEDROOMS. *Third on the left.*

I'M ON MY WAY.

BITING HER LOWER LIP, Dina skimmed the flirty conversation one more time, then returned to checking herself out in the full-length mirror because this version of her, this young woman Dina Copely who worked the front desk at a prestigious and exclusive club in Rush, California, was still mostly a stranger to her. Granted, she had stepped into this new version of herself quickly enough to find that the glove fit pretty damn well, but it still surprised her when she wasn't paying attention.

This was who she thought she wanted to be. She liked it. This version was so much better than the angry, exhausted girl from Seattle who couldn't get out from under the weight of her mother's baggage to discover who she truly was.

Though she could use a little re-up of her makeup for the night, especially if Home was about to show up after hours.

Dina stepped into the upstairs hallway, meaning to head for the closest bathroom up here where she kept her personal toiletries neatly tucked away in one of the clean, tastefully chosen drawers normally used by overnight guests or out-of-towners staying in the club. She did live here for now, yes, but the stipulations of that were that Dina ensured she left no trace of inhabiting the clubhouse, her bedroom upstairs, or any other part of the building. Pete had told her he'd made a special exception for her, given her personal circumstances, and she was more than happy to cater to the simple requests that she not look like she lived here.

On her way into the bathroom, though, a loud thump sounded from the other end of the hallway. She paused, turned around, and studied the semi-darkness with raised eyebrows. "Hello?"

There was no reply.

Of course there wasn't. Dina was the only one who stayed here after hours once the entire clubhouse was locked up for the night. No one else could have possibly been here with her.

Probably just old pipes or something.

She only got another half-dozen steps toward the bathroom before another thump came from down the hall. It sounded like it was in the exact same place as the first noise, followed by a slow shuffling and more thumps.

She wasn't a plumber or anything, but she was pretty sure pipes weren't supposed to sound like that.

More curious now than anything, Dina turned fully back around and headed to the other end of the second-story hallway. Another shuffling thump greeted her, as well as a quick scrabbling that sounded like some kind of nails on a cardboard box before all the noise stopped completely.

Before they did, though, Dina had pinned down the source of the sounds to this one bedroom at the end of the hall. The door was closed, lights off, but she knew without a doubt something was in there.

Despite knowing she was alone, Dina still thought to knock politely on the door, just in case. "Hello? Is someone in there?"

No answer, so she opened the door, let it swing slowly into the bedroom, and reached around the door frame to flip on the light.

The room was enormous, almost twice as large as the one she'd been given. On the far wall, the large, tastefully draped windows were overshadowed immediately by an enormous portrait hanging on the wall between them.

It depicted a woman in a flowy white shirt with a lace collar, her head facing directly toward the viewer while her body was slightly turned. The painting's subject didn't look happy, per se. There was a certain vitality to her, sure, but for the most part, the image left a feeling of sternness and silent yet powerful disapproval.

This was the face of a woman who knew exactly what she wanted and exactly what she didn't want.

Dina crossed the room to get a better look at the painting and found a small gold plaque mounted to the wall beneath the portrait's frame. Etched into the plaque was the name Caroline Griffiths.

The name, somehow, seemed to perfectly fit this woman's countenance, her strength and composure, the power she wielded simply by standing there and staring at the artist who'd been commissioned to create the piece. That was what Dina imagined had happened, anyway.

She tilted her head and looked into the portrait's silvery-tinted blue eyes. "Not all that happy your home's being used for whatever these men feel like doing with it, huh?"

It didn't occur to her in the slightest that talking out loud to a portrait of a woman she'd never met and never would was a little strange. In the moment, it just felt right, almost as if Caroline Griffiths were standing here right in front of Dina for a friendly and casual conversation between two women who understood what they wanted in the world, where they wanted to go, and what would be required of them to get there.

"I love this painting of you," she said. "My boss's wife, Elaine, loves it too, you know? One of the many things she's gathered about you, Caroline. I think this portrait is her favorite. She's a lot more interested in who you were than I think anyone else really knows. Elaine asked me to look into your life in my spare time. She's writing a book about the history of this place. This house. I know that's what it used to be before it was turned into the Kalamack Club. I guess for you and me, this house serves something of the same purpose, right? A safe place to stay. A roof, warmth, comfort. I wish I could thank you in person for that, but I guess this will just have to be good enough."

For now, it seemed, everything was good enough. Better, even.

This might have been exactly the life she'd wanted.

TWENTY-THREE

Sam
_____

EVEN IF SHE hadn't set an alarm for the ass-crack of way before dawn that morning, Sam probably still would have woken up around the same time anyway. She'd barely managed to fall asleep, and that sleep had been rough at best. She'd spent half of it halfway aware of the fact that she wasn't completely asleep, and then she'd looked at her phone — 4:15 a.m.

That was what she got for inviting Chris over on the same night she wanted to catch the asshole dropping flowers off in front of her trailer every morning.

Now that she was awake, listening for noises outside and fantasizing about all the things she might do to whoever this mystery delivery guy was when she finally caught him, Sam couldn't pretend she was tired enough to go back to sleep. She would be by noon, just not now.

The monotony of almost complete silence surrounding her Deville in the trailer park was suddenly punctuated by the rhythmic click-click-click of something stuck in a set of wheel spokes, the telltale jingle of a bike chain smacking against the pedal, and the soft but still very real thump of shoes pressing down onto the dirt right outside her trailer.

Sam rolled halfway over and nudged Chris's side with her elbow. He let out a growling snore that caught halfway, then rolled away from her and went right back to sleep.

So much for overnight bodyguards.

That didn't matter nearly so much now that she knew she had the guy. She just had to catch him in the act, then this whole nightmare would be over.

Well, mostly over. Once she caught him, she had to get all the missing pieces out of him, one way or the other. She knew how to make a person talk. Hopefully it didn't come to that, but bordering on harassment the way he was now, if it was necessary, Sam would do it.

This shit with the flowers just had to stop.

Tonight was the one night she had purposefully left the front door of the Deville unlocked, simply because the sound of the lock turning would have been a dead give-away that she was up and about inside the trailer. After slipping out of bed, grabbing her cell phone, and padding silently to the front door on bare feet, Sam listened again for the same noises.

There it was. More rubber-soled shoes softly crunching across dirt and a few pebbles, whispering over the grass.

She nudged the front door open by only an inch, got her cell phone ready, then all at once shoved open the door the rest of the way and activated the blinding flashlight app on her phone before aiming it right in front of the Deville's door.

There was a quick sliding scuffle across the dirt, more jingle of tire chains, and Sam finally shone her light out on the back of a black-and-white-checkered hoodie.

"Hey, get back here. Hey. Stop!"

Whoever he was, the guy was fast. He'd already gotten

back on his bike and was pedaling like hell away from the Deville toward the trailer park's exit, bumping across the uneven ground. For not having a light of his own, he sure knew exactly where to go to make the fastest, cleanest escape.

Sam was already barrelling after him. The Deville's front door squealed open, clacked against the exterior wall, then banged shut again as she took off after him barefoot across the grass. "Stop. Stop! I see you. Hey! I just wanna talk. Get the hell back here!"

A loud bang came from behind her, not in the direction of the Deville but from Syc's trailer on the other side of the firepit.

"Damnit!" he shouted in his grumpy old man roar Sam hardly ever heard. "Pipe down, will ya? A man's gotta sleep. You should too. What are you even doing out here?"

Stopping in the middle of the open field, Sam panted, catching her breath, and tossed a hand in Syc's general direction as a pervasion of a wave. "Sorry I woke you up," she said through heaving breaths.

He grumbled something unintelligible, then slammed the sliding window of his trailer shut again before disappearing back to bed.

Screw my personal bodyguard for the night. This whole damn park needs better security.

What little it already had — mainly Sam, Syc, and Dog — just wasn't cutting it.

She searched the darkness around the park one more time before heading back. Sure enough, there was yet another bouquet of pink Sophy's Roses lying there at the grass just in front of her trailer door. Sam didn't bother to pick them up this time but kicked the bouquet as hard as she could to send a lump of bound roses flying and a few ripped petals fluttering all over the place.

Stepping back into her trailer, she found Chris sitting up in the tiny twin-sized bed smashed against the back wall of the Deville. He ran a hand through his hair, his shoulders drooping tiredly as he watched her practically stomping back through the trailer.

"Some bodyguard," she muttered before dropping down into the one chair that existed at the tiny table.

"I'm guessing you didn't catch the guy," he said.

She shot him a scathing glare and snorted. "Well, aren't *you* clever first thing in the morning."

With a grunt, Chris shifted in the bed to swing his legs over the side and sit there on the edge of it. Maybe because he didn't want to get out of bed. Maybe because there really wasn't anywhere else for him to comfortably sit at the moment.

The trailer fell silent, then he shrugged. "All right. Mystery deliveries several days in a row, sure. I get how that could be annoying. But you're not annoyed. You're pissed. What's the deal?"

Sam kicked her legs out in front of her and sighed. "It just won't fucking stop. I can't even get the florist to cancel the rest of the scheduled deliveries, and this asshole just keeps showing up at my door."

Chris stared at the floor, then took a sharp breath. "Did you see the guy at all?"

"Black-and-white-checkered hoodie. Hood pulled up over his face. Got on a bike. Just a regular road bike. I couldn't even see what kind."

"Know anyone who wears checkered hoodies and rides bikes?"

Sam glared up at him again, and this time, she didn't need to say anything.

"All right, fine. I get it." He briefly lifted his hands in concession, then pushed himself up out of the bed.

"I need to find out who this asshole is," Sam said. "How he found her name, how he knows where I live, how he figured out that leaving me flowers every single day is a bad idea. Not *just* flowers but roses with *her* name on them..."

Sam jolted up from the chair and paced around what little space existed in the Deville.

She hadn't realized Chris was getting ready to leave until he'd finished gathering all his clothes and putting them back on.

"Where are you going?" she asked.

"I'm going to give you some space. Or maybe take a little for myself. It's probably both, honestly."

"I didn't say you had to leave."

"You didn't have to, Sam. Look, I'm not mad. I get it. You're pissed. This is an issue. But, you know, I thought you were joking when you said you wanted me over as a bodyguard. Still felt like you were joking last night. But I was wrong. Hey, that's on me. I didn't take you seriously. It's fine. You've got this to deal with, and I've gotta go open up the bar. So..."

"Yeah, okay." Folding her arms, she leaned back against the trailer wall and watched him. "I'll see you there, then."

"Yep." Chris opened the door and paused before stepping outside. When he turned halfway back to look at her, he seemed to seriously consider saying something that probably would have pissed her off even more but instead just went with, "Don't do anything I wouldn't step in and have your back for doing, all right? I know you wanna find this guy. Just be careful."

"So, pretty much everything is up in the air, then," she said with half a smile.

"Yeah, of course you'd say that." With a snort, Chris shook his head and left her trailer.

Sam heaved a sigh and dropped her head back against the wall behind her.

There had to be a better way to get this hoodie guy to call the whole thing off. And she just had to find it.

ON SAM'S way back from the park's public showers in her clean set of clothes for the day, she found Syc and Dog standing outside Syc's trailer this time. Dog sniffed around in the grass, then let out a happy bark when he saw her and trotted Sam's way.

"Good to see you too, buddy," she told him, pausing to scratch behind Dog's ears as he slobbered all over her wrist. "Sorry you had to spend another night with this grumpy old geezer. There just wasn't enough room for you in my trailer."

"He knows where he'd rather be any given time of day or night," Syc shot back as he shuffled in Sam's direction. "Don't go putting ideas in his head, kid. You'll only just end up disappointing him. And Dog doesn't deserve that."

"He deserves a whole lot more than having to put up with *your* shit on a regular basis." Sam's smile flickered out when she noticed the subtle yet still surprising difference in her neighbor and landlord this morning.

Syc had actually done his hair, which amounted to running a brush through it. He still wore his regular, everyday jeans and flannel shirt, though this shirt had actual buttons he'd bothered to fasten all the way up to the collar. It wasn't tucked in, but that still didn't take away from the significantly dressier look about him today. For Syc, anyway. To top it all off, it looked like he'd made at least half an effort to shine up his leather work boots. Or at the very least, they weren't covered in dirt anymore.

She stopped in front of him at the halfway point of the firepit and cocked her head. "Well don't you look fancy this morning. Who's the lucky lady? Or whatever."

Syc looked down at his shirt front, fiddled with a button, then glared at her. "Ain't no lady. I already got one living close by, and she's more than enough for me to handle. Keeps screaming in the middle of the night."

Sam snorted. "I apologized for that. But seriously, what's the getup for?"

He tugged at the tight fastening of his collar and cleared his throat. "I, uh, got a meeting with the mayor this morning. Figured it couldn't hurt to look halfway decent for it. I'm gonna go talk to him about this whole zoning thing."

Sam folded her arms. "That's actually a pretty good idea, Syc."

"Yeah, well don't get your britches in a twist just yet. So, how about it, huh?"

"How about what?"

"How about you come down with me to this appointment," he said, jerking his head toward both their vehicles. "Sit in on the meeting with me. Maybe keep an old man company. Or at least pretend like you're there for moral support."

Sam almost laughed, but the sincerity in his squinty eyes and the way he stared at her made her reconsider. "Yeah, I think I can do that. But there's a price."

"Always is."

"If you can tell me where to find Michelle Jones in town, I'll even walk into the mayor's office with you and turn on a little extra charm just for you."

He coughed out a brittle-sounding laugh. "Well hell,

kid. Your prices aren't nearly as steep as I expected. Everyone knows where Dr. Jones' son and his wife settled down after they got hitched. I'll point it out to you on the way. Pretty easy to backtrack to once we're done with this meeting."

Sam gathered up what she needed for the day, then decided to send Angela a quick text before she got on the road to head for Town Hall and the mayor's office with Syc.

I GOT *a lead on Dina's friend, Shell. If you still want my help, I thought we could stop by her place today and talk to her.*

OF COURSE *I still want your help. Let's go talk to Shell. Thank you so much for finding her. My car's still not ready yet, so do you mind driving?*

NO PROBLEM. *I'll meet you at your hotel in an hour. I've got an errand to run. And then I was gonna hit up a meeting at the Community Center. 12-Step. You in?*

I DIDN'T KNOW *this place had meetings. I'd love to come.*

THEN SHE HOPPED into her Jeep and waited for Syc to get into his old pickup before it was time to head out of Birdsong Park for the office of Rush's Mayor Wilder.

∾

WHEN SYC GOT out of his truck in the parking lot in front of Town Hall and the mayor's office, Sam looked him over one more time. "Did you have any paperwork you wanted to bring for this thing?"

"What the hell for?" He marched right past her and just kept going up the front stairs of the building.

"Nothing, I guess," she said with a shrug and turned to follow him.

The building, for the most part, was empty, which made finding the mayor's office a lot easier. To the right, down the hall, and then Syc and Sam stepped into one more room where they found the receptionist acting as gatekeeper before they could step into yet another room.

"Good morning," the woman said cheerily from behind her desk. "How can I help you?"

Syc cleared his throat. "I'm here to see the mayor," he said, then looked around the office in confusion. "Do folks come here for anything else?"

"All right, just a moment." The woman ignored his question, which Sam found commendable, although she couldn't tell whether or not Syc had been joking.

The clack of typing computer keys filled the small office. Then the receptionist paused, blinked quickly at the screen, and fixed Syc with a sheepish grimace. "I'm sorry, what was your name, sir?"

"It ain't sir, I can tell you that much. Sycamore Fox."

The woman typed again, then shook her head. "I'm so sorry, Mr. Fox. You don't seem to have an appointment scheduled with Mayor Wilder this morning. Would you like to make one now?"

"No appointment?" Sam asked, frowning up at him. "I thought you said you had a meeting today."

"Because we do," Syc replied. "I bet you everything he's expecting me."

"Well, if you don't have an appointment," the receptionist cut in, "I'm sorry, but I can't allow you past this point. I'm more than happy to schedule a time later in the week, maybe, if you'd like."

"Now's good."

Without further warning, Syc strode past the edge of the woman's desk and headed straight for the door along the wall behind her with the sign stretching across it that clearly marked the room beyond as belonging to the Mayor of Rush.

"Sir," the receptionist called after him. "Sir, you can't just—"

The door flew open under a quick, brusque flick of Syc's hand, and he kept barreling straight ahead.

Without a word, Sam darted after him, only halfway attempting to shoot the receptionist an apologetic look.

The woman gaped at her in disbelief. "Excuse me—"

"Yeah, it's fine," Sam said. That was all she could manage before she'd entered the room right behind Syc and found Little Pete Wilder sitting behind his big, fancy executive Mayor's desk with both feet propped up on its surface and his hands folded behind his head.

"Mr. Mayor," the receptionist called before she popped her head in through the open door, huffing and puffing to catch her breath. "I'm so sorry. I tried to stop him, but he just wouldn't—"

"That's all right, Annette," Pete replied. "I'll take care of it."

The receptionist quickly removed herself, and Pete's office fell silent as Syc and the mayor stared at each other. Pete still didn't change his laidback posture or cut off his feral-looking grin as he eyed his newest visitor up and down. "Sorry to waste your time this morning, too. I can't talk now. I've got a busy day, and I'm in the middle of

230

numerous important things I won't even try to get you to understand because I'm sure you just won't anyway. So, if you want to talk, you can make an appointment with my——"

"I'm here now, Mr. *Mayor*," Syc growled and took a step toward Pete's desk. "Let's talk."

Pete glanced at Sam and raised an eyebrow, but she had nothing to say. She realized then that she probably should have asked Syc a few more details about this meeting before agreeing to storm in behind him. But she'd stepped in it this far, and there weren't any options for stepping back out of it again that didn't make her look even more ridiculous.

Syc didn't wait for the other man to respond before he stabbed a finger down toward the surface of Pete's desk. "I'm here to talk about my park. Those zoning issues are bullshit. You know it. I know it. It ain't gonna stand."

"Unfortunately," Pete said, his hands still clasped behind his back, "it *will* stand. Zoning laws in this municipality are——"

"I don't give a damn what you say about zoning laws," Syc roared. "There's no issue with them at my park, because there hasn't been an issue with them at my park the whole time I've been there. And I had an agreement with the mayor of this town. Your predecessor, in case you forgot."

"Well then." Pete removed his feet from his desk and sat up straight in his chair. "If you've got a signed agreement and notarized contract between you and the former mayor, I would be happy to look over it."

"There is no signed contract," Syc snarled. "We had a handshake agreement."

"Oh." Pete feigned surprise and shrugged. "Well then,

I'm sorry. But I don't think I can honor something like that."

"You seem to honor them damn well enough down at that club of yours," Syc interjected. "If a handshake is good enough there, it's good enough right here between the two of us."

Pete stared at the man, almost looking sorry about the entire situation. He smacked his lips. "I'm afraid you just don't understand how this works. Your park is infringing on several different zoning laws for its particular type of property. Your options at this point are to file the appropriate paperwork by the given deadline in the intent orders you were served to prove that you've brought your property up to code in every possible respect. You'll also have to pay the applicable fine, or else it's no good. Or, you know, if that's not feasible for you, your only other option is to clear the land. That's how this works."

"That is not how this works and you damn well know it!" Syc pounded the side of a fist on the top of the mayor's desk.

"Hey, hold on," Sam muttered behind him, then thought better of her initial reaction to get involved.

She hadn't seen Syc this pissed off the whole time she'd known him, and she'd only seen Little Pete this self-righteously pleased with himself a handful of times.

"There's nothing wrong with my park or its zoning," Syc continued. "All you want is to whip it out and throw it around to show everyone what a big man you are sitting behind this desk. It ain't gonna fly."

"You're allowed to feel however you like, Mr. Fox. That doesn't change—"

"I ain't paying you shit!" Syc bellowed. "No paperwork. No deadlines. And that land's getting cleared over my dead body."

Pete stood abruptly from his chair and leaned over his desk toward the angry old man glaring down at him. "I'm sure that can be arranged. Because that sounded like a threat just now. And you're bordering on assaulting a public official. Not to mention harassment. Potentially public endangerment—"

"Syc," Sam said. "Maybe we should just—"

"I don't owe you a goddamn thing!" Syc shouted, spit flying from his mouth. "And you won't win this if it's the last thing I do."

"Well now I'm going to ask you flat out and only once," Pete said. "Are you threatening me?"

"You're damn right I'm threatening you, you stuck-up sonofabitch!"

Pete thumbed a button hidden beneath the edge of his desk and glared at the man towering over him without any sign of fear. In fact, he looked rather like a cat who'd just found a mouse freshly caught in a trap. "You have about thirty seconds to get out of here on your own before I have security remove you from the premises. Have a nice day."

"I oughtta wring your fat little neck!" Syc shouted. "You think just because you're mayor and your daddy owns more than half the town, you can boss everyone else around any way you please?"

"Syc, security's on their way," Sam said. "Just drop it. We can—"

"Let me tell you something, *son*," he spat, clearly not having heard a word of her warnings. "You can't get rid of me that easily. But you'll damn sure wish you never set eyes on me or my property in the first place. Just you watch. I'll make sure of it."

Heavy footsteps thumped across the outside office toward them.

Sam tried to catch Syc's attention again, but she'd run out of time.

Two enormous, hulking, muscular men barreled into the mayor's office, suddenly making the large space feel incredibly cramped.

"Sir?" one of them said as he approached Syc, "I'm gonna ask you to leave now."

"I'm not done!" Syc growled, shrugging away from the guy's hand and swatting at it for good measure.

The security guards moved.

In two seconds, the first one had both Syc's arms bent behind his back. Syc snarled and tried to shrug him off. The second one grabbed Syc's upper arm and hauled him away from Pete's desk. Then Syc was whirled around toward the open door, the security men on either side of him jostling him back and forth as he screamed over his shoulder, "Fuck you, Wilder! I ain't leaving. You can't make me leave. I had an agreement!"

One of the men had to grab a handful of the back of Syc's shirt to yank him through the doorway like a mama lion pulling a cub away by the scruff of its neck.

Sam had backed up toward the office wall the second the security guards rushed in. There was no reason for her to get physically involved with these guys, especially not two of them who looked like that. Her taser had been more or less legally confiscated months before, and she hadn't made the time to try to find herself a new one. Beyond that, she didn't think tasing anyone inside the mayor's office would do her or Syc any favors.

That didn't mean she didn't want to punch the smug smile right off Little Pete's face when he turned his gaze onto her and chuckled through his nose.

"You might wanna go help your friend, there," he told

her, leering as he calmly sank back down into his chair. "Looks like he's got a difficult road ahead of him."

Sam glared back at him. "No wonder your daddy had to put you in this office. No one else would've done it. Not by choice. Enjoy the rest of your day, Mr. *Mayor*."

The vitriol dripping from her voice was downright impossible to ignore.

He said nothing else as she stormed out of his office, and she realized how much she actually despised the little creep.

Probably because she could still feel his eyes on her the whole way out.

TWENTY-FOUR

Sam

SYC'S FURY lasted until the two security men all but threw him out of the Town Hall building, with Sam close on his heels.

He fumed after the men as they returned inside without a word. Sam opened her mouth for something quick and witty about what a stupid move he'd just made, but she shut her mouth when his demeanor changed.

Instead of raging or storming back to his truck like she'd expected, Syc ran a hand over the top of his head, sighed, and turned in an uncertain circle on the sidewalk.

He looked lost, like he'd forgotten where he was, why he was there, and who had accompanied him. When he turned to see Sam descending the rest of the front steps, he shook his head in defeat and spread his arms, worrying her even more. "What am I supposed to do about this, huh? What comes next? What the hell's gonna happen if I get kicked off my land? Sam, I've got nowhere to go. This is all I have."

"I know it is." Somehow, Sam managed to hold his gaze.

She hadn't seen Syc that angry before, but she certainly hadn't seen him looking this sad, either. All the fight had seeped out of him, and it fully sank in for her how scared he was. "You know what? I bet you can talk to the last mayor about this. Remind him of the deal you guys had. Maybe ask if he'd put in a good word for you with Little Pete. That's worth a shot."

Syc stared at her, then shook his head again. "Can't do that."

"Why not? The last mayor didn't suddenly drop dead, did he?"

"Not so far as I know. But he didn't exactly make that deal with me, either."

Sam raised an eyebrow and stopped right there in the middle of the sidewalk. "You mean you lied about that too?"

"That's one way of putting it."

"Syc..."

"I know, I know. Thought that was worth a shot too, huh? Felt like a deal to me when the last mayor didn't bother to raise a big stink about anything that's got to do with my land. I'm so far removed from town, he couldn't have cared less. This one, though..."

"This one cares about the park because *I* care about the park," Sam finished for him. "I'm so sorry, Syc. I didn't even think about how my own shit might end up getting you mixed up with it eventually."

He snorted. "You give yourself way too much credit, you know that?"

"Most people call it blame."

"Most people don't have competitions with the rest of the world for who's got it worse than anyone else, either." His haggard smile twitched.

Sam walked beside him back to their cars, then paused

while Syc got back into his truck. "I'll help you figure this out, Syc. I promise."

He pulled the driver's-side door shut behind himself and looked at her through the open window. "I just hope you have an actual plan for how to do that. Because I just used the one idea I had, and now I'm fresh out."

"We'll think of something. Together. Just maybe don't have any more nonexistent meetings or mention former agreements that don't actually exist until we have a real plan, okay?"

"If you say so. Let me know if you need any help finding the Jones Jr. place I pointed out before. Your fees are still pretty damn cheap for what I just put you through."

Sam laughed and lifted a hand in farewell as his truck pulled out of the parking lot and roared back down the road away from the center of town.

AS SOON AS Angela got into the front passenger seat, she pulled a thin wad of bills from her purse and handed them toward Sam.

Sam stared at the cash. "What's that?"

"Money." Angela looked like she almost smiled but couldn't quite manage it. "You do know what money is, right?"

"Sure I do." Sam laughed. "What I don't know is why you're giving it to me."

"For all your help, Sam." Angela wiggled the cash at her again. "You've done so much for me already. I haven't given you anything in return, and I can't in good conscience keep accepting your help like this without compensating you somehow. Please take it."

Sam grabbed the wad of cash and flipped through it, failing to hide a choking laugh of surprise when she counted out five hundred dollars.

She kept five twenties and handed the rest back to Angela.

The other woman wouldn't touch it. "No. That's all for you. I wish I had more, but at least it's something. Keep it."

"I'll keep this hundred," Sam said. "That covers the gas we've already spent, the gas we're about to spend, and most likely gas for the rest of the week. But I'm not accepting any more than that, so take this back."

"Are you sure?"

Sam chuckled. "I know. Not every day you fight with someone to take your money and not the other way around. I'm sure. Thanks for the consideration, but covering the gas will be just fine."

The other woman finally accepted the rest of the bills and tucked them into her purse again. Then she buckled her seatbelt, and in the process of turning almost completely around to find the passenger-seat buckle, her gaze fell onto the Jeep's back seat. Then she tentatively reached behind her. "Wow. Where did these come from?"

Sam recognized the rustle of foliage and crinkle of cellophane wrapper even before Angela pulled this morning's bouquet of roses into her lap.

Why had she chucked them into her Jeep before taking off after Syc this morning? She should've just left them in the grass to rot.

"Yeah, those are trash." Then shifted into drive and pulled out of the hotel parking lot. "Feel free to chuck them out the window any time."

"What?" Angela fiddled with the wrapper and gingerly ran her fingers along the rosebuds that still remained after Sam angrily kicked the flowers first thing this morning. She lifted the bouquet to her nose and inhaled deeply. "They're so beautiful. Why would you want to throw them away?"

"Because someone's trying to fuck with me."

Angela considered the bouquet a moment longer but still refused to get rid of them, even when Sam wordlessly rolled down the front passenger-side window in the hopes that the other woman would take the hint and leave it at that.

She was left hoping.

"What happened?" Angela asked.

She didn't dive into all the details.

But Sam did explain just enough about the roses and about Sophie for the other woman to get why she didn't want anything to do with that bouquet.

"Wow," Angela said when Sam finally finished. "That must be so difficult to even wrap your head around."

"Well, now you know," Sam said. "So if you feel like blowing some steam and getting a little frustration out of your system, go ahead and toss 'em. I'd do it anyway, but I just haven't gotten around to it."

"Have you considered…" Angela stopped, biting her lower lip as she stared at the bouquet in her lap.

Sam shot her a quick look but had to keep her attention focused on driving. "Considered what?"

"I only mean…" Angela paused again, then dipped her head toward the bouquet for a deep inhale of the Sophy's Roses odor that was admittedly pleasant and much sweeter compared to most other flowers. Then she sighed and continued. "Have you ever considered that whoever's leaving these flowers for you isn't doing it to harass you?"

Sam snorted. "Right. I did mention the fact that very few people know about my daughter, let alone her name, didn't I?"

"You did." Angela nodded. "But the alternative to

harassment would be, you know, wanting to show you some compassion for what you've been through. What you're still going through, even. Someone might want to show you that they care, that they understand but might not have the words to express it the way they want, so they ordered you flowers instead."

Sam said nothing. She had nothing to say to that, simply because the possibility had never occurred to her.

She honestly couldn't think of a single person who might have considered such a thing and actually followed through with the idea.

"That's an interesting theory. But if that were the case, why does the delivery guy on the bike keep running away whenever I try to talk to him?"

"Well, maybe he..." Angela frowned, puffed out a sigh, and shook her head. "I don't have an answer for that one."

"Yeah, it's okay. Me neither."

TWENTY-FIVE

Sam
___

As SAM and Angela moved down the front walkway toward the porch of the well-kept single-family home, the almost picture-perfect scene was shattered by the sound of a screaming baby somewhere inside.

When they walked up the front porch steps, a slightly older child threw one hell of a tantrum to join the screaming infant.

The second they reached the front door, all the noise inside stopped.

So Angela leaned forward and knocked.

The chaos inside erupted all over again, louder now that the women had made it all this way.

Sam wrinkled her nose. "Maybe this isn't the best time for a visit."

The front door swung open anyway. The woman greeting them on the other side bounced a baby in her arms, while the screaming toddler attached to her leg seemed nowhere near ready to let her go or stop the constant wailing.

This woman looked exhausted, her hair tied up in a

mess of loose hair clinging to her cheeks and the sides of her neck.

"Can I help you?" she asked above the screams. Somehow, through all the chaos, she managed to offer a beaming smile that said, 'I'm fine, everything's okay, I love my life, please ignore everything else.'

It was almost convincing.

Sam tried not to stare at the red-faced toddler wailing with his mouth wide open as he wrapped both arms and both legs around his mother's calf. "My name's Sam. This is Angela. We're hoping you might talk to us about an old coworker of yours from about five years ago."

"Five years?" The woman let out a tinkling laugh, then shoved the door open even farther with the edge of her hip. "That's a long time for anyone. It's a lot more fun to think about *those* days than about … well, everything now. Come on in."

She tried to open the door farther and found herself held up by the baby in her arms. Then she practically dumped said baby into Angela's arms instead. "Please come inside. Can I get you anything to drink?"

The toddler still hadn't quit screaming around her leg, even as the conversation progressed. His mother hardly looked at him as she shut the door behind them.

The living room was littered with colorful toys, some of them still blinking with bright lights or finishing annoying electric songs now that they'd been abandoned.

As soon as the door shut, the toddler stopped screaming.

"I'm so sorry," the woman said, leaping toward Sam with a self-conscious laugh and extending her hand. "I'm Shell."

They shook, then Shell remembered her baby in Angela's arms, and she laughed again. "Oh, thank you so much for taking her. I swear, this baby can't be put down for five seconds before she comes undone. But hold her, and she's an angel."

Sam nodded toward the toddler. "I would've thought *he's* the clingy one."

"Unfortunately, no. Please, have a seat." Shell gestured toward the couch, and Angela graciously pulled a fire truck off of the seat cushion before settling down. She handed it to the toddler, who took it eagerly enough, but the boy inspected her face more than he paid attention to his toys.

"Can I get you anything to drink?" Shell asked again, rocking the baby. "Honestly, I have more apple juice than anything else. Or water."

Both visitors declined, then the only thing left was to continue the conversation. Starting with confirming that this was, in fact, the Michelle Jones they were looking for.

"It's funny," she said. "People stopped calling me Shell since Matt and I got married, right before our oldest. But I still introduce myself that way."

"Married just a few years ago, then?" Sam asked, eyeing the toddler.

"No, it's been longer than that. Almost five years now."

With a quick, sweeping glance at the staircase leading up to the second floor, Sam realized there was a third child in the house — around four or five. He stood on the stairwell's upper landing, watching his mother's guests.

"Cute kid," she said, shooting him a wink.

"I'm sorry," Michelle interjected with another beaming smile. "Your name just hit. Angela Copely. Is that right?"

Angela nodded. "That's right."

"Good. I thought for a minute I was losing my mind. Happens a lot these days. I'd actually already heard you were in town. Looking for Dina. Your daughter, yeah?"

Sam and Angela exchanged a knowing look, and Sam nodded. "Well, that saves us some time."

"I really, really liked Dina," Shell said. "We had some good times working up at Rip's farm. But I haven't heard from her in years. About the time she left the farm and moved to town for a different job. It really has been about five years now, hasn't it?"

"Is that the last time you heard from her?" Angela asked.

"Unfortunately, yeah." Shell's smile faded. "I should've put more effort into keeping in touch with her but … kids, right? Oh, but I *do* have these."

With the baby still slung in one arm like it had become a part of her, she stood and went to the sideboard along the wall. She picked up an envelope sitting there, then brought it back with her and somehow managed to pull several photographs from the envelope to sift through them without setting the baby down.

Angela accepted the photos and looked through them. Her expression ranged from wide-eyed surprise to nostalgic joy, to grief, despair, guilt, and joy again.

Sam glanced at the pictures over Angela's lap. Shell was instantly recognizable in the photos, though her unmarried, childless self looked at least ten years younger instead of only five.

Hers wasn't the only familiar face, either.

"This guy right here," Sam said, pointing. "We just met him. Jordan, right?"

"That's *right*," Angela said. "He was up at the farm."

"You two already went up to the farm?" Shell asked. "Rip's farm?"

"Everyone was wonderfully accommodating," Angela said.

"I bet the place has really grown since I was there last.

245

There's definitely a picture of Dina and Jordan in there somewhere, if that's who you're talking about."

Angela held up the picture in question and turned it around for their host to see.

Shell nodded. "Yep, that's Jordan. He had a secret crush on Dina from the day she showed up. Well, not really *secret*, actually..."

"And how did *she* feel about *him*?" Angela asked, the level of suspicion in her voice overshadowing the friendliness of their meeting with him yesterday.

"It was hard to tell with Dina," Shell mused. "One minute, she could seem so naïve, like she'd never left the house or just didn't understand how the world worked. And then the next second, she was cracking jokes, making everyone around her enjoy themselves more than ever. She could be the life of a party if she wanted, especially for someone who never really partied much in the first place."

"Never partied?" Sam asked.

"Dina didn't drink. I know that for a fact. She'd smoke a little weed here and there. We all did. But it wasn't a lot. Not nearly as much as some of the other trimmers. She was pretty clean about the kinda fun she liked to have, as far as I know." Shell looked down at her now-sleeping baby, then offered another sheepish smile. "I'm so sorry. I'm gonna put the baby down and round up these kiddos for naptime. Make yourselves at home. This won't take too long."

While Shell gathered her two older children, Angela continued flipping through the photos of her daughter. Sam walked leisurely around the Jones's living room, studying their family pictures. Almost every photo included all three young children, though a few were still from before the youngest had entered the proverbial picture.

She also found shots of Shell, her husband, and an

older couple who had to be Matt Jones's parents. Two other family photos included another younger couple she didn't recognize, though there was definitely a family resemblance between the unknown woman and the other Joneses.

When Shell finally returned, Sam turned from the hearth and pointed at the photos on the mantle. "Great pictures. This is your husband, I'm guessing?"

"Mattie, yeah." Shell rejoined plopped onto the couch again with a sigh. "Dr. Reginald Jones's son, in case you hadn't heard that from literally everyone else in town." She fiddled with the hem of her shirt a moment, then sucked in a sharp breath. "Actually, there *is* something else I wanted to tell you. Didn't want to get into the details with my kids around, but I wouldn't feel right not mentioning something that still feels this important."

Sam practically skipped back toward the couch; this was the most exciting thing she'd heard from anyone she and Angela had spoken to about Dina. If a mother of three small children didn't want to talk about in front of them, it had to be something good.

Angela looked terrified.

"About Jordan," Shell continued, pointing at the stack of photos in Angela's hand.

"So he *didn't* like Dina all that much?" Sam asked.

"Oh, no, he did. I don't think Dina liked *him*. She was friendly enough with him, just like she was friendly with everybody, but he might've taken it too much to heart. *I* certainly didn't like him. I always had this feeling he was … stalking her."

"Was he?"

Shell shrugged. "I never knew for sure. But he acted really possessive around her. I heard a rumor once that she had to go to the police about it because he kept showing up at the Kalamack Club and bothering everybody there. Which obviously would've threatened her job. Honestly, I always got weird vibes from Jordan."

"Did Dina ever mention a restraining order?"

"Not to me, no. Jordan never actually *did* anything to her that I know of, but things were always a little awkward around him. Creepy. Just something off about the guy."

"Huh." Sam pursed her lips. "Good to know."

Shell sighed again, then wiped her forehead with the back of a hand. "I'm sorry. It's been hard enough to concentrate with the kiddos running around all morning. I feel like I just started this conversation now that they're all finally asleep. It's great to meet you, Angela, though I can't remember why you said you were stopping by to talk about Dina. How's she doing?"

Angela's eyes widened, then she closed them and swallowed.

Sam waited for the other woman to reply, then figured it was better she jumped in and revealed the far more uncomfortable details. "Actually, Shell, we don't know."

Shell just kept smiling. "I'm sorry?"

"We don't know how Dina's doing," Sam repeated. "Because as far as we know right now, she's missing."

"Oh my god. When … when did this happen?"

"Five years ago."

"What?"

"Dina never came home from Rush," Angela finally added, looking up again to meet their host's gaze. Then she summarized the details of her story, including the part about Dina and Angela having had a falling-out before going no-contact.

Shell looked back and forth between her guests. "Have you gone to the police about it? Filed a missing persons report?"

"The police haven't been any help at all," Angela said. "In fact, they seem to be actively trying to make things worse for me. To keep me from looking for her. They say she technically isn't a missing person and they can't file anything because they have knowledge of some witness five years ago who said they saw Dina leave town to come home to Seattle."

Shell's smile disappeared. Tears shimmered in her wide, bright-blue eyes. "It was me."

Sam leaned toward her. "What was that?"

"Me," Shell repeated. "I'm the witness. Well, at least, I'm the one who bought Dina a bus ticket home, and I took her to the station myself. So I'd be the only one who counts as that witness. Which probably makes me the last one to see her, then, right?"

Sam and Angela exchanged another surprised look. This time, Angela was one step ahead.

She leaned forward over her lap and nodded. "Shell, please tell us everything you remember about the last time you saw Dina."

TWENTY-SIX

Dina

FIVE YEARS AGO...

THE CLOSER SHE got to the coffee shop, the more uncertain Dina felt. This was probably a bad idea, but she was here now.

With a sigh, she opened the front door with a little jingle of the bell. She immediately spotted Shell sitting at a table in the corner, with her wild mane of curly blonde hair and her beaming smile.

Shell didn't seem to recognize her until Dina was almost at the table. Then the other girl leapt to her feet, her grin widening, and threw her arms open wide. "Holy shit, D. Look at you! I didn't even recognize you. You look amazing."

"Thanks. Hi." Dina accepted the hug. When they sat, neither girl immediately had anything to say, so it was a little awkward at first. "So ... we're here."

"So. We're here." Shell's smile returned, but it wasn't the same beaming grin. She kept looking Dina up and down, as if she couldn't believe what she saw, then barked out a laugh. "This is crazy. I never thought I could look right at you and not instantly know who you are. You just look so different. I'm trying to put my finger on it. You didn't cut your hair. The dress is a little fancy for coffee. Maybe that's it."

Dina looked down at the black velvet dress Big Pete had given her. "I didn't dress up for you. No offense."

"None taken. Who *did* you dress up for, then?"

"It's Sunday." Dina shrugged. When Shell still looked completely clueless, she had to explain further. "Sunday brunch. At the club."

"Wow." Shell shook her head, looking Dina over from head to toe again. "You like what you're doing? You like the job?"

"Yeah, I do. Way better than trimming. For me, anyway."

Shell shifted in her seat. "You look happy. Way happier than I ever saw you up at the farm. Sounds like a good fit. What else is going on?"

"Well..." Dina failed to hide a secretive smile. "I met someone."

"And?"

"And I'm in love, Shell. He's amazing. One of the best things that's ever happened to me, and he treats me so well."

"Okay..." Shell shot her a teasing smile. "Wait, don't tell me it's Jordan."

"Ew." They both laughed, and Dina shook her head. "Definitely not Jordan."

Shell twirled her hand, gesturing for continued information.

"That's about it."

"Bullshit. Who is he?"

"I can't actually tell you." Dina sat back in her chair and crossed one leg over the other. "Can't really tell anybody right now."

Her friend blinked. "You're in love with some dream guy, but you can't tell me who he is?"

"Because it's someone from the club."

"And you don't think it's a little weird that you can't tell me who you're dating?"

"It's not like a *secret*-secret or anything," Dina said. "They just have a pretty strict policy against any of the staff dating clients or members. So I really can't talk about it."

"Hmm." Now Shell avoided Dina's gaze altogether. "That kinda sounds like a pretty good policy to me."

Dina straightened in her chair. "What's that supposed to mean?"

"Policies are usually there for a reason, you know? And you don't seem to care much for why the rules are put there in the first place. It just seems a little weird to me, that's all."

"Oh, it's great to know you've got such a high opinion of me and how I deal with the *rules*," Dina snapped.

"Whoa, hey, hold on a second." Shell frowned across the table. "I'm not saying anything about *you*."

"Actually, Shell, it sounds like you're talking *specifically* about me."

"Listen, working at the Kalamack Club is one thing, and you already know what I'm gonna say about that, so I'm not gonna go into it."

"Well, thank you very much."

"All I'm saying," Shell tried again, "is that maybe you should pay a little more attention to the policies there. If you're going to be with those people all day every day, if you're going to be working for those people… The rules are there for a reason, D."

"You know what? I definitely didn't come meet you for coffee so you could give me a lecture about the rules," Dina quipped. The other girl looked slightly hurt by it, but that wasn't Dina's problem. Dina hadn't even wanted this little coffee date in the first place. If Shell had just asked her here to berate her some more for her choices, she'd be happy to leave right now.

Shell sighed, shook her head, and flashed Dina another smile. "I know it's all new and fun and exciting. But I've been worried about you, D. You dropped off the face of the earth after the last time we argued. And in a place like that club, it's hard to tell exactly who your friends are, you know? Your real friends. The people who actually care about you."

"And that's what you think you are?" Dina asked.

Shell paused. "Well, yeah, D. Of course."

"You know what I think?" Dina raised her eyebrows. "I think you're just jealous."

"What?"

"Because I got out of that dump and you didn't. Because I'm happy with my life. I've made changes. I'm moving up. Making way more money than anyone at Rip's. Jealous that I'm probably going to be engaged soon. So I can only imagine that would upset you after how long you and Matt have been together and he *still* hasn't popped the question."

Shell gaped at her. "Hold on a second. Engaged?"

"This guy I'm seeing? I'm expecting him to ask me any day now. And when he does, I'm going to say yes."

"Wait, what about med school? I thought that was the whole reason you came down here, isn't it?"

"And I'm still going. But plans change. I might have to

put med school on hold for another year or two while we work out the logistics, but he knows that was my plan anyway. He fully supports it. So when we're ready, we'll figure out how to make it work together."

There was little change in Shell's expression, though Dina could see the wheels turning in her mind anyway.

So she had to ask.

"What, Shell? Just spit it out."

Shell glanced around the coffee shop, then leaned forward and lowered her voice. "That seems a little abrupt, don't you think? Engaged? You've only been here a few months, and—"

"The amount of time doesn't matter," Dina interrupted. "When you know, you just know. And we know. So I don't need you to worry about me or that I'm not making the right choice. I know what I'm doing."

"Listen, Dina…" Shell sighed. "I know it might feel like you know what you're doing. But this doesn't feel like you. It doesn't feel like the right choice for—"

"That's it." A bitter laugh escaped her, and Dina scooted her chair away from the table. "If I wanted to have *this* conversation, I would've called my mother. Because that's exactly who you sound like right now."

"I'm not trying to be your mom, D. I'm just trying to look out for you. I don't want you to get hurt or get yourself into some kinda situation you don't realize isn't working for you until it's too late—"

"Thanks for asking to meet, Shell." Dina stood abruptly, her chair scraping noisily behind her across the floor. With a tense, twisted smile, she readjusted her purse over her shoulder and headed out. "Have a good one."

"Wait, D. Come on," Shell called after her. "Dina! Wait…"

Dina kept walking through the front doors of the cafe and didn't stop. She didn't look back once.

She was done with anyone else telling her what she should or shouldn't do. What she did or didn't know about herself or other people or any other aspect of her life. This was her life and no one else's.

She hadn't thought another fight with Shell would affect her so deeply. But as she stormed up the sidewalk, tears stung her eyes no matter how hard she tried to hold them back.

Instead of giving in to the hurt, she focused on her anger instead and pulled out her phone. There was really only one person these days who truly understood her. While she still hadn't changed the saved name in her phone, seeing *Home* on the screen brought an instant wave of relief.

Which had to mean texting him was the right choice.

YOU WERE RIGHT. *I should never have met her for coffee. It was a horrible idea. Turns out she can't see past her own jealousy.*

AS ALWAYS, the reply was almost instant.

I KNEW THIS WOULD HAPPEN. *That's why you should listen to me the first time I say something and just know that I'm right. I'm always right.*

SHE LAUGHED. Mostly because it was so unbelievably arrogant and a little because she finally realized just how true it was.

Then he texted her again.

ARE YOU HAPPY, *baby?*

OF COURSE I'M HAPPY. *I'm especially happy right now because I get to see you today.*

DINA REMINDED herself she'd been right about him all along. He did care about her. He did want her to be happy. They fit together in a way she never knew she could instantly click with anyone else. Especially someone like him.

If anyone in the world truly cared about her, he did. Now, Dina was really starting to think he might be the only person in the world who actually did.

TWENTY-SEVEN

Sam
_____

"I can't believe this is happening. All this time, and I just assumed..." Shell Jones shook her head, tears welling in her eyes. She looked back up at Sam and Angela sitting across from her in her living room. "I wish I'd known sooner."

"Well, whatever you know now about what happened back then," Sam told her, "we'd really appreciate hearing it. It might be exactly what we've been looking for."

The woman paused, searching her memory as her gaze flickered back and forth across the coffee table. "Honestly, I'm not sure what happened. Just that Dina showed up at my place around the middle of March that year. She looked so tired. Like she'd been dealing with something heavy for way longer than she'd let anyone else catch on. I think she'd been crying too, but she didn't talk to me about it. All she wanted was to go home, and she asked if I could help her out."

"Help how?" Sam asked.

"Not with money. Dina had plenty of it. The Kalamack Club paid her very well. I honestly don't think she was all there mentally. The last time I saw her, though, I was really preoccupied, so I just went ahead and bought her that bus ticket home. I didn't need to, but it was the least I could do. Then I drove her straight to the station because I wanted to make sure she got on the bus safely."

"Did you think she was in danger?" Sam asked.

"Not on the bus, no. At the time, I figured Dina was just homesick. That she'd had a taste of the upper-crust kinda lifestyle and found it wasn't for her. But now that I know no one's heard from her in so long, I can't help but think maybe she'd gotten herself in trouble."

"Like what?" Angela asked.

Shell didn't immediately answer. Instead, she focused on her hands in her lap and picked at her nails. "I couldn't say. We'd fallen out of touch by that point. It was just a feeling at the time. Now I wish I'd asked her about it. Tried harder to get her to talk to me——"

A high-pitched scream burst from the second story, and all three women looked up at the top staircase landing.

"Great." Shell grimaced and pushed herself off the couch. "With my luck, the second I think they're okay up there and don't actually need me will end up being the day my children kill each other. I need to go deal with this. Is there anything else I can help you with for now?"

"No, you're good," Sam said as she and Angela stood. "Go get your kids."

After another quick glance at the staircase, Shell headed straight for Angela first and grabbed both her hands. "When you find Dina, please tell her for me that I'm so sorry. And I hope she's okay."

Angela smiled, blinking tears out of her eyes once again. "I will. It was lovely to meet you, Shell. Dina was lucky to have a friend like you all the way out here."

While they shared a hug, which was bordering on a

sappy cryfest in the living room, three children screamed bloody murder at each other upstairs. Sam slowly back-tracked her way to the front door. She almost cleared her throat to tell Angela it was time to go, but Angela and Shell released each other with tight, bittersweet smiles of farewell.

Then Sam and Angela finally left Mrs. Jones to her house and her three hellions.

When they stepped onto the front porch, the driver's-side door of a dark-blue Mercedes in the driveway shut with an echoing thump. Sam found herself face to face with the man who could only have been Dr. Reginald Jones. Shell's father-in-law.

"Good morning," he said slowly, looking back and forth between the two women on the front porch and Shell standing just inside the door with the sound of screaming kids barreling out after her. "Is everything all right?"

"Morning, Reggie," Shell said. "Everything's fine. I put the kids down for a nap, but obviously someone wasn't very happy about it. None of them are. This is Sam and Angela. They stopped by to talk about one of my old friends from back in the day."

"Friend, huh? How ... nostalgic."

"Did you know Dina Copely?" Sam asked.

She definitely hadn't expected Dr. Jones to pale as soon as he heard Dina's name.

"No," he said rather quickly. "I never met her."

"Huh." Sam tilted her head. "But you would've seen her at the Kalamack Club, right? She worked there, and you've been a member for a few decades at least, from what I understand."

Dr. Jones flicked his gaze toward Shell, who was entirely distracted by her screaming kids and immediately popped back through the doorway so she could go handle them.

The man looked relieved to see his daughter-in-law had left the conversation, but he still didn't look like he could have a casual conversation without sticking his foot in his mouth. "Yes," he amended. "I had seen her at the club. I thought you were asking if I knew her socially."

"That makes sense." Sam nodded. "Enjoy the rest of your day, Doctor."

He grimaced at her, didn't look at Angela at all, and brushed past them into the house before slamming the door.

"He didn't look very happy to see we were here," Angela murmured.

Sam frowned over her shoulder at the Jones's front door, then shook her head and headed back to the Jeep. "He didn't look very happy to see anyone."

WHEN SAM PULLED into the parking lot of the Redwood Rings again, Angela sighed in relief. "Oh, thank goodness. My car's back."

Inside the pub, Angela took a sweeping look around and headed straight back toward the bar where Chris stood, cutting up garnishes and restocking.

He looked up and saw them both walking across the dining room. "What's wrong this time?"

"Something has to be wrong?" Sam asked.

"You're early for your shift. So yeah, that tends to bring a little suspicion with it."

"Nothing's wrong. Angela and I just finished our joint errands for the morning. Good thing we stopped by, though. Her car looks ready to go."

"About that," Angela cut in. "Who do I need to talk to about payment for fixing it up?"

Chris looked a bit surprised by the question as he wiped his hands on a damp rag. "No one. Don't worry about it."

"I'm sorry?" Angela's laugh sounded more like a whimper.

"I got it covered," he said. "The bill's all squared away with Ernie."

"Now why would you go and do something like that?"

"Yeah, Chris," Sam added, fighting back a smile of her own and folding her arms. "Why would you do something like that?"

She knew he wanted to scowl at her or say something snippy in response, but his intentions to help Angela won out before his smile returned. "It's no problem at all, Angela. Given all the trouble you've had since coming to this town and all the shit everyone and their mother's been giving you, it's the least I could do."

"I don't understand." Angela sucked in a quivering breath and turned to Sam next, looking as shell-shocked as if she'd just witnessed a hit and run right outside.

Sam set a hand on the woman's shoulder. "As in, you don't owe anyone anything. Your car's fixed. It's safe to drive again. And take it from the owner of the Redwood Rings speaking on behalf of this entire town when he says he's sorry for your trouble."

Angela's lower lip trembled, and this time when her eyes filled with tears again, they spilled over down her cheeks. "I don't know what to say…"

"Don't mention it," Sam said, gently removing her hand from the woman's shoulder and taking a step back. "Seriously."

Chris stared at her like she'd grown a second head, and

she held his gaze over the bar before offering a half-hearted shrug.

"I don't know *how* to thank you," Angela continued.

Chris stepped out from behind the bar. "Maybe you should start with taking a seat just for a little while. Take a few deep breaths. Plenty of space at the bar, if you want."

He gestured towards said bar, which seemed to absolutely mortify the sobbing woman until Sam stepped in to correct his mistake.

"Not the bar." She grabbed hold of Angela's shoulders to steer her across the dining area. "How about you take a seat at this table here. I'll bring you some water."

Angela huffed out a messy, wet, gurgling chuckle before sniffing and fishing a small package of tissues from purse.

ANGELA FINALLY STOPPED CRYING SOMEWHERE around her second glass of water. When she'd finally dried her tears and wiped at her face with what looked like a mountain of tissues left behind, she'd gathered her composure with a significant increase in self-control.

"Everything you've done for me in the last few days, Sam," she said. "I couldn't be more grateful. That being said, I think I'm going to leave Rush. First thing tomorrow."

"Really?" Sam looked up at her in surprise. "Don't you wanna follow this trail all the way to the end, though? To finally find out what happened to Dina?"

"I thought I did." Angela wrang her hands. "But at this point, I don't think I *want* to learn any more about what happened to her. Somehow, I can't help feeling like it'll just break my heart, and I don't think I can handle that. Not now. Maybe not ever."

She stood with a curt nod and extended her hand. "But thank you, Sam, for everything."

Sam took the other woman's hand, but she suspected something else was bothering Angela. Something the woman *hadn't* yet mentioned. "You're welcome. Anytime you feel like talking, or if you change your mind, you know where to find me."

"I do." Angela adjusted the strap of her purse over one shoulder, then practically threw herself at Sam, wrapped both arms around her, and pressed her cheek roughly against Sam's for an oddly squished hug that lasted a lot longer than normal comfort allowed.

Sam froze, fighting back the stiffness of surprise before she finally reached up to pat Angela's shoulder.

TWENTY-EIGHT

Sam

THOUGH SAM and Chris hadn't officially talked about her Back Bar privileges being restored, his actions now spoke louder than words, because that was where he put her today.

Christian had been sitting in the Back Bar since before the start of Sam's shift, which got her thinking about just how much he'd seen and heard over the course of the day. While she worked on another drink order, eyeing the other tables every now and again, she nodded at him. "I've been a little busy to pay closer attention, but something tells me you've got it covered anyway."

He leaned toward her over the pint he'd been nursing at the bar and grinned. "What do you wanna know, Sam?"

"I know you've heard about the *hauntings* at the Kalamack Club. Like everyone in this town. Has anybody decided whose ghost it's supposed to be?"

"Oh yeah..." He wiggled his eyebrows, trying — and failing — to hold her gaze as he lifted his pint glass for a long chug.

Sam rolled her eyes. "Do I have to threaten you to keep going with the details, man, or what?"

He slammed the glass down on the bar, wiped remnants of foam from his upper lip with the back of a hand, and let out a loud, contented sigh. "Nah, you can save yourself all that trouble. Just pour me another, and I'll start talking, Sam. I promise."

"You'll start talking anyway." She snatched up his empty glass and fixed him with a crooked smile. *"I* promise."

She poured him another pint anyway.

"Some girl who used to work at the club," Christian said. "That's the only ghost name on folks' lips right now. Been hearing it all over the place. Folks're saying she died there. As far as I hear, the dead girl's name is Dina something."

"Wait, what?" Sam stopped and stared at him. "Say that name again."

"Dina?" Christian shrugged, then dove face first into his next beer.

Holy shit.

"You hear anything else about this girl?" she asked, trying to make it sound as casual any other possible question. For once, the guy actually had useful information that wasn't just beating around the bush and laughing it up with Levi and Eddie.

"A few things, yeah." Christian looked particularly delighted by the fact that he had exactly what he thought Sam wanted. "Xavier sent around this photo of the haunting business the other day. Guess he was right inside the club, trying to clean it all up in secret and whatnot. Bet he knows all *kinds a* secrets from inside that clubhouse too…"

"Good for Xavier," Sam replied flatly. "Are you gonna show me the picture, or what?"

"Uh-huh." Christian fished his cell phone from his pocket, which took him at least four times longer than it would have if he hadn't been sitting at this bar all day.

Sam had to deliver this next round of drinks to another table, and only once she'd returned to the bar had Christian found the image he'd been looking for.

"Here it is." He slid his phone across the bar toward her.

Sam snatched it up with fumbling fingers and tried not to look too interested.

Red paint streaking sloppily across the wall below what looked like an anniversary-celebration banner, the words perfectly visible: *"Let Dina Go."*

"Interesting." She nodded at Christian before forwarding the image from his phone to her own cell number. "Thanks for this."

"What're you doing?" he asked with a crooked smile.

"I'm saving myself the trouble of tracking down Xavier when I can just send this to myself." She finished typing in her number, sent the image in a text, and slid the phone back across the bar toward him.

She'd never seen Christian's smile shine so brightly when he wheezed out a surprised laugh.

"Well, ain't that something? That's your personal number you just sent it to?"

Sam pointed at him. "And if you ever call it, I'll break both your arms. Fair warning."

He cracked up laughing and downed the rest of his beer in a single breath. "How about another? Looks like I'm celebrating."

"You know what? I'll pour you this next one on the house, and you delete my number from your phone."

He looked back and forth between his cell and the fresh pint glass Sam had pulled off the shelf. Then he wrinkled his nose and finally nodded. "Yeah, all right. That's good enough."

At the end of the night, Sam helped Chris close down the front and the back, and when they'd finished and he began locking up downstairs, he asked her if she felt like having any company for the evening.

"You're not trying to make up for your shit work as a bodyguard last night, are you?" she asked.

"No. You made it perfectly clear I shouldn't quit my day job."

Sam flashed him a crooked smile. "Well, I guess I could give you another chance. Feeling pretty charitable tonight, oddly enough."

He barked at a laugh. "Yeah, oddly enough."

"No bodyguard duty, though. We're past that. I'll have to shop around somewhere else to fill that position, but I guess I wouldn't mind something else tonight."

He squinted playfully at her. "You know, sometimes I really can't tell between you joking and you being dead-serious. Like now, for instance."

"It's both." She walked backward toward the staircase beside the office that led up to Chris's apartment. "I'm joking about needing a new bodyguard. Let's be real, here. That's the last thing I actually need. But I'm dead-serious about the company and staying out of the Deville for now."

"All in the name of a little distraction and switching it up, right?" he asked.

"You bet your ass."

"Uh-huh." Chris followed her across the back toward the stairs with slow, confident steps. "Sounds like you're trying to change the subject."

Sam stepped one foot back up onto the lowest stair and braced herself with a hand against either wall of the enclosed staircase. "Sounds like you're more interested in talking it out than, you know, actual company."

When he reached her, he stopped a few inches away and jerked his chin up at her.

"Or I could just shut the hell up," he murmured, leaning in.

Sam grabbed his shirt collar with one hand and pulled him closer. "Now you're talking."

THEY LAY in Chris's bed afterward, their clothes strewn all over the upstairs apartment from his front door to the mattress. Sam was still enjoying the blissful and unassuming silence between them, which, true to form, Chris broke before she was ready because that was just what he did.

"Hey." He rolled toward her and reached out to tuck a few strands of sweat-slickened hair behind her ear. "Sam."

She playfully rolled her eyes. "More conversation now, huh? There's gotta be some definition of the word 'company' that doesn't involve talking about it."

"It's not like I asked for a play-by-play," he said with a chuckle. "But I did wanna talk to you about something else."

Sam shifted in the bed to face him, lying on her side with her head propped up in one hand. "Okay, then."

He leaned slightly away from her to search her face. "I know you don't like to hear it. You don't like to hear most things people have to say to you directly, and I still gotta say it."

"Of course you do."

"I'm getting a little concerned."

"Should I tell you to join the club?"

"I *am* trying to be serious. And right now, I'm talking about all this time you've been spending with Angela. Helping her look for her daughter."

Really? Another *lecture?*

"You don't like me helping out another woman going through a rough time?" she asked.

"Not at all. You've just been pouring yourself into this whole thing with her, driving the woman around town, up into the mountains, talking to people, stirring stuff up with the police—"

"No." Sam pointed at him. "That wasn't me, that was Colton stirring shit up all on his own and trying to draw me into it."

"You know what I mean, Sam."

"And you think I'm ... what? Just gonna lose myself in this whole missing-Dina thing? You think I'm really that untethered to my own life or the present or reality right here and now that I can't separate my experiences from the experiences of a woman like Angela? Is that what you're getting at?"

Chris gazed blankly at her for a moment, then pursed his lips. "Well, I wasn't gonna say it quite in the same way. Where did *that* come from?"

Sam sighed. "Meredith tried to get up in my face about the same thing after the meeting this morning. She didn't really do herself any favors by bringing it up the way she did."

"Oh yeah?" He smirked. "Because she didn't put any effort into buttering you up first the way I did?"

Sam punched him in the chest.

"For real, though," he continued through a soft laugh. "It's been a while since I've seen you really focusing on, well, anything besides work and going back home to do nothing at the end of the night. Or maybe a few things, depending on whether or not I come with you. I just don't wanna see you get sucked up into this thing with Angela like you got sucked up into…"

His words trailed off, and he bit his lower lip through a grimace.

"Like I got sucked into things with Beth?" she finished for him. "Is that what you mean?"

Chris shrugged, which became a relatively awkward gesture for lying in bed on his side. "Maybe not in so many words."

"I don't get it." Another bitter laugh escaped her, and Sam rolled over onto her back to stare at the plain off-white ceiling of his bedroom. "What the hell is *wrong* with this place?"

"I didn't think it was *that* bad," Chris mused. "But if it really bothers you that much, I guess I'll have a talk with my decorator."

She snorted. "This *town*, Chris. Everyone's worried about how involved I'm getting in Angela's search or Beth's problems or someone else's issues. But honestly, I think more people *should* be getting involved. Especially when it concerns missing girls and this town. No one lifts a finger to help unless there's something in it for them. These young girls just keep disappearing or getting hurt or being overlooked, and no one gives a shit."

"Sam…"

"So if I'm the only one who does, fine. *Someone* has to give a shit. It's not right. It's never been right. It never will be right. But maybe I can help push this place in the right direction, even just a little. While there's still that chance, I'm gonna keep fucking getting involved, outside concerns or no."

"All right." Chris lifted both hands and backed off, though that was physically difficult while still in bed. "I'm not trying to fight you on this, Sam, okay? I just wanted to bring it up. Just put it in your ear."

"It's been in my ear, thanks. I'm good."

He studied her face, nodded, then surprised her by leaning in for a kiss that definitely got the point across.

Now he was finished talking.

SAM SPENT the night with him at his place. More because by the time she would have been ready to put her clothes back on and go home, it was already after 2:00 a.m. and less because she preferred to stay the night.

Chris managed to drift quickly and easily to sleep. He was snoring five minutes later, and Sam got left behind.

While she lay there, her brain just wouldn't turn off. Then she couldn't get comfortable in his bed. She was too hot, too cold, too cramped, too awake.

At almost 3:00 a.m., she had to throw in the towel and get out of here so she could at least try for a few hours of sleep in her own bed before having to start yet another day.

Only when she finished pulling all her clothes back on did Chris stir enough to ask her what she was doing, his voice muffled by sleep. He didn't even open his eyes.

"Going home," she told him. "I can't sleep, but I'll see you tomorrow."

He mumbled something unintelligible and fell right back to sleep.

Sam spent another two minutes looking for her jacket, which she found on the floor behind the armchair in his living room before she grabbed it and shrugged it on. Then she double-checked the back pockets of her jeans and both pockets of her jacket to make sure her things were all accounted for — including an unfamiliar crinkle in her right jacket pocket that made her pause.

She pulled out the folded wad of twenties she'd begrudgingly accepted from Angela as gas money and stared at the cash in her hand, her stomach tightening in nauseating fists the longer she looked at it.

"Fuck it," she whispered and stuffed the bills back into her jacket pocket.

∼

SAM LEFT the Redwood Rings in the darkest hour of early morning. The roads were clear and empty, with a sliver of a moon lighting up enough of the asphalt for her to have seen perfectly well even without headlights.

All she wanted right now was to get to Angela's hotel and return the money as soon as possible. It had to happen before the woman left town later this morning, but Sam wouldn't feel right until she'd handed it back. She certainly wasn't going to sleep until she'd done so.

If she had to pound on Angela's door for twenty minutes until the woman woke up and took back the hundred bucks in twenties, that was exactly what Sam would do.

Unfortunately, she didn't get as far as Angela's hotel.

Because when she slowed on her way past the Kalamack Club, which had become so much of a habit that she didn't even think about it, Sam instantly noticed something was wrong.

Severely wrong.

The first clue was the single light in the ceiling of the

clubhouse's front porch, which was left on all night every night. Tonight, though, the porch was dark.

Probably just a burnt-out bulb. It wasn't any of Sam's business if the club's staff couldn't replace the lightbulbs before closing the place down. But that wasn't the problem.

The problem was the strangely foreboding yet familiar shadow hanging across the club's front porch, stretching toward the front door in the wan ambient glow from her Jeep's headlights.

Sam slowed to a complete stop just before she would have passed the entrance to the club's parking lot and squinted.

It took her two seconds to figure out what that odd shadow was and where it came from. The back of her neck prickled with knowing before a cold wave shot down her spine and raised goosebumps along her arms.

Back in the days of her active service as an MP, she'd seen that kind of shadow before.

More times than she cared to admit.

It wasn't Sam's job to investigate anymore, but she had to do *something*.

So she turned into the parking lot, left the Jeep's engine running, and got out to head for the porch.

By the time she reached the bottom of the porch steps, there was no doubt in her mind that the man hanging there from the rafters of the Kalamack Club's front porch with a rope around his neck was Dr. Reginald Jones.

Swallowing thickly, Sam pulled her cellphone out of her pocket and didn't feel any hesitation this time about calling 911.

TWENTY-NINE

Sam

WHILE SAM WAITED for the police to arrive, she figured she might as well take a look around. Using her phone's flashlight app, she studied the front porch, taking care not to step too close to the body still hanging there or to touch anything as her shoes clomped across the wooden floorboards.

From the second she recognized what had happened here, she'd known this had happened hours ago. Part of her was glad she'd been the one to drive by and notice something was off, just to spare someone else the nightmarish shock of discovering the body like this instead.

Somehow, knowing she'd helped someone else avert a potentially horrendous start to their day made Sam feel a little better about the situation, but only a little.

She slowly circled the body, moving the bright light from her phone this way and that to investigate from as many different angles as possible. Something flashed in the light from around the vicinity of Dr. Jones' hand.

That was as close as Sam got to the body, just to get a

better look at the source of that silvery glint in the darkness.

It was a necklace.

Squinting, Sam carefully leaned a little closer and decided she wasn't seeing things after all.

That was definitely a capital letter D hanging from the end of a thin silver chain in Dr. Jones' hand. Just in case, she snapped several pictures — with the flash on — so she could study them later at her own leisure.

After that, Sam hopped off the front porch and waited by her parked Jeep.

When two police cruisers and an ambulance finally pulled into the parking lot, Sam wasn't surprised to see Chief Colton stepping out of one of those squad cars. Nor did it seem strange that he marched right past her toward the club's front porch.

"You might as well send the ambulance back now, Chief," she called after him. "You're not gonna need those guys tonight."

Colton froze, looked over his shoulder at her with a scathing glare, and said nothing before continuing on his way to investigate the body.

It did, however, take him a lot longer than she'd anticipated to finish looking over Dr. Jones' apparent suicide scene. The paramedics performed their job excellently, though there was nothing they could do for Dr. Jones. He'd been beyond anyone's help for quite some time. They marched back to the ambulance and left the site just like she'd known they would.

Then Colton and the other officers continued on as if they weren't in any real hurry to get out of here, which they weren't. This was clearly a suicide, and no one's life was in danger anymore.

Sam, however, didn't exactly want to spend the rest of her early morning standing out here in the parking lot with squad cars and Rush police and a body hanging from the porch.

"Now that you guys have showed up and seen everything there is to see, Chief," she called as she approached the porch again, "can I get out of here?"

Colton scowled at her while his officers gathered in the corner to discuss something else in low tones. "Absolutely not."

"Are you serious?"

"You really trying to test me tonight, Salazar?" His boots clomped down the steps, and in the bright headlights rising toward them from the squad cars, she distinctly made out the dark circles under his eyes that only added to his normally haggard appearance. "You're not *getting out of here*. You're a witness."

She couldn't help but laugh. "A witness? To what? All I did was find the body, Chief. I didn't see anything else. Trust me."

"Yeah, that's the problem. I don't."

After that, he instructed one of the officers to keep an eye on her while the others continued their preliminary investigation. There wasn't all that much to investigate, and Colton knew that full well.

Sam was sure he just wanted to keep her there for fun. Most likely to get back at her for ruining his arrest of Angela the other day in the hotel lobby.

If he wanted to get back at her, that was one thing. But having her stand here for no reason with nothing to do when this had clearly been a suicide? That didn't accomplish a whole lot for either of them.

Instead of standing around outside in the dark with a group of Rush police who did not seem to find her presence here all that entertaining or reassuring, Sam returned to her Jeep and climbed inside. She told the officer assigned to watch her to relax because she wasn't going anywhere. He demanded her keys anyway and said she'd get them back once the chief had cleared her to leave. Right now, she just didn't feel like arguing, so she complied without issue.

The second she climbed behind the wheel, though, she was suddenly overwhelmed by the cloying scent of flowers. Sam worried about where the smell was coming from until she remembered Angela had been fiddling with the newest bouquet of roses during one of their recent road trips.

She turned around to search the back seat, where the roses had fallen onto the floor again, looking all the worse for wear. She didn't bother to pick them up.

Her only option now was to just stay put and wait it out.

Which she did in style by reclining her seat all the way back as far as it would go and settling in until this whole thing was over.

SAM JUMPED at the sound of the quick, official-sounding knock on the driver's-side window. Blinking quickly, she sat bolt-upright behind the wheel, and it took her a minute to recognize the uniform standing just outside her Jeep. She tried to roll down the window, remembered she'd given her keys to one of the other officers, and had to open the door instead.

"Sorry, Chief," she said, blinking heavily and wrinkling her nose. "Must've fallen asleep there for a second."

"Lucky you. I need to take your statement."

"Sure."

"And I need you to step out of the vehicle for that."

Wow. For once, the Chief's actually taking his job seriously and doing things by the book.

Sam got out, pulled her jacket tighter around herself, and folded her arms. "Let's do this then."

"Let's." Colton lifted his chin to stare at her down the bridge of his nose. "So how about your side of the story, huh?"

"My side of the story?" Sam almost laughed at him. "Sorry, Chief, I don't have a story. I just have the facts, and I'm happy to offer them whenever you're ready."

"Just start talking, Salazar."

"Well first, you know I was working the Back Bar at the Redwood tonight. Chris and a whole bar full of other regulars can confirm that too, in case your memory's a little hazy. Then Chris and I closed up around midnight, and I stayed with him at his place."

"Then how'd you get over here?"

"I couldn't sleep," she said frankly. "Figured my own bed might be the better option after all. Not too odd for me, Chief. I don't usually do sleepovers very well."

He grunted. "Get to the part about how you're the one who found the body before calling it in."

Sam puffed out a sigh through loose lips and wished she could have cleared her mind from the cobwebs of sleep just a little faster. "This is my normal route on the way home. And I noticed something was different about the front of the club. That was around three o'clock. Three ten, maybe."

She wanted to check her watch to see what time it was now, seeing as the sun still hadn't come up, but she managed to refrain from that so Colton couldn't blame her for being distracted or trying to change the subject.

"Define *different*," Colton droned.

"Chief, I make this drive several times a day. At night, the front porch light is always on. Tonight, it wasn't, which I noticed, so I slowed down to check it out. That was when I realized it wasn't just a burnt-out lightbulb on the porch, but something a little *darker* all around, isn't it?"

"Now's not the time for cracking jokes, Salazar," he grumbled. "Especially not after something like this."

"It wasn't meant to be a joke."

He narrowed his eyes at her. "And you just happened to know a 911 call was necessary? Just because the light was out on the front porch?"

"No, I didn't just *happen* to anything, Chief. Listen, I've seen my fair share of dead bodies. Unfortunately, not a small number of them were suicides, though any number of suicides is too many, if you ask me. I saw something out of place here, stopped to give myself a little more time to identify what that was, and I recognized the very specific sight of a dead body swinging from a noose. So I made the call."

"Uh-huh." Colton turned halfway around to look over his shoulder at the officer still up on the porch with the body. "Any reason you decided not to cut him down when you *recognized* what this was?"

"And get my prints all over the scene before anyone else got here? Come on, Chief. I know you don't like me that much, but you gotta give me some credit, here. I'm not an idiot."

"It does seem a little strange that you wouldn't have wanted to do something to try and help the man—"

"There isn't a damn thing anyone could've done to help him," Sam interrupted. "The man was already dead. What's cutting him down gonna do? You know, I could've just gotten back into my Jeep and driven away and let someone else handle it first thing in the morning, but I did the right thing instead. And I've been here this whole time since you guys finally decided to show up, so what's with the overly unnecessary questioning?"

Colton raised an eyebrow. "And you didn't touch the body?"

"No, I didn't touch the body. I didn't touch anything. Are we done?"

"Hang tight."

"Well, then I have a question for you, Chief, if you don't mind," she called after him.

Colton had only taken three steps away from her before he turned back, his eyebrows raised in exasperation. "What?"

"I just wanted to know if you or any of your officers have any idea who that necklace belongs to."

Any sign that the chief of police was tired and annoyed by being summoned out of bed in the wee hours of the morning instantly disappeared. He didn't have to say anything.

"Is that a no, Chief? Or is there something else you wanna say about it?"

"And I don't have to tell you shit. You don't work for me. This isn't your case."

"No, you're right." Sam nodded. "Just asking. Because Angela Copely's still here in town. I'm sure she would want to hear about this. Including the cute little silver pendant dangling off that chain. It's a capital letter D, right? D for Dina, maybe?"

Colton remained steadfastly tightlipped, though she did notice one of his hands clenching briefly into a fist before he forced it open again.

"You might wanna check on that," Sam added. "Might give you a little more information as to what happened here—"

"It's already on my list." In the bright lights from the squad cars, he seemed to have regained a little color in his cheeks. "And I don't need you to tell me how to do my job. You better hope I don't find any evidence of tampering or outside interference with this crime scene or the circumstances around the good doctor's death. Because if I do, you'll be the first person I come to, and I highly doubt the twenty-four-hour café's security cameras will be able to help you this time."

"I absolutely agree." Sam lifted both hands in concession. "Just trying to be helpful. So, if you're done interrogating me, I'd love to get home. Sooner rather than later, Chief. I still haven't had much sleep. Unless there's some other important information you'd like to drill out of me right now."

The police chief sucked on his teeth, grimacing the whole time, then called out to the same officer who'd taken Sam's car keys and gestured for him to join them. He had the officer return her keys, then ordered the guy to escort Sam home.

She already knew it wasn't intended as an escort for her safety but merely for Colton to keep an eye on her all the way home. That would be their confirmation that she'd made it to where she'd said she was going and nowhere else.

Which was exactly what happened.

At first.

Sam drove two miles an hour below the speed limit all the way back to the entrance of Birdsong Park with that officer close on her tail the whole time.

Only she didn't turn into the trailer park but merely slowed down when she reached it. So did the officer. He must have assumed she'd be heading forward anyway, because he didn't waste any time in whipping a U-turn at

the end of the road and heading back toward the Kalamack Club.

Sam waited three minutes after the cruiser disappeared
from view. Then she turned around on the road herself
and booked it toward Angela's hotel.

THIRTY

Sam

SAM BANGED on the door for almost ten minutes until the sound of shuffling footsteps finally approached, followed by a clink of several locks unfastening — first the deadbolt and then the chain locks.

The door creaked open, and Angela's weary face appeared within the few inches of space. The woman blinked heavily against the remnants of sleep. "Sam?"

"Let me in."

"What's going on? Why are you—"

Sam barged inside, practically throwing the door open.

Angela stumbled backward before groggily closing the door again. By the time she turned around, she had a perfect view of Sam dropping the twenties onto the narrow desk built into the wall. "Sam?"

"We need to talk."

"And it couldn't wait until morning? It's not even light outside. What time is it?"

"I found a body at the Kalamack Club," Sam blurted.

"What?" Angela spun toward her, eyes wide. Her

already pale complexion blanched even further. "You found a *body*?"

"It was the doctor. Reginald Jones."

"*Who*?"

"Shell's father-in-law," Sam said. "He hanged himself right outside the clubhouse. And guess who drove past in the middle of the night and found him there."

"Oh my god." Angela slowly sank back to sit on the edge of the unmade bed and kicked off her slippers. "That's awful. We just talked to him yesterday."

"I know. Shit happens. That's why I'm here, actually. It seemed like a much better idea to come to you first thing than to wait for anyone else to do it."

"Do what?" Angela asked.

Sam had been flipping through her phone again. Now, she approached Angela and handed over her cell with one specific image pulled up. "He had *that* in his hand when I found him."

"A necklace?" Angela frowned. "Wait, I've seen this before."

"Do you remember where?"

"It's Dina's. The picture of her I keep in my purse? She's wearing this exact necklace. Here." The woman shuffled across the room, struggling to get her bearings before finally finding her purse to rifle through it. Then pulled out her wallet and the picture of Dina. "See?"

Sam peered into the wallet, where the flashing glint of a silver capital letter D pendant hanging from a thin silver chain around Dina's neck was clearly visible. "That's definitely the same necklace."

"Why in the world would Shell's father-in-law have Dina's necklace?" Angela asked.

"That's one of the greater mysteries now, isn't it?" Sam pocketed her phone and paced across the hotel room, shaking her head. "There's something else going on at the Kalamack Club, too. Beyond you getting arrested there or Reginald Jones choosing it as his final resting place."

Angela grimaced at the blase mention of the dead, but Sam paid no mind. She couldn't do anything for Reginald Jones, but maybe she *could* do something for the people who were still alive. That was more important.

"I know it sounds completely insane," she continued, "and it probably is. But there's been a lot of talk over the last couple days about hauntings at the Kalamack Club. Ghost sightings. Strange paranormal activity, I guess you could call it. And it's all connected somehow. I just haven't put all the pieces together yet."

"A ghost?" Angela looked baffled by this sudden turn of conversation. Then she gasped and clapped both hands over her heart. "Wait, Sam, are they talking about *Dina's* ghost?"

"Not necessarily." Sam shook a finger as she turned and paced again. "You know what? Why don't you get dressed? It's almost time for normal people to wake up anyway, so we can go get some coffee, maybe some breakfast if you're hungry. We'll talk about it at the cafe."

HALF AN HOUR LATER, as they waited for their coffees in the hotel's twenty-four-hour cafe, Sam just couldn't wait any longer.

"First of all, I want to make this perfectly clear, Angela. I do not in any way, shape, or form believe in ghosts. I think it's a load of bullshit and plain ol' wishful thinking. People seeing what they want to see. But no matter how convincing it may seem, I'm not buying it."

"Well then, what do you think's going on over there?"

"Whatever it is, it's not a haunting, that's for sure. Even with Dina's necklace on the doctor when he died, I'm still not sure she has anything to do with it. I'm definitely not convinced it's a ghost. Here's why."

She returned to her phone, pulled up the image she'd sent herself from Christian's phone, and slid the whole thing across the table. "Here."

Frowning like she had no idea what she was looking at, Angela reached for the phone, then froze. Her jaw dropped. "What is this?"

"A message from a ghost scrawled across the walls of the Kalamack Club. According to this town's gossip circle. The man who took it was called into the club to clean this off the walls. Smart of him to snap a shot like this. Then again, that's where the rumors come in…"

"So Dina *is* involved," Angela argued.

"So far, only in name. Look, even if there were such a thing as ghosts, which would be a whole different story if you're gonna get me to believe any of that, a ghost wouldn't demand to be released in the third person, right? That's ridiculous. If this really were Dina's ghost, she'd be spray-painting the walls with something like, *'Let* Me *Go.'* It's not the same thing."

"You're right."

Their coffees finally arrived, handed over by the same waitress from their first night in the café, though she no longer seemed quite as interested in eavesdropping on their conversation. Sam figured that had something to do with the ridiculously early hour and the fact that this particular waitress worked the overnight shift. Simply put, she was exhausted. Sam couldn't blame her.

"So, then, whose ghost is this supposed to be?" Angela asked, lowering her voice into a whisper once the waitress finally left.

"That's still up in the air," Sam said. "But whatever this is, whoever's responsible obviously thinks someone else at the club knows what happened to Dina. This looks more like a threat to me. Some kinda shakedown. Blackmail. One of the weirdest varieties I can think of, sure, but still blackmail. Whoever's doing this wants to rattle some nerves and seriously get under somebody's skin. Make them think the truth is about to come out. And when people don't want that, there's usually a lot of other shit that spills out before the truth eventually gets there too. That's what I think this is."

"Then we have to go talk to people," Angela suggested. "That's the quickest way to the truth, right? We go to the club, ask around, watch people's reactions, and if anyone looks suspicious—"

"It's not that simple," Sam interrupted before sipping her black coffee to kickstart her brain into thinking mode. "Pete Wilder runs this whole town, and he owns most of it. He's not just gonna sit idly by while the two of us try to interrogate his club members and dig into his personal affairs."

"Then you think Pete Wilder has something to do with this?"

"It doesn't matter if he does or if he doesn't," Sam said. "He's still not gonna let anyone question his people about anything that could remotely implicate him, his properties, his businesses, or the people protected by their social-club status. The Good Ol' Boys all look to him for pretty much everything, by the way. To make matters worse, you and I are both outsiders as far as this town is concerned. We can't just walk right in and do whatever we want."

"So what *do* we do?" Angela asked. "If we can't ask the questions, how are we supposed to…"

Her words trailed off, and her eyes widened again with something close to horror as she stared behind Sam across the diner.

Sam turned in the booth to find Chief Colton standing inside the café doors. With no one else here at this early hour, he'd already spotted them, and his gaze settled on Angela as he approached. His perpetual scowl never changed.

Sam wondered if it was always there or just whenever they were in the same room.

"What the hell are you doing, Salazar?" Colton stopped beside their table.

"Good morning to you too, Chief." Sam lifted her mug toward him in greeting. "Good to see you."

"You were supposed to go home."

"I did. Thanks to your officer's diligent escort. And now I'm here."

"Well now you need to get gone. I need a word with Ms. Copely." He nodded at Angela. "Privately."

Sam tried to discern in a single glance whether Angela could handle a conversation with Rush's Chief of Police right now.

Surprisingly, Angela nodded at her, then picked up her own mug before raising it to her lips. "It's fine, Sam. Chief, I'm happy to talk, though I'm not sure how helpful I'll be…"

"You just worry about answering my questions," he told her, "and I'll take care of the rest."

Sam stood, pulled out her wallet, and laid a twenty on the table before flashing a tight smile at the chief. "Go ahead and order yourself a little something to wake up to. On me. Angela, I'll give you a call later, yeah?"

The woman nodded. "We should send flowers."

Sam paused. "For what?"

"For Shell. Her father-in-law."

"Right." Sam turned from the table and marched across the café, feeling both Angela and Colton staring after her the whole time.

When she turned the corner to leave the hotel, she caught a quick glimpse of Colton slipping into the booth across from Angela where Sam had just been sitting.

~

SAM FOUND the entrance to Birdsong Park completely blocked off when she arrived. *Someone* had been by in the last two hours to move the town barricades from either side of the entrance, so they now stretched directly across it.

Even more surprising was the sight of Syc up and about, just before sunrise, with one of his lawn chairs pulled up to the park's entrance. He'd unfolded it there on the drying grass and settled in, facing the road, with Dog lying outstretched on his belly beside him.

She parked the Jeep, left the engine running, and headed toward them. "What are you doing?"

"Waiting for you," Syc grumbled. "These things are damn heavy. Doesn't take a rocket scientist to figure you'd come back eventually."

"You're not wrong," she said. "On either count."

"You gonna help me move these things, or what?"

Together, they heaved and lifted, grunting and huffing to move the first barricade aside. Then Sam paused. "You know what? I've got a better idea. Let's take these a little farther in. Give 'em a more permanent resting place, if you catch my drift."

Syc slowly turned his head away from her to scan this side of the trailer park, and a slow smile crept across his face. "Pretty sure I do."

WITH THE SKY a blazing pink-orange now, Sam and Syc tossed the final barricade into the firepit. Sparks and embers burst up to shower all over the place. Then Syc grabbed the bottle of lighter fluid he kept beside the pit and handed it to Sam without looking at her. "Figured you might wanna take the honors this morning."

"Don't mind if I do."

One little squirt on the already glowing coals of what was left from last night's fire, and the whole thing was blazing all over again. Flames crackled high, spitting in all directions before finally settling down. Not that these town barricades burned as easily as regular wood, but they definitely weren't fireproof.

By the time Sam finally stopped staring into the flames, Syc had already returned his personal lawn chair to the firepit, where he now sat and stretched out in his regular position. As usual, Dog joined him.

Sam left them only to retrieve her Jeep and park it in its usual spot, then she dropped into the other lawn chair beside her neighbors.

"I'm guessing you didn't get much sleep last night," Syc murmured. "If any."

"You've got a way with guessing, don't you?"

He raised an eyebrow at the fire, then picked up a random stick and tossed it into the flames.

"The lack of sleep wasn't on purpose, though," she continued. "I found a body a few hours ago. Dr. Jones hanged himself off the front porch of the Kalamack Club."

"Huh." Syc sucked on his teeth, then shifted in the lawn chair before pulling out a freshly rolled joint. "You have a knack for putting yourself at the center of things, don't you?"

"Right." She grabbed her cigarettes to light up beside him, realizing how long she'd gone without thinking about a smoke until she saw someone else doing it. It didn't even matter that Syc only smoked weed. "Because I try *so hard* to make it all about me."

"Why doesn't this surprise me?" He took a long drag on his joint, then blew it slowly out in a giant sigh of stinky gray smoke. "You make any headway on your flower culprit?"

Sam sighed out her own cloud and settled back into the comfortably supportive canvas lawn chair. "Not yet. But I will."

THIRTY-ONE

Laila

At almost 4:30 a.m., Laila ripped herself out of bed with a groan, put on a robe, and shuffled through her apartment toward the front door just to get the damn knocking to stop.

She couldn't wait to leave this stupid town.

When she opened the door, she found Chief Colton on the other side of it, his fist raised mid-knock. "What are *you* doing here?"

The man looked pissed. "Pete's not answering his phone."

"How is that my problem?"

"Because if *he* won't answer his phone, you're next on the list of people to let me into the clubhouse. So I'm gonna need you to come with me."

"Any particular reason for this?" she asked. "Because I'll tell you right now, Ralph, if this has anything to do with that stupid ghost stuff, you can forget it. I don't care how badly you need to get into the clubhouse. I'm not—"

"No ghosts, Laila." He shrugged. "Not yet, anyway. Just a dead body."

She froze, then opened her front door a little wider. "A what?"

"Reginald Jones was found hanging from the front porch of the Kalamack Club a few hours ago," Colton added, studying her expression.

"Oh my god. As in he was *murdered*?"

"That's for the coroner to decide, and whatever answer he gives me is the one I'll give you and everyone else."

"It *has* to be a murder, though, right?" Laila said. "I mean, Reginald wouldn't actually … he wouldn't—"

"Again, not my area of expertise. But investigating a crime scene *is*, and to do that, I need to get inside. Since Pete won't answer and I don't have any keys, I need you to come open up for me. So let's go."

Laila looked herself over, then frowned back up at him. "I can't go looking like this."

"So go looking like something different. And be quick about it."

As they neared the club's parking lot in Colton's squad car, he shot her several sidelong glances before murmuring, "Don't worry. The body's gone."

"I wasn't worried." Laila pressed her lips together and shook her head, staring straight ahead through the windshield.

"Might as well ask now. When was the last time you saw Dr. Jones?"

"Just the other day. He'd tried to come into the club the first morning I called you."

"When that Angela woman was giving you a bunch of trouble out front?"

"No. Sorry, the day after that. The first day of the haunting. With the writing all over the wall…"

"All right." Colton slowed to turn into the parking lot. "How did he seem?"

"He was a little upset the club was closed for the day. All the members were. But then there wasn't anything else for him to do, so he left."

"And that was the extent of your conversation with him?" Colton asked.

"Actually..." Laila readjusted her purse in her lap and couldn't help but stare at the club's front porch. Sure enough, the body was gone, but she couldn't stop staring at it anyway. "Yeah. I asked him about a necklace."

Colton jerked on the wheel to take them sharply into a parking spot right up front. His cruiser jolted to a stop before he shifted into park and stared at her. "What necklace?"

"I found a necklace on my desk," she said. "Small silver chain with a silver capital letter D pendant. I don't know where it came from, but I'd been asking everyone that day if they recognized it or knew who it belonged to. I asked Dr. Jones too, but he said he didn't know anything and just walked out. It was the same necklace I was looking for when David and I called you the other night, if you remember. After that second haunting, it just ... disappeared, apparently."

"Well, that would definitely match up."

Laila frowned at him. "With what, exactly, Chief?"

"Dr. Jones was found with a necklace in his hand that matches the description you just gave me."

"Wait, what?" Laila blinked furiously, looking quickly back and forth between Colton's serious gaze on her and the front porch of the club, *sans* body. "Wait, you think he stole it from where I'd hung it on the wall?"

"Must've been something like that. Or someone gave it to him. But you were missing a necklace, and it was found in his hand."

"You can stop looking at me like that, Ralph," she snapped. "Because *I* certainly didn't give it to him."

The chief lifted both hands in concession. "Wasn't implying anything."

Then he got out of the car, and their conversation was over.

Laila followed him. Surprisingly, her hands didn't shake at all as she found the right keys to unlock the front door. Then she went straight toward her work area at the front desk, turned off the security alarm, and let Chief Colton take the lead in investigating the first floor.

Nothing seemed out of order on the ground level. No windows were open, nothing was broken. All the other doors were still locked. Then two more Rush PD squad cars pulled up, and a group of other officers stepped inside to join their chief in investigating the premises.

Laila decided it was best to stay out of everyone's way, so she remained behind her desk as if this was another normal day at the Kalamack Club without hauntings or bodies.

It was particularly difficult to convince herself that anything about today was normal.

While the police went upstairs to search the second floor, Laila stayed where she was. Before she knew it, she found herself standing by one of the front windows close to her desk, one hand scrunching up the thick, luxurious curtains while she leaned sideways to get as clear of a view as possible. The club's front porch didn't look much different from this angle, either. There was still no evidence of a body having hung there a few hours before, but she couldn't stop staring.

When Colton came back downstairs and cleared his throat, Laila instantly dropped the curtain and spun toward him.

"One room upstairs is locked from the inside," he said. "I'm guessing you have keys to that too."

"Which room?"

"I believe it's—"

The front door burst open with a screech and violent thump against the wall before Big Pete Wilder blustered in like he had for the last several days now.

"Goddamnit! Of all the things to happen right now... Unbelievable. How were any of us supposed to know he was in a hole so big he had to fucking hang himself? And why the hell couldn't he have done that in his own home, huh? Front porch of my club doesn't even make sense. What the fuck is that about?"

His wife was with him too, looking tired but ready to work this out. Elaine cast Pete a perturbed look, then nodded at Laila and whispered, "Don't pay him any mind, honey. He's just upset that some things in this world are completely out of his control."

Colton turned toward Big Pete and nodded. "We've double-checked the entire clubhouse. The property's secure, no signs of forced entry or anything else out of the ordinary, but I do want to take a look in your office, Pete."

"So then go fucking take a look at it," Pete barked.

The chief shot him a tight smile before continuing as if this was a calm, respectful conversation on both sides. "It's locked. I was about to ask Laila to come open it for me—"

"Waste of your time," Pete grumbled before storming past the desk. "There's only one key, and she sure as hell doesn't have it."

His footsteps clomped across the floor past Laila, Chief Colton, and the desk before continuing up the back stair-case. He didn't look at either of them but hollered down the stairs, "So hurry the hell up if you wanna look. I've got shit to do."

Colton and Laila exchanged a knowing look tinged with apprehension, but neither of them would argue about who wanted to follow Big Pete's barked instructions and who wanted to stay behind.

So they both turned and headed up the stairs together.

Elaine merely clicked her tongue and followed suit.

"You can search around here all you want," Pete said in front of his study's closed door as he fished his keys from his pocket and rifled through them. "But I'm telling you right now, you're not gonna find anything in here. No one ever comes in here. Not unless they're with me, and not unless I say so."

"Just in case, though, Pete," Colton replied. "Leaving no stone unturned, here."

"Well, you fucking better find the right stone. Because I've about had it." Finally, Pete found the key, slid it into the lock, and jiggled it open. "Get ready to turn around and go flip rocks somewhere else, because there's a—"

The door whispered all the way open after Pete's enormous hand released it. The man stopped in the open doorway, his back rigid and shoulders stiffening.

"Pete?" Colton asked.

"Goddamnit!" Big Pete charged into the study, the angry thump of his footsteps interspersed with rustling, crunching, and something that sounded like a bunch of fabric moving across the floor.

Laila was only seconds behind Colton as they both entered the study behind Pete. Then they too froze.

It looked like a tornado had blown through the room.

The normally pristinely clear surface of the executive cherrywood desk along the far wall was scattered with pens, office supplies, and shredded paper. All the wiring from the internet router and the landline office phone had been stripped from the walls and thrown about. One filing cabinet was tipped diagonally into the corner, the drawers open and files strewn all over the place.

Then there were the violent slashes ripping through the leather upholstery of all the other furniture and the two potted plants in the corner smashed to bits, leaves and piles of dirt trailing all over the polished wooden floors. In the middle of the room, the 75th Anniversary Celebration banner, newly printed for the upcoming celebration at the Kalamack Club, had been cut clean through into several pieces, each of which boasted even more rips and tears and a few splatters of red.

Which must have come from the enormous letters scrawled hastily across the back wall, which made it impossible to ignore: *'Let Dina Go!'*

"Oh no." Laila shook her head. "No, not now."

It wasn't the shock of another message from this alleged ghost that got her but the fear of being the person who had shown up in the wrong place at the wrong time and therefore made the perfect target for the brunt of Big Pete's fury. Not to mention how much she did not want to spend her day trying to scrub that paint off the walls or cleaning up this mess all over his study.

That was not in her job description. This time, she would refuse to even try.

She didn't manage to escape quickly enough, however, before Elaine spoke next, clearly unamused by her husband's tantrum. "That's it, Peter. I'm putting my foot down. This isn't something we can just sweep under the rug and ignore for the rest of our lives."

He scrunched up his face. "What the hell are you talking about?"

"I'm talking about getting to the bottom of this. I'm talking about holding a séance right here in the clubhouse."

"Have you lost your goddamn mind?"

"Not in the least, and you know it."

"I am *not* having a séance at the club!" Big Pete roared. "And I don't wanna hear any more about it."

"You listen to me," Elaine said, shaking a finger at him. "I have known for *years* that there was something funny about this place. That there were spirits, ghosts, whatever we want to call them. After seeing *this*, I'm more convinced now than I've ever been that this building is haunted. And we need to find out what happened to the people who died here and how to help them move on."

Big Pete groaned. "Jesus Christ…"

"I am absolutely serious about this one, Peter," his wife insisted. "So serious, in fact, that this is what's going to happen. The Kalamack Club *will not* be holding any more Sunday brunches for any of its members, including the wives, until you agree to let me hold the séance here. And only *after* I have decided that can those Sunday brunches resume."

Laila assumed this was just a major bluff on Elaine's part. She almost laughed at the woman's attempts to strongarm her husband, but then she caught the seriousness of the warning glare in Big Pete's eyes and thought better of it.

"So you just think on *that*, Mr. Wilder," Elaine added with a snippy cock of her chin. "And I suggest you make your decision fairly soon, because it's almost Sunday."

Then she stormed out of the room and down the stairs, leaving Laila, Chief Colton, and Pete there in his office.

Laila was well aware of how little Elaine Wilder cared for these Sunday brunches — the social event looked forward to by most members and their wives. Not once since Laila started working here had she seen Elaine at the club on a Sunday.

With Elaine downstairs, Laila tried to sneak away herself.

That didn't work, either.

"Where the hell do you think you're going?" Pete shouted, kicking through the mess scattered across his study floor.

She tried to smile. "You don't need me up here, Pete."

"Oh no. You're staying. You too, Ralph." Pete shoved a finger into the chief's face. "How the fuck did something like this happen? This is my office. Mine! No one touches what's mine. Now I've got *this* shit to deal with on top of a fucking body on the front porch? Why can't anyone do their fucking job?"

With his study now destroyed, Big Pete apparently didn't see a point to containing himself. So he threw the kind of fit everyone always expected him to throw anyway, kicking through debris, smashing what little remained to be smashed, swiping scattered remnants of paperwork and office supplies off the desk with a massive arm and throwing and stomping and snorting like a raging bull in a rodeo pen.

Then it was over as quickly as it began, and Big Pete turned toward Laila and Colton again, huffing madly with fire in his eyes. "Just my fucking luck."

"I get you're upset, Pete," Colton said.

Big Pete scoffed. "Do you, now?"

"And I still have to do my job. So I gotta ask. Is there any way Reggie could've been involved in this haunting business? You know, the vandalism, breaking and entering?"

"Are you insane?" Pete cocked his head. "Of course he didn't have anything to do with it. I would know. Reggie's one of us, and he's definitely not stupid enough to get involved in something like this. He's a goddamn doctor, for crying out loud."

"Was," Laila said.

"What?" Both men turned to look at her,

She swallowed thickly and repeated herself, though this time her voice was barely above a whisper. "He *was* a doctor."

"Whatever." Pete tossed a hand toward Colton. "Any other stupid questions?"

"When you stepped into the clubhouse this morning," Colton said, "you mentioned Reggie being in some kind of hole big enough to kill himself over. What did you mean by that?"

"What did I mean by that?" Pete spun around to pace in a quick circle before throwing his hands up in exasperation. "Jesus Christ. I meant the man should've shown a little respect and offed himself in his garage or something. Hell, even his own front porch would've been better than mine. I've got nothing to do with his life, and I have no fucking clue why he'd kill himself, Ralph. You insinuating that I *would* borders on accusing me of being involved in this shit, and I don't like the way it sounds."

"Sure." Colton nodded. "Just doing my job, Pete."

"I need to clean this shit up."

Before he had a chance to say anything to Laila about the cleaning part, she spoke up first. "Pete, can I go home now?"

He turned toward her with a bristling scowl. "What?"

"After something like this, the club's not going to function as normal. We'll be closed for the day, at least, right? Again."

"The club isn't my study."

"But there was a *body* on the front porch just this morning," she said, tossing a hand toward the front of the clubhouse.

"She's right," Colton said. "We won't be finished here for a while yet, especially with multiple crimes within the same vicinity."

"Reggie hung himself. How is that a crime?"

"That hasn't yet been confirmed by the coroner, Pete," Colton reiterated. "Therefore, I'm treating everything here like a crime scene. So Laila's right. The clubhouse is closed for the day. Hopefully that's as long as it takes."

"It fucking better be," Pete snarled.

"All right, then," Laila said, trying to slip out the door again. "I'll wait to hear about when we're open again and back to—"

"Not so fast." Pete pulled his wallet from the pocket of his dress slacks, flipped it open, and yanked out a credit card. "You've got an errand to run. I don't wanna hear about anything else until it's taken care of."

He stormed toward her, and for a split second, the look in his eyes made Laila think he might actually intend to get physical with her this time. He certainly was furious enough for it. Not that he ever had, but a man like Pete Wilder didn't go through the entirety of a life like his without throwing around a few fists or open hands, no matter who was on the other side of them.

But he brushed past her through the doorway.

Laila caught a flash of silver in her periphery, and something knocked against her arm before clattering onto the floor.

"Elaine wants a fucking séance," he said as he stormed down the hall. "Well now she can damn well have it. If a séance is what gets this place back to a little goddamn normalcy, so be it."

His footsteps clomped madly down the back staircase again.

Laila wasn't paying attention to the sound anymore.

Now, she stared at the floor between her feet where Big Pete Wilder's credit card had landed. With a tilt of her head, she plastered another tight, trying-to-be-amenable smile onto her lips and bent down to pick up the card. "Great."

THIRTY-TWO

Laila

Two HOURS LATER, Laila stood on the sidewalk along the main street of Rush's town center, looking up at the marquee of the shop in front of her called Paper Moon. A shop she'd never entered and had never planned to until this morning. "I can't believe I'm here."

"It doesn't look all that bad from the outside..." One of the wait staff at the club, a young woman named Berna, stood beside Laila and folded her arms. "It kinda has a quaint feel to it, maybe."

"I'm supposed to be handling the front of the club," Laila continued. "I'm supposed to be hosting the place, taking hats and coats and gloves, leading people into the dining room, answering phone calls, scheduling events. Not being a personal assistant for the town nutjob's husband."

Berna shrugged. "At least you're not running personal errands for the town nutjob, right?"

Laila slowly turned her head toward the younger woman and raised an eyebrow. "Right. Because Big Pete is so much saner."

But Laila still had a job to do, and there was no viable way to get out of it.

They stepped inside and were blasted by the overwhelmingly powerful scent of acrid incense paired with intense floral odors and something reminiscent of baby powder. The sensation wasn't improved by the obnoxious ringing of windchimes that seemed to come from all directions. For a moment, Laila wondered how the hell there could be windchimes inside a store when there wasn't even any wind. Then she realized it was only a recording through the shop's speaker system.

Paper Moon was the only shop in Rush that fell under the esoteric-supplies category. Laila couldn't have imagined what this town would look like if it had more than one shop like this. The place was filled with candles, tables lined with crystals, glittering doodads hanging from the ceilings, colorful tapestries of trees and strange designs and moon phases all over the walls. One corner was completely devoted to several different sizes of statuettes ranging from four inches in height to almost four feet, plus countless books on magic and astrology and tarot.

Laila wanted nothing more than to turn around and blow right back through the front doors before never coming back.

Leaving without having accomplished her errand for Big Pete, however, would be far worse than staying here as long as it took to get the job done.

She hurried across the store, searching for one woman in particular.

The counter in the back of the store was covered in the same kind of tapestries and colorful cloths as the walls. It also boasted an enormous assortment of crystals. A beaded curtain covered the doorway on the other side of the counter, and a couch and matching loveseat took up the righthand corner beside a heavily laden bookshelf. A set of pewter burning dishes were laid out on the coffee table, with at least four different decks of cards on top of a purple velvet runner.

"Wow," Berna said as they made it to the back. "This place is…"

"Ridiculous," Laila finished for her before jamming a hand down on the silver bell on the back counter. The shrill ding echoed everywhere, overpowering the annoying clang of the windchimes in the background.

Then the beaded curtains were swept aside, and a tall, thin woman with immensely curly gray hair cut just below her ears hurried through with a wide grin.

"Hello," she said cheerily. "Welcome to Paper Moon. How can I help you?"

"I'm looking for the owner," Laila said, glancing at Berna from the corner of her eye.

"And you found her," the woman replied. "I'm Francine. What can I do for you today, ladies?"

"I need to book a séance for the Kalamack Club," Laila said. Those simple words coming out of her mouth made her feel like an absolute idiot.

It didn't help that Francine barked out a laugh before failing to cover it up with a hand while her giggle continued. "Isn't *that* a surprise. So Pete Wilder finally got tired of being haunted by Caroline, hmm?"

Laila leaned away from the back counter to eye her warily. "Where did you hear that name?"

"Many places, honestly." Francine spread her arms. "But most recently, the news has been all over town. Which I'm sure is only too easy for you to imagine. Working for the people you do. Everyone's talking about the hauntings now and the ghost of Caroline Griffiths. Though I've always known that old house has been occupied by spirits for quite some time. And now, Elaine finally wants to go ahead with the séance and speak to Caroline herself. How wonderful."

"Not exactly." Laila darted another quick glance toward Berna, but the young waitress looked as perfectly clueless as she truly was. Laila had only asked her along on this errand because she didn't want to be seen walking into a place like the Paper Moon all on her own. Beyond that, Berna was of no further help.

"Well, if she doesn't want to speak with Caroline," Francine said, "then with whose spirit *does* she wish to communicate?"

"Someone else," Laila replied, feeling more absurd by the second just for having this conversation in the first place. "Someone named Dina."

"Oh." Francine tapped a finger against her chin. "I haven't heard of that one."

"Well, that's the ghost. Or whatever. We need this séance to happen as soon as you're available. Tomorrow, even. Is that possible?"

"Anything is *possible*." Francine's eyes lit up with intent. "It's the cost of making it possible that might be a bit tricky. I have another event scheduled for tomorrow already, so if this is what the Wilders really want, I can cancel what's already in my calendar and reschedule it. That will, of course, cost a bit more than my going rate…"

Somehow, Laila didn't entirely believe her. What were the chances of not actually being able to fit in two séances in one day? There couldn't be *that* many people in town holding talk-to-dead-people parties.

But this had to happen. It wasn't Laila's job to haggle about it, and therefore, this wouldn't be a negotiation. Mostly because it was all on Big Pete's dime.

"So what's the price of making it possible?"

"A thousand dollars," Francine said without batting an eye.

Laila almost choked.

A thousand bucks just to set up a few knick-knacks on the table and pretend to talk to ghosts? That seemed particularly steep. But who was she to argue?

"I'll have to check with Mr. Wilder before I can give you an answer."

"Go right ahead." Francine gestured toward the couch and loveseat in the corner. "Make yourself at home. I'll be here when you're ready."

With a nod to excuse herself, Laila walked toward the couch and pulled her phone from her purse. The small corner set up like a fortuneteller's living room was cozy enough and provided a bit of privacy, but she'd be damned if she was about to sit down on that couch and try to act like he she belonged here.

Pete answered after the first ring. "What?"

"The séance is a thousand dollars," Laila told him without preamble. "That's her price."

"Are you fucking kidding me? A thousand dollars for a goddamn parlor trick? A thousand dollars to sit my wife down and tell her some bullshit story about ghosts and talking to dead people and whatever the hell else? These idiots are trying to rob me blind!"

Laila removed the phone a good distance from her ear while he rambled through another one of his fits. She let him carry on for another thirty seconds before his voice finally quieted, and she tentatively pressed her cell to her ear again.

"Fine. Take care of it. Just get it done. Whatever this swindler says she needs, let her fucking have it. There's no Sunday brunch at the club if there's no séance. And I am *not* canceling the brunch."

Then he hung up.

Laila slipped her phone back into her purse and returned to the back counter and Francine's hocus-pocus display.

I don't get paid nearly enough to deal with this bullshit.

Francine pulled away from a collection of small, colorful stones splayed out on one of the colorful cloths in front of her, which she and Berna had been inspecting together. The woman smiled at Laila and stepped back. "Well?"

"It's fine." Laila removed Pete's credit card from her wallet and slid it across the counter. "Whatever you have scheduled tomorrow, cancel it, reschedule it. You're doing a séance at the Kalamack Club."

"Wonderful." Francine delicately plucked the credit card off the counter and hardly looked at it. She did, however, hold it in front of her with both hands and smiled even wider at Laila. "To be clear, the thousand dollars is the cost of my services, my time, and of course my availability at such late notice. There's another two-hundred-dollar charge for all the necessary supplies I'll have to bring with me, plus setting everything up at the location. The total cost is due up front before I can start on anything."

"Not a problem." Laila finally returned the other woman's smile with a genuine one of her own.

Francine clearly knew exactly what kind of man she was charging for her special skills. Good for her if she had the stones to milk it for all it was worth.

"So then what time can we expect you to be at the club tomorrow?" Laila asked.

"Midnight is best for this type of work."

"Midnight it is."

"Wonderful. Now we do have a few other caveats, and this is just preparation to be done beforehand."

Laila almost rolled her eyes. Of course there was more.

"In order for this to work," Francine said, "someone who knows the spirit we'll be trying to contact must also be in attendance."

"Someone who knows the spirit," Laila echoed.

"Or who knew them in life, anyway," Francine explained. "Someone with a strong connection to them. A friend or family member. A co-worker is fine, if that's all there is, though it's certainly not preferred."

Fortunately, Laila did know of a family member who conveniently happened to be right here in Rush. "I know the girl's mother's in town. She's been here for a few days. Looking for this girl Dina."

"The mother will work," Francine said. "So go ahead and invite her to join us tomorrow night."

"Fine. I'll find her somehow. Any mystical hints as to a good place to start?"

Francine chuckled. "It doesn't work like that, honey."

Her tone dripped with condescension.

"I'm sure it won't be that hard," Berna added, looking surprisingly eager to help. "It's not like there are a whole lot of places for the woman to stay. Go ask a few hotels, see if anyone knows who she is or where she's staying. And if nothing else, we can just go by the Redwood Rings."

"I think it's a bit early in the morning for a cocktail, Berna," Laila said. "Not that I couldn't use one right about now, anyway."

"I don't mean for a drink," the waitress added. "I mean to ask around about this Dina girl's mom. Isn't that bar supposed to be the one-stop shop for information in town?"

"Fine. We'll start there."

"Wonderful." Francine extended a hand over the counter, and Laila shook it.

THIRTY-THREE

Sam

THE FIRST THING Sam did when she finally woke after not nearly enough sleep was to check for more flowers. It sucked that this had become the first thing racing through her mind every morning, but it was what it was. She couldn't bring herself to do anything else until she opened the front door of her trailer and poked her head outside.

Nothing this morning.

It was both a relief and an unexpected surprise because now she wondered what had gotten Hoodie to stop making these deliveries. It also alleviated any other chances of catching him in the act and making him tell her who the flowers were coming from.

What did catch her attention, however, were the thin plumes of smoke still trailing from the firepit outside.

Sam headed toward the firepit for a good look at the kindling she and Syc had tossed in a few hours before.

The barricades were ash now. Syc was still out here in his lawn chair, though now he'd fallen asleep in it and looked more comfortable than Sam imagined he would have been in his own bed. Dog lay in the grass at his feet, also asleep and snoring just as loudly.

Well at least someone's *sleeping well...*

After a quick shower, Sam didn't expect her first phone call of the day to come from a woman to whom she'd already said her goodbyes.

"Angela. Hi. Are you already on your way back home?"

"I definitely thought I would be," Angela replied. "But now there's something else going on, and it made me reconsider."

"Really? Something else about Dina?"

"Sort of." The other woman sounded particularly hesitant to keep talking.

Sam really didn't have the patience this morning to gently coax it out of her.

Angela had called for a reason, though, which meant she was willing to push herself into elaborating. "I think hell must've finally frozen over because I just got an invitation this morning to go down to the Kalamack Club tonight. It's completely unexpected, especially after what happened, but I was personally invited, and I do want to go. Just not alone. So will you come with me?"

"Come with you to the Kalamack Club by personal invitation?" Sam clenched her eyes shut, trying to put together the pieces of that screwed-up puzzle. Then she decided she needed a little more time to wake up and could use some caffeine before she started trying to solve those mysteries. "You know what? How about I meet you at the hotel and we can talk about it there, huh? Maybe over a cup of coffee?"

~

INSIDE THE HOTEL'S cafe with their coffee mugs in front of them, Sam and Angela could better discuss what had actually happened this morning.

"I *was* getting ready to leave town," Angela said. "Hadn't checked out yet, fortunately. Then I got a knock on the door, and it was the blonde receptionist from the club, believe it or not. And she invited me to come down to the club."

"Did she say why?" Sam asked.

"Apparently, it's for a séance." Angela looked a little embarrassed just having said the word, and she offered a sheepish shrug. "I know it sounds ridiculous, but people hardly ever get to go in there, right?"

"If they're not members." Sam nodded. "Yeah, that's pretty rare."

"She said this was a séance to speak with Dina's spirit and that they need someone there who knew her well. Who knew her better than I did, right?"

Sam studied her, trying not to frown. "We're talking about the same woman, right? The receptionist who *had you arrested* when you were picketing on the club's front porch?"

Angela tucked her hair behind one ear and dipped her head. "Yes."

The whole thing seemed wildly out of place.

"Did you two talk about anything else besides this invitation and séance?"

"Not really."

"Listen." Sam folded her arms and leaned forward over the table. "I hope you weren't coerced into accepting this invitation, Angela."

"Coerced?" The woman laughed. "No, not at all. I actually found Laila quite lovely once I had the opportunity to speak with her."

Quite lovely.

That wasn't the kind of description Sam would've chosen for the leggy blonde manning the front desk of the Kalamack Club. Then again, there were plenty of things Angela had done that Sam simply wouldn't have. This was just another item on that list.

"So the séance, then," Sam began, hoping she didn't laugh or make inappropriate faces at the mention of this hocus-pocus crap taking place in Pete Wilder's very own club.

Angela sipped her coffee. "Laila told me I'm supposed to be there at midnight tonight. Is that something you can do with me?"

"I should be able to swing it," Sam said. She'd have to leave work before the end of her shift, of course, but this was a genuine opportunity staring her in the face — to get inside the Kalamack Club, take a look around for herself, and enjoy a front-row seat to whatever weird spirit-communing crap was sure to go done.

Chris would understand if she had to dip out a little early. The opportunity likely never repeat itself Plus, Sam was insanely curious to see what hell freezing over actually looked like.

More than that, though, she couldn't shake the feeling that this whole séance thing wasn't exactly the best idea. Not for Angela, anyway. Not on her own.

"Did Laila say why *you* were getting the invitation and not anyone else who knew Dina from when she lived here?" she asked.

"I think it's because the woman putting all this together needs someone who knows the person they're trying to reach. Or *knew* them, anyway."

Saying this out loud seemed to deflate all Angela's buoyant cheeriness, which also felt out of place.

Sam couldn't blame her for getting excited about something that might off her some kind of closure when it came to her daughter, even if ghosts didn't actually exist.

It just didn't make sense why this whole town had, in a matter of mere days, instantly accepted the fact that Dina Copely was dead, that her ghost was haunting the Kalamack Club, and that her mother — who had been arrested and accosted and had her tires slashed and spark plugs screwed with — now apparently deserved to help her youngest daughter's spirit find peace.

No, of course it didn't make sense. There had to be something else going on here.

Sam just couldn't figure out what.

Now, Angela looked more uncomfortable in Sam's presence than she had since their first rocky conversation inside the Redwood Rings' front pub. But she obviously trusted Sam, or she wouldn't have asked that Sam be her Plus One to the séance.

Which meant there was a lot more on this woman's mind right now than she was saying.

Sam sipped her coffee again, waiting for Angela to continue, but she didn't.

After that, the only thing Sam could think to do was invite Angela to another meeting with her later this morning. Angela declined.

Instead, they agreed Sam would be back here to pick Angela up from her hotel at 11:30 p.m. once Sam got off work early, then they'd drive up to the Kalamack Club together.

"Oh, Sam?" Angela called after Sam had already made it halfway to the doors. "I meant to tell you something else after my conversation with Chief Colton earlier."

Sam turned around with raised eyebrows.

"He asked me about Dina's necklace. The one you showed me in that picture of Dr. Jones."

"Okay…"

"I confirmed with him that it was hers. He didn't have any answers for me about why someone like Dr. Jones would've had her necklace on him. But he did say they also found Dina's driver's license on him, too."

"Really?" Sam asked.

"Yeah." The woman fiddled with her coffee mug. "It was in his pocket."

"Well, that's one more unanswered question, isn't it?"

"Hopefully one we'll be better equipped to answer after tonight, right?" Angela gazed up at Sam with something that looked far more like pleading in her eyes.

Sam nodded. "Hopefully. I'll see you tonight, Angela. Eleven thirty. Don't forget."

The other woman let out a wry laugh. "Oh, I won't. Trust me."

∼

WHEN SAM GOT out of her Jeep in the Community Center parking lot ten minutes before the start of this morning's NA meeting, the last person she expected to see on her way back into the rooms was Chief Colton.

It sure seemed they were seeing a whole lot of each other lately.

He noticed her on her way toward the front steps, and Colton nodded before starting yet another conversation Sam had hoped to avoid. "Got a minute, Salazar?"

Sam feigned surprise, glancing over her shoulder before pointing at herself. "Me?"

"You see any other Salazars around? I know, hard to believe I'd *want* to talk to you, but here we are."

She glanced at her watch. "Sure, Chief. I've got about three minutes, then I do have an appointment to keep. What can I help you with?"

He met her at the bottom of the stairs and drew her to the side. "About that woman you've been spending so much time with lately."

"You mean Angela?"

"Yeah. Listen, Salazar. Just be careful with her, all right? She might not be the wounded but still-loving mother searching for redemption you seem to think she is. Not completely."

Sam frowned. "Is there something else you'd like to tell me about her, Chief? Or are we just spreading around as much conjecture as possible these days?"

"Just be careful. That's all I'm saying. Have a good one." Then he left her to jog across the parking lot toward his cruiser.

Sam preferred not to give him the satisfaction of seeing her rattled by that odd warning, so she stomped up the stairs and jerked open the doors without looking back.

The meeting was just like all the others, but at least Sam had gotten her ass into a seat today.

Afterward, Sam couldn't help but note how strange it was that in the last two days, both Chris and Chief Colton had come to the same conclusions before offering Sam their own variation of the same warning: *Be careful with Angela. Don't get too caught up in her problems. We're just looking out for you.*

Chris, she could understand. As far as Sam was concerned, what she did with her own time was none of Colton's fucking business.

But now she couldn't stop wondering why he'd really been here in the first place. It couldn't have been just to intercept Sam before she entered the meeting. That seemed like far too much work for him, unless Colton was also getting something fairly valuable of his own out of it.

Not likely.

"Hey there, Sam."

She spun away from doctoring up her cup of in-meeting sludge everyone in these rooms agreed to pretend was real coffee and tried to smile. "Hey, Hector. How's it going?"

"Keeping my mouth shut and putting my ass in a seat every day. You know how it goes."

She snorted. "Some days I wish I didn't."

He grabbed a Styrofoam cup and filled it with the last of the sludgy caffeine in the bottom of the pot. "I heard about the séance you're going to tonight."

"Oh, yeah? What did you hear exactly?"

"That it's happening. That it's at the Kalamack Club. That it's a séance." Hector shrugged. "Francine's been talking about it all over town, like it's Christmas morning and she's the only one of us getting anything from Santa Claus, if you catch my drift."

"Why am I not surprised?"

"Figured if it's something *that* odd at the club, you'd probably already be involved with it somehow. Turns out I was right."

"Want me to let you know how it goes?" she asked.

He dropped the plastic container of powdered coffee creamer back onto the table and turned toward her with wide eyes. "No way. I don't dabble in that kinda stuff myself. The way I see it, the dead are dead for a reason, and they should be left that way. It's disrespectful to call them back."

"So you believe in ghosts, then? Spirits? Or ... whatever?"

He considered her question, then shrugged again. "I

believe there's plenty of things in this world we humans are never gonna fully understand. Probably for the best. And I think you oughtta be careful, getting wrapped up in that kinda business. Just my two cents. For what they're worth."

"More than you think," Sam replied with a nod. "I'll keep it in mind."

She sipped her coffee, turned away, and hurried out of the Community Center to avoid being stopped by anyone else who might've assumed she was in the market for unsolicited advice or opinions.

She wasn't.

She climbed into her Jeep, turned on the engine, and pulled out her phone for a quick Google search.

Now that it had finally occurred to her, she couldn't believe how completely irresponsible she'd been not to look into Angela on her own. She'd merely taken the woman at her word from the beginning, but now, Colton's cryptic heads-up had kicked the red-flag alarm bells of Sam's mind into overdrive.

Even a quick, superficial search pulled up something about Angela Copely. It wasn't strange for people's names to turn up on the internet these days, but what Sam found wasn't all that heartening.

Barring the rare extenuating circumstance, public arrest records remained accessible in pretty much every state - to those who knew where to look.

Including Angela's single previous arrest from nineteen years ago.

She'd been busted for drunk driving and charged with a DUI. At the time, her two young daughters had been in the car with her, and the ensuing sentence had been relatively mild — one hundred hours of community service, and that was pretty much it.

It wasn't exactly damning information, no. Sam

already knew about Angela's struggle with alcoholism and how much it had affected her life before sobriety.

Sam also remembered Angela telling her on the day they'd first met that she was so embarrassed for having been arrested on the front porch of the Kalamack Club. That it was something she'd never experienced before. That this was her first time in cuffs and her first run-in with the law.

Angela had lied to her face, and that was a major concern.

~

SAM HAD ONLY MEANT to drive back home for a quick change of clothes before work. Yet another confusing surprise greeted her instead when she pulled through Birdsong Park's entrance.

Little Pete, of all people, stood on the park's property — probably for the first time — a dozen yards from Syc's trailer, with one pissed-off Syc standing in front of him and stabbing a finger into the mayor's face.

An incredibly bored-looking police officer completed the triangle of men standing in the grass, none of whom seemed to notice Sam's arrival. When the officer finally saw her leaving her Jeep to approach them, he was the only one who did and almost shrugged as if in apology.

"I don't give a rat's ass how right you think you are," Syc bellowed. "Nothing gives you the right to storm up here and start telling me what I can and can't do with my own damn land."

Sam fought off a grimace before she finally reached them. "Gentlemen. What seems to be the issue here?"

"From what I gather," the officer replied first, "there's some sort of issue with the zoning laws around here."

"And *you're* not doing your job," Syc shouted at him.

Sam placed a hand on his shoulder to hopefully quiet him down. "That's why Mayor Wilder's here, I'm guessing. But I'm wondering why *you're* here, Officer."

"I was called in. But, like I've been trying to explain, these zoning issues are a civil matter. They have their place in civil court, and I can't do a thing about any of it now. My jurisdiction covers the criminal variety. So my hands are tied."

"Just more goddamn excuses," Syc snarled.

Sam ignored him. "All right. Well, obviously, you can't settle the zoning dispute. I completely understand that part, but how about this? Was Mayor Wilder personally invited onto the Birdsong Park property?"

"You know damn well he wasn't," Syc grumbled.

The officer looked to Little Pete for an answer, and the mayor sneered as he shook his head.

"There you go," Sam continued. "Seeing as this park is in fact private property, I'd call that trespassing. Which makes this a criminal issue under your jurisdiction, Officer. So then I would advise Mayor Wilder, if I were you, to leave the premises as quickly as possible. Or my friend here could very well have him arrested for trespassing, and then it's a whole different issue."

"That's ridiculous," Little Pete snapped.

Syc nodded at the officer and folded his arms. "Do that. That's your job. That's what I want you to do."

The officer turned slowly toward Little Pete with a grimace. "She's right. Technically, that's where we are now."

"Of all the stupid fucking..." Little Pete gritted his teeth and fixed Sam with a surprisingly intense glare. If looks could impart full-fledged threats, this one was at the top of the list.

Then he spun around and marched back toward the park's entrance, on the other side of which he'd left his vehicle - presumably before Syc had noticed his presence and come out to greet him.

"Thanks for your time, Officer," Sam added.

He met her gaze, then looked at Syc and spread his arms. "Next time you call the Rush PD all the way out here for something like this, make sure it's a criminal violation and has nothing to do with municipal ordinances. All right?"

"Only if that asshole stays the hell off my property," Syc replied.

Sam swatted at his arm with the back of a hand. This had worked out in their favor this time, but there *was* such a thing as pushing it too far, and Syc had been riding that line for some time now.

With a final nod, the cop headed back to his squad car. Though Little Pete had already peeled off down the dirt road away from Birdsong Park, Syc and Sam stayed where they were until the squad car had fully disappeared too.

"This isn't how you're gonna get this issue squared away, Syc."

"Sonofabitch showed up at *my house* trying to tell *me* what to do. I didn't start it, Sam."

"I know. But let's make sure we're the ones who finish it, okay?"

"You got a plan for that?" he called after her as she headed for the Deville.

"Not yet. I'm gonna sleep on it, though, and I'll let you know if anything pops up."

Before she settled into bed to hopefully catch a few hours' sleep before work, Sam texted Chris to let him know she'd have to dip out of work early tonight, with zero explanation, and left it at that.

THIRTY-FOUR

Sam

"Part of me doesn't even wanna know because it can't mean anything good," Chris said as he unloaded a rack of clean bar glasses straight out of the dishwasher. "And the other part of me is starting to think you agreeing to this means you're losing your mind. Do I wanna know?"

"Why I'd want to accept an invitation to the Kalamack Club and get to look around the place for the first time ever?" Sam asked.

"More like why you're going to a fucking séance," he murmured. "But okay."

"And you knew it was a séance how, exactly?"

Chris shot her a sidelong look before nodding toward the bar where Christian, Eddie, and Levi sat nursing their drinks and yukking it up. "How do you think?"

"Sounds like the whole town's already heard about it," she said. "And I only just found out this morning."

"That's why you need to dip out early?" he asked.

"Does it matter?"

"Not really." Chris shrugged. "As long as you make it up to me."

Sam eyed him up and down with the hint of a smirk. "Looks like you already have something in mind."

"Uh-huh. You're closing the place down with me every night for the next month. And no shift breaks tonight before you leave. You work all the way through until…"

"Eleven fifteen," Sam suggested.

"Eleven fifteen, then. Not a second earlier. I'll be watching the clock."

She was already hurrying back toward the kitchen's swinging doors to head for the Back Bar. Grinning, she spread her arms. "Aren't you always?"

Chris rolled his eyes, but she didn't miss his crooked smile before the doors swung shut and she got to work.

ANGELA SEEMED MORE nervous than usual in the Jeep's passenger seat as Sam drove them to the Kalamack Club. She'd taken the worn, creased picture of Dina from her purse and worried at it now, switching back and forth between staring blankly out the window and gazing at the old photo of her youngest daughter.

"Anything you wanna get off your chest?" Sam asked.

"Not really. I don't know, Sam. I'm not sure how I feel about this whole thing. On one hand, if we actually speak to Dina's ghost, we might finally get some answers about what happened to her. On the other hand, if it *is* her ghost, that means…"

"Hard to think about, I know," Sam said. "So how about you just don't think about it for now, and we'll take it minute by minute?"

They pulled into the club's parking lot at 11:55 p.m. Sam had never seen the place with all the lights on at this time of night. Not to mention so many vehicles in the parking lot, but the séance's participants had to get here somehow.

The front porch was still cordoned off with yellow police tape, which made Angela pause until the front door opened and the leggy blonde greeted them on the other side.

"Don't mind the tape for now," Laila said. "That's just a formality. Just duck under it and come on in."

"Thank you, Laila," Angela replied courteously before dipping incredibly low to crawl beneath the tape before Sam had a chance to lift it for her.

So Sam lifted it for herself instead before following Angela through the front door.

I didn't actually think the receptionist would be part of a séance. But I guess even in the middle of the night talking to the dead, the Wilders still need their staff to run things for them.

"We're so glad you could make it," Laila said as she led them across the front of the clubhouse toward her desk, then past it on her way to the back staircase, occasionally looking over her shoulder at the two women. "Both of you."

"We're flattered," Sam muttered.

There was no more conversation as they headed up the stairs. Laila's heels clacked loudly at a rapid staccato pace, and she'd reached the top landing before Angela had even made it a quarter of the way up.

At this rate, the ghosts would have already gotten impatient and moved on by the time Angela finally reached the top. So Sam hurried to catch up with her and linked her arm through Angela's. "It'll be fine."

The other woman looked at her with wide eyes, her face already pale. "What makes you say that?"

Because ghosts don't fucking exist and this whole town is full of charlatans.

"Just a hunch," Sam replied.

Then they reached the top of the stairs and found Laila waiting for them at the opposite end of the hall beside a door that was already open.

The blonde gestured with a demure wave of her hand and inclined her head.

That was the room, apparently.

The silence up here calmed Sam's gnawing curiosity as they walked over the opulent runners. Nothing nefarious up here. Not a whole lot of space to concoct some elaborate production, either. This was going to be interesting.

"Right in here," Laila murmured gently.

Angela stepped through the open door and Sam came up behind her.

Whatever this room had previously been, it had now completed its transformation into the séance room. Dark strips of crushed velvet and lace hung from the walls and draped from the ceiling to give a tent-like feel. Colored beaded shades hung on the standing lamps. In the center of the room was one large round table also covered in a cloth of crushed velvet, black this time. Six chairs surrounded it.

Standing behind the chair centered on the opposite side of the table was a woman with short, tightly curled gray hair, wearing dangling earrings, necklaces, bangles, and multiple flowing layers. Directly in front of her on the table was a thick black standing candle with nine votives set around it.

The other two occupants already in the room surprised Sam even more.

On the séance lady's right stood Big Pete Wilder, and on her left was Elaine.

Laila pulled the door shut behind her with a soft click, which instantly made Big Pete look up at them.

His scowl returned with full force. "No. Absolutely not. What the hell are *you* doing here?"

His fat finger swung toward Sam's face.

"Peter, they were invited," Elaine whispered from across the table.

"I don't give a shit. I damn well didn't invite Salazar, and I don't want her in here."

"Mr. Wilder," the séance lady said, her smile calm and even despite the growing tension exuding off the man. "This ritual will only be effective with six participants. If any one of us in this room were to leave, I'm afraid the séance cannot be performed."

"Fine. I'll call someone else, then. Anyone. Hell, I'll drag David out of bed and haul his ass up here, but not *her*."

"I'm sorry," Angela piped in, surprising all of them. "I can't do this without Sam. If she can't stay, neither can I."

"Then you can get the hell out too," Pete added, tossing a hand toward her.

"Peter, this is the *mother*..." Elaine flashed a quick smile at Angela before resuming her glare at her husband. "Francine said a family member must be present if we're to commune with the spirit. Angela *has* to be a part of it."

"Then I guess it's not happening." Pete turned away from the table and only got one step in before the volume and timber of his wife's voice shocked everyone into stillness.

"Peter Anthony Wilder, not another step!" she snapped, this time pointing at him the way he pointed at everyone else. "We agreed to do this tonight. *You* agreed to do this. If you want our deal to continue as discussed *before Sunday*, you will stay in this room. You'll keep your mouth shut, and you'll be a part of this no matter who else is here, because I said so. This séance is happening. Do you under-stand me?"

The room fell awkwardly silent as Pete and Elaine glared at each other. The man's fingers drummed quickly against his thighs as he studied his wife.

Sam couldn't help but feel a strange swell of approval for Elaine Wilder in that moment. The woman had bark and bite, that was for sure. Under different circumstances, Sam probably would have even admired her for her ability to stand up to Big Pete and speak to him the way very few people in Rush could — and survive to talk about it.

Then again, Elaine had been married to the man and *stayed* married to him despite all Big Pete's … foibles. She knew exactly what kind of man he was, and still, she chose to stay.

So Sam didn't admire her *that* much.

With a growling hiss, Pete finally jerked his chair out from beneath the table with a noisy, squealing scrape and plopped into it. "Let's get this the hell over with."

"Excellent," Francine said with a wide, beaming grin Sam thought looked awfully feral.

"But I swear to Christ," Big Pete added, thrusting a finger yet again at Sam. "If you can't keep your smart-ass mouth shut, if you piss me off in any way, I'm kicking you out myself."

Sam lifted both hands in concession. "Not a peep."

His glower only deepened.

"Well then." Francine clapped her hands and rubbed them together. "Why doesn't everyone take a seat, and we can begin."

THIRTY-FIVE

Sam

SAM HAD CHOSEN the seat on the other side of Big Pete just to piss him off. He looked like he was about to snap at her, but one stern look from his wife shut him up.

Angela sat on the other side of Sam, and Laila took the final empty seat between Angela and Elaine.

The dimly lit room was so quiet, Sam was sure she could hear the hum of electricity moving through the house, but she supposed that was all part of the night's ambiance.

"My name is Francine, and I will be leading us in tonight's ceremony. The six of us have gathered here in this room to attempt our friendly and accepting communion with the spirits inhabiting this house."

Communion? Come on, can't we call it anything else?

The woman produced a long lighter and reverently lit each of the smaller candles before finishing with the wide black standing candle. Then she spread her arms and nodded. "Now, I will ask all of you to take the hand of each person sitting beside you. This is our circle. The energy that flows through it must not be broken, meaning you must not let go of these hands until I say the time is right. So go on."

Part of Sam instantly regretted her choice to sit next to Big Pete.

The other part of her got a kick out of making him even more uncomfortable.

She reached out for his hand first, which he took with a grumble and roll of his eyes. His hand felt more like a fried fish in hers — hot, dry, flaky, with very little give.

One by one, everyone else sitting around the table joined hands as well, after which Francine inhaled deeply and closed her eyes. "Remember, whatever happens here tonight, if you break this circle before the time is right, our opportunity to commune with the spirits will have passed us by. I invite each of you to focus your energy and your intentions into this circle for peaceful communion with the spirits of those who have passed over yet, for reasons unknown to us, remain here in this house."

Sam looked around the table. Everyone but Big Pete had their eyes closed. He glared at Francine as if she'd just told him the only way to appease these spirits was to give away his fortune and go live out the rest of his days as a hermit in a cave somewhere in the Sierras.

Sam fought back a snort.

"Spirits," Francine continued, "hear us now. Feel us calling to you. We offer you our full attention and our intentions to help in whatever way we can. We wish to know why you're here and what you require of us. Show yourselves to us, spirits. Give us a sign."

There was no sign of anything.

"Spirits, hear us! We welcome you. Show us you are here among us now."

Sam's foot started to bounce beneath the table. In seconds, her entire leg thrummed with restlessness.

This woman's supposed to be a professional. What's taking her so long?

A low buzz rose from the other side of the room, and Sam opened her eyes again to look.

Nothing but a flickering light on its last leg. Clearly.

But Elaine saw it too and gasped before whispering, "They're here."

Pete grunted. "This is the biggest load of bullshit I've ever stepped in."

"Please, Mr. Wilder," Francine said calmly but firmly. Her expression remained fairly passive, her smile gone. "We must all focus our intentions into the séance. And if you can't handle it, then I'm sorry, but I'll have to ask you to leave."

"He can handle it," Elaine snapped, glaring at her husband across the table. "Don't you say another word, Peter."

He glared right back at her but surprisingly did as his wife said.

The standing lamp covered in a crimson shade with black beaded fringe flickered on the other side of the room — once, twice. A wind kicked up outside, howling across the valley in which Rush sat, knocking the shutters against the old windows. The centuries-old home rattled in its frame, groaning against the elements.

"This is it," Elaine whispered eagerly. "I finally get to speak with her."

Sam pursed her lips and studied Mrs. Wilder's eager expression.

She actually believes in this crap, doesn't she?

A quick look at Angela showed very much the same thing, though the woman kept her eyes clenched shut as she nearly squeezed the life from Sam's fingers. Laila sat patiently, her eyes closed, looking neither excited nor agitated by this so-called ritual.

Francine sucked in a deep breath and announced, "We hear you, spirits. We feel your presence. Now we wish to know if this is the spirit of Dina Copely come to commune with us this night."

If any form of answer had arrived, Sam might've changed her thoughts on the whole matter of ghosts and spirits.

Nothing happened.

Francine, however, hissed out a long exhale and tilted her head back. "I'm getting something…"

"What is it?" Angela asked. "What do you see?"

The lightbulb flickered again.

"A response," Francine said. "But this isn't Dina's spirit, no. This is someone else. A grown woman. A powerful matriarch."

Elaine's excitement instantly flared to new heights, and her hold on both Francine and Laila's hands visibly tightened.

"This spirit belonged to Caroline Griffiths," Francine said.

Pete grumbled something unintelligible but didn't try to make himself heard over another gust of wind howling against the side of the mansion.

"And she's saying … she says she's not happy with the way this house is being used. She says it was once a home, *her* home, the matriarch of this mountain town that has become Rush." Francine's chest heaved. "Oh, she isn't happy at all. Caroline does not approve of the way her home has been changed. Of what it has been forced to become and to endure."

With Angela and Elaine both sitting there in rapt attention, Sam assumed Francine would have something else to give them, but then it seemed that was it. Her knee started bouncing beneath the table again.

"Well, if it's Caroline," Elaine asked, "why is *she* haunting the club with messages about Dina?"

"Caroline," Francine continued, "we wish to know which spirit in this home has been leaving messages about the girl, Dina."

The wind kicked up again, this time simultaneously with the flickering lights. Angela's eyes practically bulged from her head. Elaine grinned like a child about to dig into an entire cake.

Francine rocked against the back of her chair, her eyelids fluttering. She let out a small moan. "Caroline says *she* was the one leaving those messages. Because this house, this so-called club, this entire town needs to *let Dina go*. She says Dina was a lovely girl, that her energy in life brought joy and hope to so many around her."

Angela choked on a sob but didn't let it loose. When Sam looked at her, the woman already had tears spilling down her cheeks before she found her voice.

"Ask her what happened," Angela said. "Ask Caroline what happened to my baby girl. Ask what this place did to her."

Francine's head rolled back, then to the side and forward again. "Let Dina go..." she moaned. "*Let Dina go...*"

Then the wind died down, and the sound of Angela's quiet, shaky breath filled the room as tears kept pouring from her eyes.

"What a load of shit," Pete grumbled.

Elaine scowled at him.

"Wait," Francine added urgently. "There's more. I'm getting another image now. Caroline wants us to find something in this house. Something personal. I'm seeing a … a large desk with a red area rug beneath it."

For the first time, Laila looked surprised now. "That's my desk."

Eyes still closed, Francine tilted her head. "Caroline says we need to look in the desk. A drawer that is not a drawer, but a… Wait, no. A hidden compartment. Something difficult to find but still very real. She says to find the birds."

"Birds in a fucking secret cupboard," Pete hissed under his breath.

Francine's eyes flew open, and she gazed around the circle with a tired smile. "We may release each other's hands now. I believe Caroline has chosen to no longer commune with me until we find these birds she's talking about."

"I'll go look," Laila said. The second both her hands were free, she leapt to her feet and turned from the table.

"Me too," Sam added. "For corroboration. Two pairs of eyes are better than one, right?"

No one objected, so she headed toward the door after Laila, nodding at Angela on her way out because the woman looked absolutely terrified.

Together, Sam and Laila all but disassembled the receptionist desk in the club's front entrance. Laila started with the top center drawer, and Sam took the two stacked drawers on the right. Out came paperwork, files, office supplies, old CD-ROM disks, and a spare set of keys. But nothing indicated a secret compartment. When Laila moved to the left-hand drawers, her luck was no better.

After ten minutes of searching, Sam ran back upstairs to reconvene with Francine and through her — allegedly — Caroline Griffiths to make sure they were actually looking in the right place. The confirmation was vague, but they had nothing else to go on.

The floor of the receptionist area was covered with the scattered contents of Laila's desk when Sam returned. And still no sign of a hidden compartment or little birds.

"Do these drawers come out?" Sam asked.

"I have no idea," Laila said. "I've never had a reason to take them out."

So they experimented. When the bottom left-hand drawer rested on the floor beside everything else that had once been inside it, Sam reached in and felt along the walls of the drawer's cubby. There was the track for the wheels. One side, then the other. Then her fingers brushed across a small, barely detectable indentation on the underside of the cubby. She pushed on it, and a panel slightly larger than her palm fell away from the underside of the desk and into her hand.

Frowning, Sam drew it out again and stared at the ejected panel. On it were two tiny silver objects. It took a moment to recognize them as a pair of stud earrings.

"Look for the birds," she murmured.

"What's that?" Laila asked from the floor.

"I think we found them." Sam turned to show Laila, then both women hurried back up the stairs to join the rest of the waiting séance.

When they entered the room again, Pete spread his arms and slumped back in his chair. "Great. Now we know you didn't find shit. This whole thing is one big joke and a hell of a waste of my time, and I, for one, would love to get on with the rest of my night."

"We did find something, actually," Sam said, feeling his spiteful glare on her.

She returned quickly to her place at the table between

him and Angela. Then she set the earrings in front of Angela and took a seat.

"Little birds," she said. "And there *was* a secret compartment in that desk, just like Caroline said."

Francine was staring at the pair of silver earrings on the table, just like everyone else.

Angela let out a trembling sigh. "Oh my…" She finally picked up the earrings to study them. "These were hers. These were Dina's little hummingbirds. They're her favorite."

Francine nodded sagely, as if she'd known this would happen. "She's back. Caroline. She says … she says she's pleased Dina's belongings have been found. And that it's time to let Dina go. To let everything go. All the secrets. All the lies. And … hmm."

"And *what*?" Elaine prompted. "What else?"

"Caroline insists that until these secrets are unearthed, until someone stands up to be held accountable for what has been done in this place, she will continue to leave signs urging us to let all of it go. Dina especially."

"How great for us," Pete growled. "Any two-bit charlatan can make that shit up on the spot."

"Oh, hush," his wife said, then returned her intense stare to Francine.

"If it was all made up," Angela said, leaning slightly forward to stare at Pete on the other side of Sam, "then how did Caroline's spirit know Dina's earrings were in that desk?"

He glared at her. "It wasn't some spirit. It was all *this* woman. She's a damn phony. Probably planted those earrings in there herself."

"*Excuse* me?" Francine cut in with an indignant frown. "I do *not* appreciate what you're insinuating with that comment, Mr. Wilder. I'll have you know this is the first time I've so much as stepped foot inside this abhorrent club of yours. Me *planting* anything is impossible, and I assure you I've done no such thing."

"The woman's *helping* us, Peter," Elaine added. "Stop being so difficult."

"I don't understand." Angela shook her head. "How could Caroline know so many details about my Dina? What happened here?"

"A waste of fifteen hundred bucks is what happened here," Pete griped.

The quick glance shared between Laila and Francine definitely did not escape Sam's notice.

"I believe," Francine continued before scanning the rest of the table, "that concludes our séance tonight. I don't think Caroline has anything else she wishes us to know. I feel her presence slipping away."

"Thank Christ," Pete muttered.

Francine started to push herself to her feet, then froze, plopped back down in her chair, and closed her eyes. "Wait! There's more… Something else here." Her eyes rolled back in her head, which then whipped from side to side. She clenched her eyes shut and apparently tried to focus on whatever this new trick was supposed to be.

Sam wasn't buying any of it.

But then the woman just had to open her stupid mouth again.

"It's another spirit. A different presence with us. Smaller. Younger. With a message for someone here in this room."

"Who?" Angela asked.

"I … I can't quite tell," Francine said. "But I'm getting another image here. It's faint. The spirit's name… It begins with an S. And she … she wants to say something. If she's willing to meet me, I'll try to let her through."

Before anyone else could say a thing, Francine lurched against her seat again, throwing her head violently back before her jaw dropped open. When she spoke again, eyes closed and her entire body rigid, the voice seeping from her open mouth was not her own. It was something different. High-pitched. Squeaky.

Like that of a very young child.

"I'm sorry, Mommy. I didn't mean to leave."

Sam's knees thumped against the underside of the table in her haste to leave her chair. She hardly felt it, hardly heard the disruptive screech of her chair being shoved backward across the hardwood floor. She leapt to her feet.

She didn't give a fuck what else might have been said or discovered tonight. The whole thing was a fucking joke. And if this woman Francine was going to bring in a child whose name started with an S to give some wannabe-meaningful message like *that*, Sam honestly would've preferred the fucking Sophy's Roses.

When she stormed out of the room, the séance was undoubtedly over.

"Sam!" Angela jogged to catch up with her.

Sam didn't exactly slow down, but she didn't try to outrun the woman, either.

"I'm so sorry for the way that went," Angela said.

"It's fine." Sam tried to shrug it off as she jerked open the door and hurried down the porch steps toward her Jeep.

Her expression remained blank and hardened, but beneath the surface, a raging storm had already begun, and she had no way to escape it.

THIRTY-SIX

Dina

FIVE YEARS AGO...

DINA LURCHED FORWARD, clamping a hand over her mouth as her stomach heaved and a sheen of sweat broke out on her forehead and cheeks. She'd been so hungry before lunch, but now that lunch wasn't going to stay put.

She barely made it to the club's staff bathroom behind the kitchens, thankful to be alone here outside normal business hours. No one could hear her violent retching.

It felt like she spent hours in that bathroom, but when she checked her phone afterward, it had only been about ten minutes.

She grabbed a bottle of mineral water to help settle her stomach, no longer hungry after losing her entire lunch. It didn't help much.

After assuring herself she didn't need to run back to the bathroom, Dina went through the mini-fridge and all the groceries she'd bought this morning. Her first thought was food poisoning, but all the expiration dates were for weeks out at the very soonest, and nothing looked or smelled remotely bad.

She hadn't been drinking recently, either — which she'd tentatively started in the company of the man she now loved but couldn't tell anyone about. A few too many drinks might have caused the strangest delayed hangover in the world, but that wasn't it, either.

So what the hell had just made her so physically ill with zero warning?

No drinking last night, and dinner had been perfectly cooked, candlelit, private, just like all the other dinners they'd shared over the last several months.

A dreamy smile pulled at Dina's lips as she remembered the way last night had ended — perfectly, sweetly, with the warm, heady afterglow of—

"Oh…"

Frowning, Dina pulled out her phone to check the date, then opened a calendar app to start counting backward. She hadn't had much cause to pay close attention to this before. But now?

Now, she definitely had cause.

Her last period was almost six weeks ago.

"That's not…" Dina let out a nervous laugh and scanned the empty kitchen, unable to shake the feeling that she wasn't alone, that she was being watched, that someone else had discovered the cause of her nausea before she did.

That couldn't be possible, could it?

HER TRIP to the smallest pharmacy on the other side of town — far enough away that she was less likely to run into anyone she knew there, especially Kalamack members — took a lot longer than she'd expected.

It was all Dina could do not to take the tests with her into the restroom at the pharmacy, which would have raised questions she didn't want to answer. So she hurried back to the Kalamack Club, instantly regretting her decision to walk all the way across town because now she really had to pee. Plus, she didn't want to wait any longer to confirm whether she was paranoid and slightly off in her math, or if she was about to enter a whole new world of challenges she'd never expected when first coming to Rush.

The directions in the pregnancy test box were easier to follow than she'd expected. Pee on a stick. Wait three minutes. That was it.

Those first three minutes were agony. So were the second three when she decided to use the second one, just to confirm. She'd heard false test results were a thing, and it paid off to know for sure one way or the other.

Both tests were positive.

That certainty came with a whole new laundry list of feelings and thoughts she didn't understand, not to mention a to-do list as long as the rest of her life now. Because this was real.

The world spun around her, and Dina double-checked the lock on the shared restroom door on the clubhouse's second story, in case anyone else with a key happened to stop by. The rationalization that she would have heard anyone coming first didn't matter anymore.

Studying herself with a hand against the wall, Dina returned to the toilet and shakily lowered herself onto the closed seat.

What was she supposed to do now?

More than anything, she wanted to call her mom. This

was the kind of thing daughters called their mothers for, wasn't it? No one else in the world could comfort a young woman in a tight spot quite like her mother, and the thought of hearing Angela's voice almost made Dina cry.

They'd had such a massive fight months ago and still hadn't spoken since. Dina couldn't call her mom now just to tell her she was pregnant. Not as the first thing she said to Angela after that argument.

Maybe her sister?

No, her sister was overly judgmental. She wouldn't understand. She'd never been in love. She wouldn't be able to keep Dina's secret from their mom for very long, either.

That only left one person.

The thought of telling him now about the two positive pregnancy tests sitting in front of her on the bathroom counter made the butterflies in her stomach bash against each other more ferociously than ever.

She had to tell someone. If anyone deserved to know, he did.

She had no idea what to expect.

None of this had been part of her plan.

HEY, *are you busy? We need to talk.*

WAITING FOR HIS REPLY, even when he'd always been so quick to respond, was almost as agonizing as waiting for that second pink line to show up in the window on the plastic stick.

I'LL BE *at the club for Sunday brunch. Talk then?*

. . .

DINA'S FINGERS trembled as she typed a reply.

WE REALLY NEED *to talk before Sunday. It's important.*

HOW ABOUT I *stop by the club tomorrow after work?*

THAT'S A LITTLE RISKY. *A personal talk like this while I'm on the clock.*

RELAX, *beautiful. No one's gonna know. Just say you're taking a break, which you are well within your rights to take. State law. Then meet me in the back. You know where. There aren't any cameras there, either. It's perfectly safe.*

OKAY. *I guess I'll see you when you get to the club, then. We'll talk in the back.*

PERFECT. *Can't wait to see you.*

DINA REREAD the conversation several times before telling herself she needed to leave it alone for now. This wasn't the kind of thing a person could announce over the phone. Not in a text, not in a phone call. Not unless talking in person was completely off the table.

For them, it wasn't.

Maybe she should've explained to him how important

this really was, that it shouldn't wait for tomorrow. But now it was done. She didn't want to make a big deal out of it.

So what if she had to wait a day to tell him? She could just pretend those two positive tests didn't exist.

At least for the next twenty-four hours.

THIRTY-SEVEN

Sam

AFTER DROPPING Angela off at her hotel, Sam slipped into the autopilot functioning that had snuck up on her all the time whenever she'd made one terrible decision after another in quick succession.

Before she fully understood where her brain and body had decided to take her, undermining her at her most vulnerable moment, she found her Jeep lurching to a screeching stop in the Redwood Rings' parking lot before she leapt out and stormed toward the pub.

The noise of a packed bar, even this late at night, hardly phased her as she marched through the doors.

She didn't even notice Chris was right there until she was already behind the bar, reaching for a bottle of slightly higher quality than straight well whiskey.

"Sam?"

The weight of the full bottle in her hand when she lifted it off the liquor shelf propelled her to keep moving, to not stop, to take what she needed because she deserved it, and screw everyone and everything else.

"Hey, hold on a second." Chris's voice buzzed after her

like a goddamn fly that never showed itself despite all the god-awful noise.

Sam swerved around the corner of the bar with the whiskey bottle in hand and headed right back toward the pub's front doors.

Low conversation droned all around her.

Sam saw nothing. She felt nothing. She felt everything.

That was the fucking problem, and she was going to make it stop.

"Wait!"

Sam's free hand tightened around the door handle, and she got the door halfway open before Chris was right there in front of her, not so much closing the door or blocking her way, but almost.

Instead, he'd grabbed her upper arm gently enough not to hurt her but strong enough to catch her attention.

"Sam, hold on. Please." His grip tightened with a small tug, then he propped the door open with his other hand. "What are you doing?"

"Not tonight, Chris."

"That's not an answer. Come on, Sam, talk to me. This isn't—"

"If you don't let go of my arm right now," she snapped, "I'll break your hand, and the last thing you'll see tonight is my foot coming down on your face before you wake up in the hospital. Got it?"

His frown deepened as she finally looked him in the eye with a scathing glare that told him everything he needed to know.

A brief moment of shock across his features almost ripped Sam from her own internal madness, but not quite.

Before he could say anything else, she jerked her arm out of his grasp, shoved him aside with the door, then forced it open enough to make her escape.

The whiskey sloshed rhythmically in her hand as she stormed back to the Jeep, calling her by her true nature, if not by name.

This was where she was supposed to be tonight, it said. This was where Sam would find the solution to all her problems.

It was a warning and a promise all at once, and she no longer gave a shit about telling the difference.

The bottle of Buchanan's remained sealed in the front passenger seat as she drove, but Sam might as well have had a few swigs of it beforehand for all she remembered of the drive across town.

Next thing she knew, she was standing on the Miller Bridge again, not yet swaying drunkenly like the last time she'd come out here but absolutely pushing her way through every ounce of the same pain. Maybe even more tonight, simply because she hadn't yet opened that bottle.

But she wanted to. She was going to. It was right there in her hand, heavy, solid, comforting her with its weight.

Whispering that everything would be fine once she started.

And maybe even when she started, she would never have to stop.

Her phone buzzed in her back pocket again for probably the millionth time, and now that she was out here on the bridge, looking out over the reflection of the stars on the water with no other ambient lighting to block their brightness, she finally decided to answer. She had no idea why.

"What?"

"Jesus, Sam. What's going on?"

Chris was worried. Of course he was worried. He sounded like he was either about to start screaming at her or break down crying. She couldn't tell. She didn't care.

"You need to mind your own business, Chris. And stop fucking calling me about it."

"I've called you about twelve times since you walked out of the pub, and you're only just now answering? You haven't started drinking, have you?"

She didn't want to answer the question.

"Sam? Can you hear me? Did you open that bottle?"

"No," she said flatly.

"Okay," he said with a heavy sigh. "Good. Don't, okay? Keep it closed. You don't need to drink, Sam. Not tonight. Not any night. Just tell me where you are. Then I'll be there, wherever it is. If you need someone with you, I can be there."

"If I'd wanted you to come with me, I would've offered an invitation."

"Sam, I'm serious. This isn't what you want. It won't make anything better. You've worked way too hard to throw it all away."

She hung up. That kind of positive-bullshit thinking was the exact opposite of what she wanted.

Right now, Sam wanted to knock back this entire bottle of Buchanan's. She wanted to be numb. She wanted to drown out everything crashing around inside her to the point that she couldn't even tell where the rage and grief and shame ended and Sam Salazar began.

She wanted an end to the agony of being alive right now, in this moment, with no other viable means of escape.

Slipping her phone into her back pocket again, she took the bottle of the Buchanan's with her toward the railing of the Miller Bridge overlooking the river.

Sam wasn't wasted enough to consider throwing herself off a bridge again. She wasn't wasted at all, which meant that as she stepped up to the bridge rail and seriously contemplated opening the bottle — the crack of the seal snapping off between her hands, the rush of forty-proof alcohol stinging her nose, the semi-sweet burn of it in her mouth and all the way down her throat, setting her on fire from the inside out — she was absolutely sober enough to imagine it all too well.

She was also sober enough to remember everything else that had happened the last time she'd stopped at this bridge with a bottle of liquor in her hand.

How strange it was that on the night Sam had finally convinced herself to end it all, Beth had convinced her there was something else to keep fighting for.

That was how it worked when Sam met people, wasn't it? They were one thing on the outside, something completely different on the inside, and somehow, Sam was a magnet for the type of people who needed help making the inside and the outside match up.

She just couldn't do it for herself.

She'd tried to do it for Angela, but she'd failed again. Sam had stumbled upon some bullshit, spirit-world, séance hoax in the middle of the night and had her entire world turned upside down by two fucking sentences in a little girl's voice spewing from the mouth of a grown-ass woman.

If Angela had been here with her now, they could have shared this bottle.

Then Sam remembered the woman's DUI nearly twenty years ago. How easily Angela had gotten out of it with the legal equivalent of a slap on the wrist. How both her daughters — who had been so little at the time, probably even Sophie's age — had escaped the nightmare that night could have become.

How did any of that make sense? How was any of it fair that Angela Copely could go on a bender, drive her two children around town like it was nothing, be charged with a DUI like it was nothing, and keep on raising her daughters into adulthood like it was nothing?

While Sam had gone to work, out of town, entrusted the one precious thing in her life to a man who should have grown up enough by then to know how important Sophie was, only to lose her sweet baby just like that.

Only for Sophie to slip through her fingers like rushing river water.

And Sam hadn't even fucking been there.

"Fuck it," she hissed.

The crack of the whiskey bottle's seal separating in her hands with one quick twist felt exactly the way she remembered. Sounded exactly the way she remembered. And the smell of the entire bottle when she bent her head over the open top was better than she remembered.

It wasn't fair.

And in a way, maybe it was.

Angela had gotten away with nothing more than a DUI that night, but here she was twenty years later, not having seen or heard from her youngest daughter in five of those years and living that same grief all over again every single day because she had no idea where Dina was or what had happened to her.

Angela wasn't drinking right now. Sam couldn't know for sure, but she was fairly certain that if the woman hadn't opened a bottle at this point, she wouldn't start drinking now.

So how did Sam have more of an excuse to start?

She didn't.

She didn't put the lid back on the bottle either, but she did set that bottle down on the cement sidewalk beneath the bridge railing.

Then she scrolled through the numbers in her phone,

looking at the names of people she could call who would actually know how to give her what she needed. Not that she had any idea what that was. Chris hadn't either.

Sam came across Beth's number first, still in her phone, still tied to the number that had once been Beth's and might or might not have already been reassigned by now.

And why shouldn't it have been? Beth wasn't using it anymore.

She probably should delete it. But now just wasn't the time to clean house. Not now.

She paused again at Meredith's name, almost made that call, then remembered Meredith hadn't been her best self lately, either.

Her gaze finally settled on Hector's name with his saved number, and her thumb slid over the call button before she could talk herself out of it.

Part of her hoped he would pick up. She pressed her phone to her ear and listened to the tinny ring.

Part of her hoped he wouldn't. That he was already asleep. That it was far too late at night for anyone to help her now.

Just more excuses.

But he did answer. Though she didn't remember giving it to him, apparently, he'd already saved her number too.

"Hey, Sam. How's it going?"

"Shitty." She swallowed and forced herself to say what really needed to be said right now, out loud and in the ear of another living person who could hold her accountable to it. "I'm literally standing on a bridge right now with an open bottle of whiskey next to me, and all I want to do is drink myself into oblivion before I jump off the other side of this railing."

"Huh."

That was all he said, which confused her to no end until she wondered if he'd even heard her.

"Hector? You still there?"

"Just waiting to see if you had anything else to say."

"No." Sam stared out at the churning surface of the river again, achingly aware of how close she'd set the open whiskey bottle at her feet. "That's about it."

"All right. Why don't you come on over to my place, huh? We can talk more if you want. Or not talk at all. Whatever feels right, we'll figure it out."

Sam grimaced. "It's late, man."

"Uh-huh. Almost one thirty in the morning. Trust me, Sam, I'm still awake. And I'd rather stay awake with you coming over than head off to sleep not knowing what the hell happened. Why don't you—"

His voice cut off beneath the background noise of raucous laughter and incredibly loud music blasting to life. Hector rattled something off in Spanish, which of course Sam didn't understand. Then all the background noise faded into something less coherent but made it a hell of a lot easier to understand what he said next.

"Just come over, Sam. Don't worry about the rest of it. I'll text you the address. You're at the Miller Bridge, I'm guessing?"

"That's right."

"Then I'm expecting you to be here in twenty minutes or less. Don't keep me waiting."

He ended the call, and Sam could have laughed if she wasn't in such a damn-awful place right now.

Hector's text with his home address came through, and Sam knew exactly where it was, giving her six or seven minutes of wiggle room within that twenty-minute expectation. But trying to kill time without doing something she'd regret later felt like a total waste.

At least she had somewhere to go that wasn't straight back to her trailer in the middle of the night to sit at home alone with a full bottle of whiskey at her side.

She still picked up the open bottle at her feet, screwed the lid back on, and stuck it in the back seat before taking off toward Hector's.

THIRTY-EIGHT

Sam

HECTOR LIVED WELL beyond the populated areas of Rush, though not nearly as far outside town as the myriad farms surrounding it. The property was decent sized, with a sprawling yard of flat, closely clipped grass somehow kept relatively green even toward the end of the year when most other lawns had started to brown for the winter.

There were three homes on the property, all spread out with comfortable distance between them. Sam drove her Jeep all the way up to the middle house. The white picket fence surrounding all three buildings made the place look more like a single property on a larger bit of land than just a mobile home stuck out in the middle of nowhere with two of its neighbors. Half a dozen other cars were parked randomly in the short grass. There was no driveway after the dirt road ended far before the houses began. No parking lot.

Sam parked behind the farthest car and couldn't bring herself to leave the Jeep.

The second she opened her door to the sound of

dozens of laughing, chatting voices and the smell of home-cooked meals and some fast-paced *mariachi* music blasting from the well-lit interior of the center house, she closed it again.

Being surrounded by a whole bunch of people, whether they were partying or just hanging out, didn't feel like the best idea right now.

Instead of getting out to knock on Hector's door, she sent him a text to let him know she was here.

A minute later, the center house's front door opened, and Hector stepped out with two large, plain white paper cups in hand. He didn't stop to scan the cars haphazardly parked around his front lawn but headed straight toward Sam's Jeep.

She couldn't bring herself to get out and meet him, but she did unlock the Jeep just as Hector reached her.

He climbed into the passenger seat, set one of the paper cups between his legs, and pulled the door shut. More fast-paced, animated Mexican music and all those happy voices cut out again. For a moment, he just sat there beside Sam and stared straight ahead through the front windshield. The silence between them lasted long enough for Sam to wonder if she'd made a serious mistake by coming here.

Then Hector extended one of the paper cups her way without looking at her and simply said, "Want a Coke?"

"Yeah. Thanks." She took it, also without looking, and they stayed like that for what felt like forever.

Hector sipped his drink. Sam didn't touch hers. Somehow, holding a beverage and knowing there was nothing in it but sugar and caffeine made her feel just a little better.

"I take it that séance didn't go too well tonight, huh?"

Sam clicked her tongue. "That's a safe assumption."

"Wanna talk about it?"

She didn't think so. But with her next breath, she found herself speaking all the same, opening up as much as she dared because she'd already made the effort to call him and drive out here.

"It was supposed to be for someone else. Talking to a ghost or spirit or whatever to get information for someone else. That woman, Angela, who I've been helping out the last few days around town."

"Uh-huh." Hector nodded. "Did she find what she was looking for?"

"I have no idea. I wasn't really expecting anything, definitely not something that applied to *me* in any way. But then that fucking woman had to open her mouth about a child…" Her voice broke, and Sam finally took a huge gulp of the ice-cold Coke because that was the only way to wash down the bitterness filling her now. "A little girl whose name started with an S, apparently. And she wanted to send a message. To say she was sorry. That she didn't mean to leave."

Sam hated the way her voice quivered as she spoke. While her nose stung with the burn of oncoming tears, those tears never fully arrived. She couldn't let them. Not now. Not ever, if she had her way.

"Sounds like that tore you up a bit," Hector said.

"It shouldn't have. I don't even believe in that shit, you know? Ghosts, spirits, speaking to the dead. It's all a load of crap, and I just … I don't get why it hit me so hard. It shouldn't have hit me so hard. It wasn't real."

Hector took another sip of his drink. "Sometimes, it doesn't matter what we do or don't believe. There's still certain things out there that hit us where it hurts. Certain things out there that believe in us, whether or not we wanna see it. I did tell you it was a bad idea to go play around with dead-people stuff, didn't I?"

Sam snorted and lifted her cup toward him in a silent toast. "You sure did, Hector. I should've listened to you."

"So what happens next, then?"

Sam shrugged and dropped her head back against the headrest with a muffled thump. "Beats me. I had to drive Angela back to her hotel afterward, and she told me this Francine woman thought the Kalamack Club could use an exorcist, which honestly sounds like the dumbest fucking thing anyone could possibly say after what went down tonight."

"I wouldn't knock it entirely." Hector's next slow, burbling slurp over the rim of his paper cup filled the Jeep. "I didn't warn you away from the séance 'cause I thought it was useless or 'cause I don't believe. I believe there's plenty out there we don't know and can't battle on our own without a little help from time to time." For the first time, he turned to look at her, but Sam still couldn't bring herself to meet anyone's gaze right now. "And I believe in exorcisms. If that's really what that place needs next, and hell, there's a decent chance it does, there's only one person in this town capable of doing a thing like that and doing it right."

That finally made Sam look at him. "You know an exorcist too?"

Just the fact that she'd asked the question out loud brought the barest twitch of a smile to the corners of her mouth.

He nodded. Shrugged. Drank more Coke. "Sure I do. Watched a few of 'em myself, though I gotta admit, it's not really my thing. I ever tell you my brother's a priest?"

"Your brother."

"Eduardo. For damn near his whole adult life. Certified and ordained by the Catholic Church and the Vatican itself to perform exorcisms in all shapes and sizes."

"Doesn't that only work for, like, people who are possessed?" Sam had no idea why she was entertaining this conversation at all. She didn't believe in possession either. Or demons. Or angels. Or anything related to whatever a priest's duties entailed. But now that he'd brought it up, for some reason, she couldn't stop herself.

"The way I see it, if you're living or working or spending enough time in a place that has its own haunt, as it were, that counts as a possession of its own kind, don't it? Still takes over your mind the same way. Still feeds into fear, pain, shame sometimes. Now I don't claim to be an expert or anything. I'll leave that up to my *hermanito*. But I think it's worth looking into. Worth asking a few questions about. If they want the Kalamack Club to get its own exorcism, Eduardo's the person they should call. No doubt about it."

"Maybe I'll pass along the message," she said. "Not that the Wilders would listen to anything I have to say about it. Especially not after tonight."

"You never know. Might be useful for you too, if you're open to looking into it."

Sam frowned at him. "Open to what? Getting an exorcism?"

Hector flashed her a crooked smile and tilted his head. "Not necessarily. I suppose you could think of it along the same lines. But what I'm really referring to here is this haunting you've been dealing with all on your own."

"It's the Kalamack Club's haunting."

"I'm not talking about the Kalamack Club, Sam. Or anyone else's ghosts. I'm talking about yours."

When she looked up at him again, she couldn't look

away. The man had finally fully caught her attention, and she wanted him to both further explain and say nothing else for the rest of the night at the same time.

"You know what I mean," Hector said with another sage nod. "Little girl whose name starts with S? If you ask me, you've been haunted by that one a hell of a lot longer than just some hokey, irreverent séance tonight."

"You mean Sophie," Sam whispered.

"I mean Sophie."

"And you think I should just exorcise my daughter from myself? Wipe out my memory of her? Force her out like some demonic presence? Is *that* why you think I called you tonight?"

Hector didn't take the bait. She didn't expect him to, but she also couldn't control her flaring bursts of anger or what spilled from her mouth during them.

Fortunately, Hector had plenty of experience letting the angry words of recovering friends in pain roll right off his back. "I'm not saying any of that, either. But I do wonder if you might not benefit from ending this personal haunting of yours too."

"And how exactly am I supposed to do that, Hector?"

"You let her go, Sam."

They stared at each other for an increasingly long moment. Then she scoffed and shook her head. "I can't do that."

"Why not?"

"She's my daughter. I know she's gone. But all I have left of her is—" Sam's voice broke again, and her lower lip trembled before she pressed her knuckles into it to hold it still. Whether or not Hector had seen her brief moment of unencumbered emotion, she had no idea. It didn't really matter at this point.

"If I do that," she tried again after a deep breath, "I

have no idea what happens next. But I'm terrified that if I … if I just *let her go*, I won't have anything holding me here anymore. And then I'll just end it. Just like that. Nothing else left to stop me."

Hector mulled over her words, then finally replied, "I suppose that's more about how you wanna look at it. Whether there's nothing else to keep you here, or nothing left to push you toward leaving."

Sam thought she understood what he meant. She would've asked him to elaborate just in case, but her phone buzzed with another incoming text.

She'd left it in the cup holder in the center console, so it wasn't like she could hide the fact that Chris had sent her *another* message. Especially when her phone vibrated so loudly and his name popped up in the middle of her screen, backlit brightly enough for both her and Hector to clearly see.

"Looks like you got something, there," he said.

"Maybe."

"Not that I'm trying to pry, but when the first part of a text like that says, 'I need to know you're okay,' it stands to reason you've got someone who cares about you on the other side of that message. Someone who cares enough to worry where you are."

"Sure looks like it, doesn't it?" Now Sam couldn't stop staring at her phone.

"You should text him back, at the very least, Sam. If you're not drinking, there's no reason to make the man worry about you any more than he already does. Let him know you're all right."

She scoffed. "Like he's gonna believe that just because I replied to a text."

He shrugged. "Tell him you're fine. You're with your sponsor, and you haven't touched a drop."

It was reasonable enough. Sam found it remarkably easy to follow those instructions to the letter. Probably because she didn't have to say anything else with those three simple facts typed out in three short, simple statements. Then she sent the text and dropped her phone back into the cup holder.

"I guess you're my sponsor now, huh?"

"Guess I am."

They sat in her Jeep for another fifteen minutes, sipping on their Cokes and staring through the front windshield at the lit-up house in the center of Hector's property.

When Sam knocked back the rest of her Coke, she tossed the empty paper cup over her shoulder into the back. "Thanks, Hector. For talking. For listening. For answering your phone in the first place."

He met her gaze and nodded. "You're welcome. You wanna come inside? Something tells me you're not exactly planning to go straight home and right to sleep. Not now, anyway. Come on. Meet the family. We've got some *real* Mexican food too. Been cooking the last two days out back. Closest you're gonna get to the real thing, especially around here."

"No, thanks. I'm not hungry. To tell you the truth, I don't think being around that many people would be very good for me right now. This right here, though? This is exactly what I needed. And I — hold on." Sam turned around in her seat and reached into the back for the bottle of Buchanan's on the floor. When she lifted it over the console and straightened again, she stared at it for a good five seconds before handing it toward him. "Will you take this for me? Just so I don't have it anymore."

"Not so sure that's the best way to get rid of a thing like that," he said, eyeing the whiskey bottle with as much longing as hesitation. "But you know what? I've got a better idea. Come on."

Hector got out and waited for Sam to follow, all without taking the bottle from her in the first place.

She joined him on that side of her Jeep, wide-eyed and clueless and holding an opened but still completely full bottle of Buchanan's out in front of her like someone had stuck a gasoline-soaked rag into the top and lit the end. "What's this better idea?"

"Hold it steady."

While Sam kept a firm grip on the bottle, Hector reached out, twisted off the cap, and raised an eyebrow when the seal didn't offer that telltale crack. Sam wrinkled her nose and shook her head. He nodded.

The cap disappeared into the night when he chucked it across his neatly kept lawn.

Hector grabbed the full bottle of whiskey just below Sam's hand and whispered, "Now pour."

Together, they held the bottle upside down by two firm hands, watching the Buchanan's chug violently as they stood there in silence, neither willing to let the other slip.

Not tonight.

Part of Sam ached at the sight of so much booze soaking into the earth at their feet, especially when the air smelled like she'd already been drinking all night. It was a small part of her.

The rest of her knew this was the right thing, that she'd made the right decision after all. For now.

Only when the bottle was empty did Hector let go. "Feel free to chuck that thing wherever you want."

"Thanks for the permission." Sam folded her arms, the empty whiskey bottle dangling by its neck from her finger-tips, and studied the older man she'd known only from their shared NA meetings. "So, what's your story, huh? I haven't heard you share in a meeting yet. Figured you've either been in the rooms long enough to not need to share anymore or you're almost as new to this as I am…"

Hector clapped a hand on her shoulder and offered her one final small, crooked smile. "Good night, Sam. Drive safe."

~

SHE MADE it back to Birdsong Park at just after 2:30 a.m., which had quickly become her new normal, apparently. She noted a specific lack of both town barricades at the property entrance and any form of flowers left outside her trailer, roses or otherwise.

The rest of the park, which this time of year consisted only of Syc and Dog and Sam, was entirely silent.

Sam hadn't felt her own exhaustion until she realized that, for now, she was completely alone and could finally relax. She'd made it home without a drink or an attempt to find something stronger. She'd made it through one more night. That was what mattered.

When she opened the door to the Deville and stepped inside, a light instantly switched on farther inside. Sam lunged for the crowbar she kept just inside the front door where most people kept a coatrack or umbrella stand.

In two seconds, that crowbar was hefted in both hands and hauled back over her shoulder, ready to swing. "Stop where you are!"

Chris did exactly that.

"Whoa, whoa, hey!" The second his vision adjusted to the light he'd turned on and he saw her standing there like a pro baseball player ready to crack his head off into a home run, he lifted both hands and staggered backward. "Sam, it's me!"

She was still catching her breath. Now she looked him up and down with the crowbar still swung over her shoulder, debating whether or not it was still a good idea to use the thing. "What the fuck are you doing in my trailer, Chris?"

"Waiting for you. It was unlocked. I didn't see your Jeep, but I thought, you know, you'd probably come home eventually. Then I got your text and figured you might want somebody to talk to you when you did." He looked her up and down and raised his eyebrows. "What happened to the Buchanan's?"

"Yeah, listen...sorry about that." The crowbar swung down in front of her and clinked against the poorly laid linoleum floor before she set it upright against the wall again. "I'll pay you back for the bottle, Chris. I promise. You can take it out of my paycheck, or I'll just cough it up out of my tips next time I'm in."

"You didn't answer my question."

"I didn't drink it, if that's what you wanna know." She folded her arms. "I dumped it out all over a nice little patch of grass on the other side of town. Kinda sacrilegious, brand-new bottle and everything. I get it. But I promise I'll pay you back."

"Shut up about paying me back." Chris finally dropped his hands and headed toward her. "I don't give a shit about the whiskey, okay?"

When he stopped inches in front of her and reached up to cup her face in both hands, Sam didn't feel the need to pull away. In fact, she might have even leaned into it.

"I care about *you*, Sam," he added softly. "And that's it."

They stood like that for a moment, gazing at each other. Sam was surprised to find she could look him in the eyes for as long as she needed. Tonight, she hadn't done anything to be ashamed of or that she had felt she had to hide.

It also surprised her when a smile flickered across her lips and she lifted her face even more toward his. "Then prove it."

THIRTY-NINE

Sam

WHEN SAM WOKE the next morning at what seemed like an acceptable time — with the sun already peeking through the thin curtains covering the window above her bed — Chris was gone.

She hadn't expected that, though she couldn't blame him.

Chris wasn't the only thing missing from her morning.

There were no roses outside her Deville, either.

She wasn't sure how she felt about that, whether she wanted to be relieved and take it as a good sign that the harassment had finally stopped or if she actually felt disheartened by the lack of bouquets on her doorstep, knowing there were supposed to have been seven and she'd only received three.

It didn't matter.

After splashing some water on her face, Sam grabbed her phone and found a new voicemail waiting for her. The missed call came from an unknown number, but curiosity had always been one of her more endearing attributes — when it didn't get her into insane amounts of trouble.

She put her phone on speaker and played the voicemail before heading into the Deville's tiny, cramped kitchen to start a pot of coffee.

"HELLO. *This message is for Sam Salazar. It's Greg. Dr. Greg Masterson. You and your friend, Angela, I think it was, came up to my cabin a few days ago, asking questions about the Kalamack Club. I'd actually like a chance to speak with you again about that, if you don't mind. Just you this time. Don't bring your friend. It's hard enough to talk about on its own, but I only want to have the conversation just the two of us. If that's something you're still interested in, you can give me a call back or just stop by whenever's convenient for you. You know where I live, and, well, I'm retired, so I'll be here. Hopefully, I hear back from you or see you pulling up again in the near future. If you have any questions first, this is my number. Obviously. Feel free to call me back. All right, thanks."*

INTERESTING VOICEMAIL.

She played it again from the beginning as she finished filling the coffee pot and turned it on to start brewing.

Couldn't hurt to have one more friendly chat with the good Dr. Greg. Anyone who said they wanted to speak with her privately and in person obviously had something fairly juicy to say.

That was fine by her. Sam could go up there, give this retired Dr. Greg a few minutes of her time to hear him out, and if it was important enough to share with Angela, she'd share it with Angela later.

After coffee, she showered and dressed for the day, then piled into her Jeep and set out.

Only she didn't make it any farther than the turnoff entrance to Birdsong Park because lo and behold, someone had replaced the town barricades blocking off the park's entrance. Even after she and Syc had burned the last batch.

With those new barricades came a typed-up missive printed in large, bold black letters and tacked to the center barricade right in plain view.

It had even been laminated, for crying out loud.

To Whom It May Concern:

All renters, residents, and visitors within Birdsong Park Trailer Park claiming this property as their own personal residence, either permanent or temporary, are hereby served with this legal notice to vacate the premises within the next thirty (30) calendar days from the date of this document.

Failure to comply will result in legal action and possible fines of up to $15,000.

Thank you in advance for your understanding and timely cooperation.

Mayor Pete Wilder

Rush, California

BELOW THAT GODAWFUL send-off was Little Pete's signature, immediately followed by incredibly small print at the bottom referencing whatever sort of town zoning laws the man and his attorneys had dredged up from the bowels of Rush's founding legal structures. A bunch of legal-citation bullshit to claim precedence and potentially dissuade any and all residents from trying to fight such a declaration.

Sam wasn't about to sit here and try to make out the incredibly small type to then go looking up the town zoning laws and property codes or whatever other official bullshit was involved.

She did, however, get out of her Jeep to kick the

notice sign around a few times until it fluttered into the browning grass. Then she spent the next five minutes yanking and pushing the new set of barricades out of the road all by herself so she could actually get out into town.

Thirty days was long enough, and Sam was sure she and Syc could figure out how to reverse this insanely banal issue before their time ran out. Right now, she had to get out of the park, down the frontage road to the highway, and all the way up past Rip's farm one more time to talk to a young yet retired doctor who apparently had more to say.

~

THOUGH SHE'D BEEN SPECIFICALLY LOOKING for it, Sam missed the turnoff to Greg's property again and had to turn around on the narrow, bumpy, poorly maintained dirt road before slowly scanning the overgrown sides of the frontage road just to find the damn thing.

There was no Dr. Greg standing outside by the tree stump, coming down on hunks of wood with his axe. In fact, there was no sign of the man at all.

Even more unusual was the front door of Greg's cabin had been left wide open, as if the man had left in a hurry and forgotten to close up behind himself.

Or as if someone else had gone through his home without knowing how to clean up after themselves.

Sam parked in the dirt lot, then scanned the openness of the property surrounded by trees as her sneakers crunched across the dirt and pebbles leading to the front of the cabin.

But when she reached the front porch and that open door, it still felt prudent to knock anyway.

There was no response from inside or anywhere else on the property.

"Hello? Greg? It's Sam. I got your message. Obviously. You home?"

Still nothing.

She turned around, studying the long dirt road through the trees.

Something niggled at the back of Sam's mind.

Greg had called her because he'd wanted to talk. Alone. He wouldn't have made himself this difficult to find, and he'd sounded particularly genuine in his voicemail.

She stood on the front porch for another two minutes before finally deciding to walk inside anyway. If she stumbled upon him getting out of the shower or something, she could apologize for the oversight and promise to call ahead next time.

But if something had happened, if Greg was in danger somehow or missing altogether, Sam couldn't live with herself knowing she'd had her suspicions but had done absolutely nothing to disprove them.

She headed into the house, calling out his name gently at first but then louder. Her footsteps echoed on the smoothly sanded wooden floors. Still no response, no sign of the man's presence in his own home.

Sam made her way across the cabin, meaning to walk down the short hallway toward what she assumed were the back bedroom and maybe a bathroom.

On her way, she passed the large tables in the back set closely together as a spacious kitchen counter, and all it took was a single look behind them.

There he was, lying on the floor behind the tables, limbs akimbo, his nose, cheeks, and mouth smeared with blood.

Sam raced toward him and pulled out her cell to dial 911 as she dropped to her knees at Greg's side.

She turned the call on speaker, set her phone on the floor, and felt for a pulse at the side of the man's neck.

It was definitely there. Good info to have.

While the 911 dispatcher asked about her emergency, Sam hefted a surprisingly heavy, unconscious Dr. Greg away from the floor and into the recovery position, propping him up against the corner of the kitchen's far wall and the row of cabinets.

He was still out cold.

She offered emergency dispatch what few details she had, but she did make sure to include a heads-up for the paramedics and EMTs to pay close attention to the overgrown turn-offs along the frontage road so they could avoid having to make a hundred-point turn in an ambulance.

After ensuring dispatch that she would remain on the premises until the qualified authorities and first responders arrived, Sam ended the call. She checked Greg's pulse and breathing again and decided he wasn't in any immediate danger. He stirred a bit now that she'd pulled him slightly up off the floor, but he hadn't regained consciousness.

After that, all Sam had left to do was wait.

If there hadn't been a bloodied, unconscious man half-sitting up, half-laid out in his own kitchen, she would have preferred to wait outside. But seeing as she and Greg had something of a previous rapport and he'd just recently invited her to his home, it felt more appropriate to do her waiting inside instead.

So she perused the man's cabin again. When she stopped at the small side table in the main room and stared down at the landline phone sitting there — amazing that anyone still had a landline anymore, but this was Rush — she couldn't help herself. She grabbed the phone off its cradle, pressed the Redial button to pull up the last number called from this phone, and found herself reading the Caller ID name scrolling across the phone's small, digital window above the keypad: *Hank Topping Real Estate*.

Interesting. At least it wasn't *Sam's* number.

Looked like Dr. Greg was getting busy with his phone calls. Especially for a man who'd physically removed himself from the rest of Rush so many years ago on purpose.

She heard the sirens five minutes before the ambulance and two police cruisers finally pulled down the aggravatingly long dirt road of Greg's property. Then Sam stepped outside to silently alert them to her continued presence here.

Just her luck that Chief Colton happened to be one of the dispatched officers sent out this morning. The man wasted no time in leaping out of his squad car and angrily marching toward her the second he noticed Sam on the porch.

She figured she'd help him out a little and meet him halfway, lifting a hand in greeting as she walked down the stairs.

He said nothing until they stood face to face. "What the hell are you doing here, Salazar?"

"Oh, you know. Just passing the time. Thought it would make for a fun morning. What about you, Chief?"

His scowl never wavered. "You know exactly what I mean. Every time there's some kind of upset in this town, I find you on the other side of it. Care to explain why that's suddenly become your new hobby?"

"I wouldn't call it a hobby. But today specifically, I was invited up here. The doc and I had an appointment. When I showed up, I found him laid out on the floor in his own kitchen." Sam jerked her head toward the open front door where two paramedics had just disappeared to tend to Greg.

Colton ignored them. In fact, he seemed oblivious to all the other hurried activity on the premises. She couldn't blame him. The chief had to be used to all the bustling back and forth like this by now.

Unfortunately, he ignored everything else in lieu of continuously scrutinizing Sam almost like he had it out for her personally.

Which, looking at it from his perspective, she could also understand.

"Bullshit you had an appointment," he growled.

"No, really. He left me a message and everything. Invited me right on up. You're welcome to listen to it if you want."

He looked over, then nodded brusquely and grunted.

So it had devolved into grunts and nods and zero words now, huh?

"Fine." Sam fished out her phone and pressed play on the most recent voicemail. Greg's tinny, virtually recorded voice rang through the clearing above the conversation of the other officers, the paramedics, and over multiple radios. When the voicemail finished, Colton looked even angrier to have heard the whole thing than he'd been to find Sam Salazar already on the scene.

"So he asked you up here for a chat? Great. What did he wanna talk to you about?"

"If he'd wanted me to know beforehand, Chief, that probably would've been included in the voicemail."

"Just answer the question," he snapped.

"I have no idea. And it's really none of your business. So I'd start asking different questions if I were you."

She shouldn't have said it like that, but Sam was also at

the end of her own patience, and now she'd clearly pushed Colton to the brink of his.

He snarled and stepped closer, lowering his voice amidst the chaotic noise all around them. "You don't wanna tell me? That's fine. But then I have to tell *you* that it just makes you seem all the more suspicious. You know that, right?"

Sam cocked her head. "You mean there's a time when you're not automatically suspicious of me from the start?"

"You know what I think, Salazar? I think you've been up here a while. I think the doc said something you didn't like, and you're the one who knocked him out and left him on his own kitchen floor. Then I think your guilty conscience got the better of you, and you thought you could call 911, get him the help he needed, and skirt right through this whole thing with none of us the wiser."

Sam snorted. "If I was the one who made this mess, that's a pretty stupid move. Call 911, provide all my personal information as requested, then stick around to wait for an ambulance? Doesn't exactly scream criminal self-preservation, Chief. What do *you* think?"

"I don't know what to think when I see you where you're not supposed to be. But I do know I don't like it."

"The facts don't change based on whether or not you *like* them. Trust me, I know. Besides, do I look like I've just been in a fight with anyone?" Sam spread her arms and gave him an extra second to look her over. "I'm not out of shape or anything, but Greg's been up here playing lumberjack all by himself for the last several years. I'd be seriously impressed by anyone who could fight the guy, do what they did to him, and walk away without so much as a scratch."

Colton shook his head. "You just keep running your

mouth, don't you? One of these days, that mouth is gonna lead you straight behind bars."

"That's an interesting theory. Wanna place a wager on it?"

He sneered at her, then forced himself to look away. "You know what, Salazar? If you don't have anything useful to add, why don't you just go back to your vehicle. Wait there. I'll let you know what happens next."

"Sure thing, Chief. You're the one calling the shots."

She did as he said, only because it wasn't worth either of their time for her to fight emergency-response protocol based on principle alone. No, she and Colton weren't fond of each other, but that didn't mean she had to make things significantly more difficult for him here, especially when she'd looked forward to hearing exactly what Dr. Greg had sounded so eager to discuss with her.

She didn't make it to her Jeep, though, because when her gaze fell on another officer standing beside one of the squad cars, Sam couldn't help but seize the open opportunity.

One more glance over her shoulder confirmed that Colton had finally entered Greg's cabin and was therefore out of earshot for the moment, so she headed toward the lone cop.

He didn't seem surprised to see her approach.

"Hell of a way to start the day, huh?" she asked, stopping beside him and turning to face the cabin.

The officer acknowledged her with a sidelong glance and half a nod.

"I don't know if you were told any of this," she said, "but I'm the one who found the doctor on the front porch of the Kalamack Club. The *other* doctor. Reginald Jones."

The officer nodded. "That was a tough day too."

"Yeah, no kidding. Actually, I never heard anything

more about him after the fact. Chief Colton told me the coroner would have to decide on the cause of death after the autopsy, obviously. Did they figure out exactly how he died?"

The officer finally turned to look at her for what felt like the first time, or at least with more attention before. "I thought you said you were the one who found him."

"I was. But there's always a chance that what looks like a suicide is actually something else just dressed up to keep looking like a suicide so people stop asking questions. I've been worrying about it this whole time, you know? It would just be *devastating* to hear there was some kinda murderer on the loose in our town. Someone who's either brave enough or stupid enough to commit such an awful crime right there on the front porch of the Kalamack Club. People won't be happy when they hear *that's* the real story…"

She'd hoped this guy would take the bait, and maybe it was due to the extra hustle and bustle around Greg's cabin today, but the officer seemed completely ignorant to her intentions, and he bit.

"Yeah, the coroner confirmed it as a suicide," he said. "And you can tell anyone who tries saying otherwise to mind their own business and quit spreading rumors about something like that when they have absolutely no idea what happened."

Sam shot him a quick smile and nodded. "Absolutely, Officer. I can do that, no problem. Thank you."

After that, she headed to her Jeep, ready to get the hell out of here now because she clearly wasn't having that secretive last-minute discussion with Dr. Greg the way she'd wanted. When no one tried to stop her from climbing behind the wheel, she figured it was safe to leave.

It was all she could do not to peel out of Dr. Greg's

private dirt drive and race back around the twisting turns toward the frontage road. No one came after her then, either. Once she turned back onto the highway again, she stepped on the gas to book it back into town.

SAM DIDN'T KNOW where she'd go next or what she'd do when she got there, but something didn't sit right about Dr. Greg's whole situation. Especially the fact that the man had apparently been speaking with Hank Topping or someone in the man's employ mere hours or even minutes before being attacked in his home.

The call he'd made to Sam obviously hadn't been his last, but somehow, she couldn't imagine Hank Topping driving all the way up to the middle of nowhere in the mountainous boonies just to trade a few punches with the retired doctor who'd been socially exiled for years.

Then another face entered her mind, and immediately, Sam settled on a new last-minute plan, which she intended to carry out now simply because it felt right.

Fifteen minutes later, she'd parked in Michelle Jones' driveway and now marched up the steps of the woman's front porch. This time, there were no screaming children inside, no baby wailing, no shouting voices. The door opened in a matter of seconds.

No surprise that Shell stood on the other side. What was concerning, however, were the woman's puffy, red-rimmed eyes and the bright-red splotches across her cheeks and flushing down the sides of her neck.

Sam didn't know this woman very well, but she did know what any woman looked like after spending significant time crying and fully expecting no one else would be around anytime soon to see it.

FORTY

Sam

"SAM. HI. COME IN, PLEASE." Shell backed away from the door to make room.

The place looked completely different since Sam was here last.

All the toys were put away. No dishes left out on the tables or counters. Zero screaming toddlers or five-year-olds chucking toys from the top of the stairs.

"I'm sorry. I'm a mess." Shell spun back and forth, looking like she had too much to do but couldn't decide where to get started.

"Get the kids down for an early nap?" Sam asked.

"No, my mother-in-law stopped by earlier to pick them up. She wanted all three with her. Said it's because she doesn't want to be in that giant house of theirs all alone... I can understand why."

"Benefit of having grandkids," Sam said. "And I'm so sorry for your loss, Shell."

"Thank you." The woman finally stopped fidgeting on her feet and met Sam's gaze. "I appreciate that. Oh, and thank you so much for the flowers. They're lovely."

378

"Flowers?"

"I put them on the dining room table. They add a little life and color to the day. For as much as it counts, anyway." Shell gestured toward the table, at the center of which rested a clear crystal vase with an impressively large and elegantly arranged bouquet of flowers in darker seasonal colors.

Angela must have immediately purchased them for Shell and her family as soon as Sam agreed to it. At least the woman hadn't bought one of those god-awful funeral wreaths.

"*That's* what I was about to do!" Shell snapped her fingers, then pointed farther into the house. "I need coffee. Obviously. Would you like some?"

"That's one thing I'll never turn down," Sam said. "Even if it's awful, which I'm sure yours isn't."

"You'll have to try it first." Shell led her through the house, which was startlingly quiet without the Three-Jones-Kids circus in attendance.

That provided them an opportunity for uninterrupted conversation, which was exactly why Sam had driven out here in the first place, though she waited until the coffee had finished brewing and Shell brought two freshly filled mugs and all the extras to the round kitchen table.

"What can I help you with, Sam?" Shell asked as she sipped her coffee. "We've been getting a lot of condolences and care packages, and that's all been nice. For what it's worth. You already sent flowers. You stopped by in person. Now you still wanna talk. Something tells me you're not exactly the kind of woman who sticks around just for fun after checking anything off her to-do list."

Sam finished stirring the sugar around in her otherwise black coffee and left the spoon in her mug. "You're right.

Actually, I wanted to talk to you a little more about Dr. Greg Masterson."

"The one who moved all the way up into the mountains past Rip's farm?" Shell asked.

"The one and only."

"I don't know him all that well…"

"That's fine." Sam sipped her coffee, held back a grimace, and added more sugar. "I just wanna pick your brain about the guy and whatever relationship he might've had with Dina."

Shell's eyes widened. "You're still checking into Dina?"

"Yep. And something tells me Greg knew a little more about her than he let on when Angela and I went up to his place the other day."

"What did he tell you?" Shell asked.

"Not much."

"Then he was definitely holding something back." Shell didn't seem to taste her coffee as she stared blankly at the tabletop. "He was in love with her, for one."

"Really? So Dina had more than one secret admirer, huh?"

"I don't think any of her admirers were all that secret, actually," Shell said. "She was insanely charismatic. I've already told you how quickly she settled into life in Rush, being part of the Kalamack Club, getting all the members and their families on her good side, ingratiating herself with the upper crust, blah blah blah. Back then, at least, she was the kinda person who appealed to literally all walks of life."

"As evidenced by first Jordan and now Dr. Greg having been head-over-heels for this girl, right?" Sam asked.

"Exactly." Shell nodded. The soft, nostalgic smile briefly flickering across her expression snuffed out just as quickly into a pained grimace. "Maybe it was all the secrecy and sneaking around that did it. Maybe she was just one of those girls who'd been cooped up in her childhood for so long, she went in the complete opposite direction the second she got a taste of freedom. But Dina really went after it when she got that job at the Kalamack Club. She was part of high society just like that. Just as beautiful and just as ruthless as the rest of them."

"What happened with Greg, then?" Sam asked.

"Nothing, I imagine."

"Did he ever tell her?"

"He didn't have to. Everyone knew. It was painfully obvious. But Dina was already in love with someone else. I don't think she felt much of anything for anyone else once that relationship started."

"You mean the secret boyfriend from the club?" Sam asked.

Shell nodded, pressing her lips tightly together.

Sam studied her reaction and decided to go with her gut here instead of being gentle. "Dina told you who he was, didn't she?"

Shell stared back at her, eyes widening by the second, but her lips never moved.

That was a yes.

"Shell, I need to know who he was," Sam continued. "This whole thing with Dina has gotten way too complicated, way too fast, and ninety percent of it is because people refuse to talk. Generally, with secrets, that's a good thing. But in this case, when a young woman goes missing, when your friend goes missing and her own mother doesn't know what happened to her, I'd say opening up a little is the least you can do to help."

"She made me promise not to tell anyone," Shell said softly.

"Same thing goes for promises. All bets are off when someone's life is on the line."

Sam didn't want to get her hopes up and preemptively prepared herself to leave without the information she needed.

Then Shell sighed heavily, took another sip of coffee, and closed her eyes. "It was Hank. Hank Topping."

"Thank you, Shell," Sam said. "I know that was hard. And this is still really important, so don't beat yourself up too much about it, okay?"

"That's easier said than done, I think."

"So what can you tell me about Hank?"

Shell shrugged. "I really didn't like him back then. Honestly, I'm not sure I like him now either, but it doesn't really matter what I think. Have you met him?"

"No. But I've heard the name tossed around a few times."

"He's a big guy. Almost Big Pete big, you know? Just as full of himself for different reasons. Carries himself like he knows more than everyone else. Like he's always right. Like he can do no wrong, and so far, no one's really tried to correct that misconception. It annoys the hell out of me."

"Dina clearly appreciated those character traits," Sam suggested.

"I kinda told her the same thing, then Dina tried to explain to me Hank had a whole different side to him he didn't let most people see. A gentle side. Tender. Selfless. All the things a young girl with the rest of her life ahead of her would wanna see in a married man she was seeing in secret. I never saw them together, so I couldn't say if it were true one way or the other."

"So Dina and Hank were seeing each other in secret," Sam confirmed, "and no one at the Kalamack Club knew? What about Hank's wife? Did she ever find out?"

"I have no idea."

"Five years ago," Sam mused. "That was about the same time Greg got himself kicked out of the club for good and his membership revoked, right?"

"I think so." Shell traced the lines of wood grain on her kitchen table's surface with a slow, absent finger. "I didn't really pay that much attention to town stuff back then."

"You think that might've had something to do with why Greg got kicked out?" Sam asked. "Maybe he found out about Dina and Hank, and somehow Hank managed to come out on top and kick the doctor out of the good life to keep him quiet?"

"No. Greg losing his membership had nothing to do with Hank. It didn't have anything to do with individual club members, either. Greg got himself booted because he finally decided to say something about his issues with the Sunday brunches. And probably a little because he didn't approve of Dina's involvement in them, either."

Sam cocked her head and frowned, waiting for the other woman to finish explaining so that single odd comment might actually make sense.

Shell just looked incredibly uncomfortable. So Sam once again had to push for more.

"I'm sorry. I've obviously missed some crucial connection here, because that picture just isn't adding up. Dr. Greg got himself thrown out of Kalamack Club because he didn't like Sunday brunch?"

Shell couldn't meet Sam's gaze for longer than two seconds. She merely nodded. "Right…"

"That doesn't make sense. It's brunch. On a Sunday, sure, but a lot of brunches are. Is Greg religious or something?"

The other woman still said nothing. Then she stared

directly at Sam, as if silently daring her to stop asking questions to which she didn't want to know the answers.

"Shell. I really need you to tell me what the hell I'm missing right now."

Finally, the woman caved and squirmed in her chair, looking everywhere but at her guest. "Sunday brunches. They're ... Shit, they're not brunches. I mean, I'm sure there's some kinda food in there somewhere, but it's more like an all-day swingers' party at the Kalamack Club. Mixed with ... I don't know. Some messed-up masquerade ball that eventually turns into an orgy."

Sam blinked, pushed herself slowly away from the edge of the table, and thumped back against her seat. "The fuck?"

"I know." Shell rolled her eyes. "It's insane. That's what happens. Every Sunday, all the active members get together, and it's basically a free-for-all. They get to play dress-up, wear a mask, pretend they're someone else, and fool around with whoever they want."

Sam still couldn't wrap her head around the whole thing, and it took her a moment to get past the shock of it. "I thought all the wives joined their husbands for the Sunday brunch, though."

"Membership is just for the men, yeah. But the women? The wives? They're actually pretty into it too. Most of them." Shell paled considerably as she described one of Rush's biggest secrets to date. "Everybody's in. The wives go, and they get to hook up with somebody who isn't their husband, and there are zero rules. Nobody talks about it after the fact. Nobody connects with whoever they were with during brunch. Not that everyone always knows who they're with. They wear masks."

Blinking quickly, Sam searched for the words she

wanted and just couldn't find them, so she settled for, "Shit."

"I actually consider myself pretty lucky that I found out about it the way I did," Shell added. "Dina told me, eventually. That's why I wouldn't let Mattie join up after he graduated. Reggie wanted him to. I don't think my husband had any idea what the brunches really were, but I couldn't let that happen."

Sam clicked her tongue. "I would've made the same decision. Kinda weird that your father-in-law wanted his son around for something like that. His daughter-in-law too."

She'd been thinking out loud, not paying attention to how her shared thoughts might affect the woman across the table until Shell cleared her throat.

There were tears in her eyes again, and she looked like she wanted to spit, preferably at Reginald Jones's feet. But it was too late for that now. Dr. Reginald Jones was dead and had probably offed himself just to avoid getting exactly what he deserved once these secrets came out.

"Reggie definitely wanted my husband there," she said. "He wanted me there too. No way in hell. Hey, I've had my days of partying and travel and living fast and loose, sure. But that's disgusting. Not that I would put much of anything past Reggie. He didn't have a whole lot in the way of morals."

"Sounds a little counterintuitive for a successful medical doctor," Sam said.

"Not when he had the Kalamack Club to support all his more *taboo* interests," Shell snapped, the words hissing out of her in pure disgust. "It wasn't just that he went to Sunday brunches but that he wanted his son and daughter-in-law to be there too. Until I finally pretty much told him he could go fuck himself."

"Good for you," Sam said.

"I wish I felt the same way. It didn't even faze him, really, but I guess he had plenty of other diversions anyway. Reggie was the man to see during those brunches. You could get anything you wanted from him. Substance-wise."

Sam wished she hadn't just taken another sip of her over-sugared coffee, because now she was choking on it. "Wait a minute. Your father-in-law was dealing drugs out of the Kalamack Club?"

"Every Sunday. I guess it's not a real orgy without a bunch of illicit substances, right?"

"Wow."

To date, Sam hadn't been this surprised by anything she'd discovered about either of the Petes or the town of Rush as a whole.

Screw ballpark — this was a whole different game all on its own, and she had no idea what the rules were.

"Well, that's enlightening. So Dr. Greg had an issue with these Sunday not-brunches, then he brought it to someone's attention. Started getting vocal about it. And that's why they kicked him out?"

Shell nodded. "Probably threatened him somehow into silence too. I have no idea why he didn't just pick up and leave town altogether. But it's really none of my business."

"It's possible Greg was finally speaking up and saying something about these brunches because he didn't want Dina involved, yeah? Did she ... participate?"

One quick, wide-eyed look from Shell answered that question instantly. She didn't even have to say it.

"And she talked about this with you freely?" Sam asked.

Shell nodded. "It took some coaxing after a while, but yeah. Eventually, she described everything. Maybe in a little too much detail."

"Are you sure she wasn't trafficked into this somehow?" Sam asked. "Maybe blackmailed or threatened? Forced into participating in these things to protect someone or her own physical well-being?"

"That was my first thought too, when she told me," Shell said. "But no. According to Dina, she actually enjoyed it. Said it was exciting. That she got high off the thrill of it all. I mean, she didn't do any drugs there. I know Dina didn't touch anything harder than a joint. But she did mention getting paid a hefty bonus for *participating* in Sunday brunches. I'm pretty sure she participated in a *lot* of them."

"And she never gave you any indication that it was starting to get old? Or that she wanted out somehow?"

"No. She was weirdly happy with the arrangement. Until the day she showed up on my doorstep asking for help."

"Sounds like something must've happened to her to make her change her mind so abruptly," Sam mused. "Any idea what that was?"

Shaking her head, Shell curled both hands around her coffee mug but didn't drink any more of it. "She didn't tell me that day, or any other day, and I honestly didn't feel I had a right to pry. At that point, we hadn't talked for a while."

They sat there for a moment longer, Sam still stunned by the recent revelations and Shell stewing in a mixture of her own disgust and guilt. Then, once Sam's mind had settled, she changed the subject. "Have you heard about the whole ghost-haunting thing at the Kalamack Club the last few days?"

Shell cracked a smile for the first time since they'd sat down. "I'm a stay-at-home mom of three kids under five, Sam. Not a hermit."

"Fair enough. Maybe you've heard about the message this alleged ghost's been leaving all over the walls? 'Let Dina Go.' What do you think it means?"

"Sounds pretty self-explanatory to me," Shell said.

"As in someone at the club is responsible for trapping Dina somehow?"

"Maybe. From what I heard, the clubhouse's entire second story is basically living quarters. Could've been turned into a real cute bed and breakfast or something, but instead, the Wilders decided to do what they did with it. Just a bunch of private guest rooms up there. For even more privacy during Sunday brunch. I'm pretty sure members have full access to those rooms any other day of the week, or night, as long as they book it out in advance. That would've gone through the front desk too."

"Through Dina, you mean," Sam clarified.

"Yeah. I know Dina was living in one of those rooms. That's where she moved to when she left Rip's. She definitely hadn't made enough money from trimming for only two weeks to get herself an outside apartment somewhere. So I guess Big Pete offered her one of the rooms. I don't think she ever left."

"Is it possible Dina's still there?" Sam asked. "Maybe this whole 'Let Dina Go' thing is a legitimate cry for help."

Shell snorted. "What, you mean, like, do I think the Wilders have literally been holding her hostage in one of those extra rooms upstairs for the last five years straight and no one figured it out? That a little far-fetched. Even for this crowd."

"So no, you don't think it's possible."

"I really don't." With another sigh, Shell sat back in her chair and folded her arms. "Besides, I took her to the bus station myself. I watched her get on that bus from Rush straight back to Seattle. She'd already gotten out, as far as

Rush is concerned. It wouldn't make sense for her to have come back after that."

Sam mulled over everything she'd been told this morning, then knocked back the rest of her coffee, which had finally cooled enough to chug while also still warming her stomach. "Thank you, Shell. For telling it to me straight like this. I know it was hard, especially at a time like this with Reginald."

"That son of a bitch can rot, for all I care," Shell said as she also stood. "I just really don't like breaking promises."

"I get it. Thanks for the coffee, too, by the way. It was good." She hoped the lie held up long enough for Sam to get out the front door and back to her Jeep, though Shell didn't seem to notice her coffee this morning hadn't quite held up to quality standards.

"Yeah, thanks for coming by again. I'm sorry I didn't tell you the first time. Dina's mom was here with you then, and the kids... It just seemed..."

"Makes perfect sense. If anything else comes to mind in the next little bit that we didn't talk about, you can pop into the Redwood Rings. Sit down. Take a load off for a while. Come in when I'm working, and your drink's on me."

Shell walked Sam to the door, then gasped like she'd just stepped on a thumbtack. "Wait. I'm sorry, there *is* something else. I didn't confirm it then, and I can't confirm it now, obviously, but I did think there was something else going on with Dina the day I helped her get on that bus home."

"Okay..."

"I wouldn't have recognized it then," Shell continued, "but I've been through it a few times myself now. Easier to see in someone else after the fact. I think Dina might've

389

been pregnant before she left Rush. Like she'd just found out when I saw her last."

"What makes you say that?"

"It was just the way she looked. The way she talked to me. The way she seemed so desperate, almost. Terrified. Ashamed. I remember how *I* felt when I found out I was pregnant with Mickey. It's one of the few things that completely changes you in a split second while also leaving you exactly the same as you were before."

"Easy enough to recognize if you've been through it yourself," Sam repeated. "I totally get it. Thanks for everything, Shell. And again, my condolences."

SAM HAD no idea what the hell to do with the rest of her time after that. Everything Dina's so-called best friend from five years ago had just revealed had shaken the entire picture of Dina's life in Rush upside down and inside out.

Even with knowing it was Hank Topping who'd had the affair with Dina, Sam still couldn't siphon out what felt like the last seemingly important, laughably obvious part of this entire equation.

And for the life of her, she couldn't figure out why the fuck she was still so blind to it.

FORTY-ONE

Laila

LAILA COULDN'T BELIEVE it had come to this, but it was her job to do what Big Pete Wilder instructed — or commanded.

Today, she'd led Father Aguayo, Rush's resident Catholic priest, through the entirety of the Kalamack Club for an exorcism. And now, she led him back down the staircase toward the front of the club to find both Big Pete and Elaine milling around the front entrance.

Pete saw Father Aguayo. He didn't have to change much in his expression, because apparently, he'd shown up to the club already scowling. "Tell me it's over, Padre. Tell me you did everything you need to do, and we can put this whole fucking thing behind us."

"It's over." Father Aguayo nodded as he approached Pete, then extended a hand. "Anytime you ever need my help in the future, Pete, you know where to find me."

Pete stared at the priest's hand as if Aguayo had wiped his own ass with it first. Then he took it anyway in a grip that looked like it would have made any man grimace in pain. If he felt anything, though, the priest was certainly well-experienced in hiding it.

Then Father Aguayo nodded at Elaine and finally at Laila before taking his leave.

Laila had already made her way toward her employer's wife, slightly alarmed because today, the woman looked indescribably sad. Laila couldn't help but want to provide the woman with whatever comfort she could. Elaine had always been good to her, even if she was still married to the crudest, most demanding, most disgusting employer for whom Laila had ever worked.

"Elaine? Are you all right?"

"I'm fine, dear," the woman replied. "Really." She sniffed and dabbed at the corner of her eye with a small tissue pulled from a miniature packet in her purse. "Just a little sad, I suppose. One might even call it mourning."

"Mourning?" Laila looked quickly back and forth between Elaine and Pete, who snorted and rolled his eyes as he stomped across the reception area toward the back staircase.

"I had hoped I might have at least one more chance to commune with Caroline's spirit," Elaine added. "I know it sounds strange, but I actually enjoyed having her here with us, you know? Her presence. I could feel her energy in this house, especially up in her old bedroom where we'd hung the portrait. Now, well, if that priest is as good at what he does as everyone seems to think he is, I suppose that's all over."

"Shouldn't have had to deal with any of this fucking bullshit in the first place," Pete growled before clomping up the stairs.

"Where do you think *you're* going?" Elaine snapped, transforming in an instant from a saddened, teary-eyed woman to the fiery challenge Big Pete had unknowingly taken on the day he'd married her.

His irritated growl echoed back down the staircase. "It's my office, woman. Finally put a goddamn camera in there last night. So, whoever's been fucking with that lock and breaking into my office is gonna get one hell of a surprise when I tell them I caught 'em red-handed this time."

"He finally relented," Laila murmured.

"It takes that man fifty times longer than it should to do anything with any benefit to anyone else but himself. But yes, he finally gave in."

"Listen," Laila said. "About Caroline. I'm sorry it got to this point, you know? And that it went so far, we had to call in Father Aguayo to exorcise the house just so we can all move on with our lives. I know how interested you were in Caroline and getting to know more about her life."

"That's very sweet of you, Laila." A surprised smile flickered across Elaine's lips. "Thank you."

"Speaking of the spirits that were here, at least," Laila continued, "what do you think happened to her? To Dina, I mean."

"Oh, well that's a question on everyone's lips these days, isn't it? I honestly couldn't tell you, dear, but it has been awfully exciting, hasn't it?"

When Elaine flashed her a brilliant, beaming grin, the ferocity behind her eyes made Laila catch her breath. Which made it all too easy for Laila to imagine what Mrs. Wilder had been like in her younger days. A force to be reckoned with on multiple accounts, that was for sure.

She was about to pull something witty out of thin air, if only to further ingratiate herself with Big Pete's wife — which was incredibly advantageous for someone in Laila's position. But she was cut off by Big Pete's furious roar directly above their heads, followed by violent pounding and banging back and forth across the floor.

Elaine tipped her head back to study the ceiling, and her demeanor remained remarkably calm and composed, completely at odds with her next words. "I don't suppose it's possible he's having some sort of heart attack up there, do you think? Maybe an aneurysm of some sort?"

Laila almost burst out laughing. She managed to cover it up just in time before softly murmuring, "Knowing him, I wouldn't bet on any of those things."

Mrs. Wilder clicked her tongue. "Yes, I've believed very much the same thing for years now, unfortunately."

"Laila!" Big Pete's thunderous roar shook both women out of their shared musings on the topic of his health, and Laila had no choice but to hop to it.

"Do feel free to take him down a notch, won't you?" Elaine called after her as Laila hurried toward the back staircase. "I seem to have run out of energy for it today."

"I'll do my best," she replied, then headed up. Her stiletto heels clicked against the wood with each step, her strides automatically shortened by the cut of her business-style pencil skirt.

Part of her expected another disastrous mess inside Pete's office. But instead, Laila merely found her employer bent over his desk, looming above the keyboard as he swiveled the computer mouse and clicked around, his giant ham of a hand threatening to break the plastic into a million pieces if he squeezed any harder.

"What happened?" Elaine called breathlessly behind her before she also entered the office.

"What happened?" Big Pete blustered. "*What happened*? I'll show you what fucking happened. Come here."

Laila did as instructed, more curious now than wary

because this was the first time she'd seen Big Pete get so dangerously flustered by nothing more than technology.

"Something on your computer?" Elaine asked. "Pete, don't you think you might be overreacting just a little?"

"I said come here," he growled. "You just take a look at this and *then* tell me whether or not I'm overreacting."

Both women approached his desk to view the large flatscreen monitor.

Pete clicked around a some more and started the video recording from the most recent camera footage of his office last night. Then he had to fast-forward before he stepped back and folded his arms with a grunt. "Just watch."

There didn't seem to be much of anything going until a subtle shift in the light appeared on the video feed. Apparently, Big Pete had sprung for a full-color surveillance system. Which wouldn't really have mattered beyond giving the footage a much more realistic feel as Laila watched.

Then she realized the figure caught on camera was David, the club's manager, making his way across Big Pete's office in the middle of the night. According to the video's timestamp, it was just after midnight. He went directly to Pete's desk and opened one of the drawers. When he stood again, he held a medium-sized silver box in both hands. He put this down on the desk, jiggled it open with a key, and removed several items he then swiftly deposited into his jacket pocket.

Then the box closed, he returned it to its place in the desk drawer, and David disappeared from the camera's view again before the lights switched off and the office was plunged into almost complete darkness, all neatly locked back up again as if nothing had happened.

As soon as the shadow of the office door closing all the

way fell across the screen, Big Pete stabbed a finger down onto the keyboard, and the footage paused. "Fucking David."

"What?" Elaine said. "Why? What was that? What was he doing?"

"Taking his own little private dip into the petty cash box," Pete snarled. "That son of a bitch has been stealing from me. This whole goddamn time. Right under my fucking nose." His fist pounded onto the desk's surface before he spun away from the furniture and bellowed in anger. "The manager of my fucking club for *years*, and he's been stealing from me! How the hell did he get a key to my office? How the hell did I not know about this? Who the fuck does he think he is?"

"All right, Peter," Elaine said. "Let's take a moment to—"

"I don't need a moment for shit. I'm gonna kill him. That's it. He's forced my hand. I'm gonna fucking kill that sniveling little—"

"Peter, please." Elaine stepped toward him again, scowling in disapproval even as she reached toward him with both hands, still trying to calm her husband. "That's not the right way to handle this."

"I'll handle it however I goddamn please," he roared.

While her employer raged again, likely not for the last time today, Laila took the opportunity to slip out of his office and back downstairs.

It was impossible not to hear him in his office, which was almost directly above her desk, but at least she was no longer in his immediate vicinity and therefore wouldn't find herself at the receiving end of his rage. Not that she wished it on anyone, even Elaine, who might have been the only person alive capable of talking some sense into the man.

～

THOUGH THE CLUBHOUSE itself had not reopened to the public, the staff was still here every day, preparing a soft reopening for whenever Big Pete told them it was time to start letting members enter the premises again after the hauntings.

The first thing David did when he stepped inside was walk straight across the front entrance toward the reception area where Laila sat at her desk. These were still normal working hours, despite the actual clubhouse being temporarily closed.

All of Laila's aggravation with the day so far disappeared as soon as she saw him heading her way.

"Motherfucker!" Big Pete boomed from his office.

Laila tried to smile at David, but it came out as a grimace, and there was nothing she could do about it.

"What's the problem this time?" David asked, nodding at the staircase.

"Pete's been up there for about an hour now," she said. "Reviewing security footage."

"Huh. Why? Something happen in the parking lot?"

"The security footage of the inside of his office," she added. "From last night."

He paled instantly and froze, his eyes wide. Then he started fiddling with his light jacket folded over one arm, and the blank stare he fixed on her said it all. "I didn't know there were cameras inside the club. Even in Pete's office."

"There didn't *used* to be. But he just had them installed yesterday, so ... there are now."

The man looked like he was about to fall over. He just stood there, then frowned and pressed a hand to his lower stomach. "You know what? I'm starting to feel a little under the weather. I think I might've eaten some bad sushi last night."

"That's awful."

He didn't look at her. "Yeah, I'm gonna go home, I think. Try to sleep it off. See if I can't fix this sooner rather than later."

"Home. That's probably a good idea. Though, if it were up to me, David, I'd probably go a lot farther than just back home. You know, put as much distance as physically possible between me and this clubhouse and the man upstairs who owns it."

That made him look at her again, his gaze filled with pure terror before he spun quickly around and booked it out of the clubhouse.

He couldn't have said much else, given the circumstances. Laila would have wished him luck, or told him to be careful, or tried to provide some type of parting words, but it seemed useless.

They both knew the current and soon-to-be former manager of Rush's Kalamack Club was well and truly screwed.

FORTY-TWO

Sam
_____

SAM DIDN'T BOTHER to text Angela first before heading to the woman's hotel. She'd been knocking fervently on the door of Angela's room for what felt like half an hour but was most likely more like half a minute.

"I'm coming, I'm coming. Hold on," Angela called, joined by the sound of hurried footsteps and a few thumps and thuds from inside.

Then the door opened abruptly, and she looked entirely surprised to see Sam standing there.

"Sam. Hi. Um, is everything okay?"

Usually, this was the part where whoever answered the door opened it a little wider and invited their visitor in. Angela, however, did the opposite. She'd only opened the door a few inches and kept it mostly closed.

Sam huffed out a laugh. "You trying to keep me from seeing into your room, Angela?"

"What? No." Her gaze and darted around the hallway before finally landing on Sam's eyes. Then she smiled. "Can I help you with something?"

"Yeah, I wanted to go over some new information with

you." Halfway pretending to try peering around Angela, Sam couldn't help but laugh. "Are you hiding something in there? Company, maybe? That'd be *some* surprise. You haven't even been here that long."

"Hiding someone?" Angela scoffed. "Don't be ridiculous. My room is a total mess right now. Let me grab my things, then we can go talk at the cafe."

The door closed in Sam's face.

Fortunately, she didn't have to wait long before Angela came bustling out with her purse slid only halfway onto her shoulder, her feet not quite fully fitted into her shoes, and her hair partially tied back in a ponytail she struggled to tighten and correct as they headed for the hotel's cafe.

Sam didn't want to stare. She didn't want to jump to any conclusions, either, but this was the most scattered she'd seen Angela since they'd met.

Something had happened. Something was different.

Angela would eventually share when she was ready, assuming she thought it was important enough for Sam to know.

They went with their usual coffee orders at the café, and Angela immediately dug into a slice of blueberry cobbler this time instead of the cherry pie.

"Angela, did you know Dina was seeing someone while she was here?" Sam asked. "Not just casually dating, either. I mean something serious."

"No, not really," Angela said. "I figured there might've been some boy trouble involved. That tends to turn things upside down for anyone. But no, Dina never mentioned someone specific."

"She was definitely seeing someone. I managed to confirm it this morning."

Angela's eyes widened, and she leaned forward. "That's good news. Please tell me you also confirmed his name."

Sam nodded, sipped her decent diner coffee, and said, "Hank Topping."

"I've not heard the name. Dina certainly never told me about this Hank person. Are you sure that's who she was seeing?"

"I'm sure," Sam said. "I wanted to let you know I'm gonna go talk to him in person today. See what he'll tell me about their relationship. Maybe he knows something about what happened to her."

"When are you going?"

"Right after talking to you. That was the plan."

"I want to come with you," Angela blurted.

"Oh." Sam eased another sip of coffee to stall for time. "Well, I wasn't really planning on inviting you to come with me."

"That's fine." Angela shrugged. "I would still very much like to come."

"Angela, I'm not so sure that's a good idea. These kinds of conversations are pretty sensitive. People generally don't wanna talk about stuff from the past with practical strangers. Hank doesn't know me, but I'm not nearly as involved. Bringing the mother of the young woman he was intimately involved with five years ago to talk to him about her missing daughter? That's something totally different."

"We don't have to tell him I'm her mother," Angela said quickly. "We can just say I'm your friend, that I'm helping you out for the day. You're good at finding the right kind of answer, Sam. I'm sure you can come up with something."

"Still." Sam shrugged.

"Please," Angela insisted. "Please let me come with you. I promise I won't get involved. I'll let you do all the talking. He won't even know I'm her mother. I just wanna see this man with my own eyes, face to face. And if you're going now, it's the perfect time. Great excuse for me to get out of the hotel. I feel like I've been holing myself up in that room longer than I should've. Staying there isn't all that healthy for me right now, you know?"

Yeah, Sam knew the feeling all too well. She still didn't think it was a good idea, but she wasn't completely heart-less, either.

"All right," she finally relented. "But I'm gonna hold you to that promise, understand? I'll do the talking. You just stand there, listen, keep your mouth shut, and pay close attention. Deal?"

"Absolutely. Yes!" Angela's buoyant smile carried far more energy than Sam had seen in the woman. "Perfect. Just let me finish this cobbler first. You sure you don't want a piece, Sam? It's surprisingly good."

IN TWO YEARS of living in Rush, Sam hadn't had reason before today to drive down the side streets past the main part of town toward Hank Topping Real Estate. If she'd had any intention of staying in Rush long-term when she'd first come up here, things might have been different. But after Syc's generous offer of a spot at Birdsong, the need for real estate agents and official renting had gone out the window.

The office was relatively small but very well put together, tastefully decorated, and sectioned off with half a dozen smaller offices throughout the building for any part-ners or collaborators. All Sam and Angela had to do was step through the front doors and look around before they found Hank Topping with remarkable ease.

"Well, hello, there," he said. "Come in, come in, please. It's good to see ya."

Sam stopped herself from bristling and asking if she knew the guy from somewhere. He was just being friendly, and this was all part of his sales tactics. It had to be.

She and Angela walked across the small, cozy lobby toward the man in his late thirties or early forties now heading toward them from the other side of his desk.

"How can I help you today?" he asked.

Sam took a slow, sweeping glance around the main room. "We're looking for Hank Topping, actually. Can you help?"

"I can do more than that." He laughed, pushed his already rolled shirt sleeves farther up his forearms, and finished walking around the desk toward them before extending a hand toward Sam. "Hank Topping, at your service."

She smiled and took his hand. "That was easy."

That was as much as she was willing to say right off the bat, and the way the rest of this conversation went was entirely dependent on how Hank reacted after this.

"Off to a good start, then." Hank flashed both women a brilliant smile, and Sam supposed she could see why a girl like Dina had fallen for a man like him. He was certainly confident, though she hadn't yet noticed the vain, self-centered qualities Shell had described. Not yet, anyway.

When he shook Angela's hand too, she said nothing, just as she'd promised. Then Hank clapped his hands together, spread his arms, and acted as if he'd just done something particularly heroic. "Now we've covered the basics, I feel better about asking why you're looking for *me*."

Sam glanced at the photos on the desk behind him. One in particular contained multiple familiar faces.

The same faces she'd seen in family photos at Shell

Jones's house. Shell was one of the people in this photo now on Hank's desk, as well as her husband Matt, Reginald and his wife, plus Hank Topping himself and another woman around his age who stood between Hank and Reginald with a brilliant grin and her hair perfectly curling over her shoulders.

No wonder Hank had looked familiar.

"Sorry to change the subject," Sam said as she pointed, "but that's a great picture."

Hank looked over his shoulder, then chuckled. "Ah, yes. The whole family. Most of us, anyway."

"Family, huh? Are you related to the Joneses somehow?"

"Only by law. I married Reggie's daughter Valerie."

Sam tried to hide her surprise at that one.

So this guy's technically Shell's brother-in-law. That's an interesting twist. Why wouldn't she have mentioned that fun connection?

"Small world, then," Sam said with a nod, then her smile faded. "Even in a town like this. In that case, Hank, I offer my condolences for your recent loss."

He looked surprised to hear those words from a stranger.

Angela looked just as surprised and turned slightly to gape at Sam. She still didn't say anything, but she also clearly wasn't trying to play it cool or not give herself away. Her thoughts seemed beyond obvious in her expressions today.

What had gotten into her lately?

First the secrecy inside Angela's hotel room, then the scattered disorientation and all the eager excitement in the coffee shop. And now, she looked at Sam like Sam had just turned into a human-sized porcupine.

Sam could save that mystery for later.

"Are you the only one in the office right now?" she asked Hank.

"Yes." He adjusted his hands on his hips and gazed around. "For the rest of the afternoon, actually."

"So I guess that also means I don't need to ask if we can speak somewhere a little more private." Sam looked around, then fixed him with a no-nonsense smile. "Since it's just the three of us, we might as well have this conversation right here."

Hank tried to hide a flickering frown behind a salesman's hospitable smile. "Sorry, I don't quite follow."

"No need for privacy when we're already alone." Sam folded her arms. "So now you can go ahead and tell us about Dina Copely."

Hank looked back and forth between the women and blinked. "Come again?"

Sam nodded. "I know about you and Dina. And I'd like to hear more about it directly from you. In your own words, of course."

Hank's brilliant smile tightened, his eyes narrowing as he held her gaze. "You'll have to forgive me. I'm a little confused here. I don't know any Dina."

"I know it's been a while," Sam added, "so I'll refresh your memory first. She worked at the Kalamack Club, of which, I take it, you're currently a member. Is that correct?"

"I am a member." The suspicion quickly grew in his gaze and his voice, but he maintained that killer smile through all of it. "But I still don't know any Dina. And believe me, I know all the staff at the Kalamack Club. By name, even."

"She doesn't work there now," Angela cut in without preamble, immediately adopting a healthy dose of spiteful venom in her voice that made Sam instantly regret letting

405

the woman come with her. "But she worked there five years ago. Did you know all the staff members by name back then, Hank?"

His mouth popped open, and he paused for a moment before slowly nodding. "Yeah. You know what? I think I vaguely remember a Dina at some point back then. That was a long time ago, though. A lot happens in five years."

"And at the same time," Sam added, "even five years can go by in the blink of an eye, just like that." She snapped her fingers, vaguely aware of Angela jumping a little beside her.

What was her *deal*?

"Sure." Hank tried to laugh again. "Sorry to disappoint you, though. If you're trying to ask me about this Dina person, I can't help you there. I didn't know her personally. Is there anything else?"

Sam nodded at the man's hands propped on his hips; she'd noticed the second he'd reached out to shake her hand that his knuckles were bruised, the skin on the back of his right hand red and raw and covered in tiny cuts. "You getting into a lot of fistfights lately, Hank?"

He immediately looked down at the backs of his hands, then shrugged. "Oh, this? Nah, I was installing some drywall earlier. Got a little too eager with it."

"A real estate agent who does a little construction on the side? Nice. So if I drove by your house, the place would be under construction, huh? Drywall and everything. I bet your wife can't *wait* for you to finish the project so she has her clean house back."

This time when Hank replied, his voice fell flat and emotionless. "I didn't say on my own house. It's one of the properties my agency represents."

"Ah…" Sam pursed her lips and nodded. "Makes sense."

"You know, I'm starting to get the feeling you ladies didn't come here to talk about real estate in even the vaguest sense. If there's nothing I can help you with in that respect, I'm sorry, but I'm gonna have to ask you to leave. I've got a busy afternoon ahead of me, and I need to catch up on the workload."

"I'm sure a man like you who works for himself and owns his own business can spare another couple minutes, at the very least," Angela blurted. "Unless, of course, you're just trying to hide something."

Sam reached toward her, wanting to wordlessly remind Angela that she'd promised to keep her mouth shut, but now it was too late.

Angela was already on a roll.

"Excuse me?" Hank asked.

"You know exactly what I'm talking about, Hank," the woman spat, pointing an accusatory finger at him. "And you know *exactly* what happened to Dina, don't you?"

"Okay, there's been some kind of mistake."

"The only mistake," she shouted, "was that she ever met *you*! You *ruined* her, Hank! And now you owe me an explanation!"

"Angela," Sam warned.

"What did you do to my daughter?" she shrieked, stepping toward him with her face now a mottled, blazing red and her eyes wide with fury. "What did you do? What happened to my daughter? You tell me right now!"

Hank threw both hands up in concession. "I didn't do anything."

"This isn't helping," Sam added.

Angela evaded Sam's attempt to grab her arm and lead her away. "I call bullshit. Everyone in this whole town is full of shit. Everyone's a liar, and I deserve the truth. I want to know what you did to my daughter!"

"This is ridiculous." Hank stepped behind his desk again and reached for the phone. "I need you both to leave right now, or I will be calling the police, and *they* can escort you out."

"You think I care about the police?" Angela screamed. "You think they're enough to stop *me*? Like that's an actual threat? Ha! This whole town is a goddamn joke—"

"All right, that's enough." He picked up the phone and started dialing. "Last chance to get out of here before you no longer have a choice."

"I will *not* be bullied or threatened into backing down about this. I want to know! And you're going to tell me!"

"Well, *this* just went to shit," Sam murmured.

"Hi. Yes," Hank said into the receiver. "This is Hank Topping. I need you to send an officer down to my office. There's a woman here harassing me, and it wouldn't surprise me if she turns violent. She's crazy and refusing to leave the premises."

"I am *not crazy*! This is your fault! You ruined her! You ruined everything!"

"That's it!" Sam snapped. She didn't care how loudly Angela screamed or how fervently the woman struggled in her grip; once Sam had decided it was time to physically remove this woman from Hank's business, nothing would change her mind.

Angela struggled against Sam's harsh grip on her upper arm, but Sam was much stronger and had far more experience escorting emotionally charged people out of various situations.

"We're leaving," Sam warned. "Now."

"No! You said you would help me, Sam. You said he was—"

"Not another word," Sam snarled, then yanked the struggling woman toward the front door. "Don't worry about the police, Hank," she called over her shoulder. "We're gone."

"Yeah, that doesn't make me feel any better," he said with the phone still pressed against his ear. "Oh. No, I'm sorry. I was talking to someone else… Yeah, sure. I'll stay on the line."

Short of kicking and screaming, Angela continued her struggling until they'd almost made it back to the Jeep. Then Sam grabbed her by both shoulders and gave Angela a rough little shake. "Get ahold of yourself, will you?"

Tears poured down the woman's cheeks, and she tried to escape Sam's grasp one more time before finally giving up.

"What happened to her?" Angela sobbed. "I just need to know what *happened*…"

"Well, you're not gonna figure that out with the way you're acting right now," Sam said firmly. "Pull it together."

She opened the passenger-side door of her Jeep and finally let Angela go, pointing into the vehicle. "Get in. Now."

All the fight seeped out of Angela the next second, and she practically sagged against Sam before dragging herself up into the Jeep and plopping down into the passenger seat. Then she burst into sobs.

Sam slammed the door shut before rounding the vehicle to climb behind the wheel.

After giving the woman another five minutes to hopefully cry it out of her system, Sam sighed and failed to find anything in her vehicle that might act as an effective tissue.

"What the hell was that?" she finally asked.

"I'm sorry," Angela whined.

"I told you it wasn't a good idea to come with me, but *you* convinced me it'd be fine. You promised me you'd keep your mouth shut. That we wouldn't tell him you're Dina's mother. That you wouldn't get involved. You gave me your word."

"I'm *sorry*," Angela almost shouted before letting out another strangled sob. "I just can't… It's all wrong. Everything just went so *wrong*, and I can't fix it, and I still don't know what happened…"

Sam waited until the woman's tears had calmed again. Now that she had another moment to consider Angela's erratic behavior today, she found herself unable to keep her new suspicions to herself.

She shifted in the driver's seat to more fully face Angela and dipped her head. "You're not gonna like what I'm about to ask you, but I need you to be honest with me for both our sakes. Have you been drinking again?"

That stopped Angela's tears immediately, which was enough of an answer in and of itself. She sniffed twice and slowly looked up to meet Sam's gaze with a pitiful expression.

"Is that why you didn't want me seeing the inside of your hotel room this morning?" Sam added. "Because you slipped?"

Angela said nothing, and now she couldn't even look Sam in the eye. Instead, she dropped her gaze to her lap, where it stayed.

Sam gave her another moment to say something, but Angela clearly wasn't talking. She also wasn't crying anymore, which was a plus, but Sam had already had enough.

She couldn't deal with this on her own right now.

Angela needed more help than Sam was capable of giving her.

So she started the Jeep with an irritated crank of the ignition and headed out of Hank Topping Real Estate's parking lot toward the one place in town she knew someone like Angela would be accepted, no questions asked.

And, more importantly, where she would be safe.

~

ANGELA DIDN'T PUT two and two together until Sam was literally escorting her through the front doors of the Community Center with a firm but gentle grip on her elbow.

Then it hit her, and Angela rolled her eyes. "Sam. I really don't need—"

"You know what? Right now, I'm not sure you're the best person to say what you do and don't need. You're going through some shit. I get that. I'm not taking you back to your hotel room, which would be just as bad as dropping you off outside the liquor store at this point, and I can't keep you with me."

"I promise I won't do anything like that again," Angela pleaded. "Let me go back to the hotel at least. I'll clear out my room."

"You're right," Sam added as they turned a corner, "you won't pull that crap again. Because you'll be here with someone who can offer you a lot more help than I can right now."

"Sam, really. Is this entirely necessary?"

"I'd say more than entirely, to be honest."

Sam knocked briskly on the door to the office she'd been looking for, the label of which read *Program Director*. She was already pushing the door open before the woman inside finished calling out for them to enter.

Meredith sat behind her desk, looking a little tired and partially annoyed. "Sam. And Angela. Hi. Didn't expect to see you in here this morning. Unfortunately, our meeting isn't until later."

"Not here for a meeting," Sam said. "I'm here to drop off a friend in need because I've got a few things to do, and I don't think Angela should be alone right now. If you catch my drift."

Meredith stood behind her desk, nodding as she looked Angela up and down. Leave it to that one simple phrase 'shouldn't be alone right now,' and any recovering alcoholic or addict's mood instantly changed; the only other thing that could have garnered such a quick response was bringing a bottle of liquor into the Community Center, and that was just hitting below the belt.

"We'll be fine here, Sam," Meredith said. "Though I'm curious as to what's so important that you're too busy to stay awhile."

Seriously?

No thanks.

This wasn't a meeting, and Sam sure as hell hadn't raised her hand to share.

Even if she'd had something pressing on her schedule, she just didn't want to be around a woman who couldn't get a grip on herself, couldn't keep her mouth shut, and couldn't stay away from the bottle.

"That's *my* business," Sam replied, then headed back through the door. "But I'll be back later. I'll be busy, but if you *really* need me, you have my number. I'll get back to you when I can."

She didn't wait for either woman to return the farewell.

All she wanted now was to get away from both of them and find some space and time to think.

She didn't get any.

The second she stepped out of the Community Center, her phone buzzed with an incoming text. She didn't recognize the number, but the text's included picture stoked all the curiosity she needed.

It was a picture of Jordan, for whatever reason.

Sam glowered at it and almost put her phone away before a new text stopped her.

THIS IS KEVIN. *From the grocery store. Deli department. You said to let you know if I found anything. Sent a photo of the guy who picked up those special roses. Thought you might wanna know.*

KEVIN FROM THE DELI DEPARTMENT...

Sam barked out a bitter laugh and booked it toward her Jeep.

Jordan from Rip's farm. That greasy, stringy-looking little shit who'd somehow managed to slip right through her fingers more times than Sam appreciated.

Once was one time too many, but this kid?

Yeah, this kid was in for an earful.

FORTY-THREE

Sam

THE PROCESS of getting onto Rip's Farm and escorted to his temp-building office by his security people was just as convoluted as her last time up here. Today, though, she had enough fire inside her to fuel her patience until Jordan arrived. And then...

Who knew? She'd probably snap on the kid. At this point, he deserved it.

Rip looked surprised to see her again but instantly caught on to her urgency when she asked him to call Jordan to his office for another chat.

The farmer told her she could wait inside with him until Jordan arrived, but after three minutes of Sam's pacing, Rip looked up from the work scattered across his desk. "Come to think of it, why don't you go ahead and wait outside? There's a lot more fresh air out there."

She didn't stand directly in front of the office door, knowing full well the moment Jordan showed up, he was going to recognize her. If he really was Hoodie, he might already know why she was up here asking for him. So instead, Sam paced behind Rip's office trailer, biding her time and listening for sounds of Jordan's approach.

When she finally heard footsteps, she practically leapt out from behind the temp building. The first thing she saw was a twenty-something-year-old man with the exact same build as her mystery delivery guy walking straight toward her...

Wearing the exact same black-and-white-checker hoodie.

With his hood pulled back from his head now, Sam also recognized the long, unkempt, greasily stringy hair that would've looked a million times better with a single brush and pulled back into a ponytail or something.

It was Jordan, all right.

"Son of a bitch," Sam muttered.

As Jordan approached the door to Rip's office, Sam emerged from behind the trailer and stepped in his path to cut him off. The kid stopped and stared at her like he'd just awakened from a dream and found himself not in his own bedroom but halfway across the world instead.

It gave her enough time to raise her eyebrows and say, "We need to talk."

Jordan swallowed thickly, looked her up and down, then bolted.

"Hey!" Sam took off after him, arms pumping as she chased the guy around the back side of the main lodge and toward the front of the farm.

By the time Sam rounded the corner of the lodge after him, she found that checkered hoodie popping up onto a slightly dented bike, its frame off kilter but still otherwise perfectly usable.

"No, no, no, Jordan, stop!"

The seconds he'd lost by hopping onto his bike and

slapping his boots down onto the pedals was all the extra time Sam needed.

She barreled forward and straight into him, dipping her head and shoulder at the last second for a much more effective tackle as she wrapped her arms around his body and took them both to the grass.

He was a hell of a lot skinnier than she'd expected, even of a young-ish guy who already looked skinny and well-worked.

They both toppled to the ground with a thud, the jangle of bike chains, and the scattered click of something caught in the spokes — arms and legs twisted up all over the place. Sam thought for a moment the kid was actually trying to kick her in the face before she realized he'd gotten his boot tangled in the bike chain and was trying to kick himself free.

By the time he finally freed himself, Sam had pushed herself off the grass. Jordan scrambled to his feet and took off blindly again, too terrified to pick the smartest escape route.

Which meant Sam was up and in the guy's face again a second later, this time with both fists bunched up around handfuls of that stupid checkered hoodie. "Jordan! Just hold on for a second and let me—"

He twisted sideways, bringing an arm up and over his head before he chopped it down between them right into the creases of Sam's elbows.

She lost her grip as he spun and tore away from her, then he was off again.

"Goddamnit," she spat.

That move was definitely a surprise.

Snarling, she took off after him.

Should be a hell of a lot easier now that the guy had abandoned his bike again.

She was wrong.

Jordan led her all the way across the open field of Rip's farm, back behind the main lodge again, then straight for the forest's tree line.

Two of the farm's security men on patrol slowly walked that tree line. They paused when they noticed Jordan booking it toward them.

"Hey, stop him, will you?" Sam shouted, pointing after Jordan as she kept up the chase.

Jordan crashed into the woods, snapping branches and rustling leaves.

She was close on his heels, but she had enough time to glimpse the security guys sharing a confused look before one of them snorted before they resumed their patrol.

A chase on foot through the woods wasn't anywhere on Sam's list of best places to pursue a suspect, but it was surprisingly easier than trying to gain on him riding a bike.

Jordan was terrified enough to have stopped paying attention to where he was going. He crashed and bumbled into the underbrush, nearly running headfirst into huge tree trunks every time he looked over his shoulder to check behind him.

The next time he did, it wasn't his face against tree bark that took him down but the toe of his boot snagging on a thick root protruding from the spongy forest floor littered with decaying leaves and dry pine needles.

He went down hard with a grunt, sprawling across the ground and narrowly avoiding cracking his head open on a rock a foot away.

Sam was on him before he could recover. This time, she didn't bother with his hoodie.

She skidded to a stop beside him, dropped one knee onto his upper back, and grabbed his wrists to pin both arms behind him. More than half her full body weight now pressed into the middle of his spine.

He cried out with a breathless groan, and she eased up a little. This wasn't about taking the guy down permanently, arresting, or incapacitating the kid.

It was his own damn fault, though. He just kept running.

"I'm not here to hurt you," she said, breathless herself. "Okay? I'm just here to talk. We could've talked a long time ago if you didn't always bolt every time we see each other. So now you're not going anywhere, understand?"

Puffs of brown-red dust burst away from his face as he panted against the ground.

"Understand, Jordan?"

"Yeah, yeah," he squeaked. "I fucking get it, man, okay? Jesus." The terror in his voice wasn't for Sam. In fact, she'd loosened her hold on his arms and had started to remove her knee from his back.

Something else terrified him.

Maybe one too many things in his past had required running before he'd found a steady job at the farm.

"You're not gonna run," Sam told him, just to be sure.

"No, man, no. I won't, okay? I promise."

Grunting, Sam fully removed her weight from his back and pushed herself to her feet.

Jordan instantly spun away from the earth to sit up with his legs sprawled in front of him, still catching his breath. He glared up at her and smacked clumps of pine needles and a smattering of dirt off the front of that damn hoodie.

"All right." Smoothing her hair away from her face with both hands, Sam took a deep breath. "This is the part where you tell me exactly what's going on here. And I want the whole story. No half-assed bits and pieces, got it? I know you're the one who's been dropping those fucking bouquets at my house after you picked them up from the grocery store. I know you've snuck into Birdsong Park to leave them outside my front door three days in a row. What I *don't* know is which shithead in this town paid you to pull this off. So you're gonna tell me."

He gaped at her. "Wait a minute. You mean you don't know?"

"Now!" Sam growled. "Who was it?"

"Okay, okay! Shit, man. It was that lady, yeah? Your friend, uh … shit. Dina's mom, okay?"

His final shout echoed for half a second before the trees and layers of underbrush coating the forest floor sucked up his voice.

But it still echoed around over and over in Sam's mind a bit longer.

"Angela?" she finally asked, scrunching up her face.

"Yeah. Angela. The lady who came up here with you the first time." Jordan sniffed, wiped under his nose with the back of a hand as if he expected to find blood there, then shook himself off. After that, he looked her up and down and rolled his shoulders back. "Damn, dude. Were you, like, a linebacker in a past life, or what?"

"Military police," Sam muttered. She was already turning away from him, blankly scanning the forest floor. Because now, the shithead who'd been harassing her and playing such an awful fucking joke with those Sophy's Roses had been Angela all along, according to this yahoo. That didn't even make sense.

"You sure it was her?" she asked.

He started as if he thought she'd tackle him again. "Yeah, I'm sure. Talked to her and everything."

But those flowers had shown up at Sam's front door *before* she and Angela had even met.

"Did she tell you *why* she wanted those flowers delivered to my house every fucking day?" Sam asked.

"No. I don't need to know why someone wants a job done. I just do the job and get paid, you know?"

"So then tell me about the job, Jordan." Sam stepped toward him, recovered from her shock but now fueled by her boiling rage again.

He must have seen it in her eyes.

The kid took a step back away from her to mirror the action, then lifted both hands in concession. "Okay, I'll tell you! Look. This lady, Angela, whatever. She showed up in town, like, two weeks ago. I don't know how she found me, okay? Ask all you want. Try to torture it out of me, whatever. But all I know is she found me.

"We talked a little about Dina. About when she worked at the farm and then after, when she went into town. Then the lady asked if I wanted to make a little extra cash delivering flowers for a week, and I said hell yeah. Why not?"

He snorted, then scratched his head. A clump of dry leaves fell from his stringy hair and fluttered to the forest floor. "You're not gonna tell her I stopped, are you?"

Sam frowned at him. "Why would I do that?"

"I mean, 'cause I already spent the money. She paid to deliver bouquets for seven days, and I only got through three before you started chasing me off every time. Damn."

"I'm not gonna tell her you stopped, Jordan." Sam puffed out a sigh. "She should've just *told* me herself. What did you do with the rest of the flowers?"

He looked her up and down again. "Why? You want 'em all of a sudden?"

"Just show me."

~

"THERE YOU GO." Fifteen minutes later, Jordan gestured toward the far wall of the small, cozy cabin situated away from every other building on Rip's farm. The cabin in which he'd been living on his own for the last several years of his employment here.

Sam peered at the large metal bucket on the floor, filled with water and four more neatly wrapped bouquets of those small, sweet-smelling, mostly fresh Sophy's Roses, a dozen in each.

"Four left. Just like I said. Looks like they're kinda starting to head out. I mean, I've been refilling the water and stuff just in case, but it's not like they're mine. You want 'em?"

Sam ignored the question and turned away from the bucket to peruse Jordan's cabin. "So she came to you first and wanted you to deliver flowers. That isn't... Wait, you said she showed up two *weeks* ago?"

Staring intently at her, the kid slowly nodded. "Give or take a few days."

If she'd heard it from anyone else, Sam wouldn't have believed it. But this kid had no reason to lie to her about either Angela having commissioned the deliveries or the actual day she'd arrived in Rush. Sam believed him.

What she didn't get was why Angela had felt the need to lie to her about it.

"How did she know where to find you?"

Jordan shrugged. "I don't know. She didn't come up to the farm like you did. I just got a phone call. Said she was Dina's mom. Said she was in town and asked if I could meet her. We met at that cafe on the corner on Main Street. The one that's open real early. She probably found my number in Dina's phone or something and figured Dina and I were friends."

Or maybe that he'd been Dina's stalker back in the day...

But if Angela truly believed that, she wouldn't have called him to meet in person for an innocent chat over a cup of coffee and a scone.

"And she didn't tell you anything about me specifically?" Sam asked.

"Just that you live in Birdsong Park. You know, so I could drop the roses there."

"So why'd you keep running?"

"Shit, lady," he said through a nervous chuckle. "If *you* saw you charging right up in your face, you would've run too."

Sam raised an eyebrow. "I'm that scary, huh?"

"Only when you look crazy-pissed like that," he murmured.

She ignored that too and swiped at the corner of her mouth so he wouldn't see her twitching smile. "Why'd you change up the hoodies, then?"

"What? A guy can't have a little variety in this wardrobe without being interrogated about it?"

Sam stopped a few feet in front of him and folded her arms.

The kid was as easy to break as a damn waffle cone.

"All right, fine," he said with a sigh. "Yeah, I normally wear this one. But then you saw me that first morning at the trailer park, and then I saw you and Dina's mom around town together. Figured it was probably best if you didn't recognize me. So I stopped wearing it for a few days."

"When she asked you to deliver these flowers, did Angela say that I couldn't know who you are or that she was the one sending them?"

"I mean, she didn't flat-out *say* it, but I can take a hint. When somebody tells you, 'Make sure she doesn't see you delivering these,' it kinda feels like a secret."

"She didn't say anything about why she was doing this? Sending me flowers? Or why she picked these specific roses or anything?"

"Listen, lady. I just do the work. You tackled me off my bike and into the woods, and I still brought you here. To my place. To show you the proof you wanted. What else you think you're gonna get outta me?"

Clearly, she'd pushed him to his breaking point now, and she didn't want to push him past it. There was no telling what Jordan might do after that.

"No, you're right. Thanks for bringing me out here and finally talking. And sorry if I hurt you. Or whatever."

He narrowed his eyes, then exaggerated a wide roll of his shoulder before grabbing it and wincing. "I'll be fine. Kinda weird Dina's mom didn't tell you what was up, though."

"Why is that weird?"

"You've been running around with her the last ... what? Almost week? Trying to dig into what happened to Dina. I figured maybe the roses had something to do with it."

"No, you left that first bouquet before Angela and I even met," Sam replied automatically. Then her thoughts snagged on one very specific thread in this seemingly pointless conversation. "Hold on." She turned back toward him. "Did she tell you why she came to Rush in the first place? When you guys had coffee."

"She mentioned it. Said something about looking into

what happened to her daughter. That she and Dina hadn't spoken in years, and she came all the way down here to figure out what happened to her."

Something itched in the back of Sam's mind, and she cocked her head as if it would reach some kind of mental backscratcher all the way into that dark corner where she couldn't quite get to the itch on her own. "That's what she said? Verbatim?"

"I guess."

"Jordan, I need you to tell me *exactly* what Angela said about why she came here. I need you to try to remember the exact words she used."

Jordan shoved his hands into his jeans pockets and stared at the floor. "I guess she said she was here to find out what happened to Dina."

"And that was it specifically? She said *what happened* to Dina, not that she was here to find her daughter? Or to find the person who took her daughter? Or that she'd come to make people pay for her daughter's death or something else like that?"

"Her death?" Jordan quickly looked back up at her with wide eyes. "Is she really dead?"

"No, that's not what I'm saying." Sam had no idea if Dina was alive or dead, but this kid clearly wasn't the person to give her that information. Definitely not now. "Just answer the question, Jordan."

"Yeah, man, that's what she said. Pretty damn specifically. The lady came to Rush to figure out what happened to her daughter. That's it."

"All right. I believe you. Thanks." She felt the kid's gaze on her as she turned, perusing the inside of his bachelor cabin.

"You seem like a pretty high-strung person," he said.

"You sure you don't want a little something to help take the edge off?"

"No, I don't drink." The words tasted sour, but at least she wasn't lying. Not for the last few months, anyway.

Jordan high-pitched giggle was unexpected. "Yeah, me neither. I'll stick with the natural shit any day. It's way better."

The flick of a lighter caught her attention, and she found the kid with a freshly rolled joint between his lips and a lighter raised toward the end. The thing didn't seem to want to light, so he flicked it a few more times, then paused and looked at her. "Want some?"

"No, I'm good."

He shrugged, finally got the lighter to work, and puffed on the joint a few times before taking a deep pull and holding his breath.

At this point, Sam felt dangerously close to not being able to tell the difference between up and down, left and right. She thought the Sophy's Roses had been from some douchebag who wanted to stick her heart in a blender and force her to drink it.

It had been Angela the whole time.

Angela, who'd said people generally send flowers out of compassion.

She finally decided to take a seat across from Jordan at the table, took a deep breath, then leaned back in the chair and crossed one leg over the other. "What do *you* think happened to Dina?"

Jordan's bright eyes flickered up to meet her gaze. He slowly licked his lips, as if debating whether or not to be honest with her. To his credit, he seemed to have learned a lesson by avoiding her, so he decided to answer instead. "Honestly, I think she's dead."

"Really?" Sam asked, genuinely surprised.

"Why? You know something I don't?"

"No, I just didn't expect to hear you say that."

"I mean, she *has* to be, right?" He took another puff of his joint and tapped the ashes off on a plate in the center of the table. "If she's the one haunting the Kalamack Club lately. Can't really do that if you're not dead."

Sam couldn't hold back a snigger. "Come on, Jordan. You're a smart guy. You don't actually believe in that bull-shit, do you?"

"Hey, I'm smart enough to know I have no fucking clue."

"There's no such thing as ghosts. Trust me. Every time people think there is, it always turns out to be something else, and then everyone's disappointed. There aren't any ghosts haunting the Kalamack. Definitely not Dina's."

"And what *do* those ghosts usually turn out to be?" he asked.

She held his gaze. "Just regular people, most of the time. Live ones. So how about it, Jordan? Are you Dina's ghost? You the one who's been breaking into the clubhouse and writing those messages all over the walls?"

The kid's eyes bulged from his head before he lurched forward in his chair and burst out laughing. "Are you kidding me? That's the stupidest thing I've ever heard. Why the hell would I do something like that?"

"It's hard to tell why anyone does anything in this town, honestly," she said. "But I'm still trying to figure out why you think Dina's dead."

"After five years?" He shrugged. "That's mostly what happens, right?"

Jordan reached for the joint in the ashtray, paused without touching it, and looked up at her before deciding not to light up again. "I'm not, like, in some kinda trouble about those flowers or anything, right?"

"Not as far as I'm concerned. Between you and me, I'd say you made up for it. And I won't tell Angela you have the rest of the bouquets, all right?"

"Yeah." He snatched up the joint again anyway and leaned back in his chair. "Yeah, thanks a lot."

～

WHEN SAM MADE it back to the Community Center, the door to Meredith's office was wide open and the room empty.

Meredith came around the corner and stopped when she saw Sam. "Hey. Did you get all your important errands done?"

"Where's Angela?" Sam asked.

Meredith's eyebrows shot up, and she resumed walking toward her office. "She left about five minutes after you dropped her off."

"What do you mean she left?"

"It's pretty self-explanatory, Sam. She's not here anymore."

"She just walked out the door to go exploring on foot? This place is miles from anything."

"No, she didn't just walk out," Meredith replied curtly. She crossed her office and sat down calmly behind her desk. "I tried to tell her the same thing, you know, about it being quite a walk to literally anywhere. But she told me she had a ride, and I saw her get into a car in the parking lot. After that, it was out of my hands."

"Whose car?" Sam asked.

"Someone else's," Meredith said, now with a hint of overwhelmed annoyance in her voice. "I appreciate you bringing Angela here, but I can't help anyone who doesn't want to help themselves. You know that. Angela clearly wanted to leave, and that's exactly what she did. I'm not a babysitter or a jail or an inpatient rehab, all right? I don't know who picked her up. All I know is Angela wasn't driving, and that's probably for the best today."

So Meredith obviously knew Angela had been drinking again.

"Great." Sam spun away from the open door to head out again. "Thanks for all the help."

Apparently, Angela had been lying to her all the way up until right before Sam had dropped her off here. There was no way to tell exactly who had picked her up, but now Angela had completely escaped Sam's grasp. She was with who knew what kind of person, and she could be anywhere right now, doing absolutely anything.

The chances of it being something constructive and beneficial to Angela's sanity and recovery didn't look so hot.

"Fuck."

The only other place Sam could think of to look for Angela right now was back at the woman's hotel room. But no one answered the door, and Sam didn't hear anything on the other side of it. She even went to the clerk manning the front desk to ask around.

The clerk confirmed Angela had been staying in that room for the last two weeks — fifteen days, to be exact — and that she'd checked out about half an hour ago.

"Was there anyone else with her?" Sam asked.

The guy scratched the side of his chin and shook his head. "Didn't see anyone."

Then Sam was out of leads and out of ideas.

She spent the next hour and a half cruising through town in her Jeep, searching for Angela's car. She checked parking lots in front of bars first, drove by the liquor store, and got a whole bunch of angry car horns honking up behind her when she drove way below the speed limit down the main streets of Rush's town center, in case Angela somehow got it into her head that binge-shopping was worth her time today.

There was no sign of Angela's car, no sign of Angela, and no sign of what Sam was supposed to do next.

What the fuck was going on?

FORTY-FOUR

Sam

WHAT SAM DID know was this: the person "haunting" the Kalamack Club obviously wasn't Jordan. He thought Dina was dead — or at least he suspected it — and with all the extra errands he'd been running lately, like leaving flowers in front of Sam's trailer at ungodly hours of the morning and running away from her every time they saw each other, she didn't see how it would've been possible for him to get into the Kalamack Club anyway. Beyond that, he was admittedly a little scatterbrained.

No one else came to mind after that, because there *was* no one else. No way in hell would Big Pete have forced this kind of situation onto his own establishment, haunting the place himself just to scare people, forcing him to close the club's doors for several days to hold a séance and then an exorcism on the premises. The man was screwed in the head, sure, but he wasn't *that* loony. In fact, Sam knew just how smart Big Pete Wilder was, which matched his ruthlessness in equal parts.

After the séance, she also didn't think Elaine could've had anything to do with this. The woman had been far too excited about communing with ghosts and spirits. She also knew the risks of messing with her husband's businesses just for a good laugh.

All the usual suspects were now off the table. Even the leggy blonde working the club's front desk — this Laila woman — couldn't have possibly pulled off something like this. She was Big Pete's employee, for crying out loud. Nobody in their right mind would put themselves through that kind of emotional and energetic turmoil just to convince the man his place was haunted. What would Laila have gotten out of it?

Sam couldn't think of anyone else, but she kept running through her conversation with Jordan. She'd told him these ghosts' hauntings almost always turned out to be acts performed by real people with real lives. Or if hauntings weren't some kind of practical joke, they were freak accidents instead and nothing else.

Nothing in the world could have convinced Sam that writing the words "Let Dina Go" on the walls several different times at the Kalamack Club could have possibly been a freak accident.

Which meant *someone* knew who this ghost really was.

Someone *was* the ghost. They were still alive and kicking. And whoever it was, they were also impressively skilled at covering their tracks.

Almost as if they'd done this before.

Sam groaned when it finally hit her. "Oh, for fuck's sake…"

Of course. It made so much sense. If she hadn't been so damn emotional about the whole thing, she would've picked up on it immediately.

But no, she'd let her fucking feelings get in the way and had to go have a little pity party before Hector talked her out of doing something stupid and actually worth pitying.

Thumping the heel of her fist against the steering wheel, Sam huffed out a sigh, mentally berating herself for letting her emotions get in the way.

Which was probably exactly what the person behind the club's hauntings had been going for all along.

~

SAM BARRELED through the front half of Paper Moon, looking left and right for someone to come greet her. At least she had the one simple rule on her side that the customer was always right.

Not that she was going to buy anything.

The back of the store looked like its own private living room. Then she noticed the beaded curtain hanging over the doorway behind the counter, as well as the little silver bell beside an old-fashioned cash register surrounded by large, globe-shaped stones resting on pedestals. As Sam approached them, the little placards in front of these stones marked them as Crystal Viewing Orbs with a price of a hundred fifty dollars each.

Jesus Christ, do people really shell out this kinda money for a big rock stuck on a metal stand that probably cost two bucks at the craft-supply store?

Ignoring the so-called "viewing orbs," Sam slammed her hand down on the bell. Its obnoxiously high-pitched ding reverberated around the back of the store, and Sam waited all of three seconds before she hit it again, and again, and one more time.

A hand finally slipped through the beaded curtain and drew them all aside.

Then out walked Francine, her eyes wide with curiosity as her short, messily curly gray hair bobbed up and down with every step.

"I'm coming, I'm coming. Yes, so glad you've found the bell." She stopped when she saw Sam, then broke into an enormous grin. "Well hello, there. Good to see you again. And so soon. What can I do for you?"

"How did you do it?" Sam snapped, remaining at the end of the counter but preparing herself to move if Francine reacted like Jordan and decided to run. "That's what I can't figure out. So now I need you to tell me."

Francine chuckled politely and shook her head. "I'm sorry, I'm not quite sure I understand."

"How'd you get in?" Sam clarified. "To the club, Francine, huh? You're not a member. So what did you do? Steal somebody's key? Bribe one of the staff?"

Francine's smile never wavered. "You'll have to forgive my ignorance, but I have no idea what you're talking about."

"The earrings, Francine. I gotta admit, that one really got me. Hidden compartment in the desk where Dina's favorites would be found. The hummingbird earrings. That was a nice touch. Very believable. So how did you do it? Couldn't have been in broad daylight under anyone else's nose. I know for a fact that woman Laila in reception doesn't let anyone in unless they paid an arm and a leg for an active membership. So what did you do to get those earrings in that desk drawer? I just can't put two and two together."

Francine sidled down the other side of the counter until she stood directly in front of Sam with the crystal balls between them. "There's obviously some kind of misunderstanding here. It's Sam, right?"

Sam raised her eyebrows. She knew this woman knew her name and that she was still putting on an act here. That was the only thing that made sense.

"Listen, I know the séance got a little choppy," the

woman added. "They do that sometimes. It's all part of the risk we take by communing with the dead."

"You can cut the bullshit. I'm on to you. I know you were involved in this. Now I need you to tell me how you got those earrings into the secret compartment in that desk, which I saw myself, so I know at least *that* was real."

Francine pressed her lips together, then inhaled deeply through her nose. "I'm sorry I can't help you, Sam. Unfortunately for your theory, the only time I've ever set foot inside the Kalamack Club was last night for the séance, and that was it."

"Then you got someone else to do your dirty work for you. You know Dina, don't you? Or you knew her five years ago when she was still in town."

"I'd seen her around a few times, yeah," Francine finally relented. "She came in here every once in a while to browse through our reading materials or look through the clothing. Never bought anything, though. I think sometimes she was just looking for a little change of pace, but I didn't know her well. Every time she came in, she was polite, kind, a real sweet girl from what I hear, and that's the extent of it."

"So how'd you get the earrings?" Sam asked again. "And how the hell did you plant them in that desk?"

"The answer you're looking for just doesn't exist, Sam," Francine replied, spreading her arms. "I'm sorry to have to be the one to tell you that, judging by how obviously unwilling you are to accept it. I can also tell you I absolutely did not plant those earrings."

"Then who the hell did?" Sam almost shouted.

The other woman merely shook her head.

It was a perfect facade of cluelessness, that was for sure.

And yet Sam just couldn't let this one go.

"If you don't tell me who planted those earrings," she said, leaning closer over the counter between them, "I'll have to start talking about the hauntings being one giant hoax. And, of course, pointing the finger back at you, Francine, and your store. You're the only one in town who holds séances, after all. I can't imagine a woman like you with experience like yours has absolutely no idea how certain things happen. So tell me who planted the damn earrings."

The other woman blinked quickly, then her gaze dropped toward a small, brightly painted wicker basket sitting on the counter beside the crystal balls.

Sam followed her gaze and found herself staring at a bunch of silver angel pins thrust through small pieces of cardstock, which were printed with first a name in larger bold letters and then a description typed out below.

Great. Sam had already been forced to sit through an entire séance that hadn't gone anywhere. And now this nutjob was answering her questions with angels. What came next? Seeing some future of Sam's horrifying demise in one of these crystal balls right here?

But then a name on one of the angel cards caught her eye, and she couldn't help but snort. "Why does that one say Dina on it?"

"It's the name of an angel," Francine replied matter-of-factly, as if this was something everyone automatically knew. "The seventh angel of heaven, believe it or not."

Pressing her lips together, Sam reached into the basket for the same type of angel pin stuck through the same type of card, though this one had a different name and a different description. She picked it up and turned it around for Francine to see. "And this one?"

The woman nodded sagely. "I'm not just making these things up for my own personal amusement, by the way. But anyone who knows anything about angels could also tell you this. Yes, Laila is the name of another angel."

Biting back a snarl, Sam dropped the card and the pin back into the basket with a soft rustle of paper against paper, then fixed Francine with a bitter smile. "Thanks a lot. You've been so forthcoming."

"Are you sure I can't interest you in some crystals to take with you on your way?" Francine called after her as Sam stormed back across the store. "It never hurts to have a little extra help on your side."

Sam didn't respond. She was too focused on getting the hell out of this store without anything else holding her back. Because Jesus Christ, how could she have been so incredibly stupid about this whole thing?

Naming one child after some seventh angel of heaven was one thing. But naming both children after specific angels? That was a theme.

Angela never had told Sam the name of her oldest daughter.

And Sam had been so caught up in what was missing, she hadn't stopped to take a good look at what was already right in front of her.

When she reached the shop's front doors, though, she paused, not sure why she couldn't yet bring herself to step outside again until she heard footsteps behind her.

Francine stood there with an armful of books.

Sam gritted her teeth and headed back toward the woman. "One more question."

Francine looked up at her as if she hadn't realized Sam was in her store. "Hopefully I have one more answer."

"Why did you have to bring my daughter into it?"

The confusion on Francine's face would have been incredibly difficult for even the best actor to reproduce artificially. "I'm sorry?"

"My daughter," Sam repeated. "At the end of the séance. That message from the little girl. Why did you have to bring her into it?"

The confusion quickly melted into another of Francine's warm, inviting smiles Sam was quickly growing to loathe. "I didn't do any of it, Sam. The spirits spoke to me, as they sometimes do, and I simply gave that little girl's spirit a voice."

Seriously? That was the best answer this phony had?

Sam grimaced, then spun on her heel and slammed both hands against the glass front doors before marching swiftly back to her Jeep.

She'd let herself be blinded by all the other emotions and all the other mysteries and possibilities, she'd basically made herself one of the easiest, most willing targets ever. All while eating up all the bullshit like candy with an idiot's grin and a please and thank you.

Angela's daughter wasn't back in Seattle, waiting for her mom to come home after her search in Rush.

She'd been right here in town this whole time, right under Sam's nose and everyone else's, working diligently away at the goddamn Kalamack Club.

SAM'S recent discoveries fueled her all the way across town and out down the frontage road to the Kalamack Club. Then she was storming through the front door like she was Big Pete Wilder himself, barging in to make heads roll.

In fact, Laila seemed to expect her employer after the door cracked so loudly and violently against the club-house's interior wall. But her expression of forced patience transformed into horror when she realized it was Sam Salazar blasting through.

Sam didn't give a shit what the leggy blonde thought of her.

She stormed toward the front desk, fists clenched at her sides as she opened her mouth to start raining hell on this woman who'd jerked her around one too many times in one too many different ways.

"I'm so sorry," Laila said a little louder than necessary as she hurried around the side of her desk. "I can't allow you to come in here. The Kalamack Club is for members only, and our all-male membership is only allowed to bring women inside as guests. But all guests must be accompanied by a member."

"I think I've got a pretty clear picture of the rules," Sam snapped as she stomped stopped a few feet from Laila. "You think Big Pete will hand over an honorary membership to me anyway once I tell him *you're* the fucking ghost haunting his club the last couple days?"

Laila's eyes widened, and she froze.

"I don't know, maybe he'll go easy on you, right?" Sam added. "All I'd have to do is tell him your *mother's* the one doing all the real hard work. Mothers always are. It's not like Angela has much of a reputation to uphold in this town anyway, huh?"

"Sam," Laila began, her voice still incredibly calm. "Listen. I can explain."

"Great," Sam practically shouted. "Why don't you explain it to both of us at the same time? It might actually be the one thing that doesn't piss Big Pete off about being forced into a room with me. Should we go get him?"

"Seriously, I need you to keep your voice down. And I *will* tell you everything, Sam, all right? It's about time anyway."

"You're damn right it's about time."

Laila glanced nervously around the front part of the

clubhouse, then stepped toward Sam. "I promise. I just need you to go right now. You can't stay here. And there's nothing I can do or say today that's gonna make it all right for you to be inside this building. So I'll meet you at my apartment later, okay? I'll text you the address. But I need you to leave now."

Sam bit her lower lip to keep from spewing even more hot air. "You don't have my number."

Laila tilted her head and fixed Sam with a poignant look.

Of course. Mothers and daughters shared all kinds of things, didn't they?

"You better not be trying to drag me around in circles," Sam warned.

"I promise. No more secrets. No more hiding or sneaking around. I will tell you everything, Sam. I promise. But you have to go."

Pounding footsteps from directly overhead cut off whatever else she might have said. Then Laila tried to shoo Sam back toward the door as those footsteps clomped down the staircase.

"Laila!" Big Pete roared before emerging at the bottom landing. "I need you to call—" His words cut off, and his jaw clenched visibly as he now glared at Sam standing beside the desk. "What the fuck are *you* doing here?"

"Just waiting for a charming hello like that one," Sam quipped.

"You know what? I don't actually give a shit. If you don't get the hell out of my club in the next five seconds, I'll have you arrested for trespassing. Wouldn't be the first time that's happened in the last few weeks. And I don't care that it's you, Salazar. I'll fucking do it again."

"Sam just stopped by to ask if I'd seen her necklace," Laila added quickly. "She had it at the séance when she came by and hasn't seen it since, so she thought she might've dropped it here somewhere."

Sam didn't miss a beat in the lie, but she couldn't bring herself to look at the blonde woman actually trying to save her ass right now. Or maybe Laila was just trying to save her own ass. "It's a thin silver pendant on a chain. About the size of a quarter. Has a little symbol etched into the front. I realized it was missing this morning, so I thought I'd just retrace my steps."

"Here." Laila leapt behind her desk again, snatched up a pen and a pad of sticky notes, then got busy scratching away as she spoke. "This is my direct number here. Call again next week. I'll talk to the staff and have them keep an eye out for your necklace over the next few days. Maybe one of the janitors finds it. If they do, I'll make sure I hold onto it for you."

The pen clattered onto the desk. The sticky note whispered swiftly off the top of the pad, and Laila handed it to Sam with a curt nod.

Sam accepted the note and in a quick glance of half a second saw it was an address, not a phone number.

Damn, this woman could've made one hell of a living as a professional liar.

She folded the sticky note in half and shoved it into her pocket. "Yeah, I'll do that. Thanks. Good to see you, Pete."

Big Pete sneered at her and said nothing.

Then Sam was out the door, hurrying across the Kalamack Club's front porch and barely keeping herself from breaking into a full-on run toward her Jeep.

AT LEAST THE address on the sticky note hadn't been a complete lie too.

Sam drove around Laila's apartment complex, scanning everything in sight until she came to Building 3.

There were two dumpsters behind this building, behind which she caught a glimpse of Angela's Honda parked haphazardly as if the woman had tried to hide it from view.

Probably after the drinking binge that had led her to her daughter's apartment in the first place.

The fact that Sam hadn't figured out the women's relationship until now infuriated her every time she thought about it. Which was nearly every second, because that was why she'd come here in the first place.

They'd better have a damn good reason for lying to her.

She found Laila's apartment easily enough after stomping up the exterior stairs to the second floor. Then she pounded on the door, not giving a shit that her knock absolutely carried that official-sounding weight and cadence so often attributed to visits from local police.

She just didn't have the energy to act like she was anyone or anything else.

Or that she wasn't completely pissed.

A muffled thump rose from the other side of the apartment door.

"Oh. I guess someone's just a little scattered, huh? What is it, honey? Did you forget your keys?" The door opened to reveal Angela's face, already grinning. "I haven't seen them—"

Her words cut off the second she recognized Sam standing there, and her smile disappeared.

"Actually," Sam said, "I'm pretty sure *you're* the one who forgot something."

Angela blinked, then instantly swung the door shut with both hands.

Sam stuck her foot through the door, which thumped against the side of her sneaker instead of its setting in the doorjamb. She grabbed the doorknob before putting her shoulder and most of her body's weight into it. "Don't look so surprised, Angela. Your *daughter* sent me."

That was all it took to shatter Angela's resolve.

The woman's expression slackened. Her faced paled into sickly yellow hue. She released the door before staggering backward down the entryway. "Sam…"

"Yeah, we all know who I am." Sam entered, then swung the door shut behind herself.

"I'm so, so sorry," Angela repeated, staggering farther away with each of Sam's steps inside. "I never meant to hurt you. I never meant to cause any more chaos in your life. You've been so incredibly helpful. Better than I ever could've imagined. Everything you've done, I appreciate so much, and I don't want you to think—"

"Just shut up," Sam snapped. Then she headed for the kitchen table, hardly able to look Angela in the eye. Not that she could have given the way Angela's gaze darted all over the room.

The woman sniffed heavily and still hadn't regained any color in her cheeks.

Her eyes were red-rimmed, just like the tip of her nose, and she seemed to have a particularly difficult time maintaining focus on much of anything.

So she'd definitely been drinking.

Sam definitely didn't need to be looking that in the face right now either.

"This whole time, you never actually gave a shit what I think." Sam noisily yanked a chair out from under the kitchen table. The legs caught on the linoleum floor and skidded, clanging about until she finally decided to sit. She kicked her feet out across the floor with one ankle over the other and folded her arms. "So I don't wanna hear a goddamn thing from you about what you did or didn't want me to think."

Angela looked quickly back and forth between Sam and the front door. "Then why are you here?"

"I already told you. Your daughter sent me. If that's not enough of an explanation for you, I guess you'll have to wait for the rest of it, just like me."

Angela didn't say anything else. Instead, she scuttled around the apartment, wringing her hands and muttering to herself and occasionally darting quick glances in Sam's direction, which consistently went ignored. Eventually, she disappeared into the kitchen, where she clanked and banged around with cabinets, cupboards, drawers, and various appliances. The sink turned on and off. More clunking. Then came the soft, telltale burble of a coffeepot brewing a fresh batch.

Great. I'll probably never enjoy coffee again after this.

When Laila finally came home, she found her terrified-looking mother and one furious-looking Sam both sitting at the kitchen table.

Angela instantly stood and disappeared into the kitchen again, from which the sounds of coffee pouring into empty mugs emanated.

Laila glanced that way, slipped her purse off her shoulder, and hung it on the coatrack. Then she met Sam's gaze and nodded. "How's she doing?"

"You tell me. That's why I'm here, in case you forgot."

Laila kicked off her work heels and shrugged out of the light sweater before hanging it over the half-wall partition separating the dining room from the kitchen. Then she headed toward the table. "No, I haven't forgotten. But I had to come up with a good excuse to get out of the clubhouse. Told Pete I was coming down with something, so he was happy to kick me out and tell me not to bother coming back in tomorrow unless I felt like a new woman. So there's that…"

"How lovely to hear your position at the Kalamack Club wasn't compromised." Sam's voice dripped with sarcasm, which Laila obviously recognized, though without comment.

That only frustrated Sam all the more. "Because I'd just feel *awful* if all your lies somehow got you into even more trouble."

"Okay, Sam, you've made your point." Laila shot her a curt look before pulling out another chair and slowly settling into it. "And you have every right to be upset with us, which is why I wanted you to come over. We should've cleared this up a long time ago."

Sam folded her arms again and shrugged. "I'm still waiting for you to tell me something I *don't* know. Which at this point is a whole hell of a lot. So I suggest we get a move on before all three of us run out of time."

Neither Sam nor Laila said another word until Angela rejoined them with a large plastic serving tray in hand. The whole setup looked like it had come straight off a Backyard-Summer-Picnic-in-Suburbia display. On it were three coffee mugs, a surprisingly wide selection of things to put in the coffee, and a lime-green teapot with the lid on.

Sam only knew it wasn't actually tea because she could smell the coffee.

"Here we go." Angela stumbled a little as she approached the table but managed to get the whole tray down without incident. "Can't start a heavy conversation without a good cup of coffee, right?"

A nervous chuckle escaped her, and she sidled around the table toward the closest empty chair before dropping into it.

Laila stared at the lime-green teapot. "Mom? You did make *coffee*, right?"

"Well, I thought that was fairly obvious. That pot in the coffeemaker doesn't keep it hot, Laila. And we're gonna be here a while, so I want to make sure the coffee *stays* hot. Nobody likes to drink cold coffee."

"Not the most important detail right now..." Laila muttered through clenched teeth. Then she inhaled deeply, let out a calming sigh, and looked up at Sam. "How much time do you have?"

"As much time as it takes," Sam said. "And I wanna know everything. Every last detail. Starting with the daily flower deliveries for a week."

FORTY-FIVE

Sam

"FIRST OF ALL," Angela began, "I just really want to apologize, Sam. I never meant to hurt you with any of this, and I know the details just kept getting buried under so much…" She looked up at Sam and must not have liked what she saw there; her lower lip trembled, and tears sprang to her eyes. Amazing that the woman could somehow look so violently ill, genuinely apologetic, and like she'd spent all morning drinking all at the same time.

"The flowers first, Angela," Sam reminded her.

"Right, the flowers…" The woman licked her lips, stared at the contents of her coffee mug, then continued as best she could. "The flowers were my attempt to reach out to you, I suppose. Before I decided to come down to Rush and help Laila, she told me she knew of someone here in town who we could trust with this whole thing. Someone who would want to help us, not necessarily because there was anything in it for her but out of the goodness of her heart. Someone who couldn't be bought by the Wilders, no matter what, which obviously was incredibly important. And, well, someone who knew firsthand what it was like to lose a daughter. It's not one of those things just anyone's gonna understand. So I thought the flowers were the best way to connect with you first."

"I don't think I've said more than two sentences to you about my daughter since we met," Sam slowly replied. "Two very short sentences."

"I know that. See, Laila had done some digging on you before, and she managed to find out a little bit more than you would've told me anyway. I just wanted to show you that I — that *anyone* — was thinking about you. That I understood the pain of—"

"Don't tell me you understand my pain," Sam interrupted. "You never knew my daughter. You hardly even know me. That's not for you to decide, whether or not you understand it. And inserting yourself into my personal life like that, no matter what your intentions were, doesn't show understanding. It shows the exact opposite."

"Y-yes, of course, Sam. I ... I know that too," Angela stammered. "I mean, I know that *now*, obviously. I thought the Sophy's Roses would've been a sweet touch. Something to connect the two of us in a positive, compassionate way. They're *flowers*. But I realized as soon as I saw how upset they made you that I was wrong, which is why I decided not to bring up the topic of your daughter after that. I'd meant to ... but I didn't."

"That might just be the only good decision you've made since you got here," Sam quipped.

Tears welled and slid out from beneath Angela's lashes again. She wasn't full-on sobbing, which probably had more to do with the booze in her system than anything else. But she still looked physically ill.

Sam hadn't seen her drinking since she'd arrived at the apartment, so she didn't know how far gone the woman was. She was willing to bet it was far enough to numb

Angela for this conversation but not far enough to help her avoid feeling everything.

"I deserve that, I guess," Angela said.

"Okay, so then the way we met," Sam prompted. "That was all prearranged too, yeah?"

Angela nodded, returning her gaze to her coffee with more cream and sugar in it than coffee this time. "It was. I already knew you worked at the Redwood Rings, obviously. Laila told me all about it, and I knew you'd be there. My explosive reaction to you just trying to be friendly wasn't part of the plan. That was all in the moment."

"And you sitting there afterward because your tires had been slashed and the spark plugs removed?"

Angela glanced at her oldest daughter, and Laila responded with as encouraging of a nod as she could muster to help her mother continue.

"That was me too," Angela finally admitted. "I did it to my own car. We decided I needed a valid excuse for sticking around in town as long as I had. Slashed tires weren't quite enough to do the trick."

"Hell of a way to put me off the scent," Sam said. "It always seemed a little off that someone else would destroy the fastest and easiest way for you to get out of town if they were trying to force you to leave."

"I needed a better reason to stay," Angela confessed. "To spend more time with you, if I couldn't drive myself anywhere. And you offered, just like Laila expected you to."

Sam glanced at the blonde sitting quietly across the table. As if she could feel that gaze, Laila looked right into Sam's eyes and pressed her lips together.

"Sounds like Laila put an awful lot of effort into building this file on me," Sam said.

"It wasn't because—" Angela choked on the words, her

tears flowing more freely now. She shook her head over and over, which made her look like she'd completely forgotten how to carefully choose her words and had therefore given up altogether.

Simply put, she was just too upset — or too drunk — to keep going.

Sam's brain kicked into overdrive as she reviewed the various oddities of Angela's reactions over the last several days.

"That's what you were trying to hide," Sam said. "Earlier today. I was joking about you having a secret visitor in there, and then I thought you were trying to hide your drinking from me, which honestly made more sense than anything else. But that wasn't it at all, was it? You actually did have someone in your room. Not a man. It was Laila."

Mother and daughter stared at her from their seats around the table. Angela nodded. "That was definitely part of it. But I have to be perfectly honest with you, Sam. I did start drinking again the other day. That's why I wanted to leave town. This place just isn't good for me. I keep thinking—"

Another choked sob escaped her before she tried again. "I keep thinking that if someone would just…"

Then she really did break down crying — small, silent sobs that shook her entire body. She slumped forward in her chair and buried her face in her hands.

Sam and Laila waited patiently for Angela's crying to stop, but when it became clear that wasn't going to happen anytime soon, Laila took over for her mother and continued.

"Everything you already know so far about my mom, about Dina, it's all true. Five years ago, Dina hopped on a bus from Seattle to Rush by herself. She came down here to work as a trimmer on a pot farm and save money for med school. She got offered that job at the Kalamack Club, and she took it. Easier work, nicer environment, way better pay. She and my mom did have a huge falling out while Dina was still here in Rush. Mom was still drinking. Those things all happened. We didn't lie to you about any of it."

"So what *did* you lie to me about then?" Sam asked.

Laila shook her head. "Nothing. We didn't lie at all. We just left a few things out. Mainly the part about Dina making it home after Shell put her on that bus back to Seattle."

Sam straightened in the chair. "She made it home."

Laila nodded. "Right on schedule. I picked her up from the bus station in Seattle myself."

Despite these not-so-fun revelations, Sam had to admit Angela technically hadn't lied to her at all. She'd never once said she'd come to Rush to find her daughter or to find answers to why she went missing or why she disappeared or to find whoever was responsible for kidnapping or abducting her. Those words had never left her mouth.

Every single time she'd mentioned it, Angela had always said her reason for being here was to *find out what had happened to her daughter*. It was only too easy for everyone else to assume that meant she thought Dina was either dead or missing. Clearly, that just wasn't the case.

"So Dina came home," Sam repeated. "And … what? I'm guessing there was something incredibly different about her, right? Something wrong? Like she'd changed somehow?"

Angela lifted her face out of her hands to gape at Sam. "How did you…"

"That's the only other explanation to you saying over and over you came here to *find out what happened to her*."

"Because something *did* happen to her," Laila added.

"Something awful. She was a mess when she got off that bus. Over the next few weeks, we realized it wasn't just some small thing she could quickly get over. Something terrible happened, and Dina wouldn't talk about it. No matter how long we waited or how patient we were or how often we told her we were here for her."

This time, Laila's voice quivered, and her eyes misted a little, but she didn't break down like her mother. Then she cleared her throat and continued. "She was depressed. I don't throw that word around lightly. I mean she was *really* depressed. She'd brought home everything she'd saved working in Rush and used some of it to enroll in medical school. Mom and I encouraged her to go, thinking that might bring some of the spark back, but she dropped out after the first semester…"

Laila puffed out a heavy sigh through trembling lips and closed her eyes, shaking her head against the painful memory.

Sam noticed Angela reaching toward her daughter to gently pat Laila's thigh before taking it upon herself to continue their tale.

With tears still streaming down her face, Angela looked directly up at Sam and said what needed to be said in an eerily detached way. "Dina committed suicide three months ago. My daughter, Laila's sister, is dead. It's still fresh for us. For five years, she wouldn't tell us what happened. We still don't know what happened to her here. We don't know why she came back as some empty shell of the beautiful, vibrant, amazing young woman she was before she left. So what we really came here for was information. We're here for the truth."

"And revenge," Laila added, the intensity of furious determination in her voice putting even Sam a little on edge.

Angela scrunched up her face and didn't look nearly as gung-ho about the idea. "I still haven't made up my mind about that part just yet. Really, all I'm looking for is the why. Some kind of explanation so I can finally have the closure we've been looking for for the last five years."

Sam nodded, still trying to work out all the various pieces for herself. "I spoke to Shell again. She told me she thought Dina might've been pregnant."

Both Angela and Laila looked up from their coffee cups, each woman's cheeks stained to various degrees with tears, though Angela looked far worse for wear.

"Well that's new," Angela said. "If she was, Dina would've had to have an abortion or a miscarriage before she came home. There was no baby."

"She never mentioned anything about it to us either way," Laila added. "It would make sense, though, if that's what actually happened. We don't really have any way to prove it, do we?"

"Not yet," Sam said.

The apartment fell silent beneath the heavy weight of all these new truths these three women now shared.

Then Laila nodded as if she'd made up her mind and pushed herself to her feet. "There's something I want to show you, Sam. If now isn't the time, I don't know what would be better after this. I should've said something sooner."

This time, Sam didn't have any biting quips in response. Her curiosity overshadowed any frustration or anger she might've still harbored.

Laila disappeared into her bedroom, then returned shortly thereafter with an envelope, which she set gingerly down on the table in front of Sam as if it were some precious, fragile heirloom — or an unstable stick of dynamite.

"What's this?" Sam looked up from the blank front of the standard-letter-sized envelope, then slowly picked it up and turned it over.

"I think you should just read it," Laila replied.

The back of the envelope had been left unsealed, and the piece of plain white paper inside couldn't have been unfolded and folded again more than two or three times. The creases were still crisp and stiff. Unfolding that paper now made Sam feel like an intruder, but she focused on the surprisingly difficult-to-read handwriting and devoured the letter's contents.

'PETER,

I know we had an agreement, but I can't continue to keep my end of it. What we did was beyond reprehensible. I'd even go so far as to call it evil. And after all this time, I still haven't been able to let it go. I can't keep living this lie with all its secrets. I can't let the truth out and keep living with that, either. This is the only way. I hope you find your conscience too someday. Sooner rather than later. I did my best.

Reginald'

SAM READ the letter two more times, just to be sure the words she'd thought she made out in Dr. Jones' nearly illegible chicken scratch were in fact the words he'd penned himself.

"How did you get ahold of this?"

Sighing deeply through her nose, Laila sat in her chair again and swallowed. "I don't think Dr. Jones had any idea I was still at the club the night he hanged himself. He'd slipped this letter under the front door, probably thinking Pete would find it the next morning. He clearly didn't consider the fact that Pete's not the first one to walk into the building every morning or the last one to leave. I guess the man wasn't really thinking at all, anyway. Scared me half to death when I stepped onto the front porch that night and found him hanging there. Already cold…"

"The club closes at ten generally, doesn't it?"

Laila nodded.

"So you weren't there just locking up for the night, were you?"

Laila glanced at her mother, then back at Sam again and dipped her head. "No. I couldn't call the police because there was no way to explain what I was doing there almost two hours after I usually leave. That would've only led to more questions I couldn't answer because, well, I was busy…"

"Haunting the Kalamack Club," Sam finished for her.

"Yeah."

"So, Dina's necklace, then. The one found in Dr. Jones' hand when the police arrived on the scene. The one he was holding when I got there first. Was *that* you?"

"I've never done anything like that before," Laila said. "I promise you that's the truth. I just … well, we'd already put our plan into motion, and I saw an opportunity. So I took it. Slipped her ID in his pocket too."

"At least the man wasn't murdered and we don't have to cover *that* up," Sam said with a shrug. "Plus, we've got a suicide note to prove it." She gingerly folded the letter back into thirds, slipped it into the envelope, and set the envelope down on the table before staring at it for a moment. "Actually, now that I think about it, this letter could be the one thing that helps us solve a whole number of different problems all at once." She looked up at mother and daughter sitting around the table with her and hoped she wasn't shooting in the dark here. "Would you be interested in staying undercover just a little longer and tackling one more thing with me? Now that I'm in on the whole thing, I don't have to tell anyone else until it's all wrapped up. Or ever, really, since it's none of my business. As far as I'm concerned, Laila breaking into her own place of employment is on the same level of punishable crimes as Angela picketing the club's front porch. And I can't believe you had your own mother arrested."

"The arrest was her idea, actually," Laila added.

"Remind me not to screw with the two of you in the future," Sam said. Tight smiles and less-than-sincere chuckles rose around the table. "So how about it? Do you guys wanna help me finish this?"

"Absolutely," Angela said, nodding fervently. "Though honestly, I'm surprised you'd want anything to do with us after this."

"Well, you came clean eventually. Might as well use it to our advantage. I'm in the same boat as Laila on this one. This looks like an opportunity, and I think the three of us should seize it while we can."

Laila scooted forward to the edge of her chair, clasping her hands together in her lap. "I'm in."

"Good. Listen, I have to get to work soon, so I'll make this quick. Just the basics of a plan, but I really do think we can pull it off." With the full attention of both Copely women, Sam walked them quickly through the steps of what her mind had drummed up all on its own.

One more shot at digging up the truth. One final message. One last chance for the people of this town to come clean and do the right thing.

When she'd finished, they all agreed to meet back here at Laila's apartment at midnight, after which they'd get busy putting Sam's plan in motion.

FORTY-SIX

Sam

SAM HAD JUST enough time to stop back by the trailer park for a change of clothes and to grab a few necessary items before heading out again.

The town barricades were right where she'd left them after pulling them aside the last time, but when she rolled up to her usual parking spot between the trailers, she found Syc standing at the firepit, the canister of lighter fluid once more in hand while flames blazed in front of him.

He didn't seem to have noticed her arrival as usual when she shut the door to the Jeep and headed toward him. Dog barked happily a few times before bounding off across the open field and leaving the humans to their business. Syc still didn't say anything. The man scrunched up his face and lit another joint as he glowered at the roaring flames.

Sam stopped a few feet away from him. "What are you burning this time?"

"You telling me you don't recognize these?"

Sam squinted into the flames and made out the edge of a laminated corner and some bold blocky letters a few

456

seconds before they shriveled up into acridly stinking black smoke. "My guess is you decided to liberate our community eviction notice."

"You guessed correctly." He shrugged and puffed on the joint. "Guess you're smarter than you look after all."

She huffed out a laugh and folded her arms. "What's the plan with this, then? Notice said thirty days."

"I bit the bullet and hired a lawyer to look into it. So we're getting real legal help from a real legal professional. Apparently in this day and age, zoning laws are actually a thing, and folks actually give a shit about 'em."

Sam clicked her tongue and shook her head. "Times are a-changin'."

"Don't even get me started, kid."

"Let me know if you need any help. Or if the lawyer needs any help." Sam snorted. "Or if you need help with the lawyer, I guess. It's gotta be one of those."

"I'll handle my end of it just fine. You keep doing what you're doing on your own. If I need ya, I'll say something."

"And I can trust you not to storm into the mayor's office again on your own?"

His only response was a non-committal grunt that made her laugh before she took off toward the Deville.

Sam dressed quickly in all black, which no one at the Redwoods would question on a bartender. She gathered everything else she thought might be useful for her planned outing tonight and headed for the door. On the way out, her gaze fell one more time on the emptied-out coffee grounds tin she'd transformed into a flower vase. The first bouquet of Sophy's Roses was still there, still with plenty of water despite the fact that Sam hadn't touched it in days. She reached toward the soft pink flowers that had now reached full bloom, then decided against it.

❧

SHE DIDN'T KNOW what it was about hospitals, but even in a town as small as Rush, the nurses still refused to hand out information like where certain patients were being kept in recovery rooms to anyone who couldn't immediately prove their familial relationship to said patient.

So Sam resorted to sneaking around the regional hospital and eventually found where Dr. Greg Masterson resided for the moment, only because one of the nurses had left out a check-in sheet on a clipboard right where anyone could see it.

He was awake in the hospital bed when she knocked on the door and slowly opened it.

"Sam?"

"Hey, Doc. How you doing?"

"Well, I'm not dead. I guess that's a plus. Colton told me you were the one who called in for me."

"For once, Chief Colton isn't full of shit." Sam laughed at her own half-joke. Greg didn't laugh, but he did crack a partially amused smile. "Yeah, I called it in. I realize I probably should've called you back to say I was heading up, but that would've just ruined the surprise, don't you think?"

"Thanks. For all of it."

"Don't mention it. I'd say you could make it up to me by telling me now what you were going to tell me at your place, but I've already figured it out." Sam approached his bed and stopped a few feet away, glad to see the man's injuries weren't as bad as they could've been. His arm was in a cast and a sling, and he had had several rounds of stitches, but otherwise, it looked like he'd recover just fine.

"I know it was Hank," she added.

He widened his eyes. "You know it was Hank what?"

458

"Couple of things, actually. I know it was Hank who put you in this hospital bed, and I know it was Hank having an affair with Dina when she worked at the Kalamack Club five years ago."

"Oh. Then I guess that conversation we never had is a moot point."

"I appreciate your willingness to talk about it anyway." Sam decided her shift at the Redwood could wait a few extra minutes, so she grabbed one of the god-awful hospital chairs, pulled it toward the bed, and sat. "If there's anything else you'd like to say, I'm here now."

"I guess you got most of it down already." Greg shook his head and stared at the drab hospital sheets draped over his legs. "Hank and I used to be best friends. One of the coolest things ever was when my best friend proposed to my business partner's daughter. Did you know Reggie and I used to work together at the same practice in town?"

"I figured as much."

"Everything felt perfect back then. Like nothing bad could ever happen because here we were, being adults, living the life, knowing what people in this town do day after day. I guess Hank and I drifted apart over the years for various reasons. Definitely didn't hurt that I moved up into the boonies. But I still felt I should say something to him, you know? That I'd called you to give you the rest of the story about him and Dina. I felt he deserved not to be blindsided by that. No way in hell were you going to take the information I gave you and not go to him with it."

Sam's smile widened. "Sounds like I left an impression on you, Doc."

"Seems like everyone does these days. I'm glad you got the story straight, even if you had to figure it out on your own."

"I'm glad you got to the hospital on time," she said. "Has he ever done something like this to you before?"

"What? No. Pretty sure that was a one-time thing. Last desperate attempt, you know?"

"Sure. Did he ever do something like this to Dina?"

Greg looked even more horrified by that thought, then slowly shook his head. "I really don't think so. Hank's got a temper on him, sure, and he could get loud and mean if he felt like he had to. But he's never raised a hand to a woman. Especially not Dina. Even after all this time, I'm still convinced he really was in love with her."

"What makes you say that?"

"Just the way he was about it. I knew about them. That was all back when Hank and I were still talking. We were still friends, before the club kicked me out. But I really don't know what happened between them afterward. Why she left the way she did, or why she even left at all, honestly. All I know is he was torn up worse than I've ever seen after she left."

"Thanks for your help, Doc." Sam nodded and shot him an appreciative smile. "Turns out you're still useful even in a hospital bed."

"Very funny." They both chuckled, because almost nothing was as painful as taking oneself too seriously when shit got too serious.

Sam cleared her throat and figured it was time to cover one more topic. "Listen, I gotta get to work, but I have another favor to ask of you. If you don't mind."

"I'm not sure how much help I can be, but sure. Let's hear it."

"Can I borrow your house?"

Greg's face scrunched up in a confused, partially laughing frown. "My what now?"

"Your house. Your current home. You know, the cabin

in the woods where I found you beat to shit on your kitchen floor. Ring any bells?"

He barked out a laugh, then winced at whatever pain it caused him before pulling himself together again. "What do you want with my cabin?"

"Thing is, I'm ridiculously close to figuring out exactly what happened between Dina and Hank right before she left Rush for good. I just have to put a few pieces into play. And I was hoping to use your cabin to get that ball rolling. I won't touch the house, though, Doc. I promise. Just use of the property. You won't even know I was there once this place releases you. And if you say no, I totally get it. It's your exile."

He laughed harder at that than anything else before Sam felt it was an appropriate time to continue.

"But if you agree," she added, "this could seriously help Angela find some closure around her daughter and their past and everything that happened here. Though you're not practicing on the regular anymore, Doc, it's still a good chance for you to seriously impact people's lives again in a positive way."

Greg studied her for a moment, then smirked. "You had me at 'close to finding out what happened between Dina and Hank'."

"Oh, great. Thanks for stopping me."

He shrugged, made ridiculously awkward by his arm in a sling and all the other physical discomfort that came with it. "Don't worry about it. I'm doing what I can. House keys are over there on the table. Right-hand jacket pocket."

"Excellent." Sam spun around to go find his keyring, then lifted it toward the man with a playful little jingle. "I'll make sure to bring them back."

"If you don't, I'm sure it's fairly easy to figure out where you live."

"Careful, Doc. Someone might overhear and think you've started threatening people all of a sudden. Seriously, though, I appreciate the help."

"I hope it's enough," he said. "I spent way too much time sitting on all these secrets as it is."

"Trust me, you're not the only one."

She knew full well what she was walking into for her shift on a Saturday night. Both bars at the Redwood Rings were packed almost to capacity.

They were so busy, in fact, that Chris didn't say a word to her when she finally showed up a whole twenty-three minutes late. He simply caught her gaze from across the front pub, raised his eyebrows, and pointed at a wristwatch he wasn't wearing.

Sam jerked her chin up at him in greeting, then marched through the kitchen and into the Back Bar like this was all just part of their usual routine.

Because it was.

She didn't get a chance to talk to him until about halfway through her shift.

"Hey, real quick. I just wanted to let you know I need to leave early again tonight."

He fixed her with a deadpan stare. "On a Saturday night. One of our two busy nights of the week where we make the most of our money across the board. And you have to skip out early."

"Chris, I know it's not ideal…"

He snorted and nodded at another customer trying to shout their drink order over the noise before he got to work making it.

"But it's important," Sam added. "And I promise I won't leave work early for as long as you need after that. For a reasonable amount of time."

"I'd rather you showed up for your shift on time instead," he replied without looking at her.

"Nah, that's not on the table tonight. Sorry."

He finished ringing up the next customer and delivering their drinks, then scanned the bar for the next person and spared Sam a quick, very clearly amused glance. "You got another séance?"

"Maybe. I mean, someone's gotta die first, though, so not tonight, anyway. I hope."

Shaking his head, Chris chuckled, then listened to another drink order shouted out at him. "Get to work. I'll get someone to cover you when you're gone."

She didn't bother sticking around to thank him.

They took Laila's car when Sam showed up at her apartment just after midnight. Laila drove, then pulled over down a dirt sideroad about half a mile from their destination. Neither woman knew exactly where that road led, but they were pretty sure it was hardly ever used these days.

Then came the half-mile walk in the dark in the middle of the night, both of them dressed in all black, which wouldn't have been all that bad if it hadn't felt like it took forever.

They slipped around the back of the building, paused to each don a pair of neoprene gloves, then Laila slipped a key into the lock and opened the door.

They entered quickly, Sam keeping an eye out while her accomplice went straight for the keypad on the silent alarm to turn it off the way she'd done several times over the last week. By now, she was practically a pro.

Only this time, she had Sam here with her.

FORTY-SEVEN

Sam

"HERE IT IS." Laila dug through the back of the empty coat closet where they kept members' belongings. A soft click followed, then she pulled aside a loose board of siding from the back of the cupboard and handed it behind her.

Sam took it and set it against the wall before Laila started handing her all the myriad haunting supplies she'd used over the last week — red paint, an old brush, a stir stick. "And you've been keeping it all here in the coat closet this whole time?"

"It wasn't like I had anywhere else to keep it."

"Why'd you pick that phrase specifically, huh?"

Laila turned away from the closet before rising off her knees. "I don't know. It just came to me, I guess. Part of me feels like Dina's still here, you know? The version of her that came to Rush in the first place. *That* girl never left. Whatever happened to her here, it locked her up tight with all the other secrets these fucking people keep."

"I saw lights flickering all over in the middle of the night a few times. When I was driving home after work. That was you too, wasn't it?"

Laila nodded. "A lot of the interior lights, even in the bedrooms, are connected to a building-wide system timer, so I set a few of them to go off at random intervals just to help cover my tracks. Not that it got past *you*, though. I've gotten the feeling very little does."

Sam snorted. "You'd be surprised. Lately, I've let way too much slip right past me. Believe me."

"Come on, let's head upstairs."

Sam was only too happy to oblige, and they made their way up to Big Pete's office on the second floor. Laila pulled out a keyring and stuck a key in the lock.

Sam almost burst out laughing. "He actually trusts you enough to give you a key to his office?"

The door swung open, and Laila looked back over her shoulder in surprise. "What? Oh, fuck no. I had to go a little old-school and made a soap mold, actually."

"No shit."

"Had to drive two hours out of town to a key maker who wouldn't recognize me or start asking a bunch of questions. But it worked. Copier's over there." Laila pointed towards the copy machine on the far side of the room, and Sam instantly went to go make dozens of copies of Dr. Jones' suicide note.

Laila rummaged around in the desk drawers, pulling out thumbtacks and paperclips among various other office supplies. Sam didn't feel the need to question her about it; the woman obviously had a knack for this kind of thing. And if Laila had some of her own ideas for how to pull this off even better, who was Sam to stop her?

They took everything back downstairs after Laila made sure to lock the office again. Then they went straight into the fancy dining room that had already been prepped for tomorrow's resumed Sunday brunch.

Sam handed the photocopies of Dr. Jones' final letter

to Laila so the woman could start tacking them up all over the dining room walls. Then Sam grabbed the bucket of red paint and the old paintbrush and found the perfect spot on the wall, front and center, where everyone who entered the dining room would immediately see the final message from Dina's ghost. She took the liberty of adding a little something extra.

It didn't take her long to slash out a markedly sloppy rendition of a ghostly message across the wall: *'I tried to warn you. Let Dina Go.'*

Once they finished, both women stepped back to take a look at their handiwork.

Sam turned down the corners of her mouth in consideration and cocked her head. "That's not half bad."

"Yeah, that's a nice touch." Laila stuck her hands on her hips. "This is actually the first time I've stopped to really appreciate being my sister's ghost."

Sam snorted. "Don't act too excited, or I might start to think you're gonna take this up professionally."

"Very funny. No, as soon as this is over, I'm getting the fuck out of this town. I've already been here way too long for my own sanity."

Sam picked up the paint bucket and brush. "Tell me about it."

They had everything cleaned up and put away behind the secret compartment in the coat closet, then it was time to go.

Before they could head out of the clubhouse, Sam caught the sound of tires crunching across gravel and stopped short.

"Laila, hold on," she said softly, holding out an arm for the other woman to stop.

Fortunately, Laila actually listened to her, then both

women clearly heard the sound of multiple vehicles pulling into the Kalamack Club's front parking lot.

"Shit," Laila whispered. "Why are the cops here?"

"You definitely turned off the alarm, right?"

Laila shot her a scathing glare.

"Just asking. If it's not the alarm, I'd say Big Pete commandeered a few of Rush's finest to keep an eye on the place tonight and make sure there aren't any more ghost problems."

"Of course he did." Laila puffed out a massive sigh and shook her head. "Tomorrow's the 75th anniversary celebration. Pete *would* expect somebody to try pulling something the night before. I should've thought of that. What are we supposed to do now?"

"We can try heading back out the way we came in." Sam stuck a thumb over her shoulder toward the rear of the clubhouse before they headed that way.

Unfortunately, two more police cars had circled around back toward the bit of dirt where employees and staff were expected to park their vehicles.

"Shit," Laila said. "They're everywhere."

"Looks like it."

"What are we supposed to do? They can't find us here. If we're caught…"

"We won't be caught, Laila. I need you to calm down." Sam lifted a hand, signaling for the other woman to take a deep breath and chill while she thought for a minute. "Okay, I have a plan. Mostly. You're gonna have to do exactly what I say without arguing because at this point, it's really the only out I see for either of us. Got it?"

Laila nodded.

"I'm gonna distract them. And—"

"How?" Laila interrupted.

"That's for me to worry about and you to forget," Sam

snipped. "I'll take care of it. Just give me a second. I need to think this through before we get you out of here."

"What about you, though?"

"I'll be fine. It's not like this is the first time I've had to think on my feet. And I've made it out of all the other hairy situations in my life. I'll make it out of this one."

Laila didn't look too happy about it, but she didn't have to be. Sam just wanted to get the woman out of the building, then she'd take care of the rest on her own, somehow. Inspiration always struck best during the thirteenth hour anyway, when she was literally out of all other options.

Thinking quickly, Sam scanned the dining room. Her gaze fell on a large, fancy-looking chest decorated with gold embellishments and boasting an intricately designed keyhole right there in the center.

I'd bet anything this is where they have their Sunday-Funday orgies.

"Hey, Laila? Just while I'm thinking about it, did you ever participate in these Sunday brunches?"

The woman's disgusted grimace was more than enough answer. "Are you fucking kidding me? Absolutely not. Couldn't have paid me to sit in on that kinda thing. Any progress on this so-called distraction?"

"Yeah, I think so. But we need to get upstairs."

They hurried up the staircase, careful not to use the flashlight apps on their phones or make so much noise that they might be discovered by at least four police cars parked around the building.

Sam picked one of the so-called guest bedrooms at random, which Laila helped to open far more quickly because she actually knew which keys belonged to what.

"You know what?" Sam said when the door was open. "Go ahead and unlock all the other ones too."

Laila did so without question, then bit her lower lip. "Now what?"

"Now I want you to go back to that first bedroom," Sam said. "When you're in it, shut the door behind you and count to thirty. Then get one of the windows open. That's how you're getting out of here, so I hope you don't have a fear of heights or anything. Otherwise, you'll have to get over it pretty fucking fast. The windows do open, right?"

"In that room? Yeah. As long as the security alarm stays off, there shouldn't be a problem."

"Good. Once you get up onto the roof, you're gonna go around back. This house is built like all the others were back in the day. Easy to climb up and over toward the back of the building. Shouldn't be too tricky. Then you'll have to find a way down."

"There's a commercial dumpster out back," Laila said. "I think I can climb down low enough to drop onto that if I have to."

"Great. Do that. And no matter what, don't stop. You go right back to your car, get in it, go to your apartment. Understand? Don't wait for me. Don't look back. Just move as quickly as possible because once we start this, we can't stop it. And the last thing either of us needs is to get caught here right now, especially tonight."

"I got it, Sam."

"Remember, thirty seconds. Then you open a window and get the hell out."

Laila nodded. "Thirty seconds."

"Looks like Dina's ghost is coming out to play one last time." Then Sam stepped into the guest bedroom at the very end of the hall, ducking and crouching as low as possible while reaching up the wall inside the doorway for the light switch. She turned it on, waited three seconds, then flipped it off again.

As soon as she did, she darted into the hallway, down three rooms, and did the same thing again.

Her third mystical ghost-haunting lightshow came from the room just next to the one where Laila waited by the window, counting down her thirty seconds. Sam figured lights flashing on and off consistently in one direction might lead even the police to think there was some rhyme or reason to the happenings right now.

Then Sam darted from room to room, switching the lights on and off again and again. She doubled back twice just to make it seem as close to random as possible. Then she started messing with the light switches in the rooms at the very end of the hall opposite the room Laila had chosen to make her escape.

She heard the window sliding and squeaking open and hoped it wasn't loud enough to carry down into the parking lot.

By this time, she could also clearly hear the Rush police parked out front, getting out of their cars and talking to each other and trying to figure out what the hell was happening on the second story.

Then someone let out a startled shout, followed by bursts of radio static and a series of half-discernable conversations coming through those radios.

"...*suspect on the roof...*"

"...*attempted break-in...*"

"...*moving toward the west side of the building...*"

"...*get your ass over there and cut him off!*"

Sam didn't wait to hear any more. She instantly resumed flickering the lights on and off as quickly as possible, jumping from room to room and hoping she didn't get sloppy enough in her haste to help Laila that she ended up giving the police down below a perfectly clear view of herself messing with the lights upstairs.

There was a moment of confusion, with plenty of shouting and scuffling footsteps across the dirt in the back lot and the gravel in the front. Then more radio communication cited one unidentified suspect trying to enter the premises.

"...*pursued the suspect on foot but lost them during the chase. Whoever it is, they sure as hell aren't breaking and entering anywhere tonight. Definitely not here.*"

Sam let herself puff out a sigh of relief. That suspect on the roof was her best shot at finally getting to the bottom of this whole thing. She and Laila both knew it. At least the cops had lost track of Laila now, and she could get back to her car, her apartment, and her mother without further issue.

As long as she did what Sam had told her and didn't try to come back for a stint at playing hero.

Laila had gotten away, which was a major plus.

On the other hand, the cops were still outside the building, now with even more incentive to stay after they believed one person had already tried to break into the Kalamack Club. And now Sam was trapped inside on her own until the Rush PD decided it was a good time to leave, however long that happened to be.

Honestly, she'd been in worse situations than this. Much worse. All things considered, the Kalamack Club was pretty fucking cushy in comparison.

At this point, she really only had one option. Hole up here for the remainder of the night and hope to find a successfully unnoticed way out so she could continue her day pretending like she'd never left Birdsong Park. That left her with plenty of time, and once curiosity got the better of her, as it always did, Sam started snooping.

What she was really interested in the most was that fancy-looking chest in the dining room.

When she finally got the lid open, she lifted it all the way back to settle on its hinges before using her cell phone's flashlight to take a peek inside.

The thing was full of masks.

The fancy kind, intricately and deliberately decorated with beads, sequins, feathers, and lace. They came in all different shapes, colors, and sizes. Most of them included headbands to keep them on hands-free, while a smaller portion were mounted on sticks, which the wearer presumably had to keep holding up at all times if they wanted their face to remain as hidden.

Who wanted to have to hold a stick mask up to their face during an orgy?

Despite the weirdness of it all, made even weirder by the fact that Sam knew exactly what these masks were for, she took one.

She did a little more perusing after that and found to her disappointment that the rest of the Kalamack Club on the inside was just another normal clubhouse. No sign of actual ghosts, no sign of actual hauntings, no deadly secrets, or even dead secrets to be discovered. Not with what she had to work with tonight.

She did, however, feel like she hit the jackpot when she found a filing cabinet in the rear hallway behind the club's main dining room. This must have been an infrequently used area of the clubhouse, because none of the metal drawers were locked. Anyone could just stumble across said filing cabinet, open a drawer, and take a peek at the contents.

Which of course was exactly what Sam did.

"Wow. Would you look at that," she muttered with a snort.

472

Every drawer was filled with various file folders stacked neatly together. Lo and behold, they were also organized in alphabetical order, which just made it much easier for Sam to get a good look at the labels as she sifted through them.

The file folders were organized by last name, and every single last name Sam found belonged to someone who either considered themselves a townie here or wielded significant enough influence to make the list in the first place.

Except that theory didn't entirely hold up when Sam found a file with *her* name on it: 'Salazar, Samantha.'

She wrinkled her nose. The only time she was ever Samantha was on official legal documentation.

"Must've left a real impression on you, huh, Pete?" she murmured, pulling her own file out of the drawer.

Sitting on the floor beside the filing cabinet, Sam gave herself as much time as she needed to go through the collected information in her file. It was thoroughly disappointing. There wasn't really anything good on her, just the basic facts about her childhood and her past and her active service in the US Army. There *was* mention of Sophie, however brief — just the pitifully short date range of her life beside her first, middle, and last name. But that was enough to catch Sam's attention, and it was certainly enough for her to not want anyone else to get their hands on something like this.

So she removed every piece of paper from the file with her name on it, folded it in half, and took it with her. It was easy enough to pull the same number of sheets from the office printer on Laila's desk, all of them blank, which she used to fluff up the now empty folder before she returned the whole thing to the filing cabinet drawer and pushed it closed.

At least now, she had a better understanding of how

Francine knew about Sophie to deliver that stupid fucking made-up message at the séance. Which, she knew now, was also exactly how Laila had figured out so much about her. All thanks to Pete's penchant for keeping personal folders on people of interest in what he clearly still considered to be *his* town.

After that, Sam let herself into one of the empty guestrooms upstairs and figured it was best to settle down there for the night.

Wait for morning.

And maybe even find herself dreaming about Sophie.

FORTY-EIGHT

Laila
_____

With no word of Sam all night, Laila hadn't slept. Now, just before sunrise, she decided to head to the club a little early. She thought she'd have at least half an hour there first to finish pulling herself together, reining in her emotions, and effectively covering up any and all sign of discomfort or misgivings before she had to deal with anyone else today.

Unfortunately, she was wrong.

For whatever reason, Big Pete had chosen today of all days to show up extra early. Which meant he was already there, waiting for her beside her desk, when Laila walked through the front door.

"I swear to Christ you better have a good goddamn excuse for this," he roared.

Laila stopped in her tracks, trying desperately not to look desperate while she fought to collect herself in the face of this new verbal onslaught.

"Good morning to you too, Pete," she replied as calmly as possible before continuing toward her desk.

"The hell it is." He thumped a fist down onto her desk,

making pens jump in their holders and a small loose stack of paper fluttering sideways away from the violence.

Laila fervently wished she could flutter away with them right out of this fucking clubhouse and the whole goddamn town. But she couldn't. Not just yet.

"I don't know what the hell's gotten into you lately," Big Pete snapped, "but you fucked up when you went home last night without turning on the alarm. And if I'd been anyone else but me trying to get in here this morning, I could've just waltzed right in, gotten into any goddamn room I pleased, and taken whatever I wanted. So? Do you have anything to say for yourself, or what?"

She paused a few feet from her desk, mostly because she didn't want to walk around him to her chair and risk coming within snatching distance of Big Pete's enormous arms. But she forced herself to look up at him and hoped the attempted expression of sincere horror and apology she tried to pull up was convincing enough this morning. "Pete, I am so sorry. I don't know what happened. I can't believe I didn't turn on the alarm."

"You calling me a liar?"

She forced herself not to exaggerate a deep breath and shook her head. "No, absolutely not. I take full responsibility for that. I've just been distracted lately. A little flustered with all this ghost business going on."

"That's no excuse," he growled. Then he looked her up and down and sneered. "Neither is the way you look this morning. Christ, Laila, you look old as hell. No one wants to see that first thing when they walk through these front doors. Go pull yourself together. Put on some damn makeup at least. And make it quick. I'm not waiting around all morning for you, but I wanna see you in my office before any of the other members get here."

She couldn't shake the feeling that something abso-

476

lutely awful was about to happen. Then again, she'd been harboring that same feeling for the last several days after the second so-called ghost haunting at the Kalamack Club. She'd been cutting it close every single time. Closer and closer with each haunting, in fact. She wasn't sure how much longer she could keep a firm hold on her own emotions, especially now that they were so close to the end.

It didn't help that she was certain Sam was still here inside the clubhouse. But now her window of opportunity to help Sam exit the building had already slammed shut in her face before she'd even had a chance to open it.

She took her purse with her to the staff restroom in the back hallway, where she applied a little extra blush to her cheeks to avoid looking so desperately pale and haggard. Then she combed her long, wavy, unnaturally platinum-blonde hair with her fingers and stared at her reflection.

"You can do this. Just a little longer. Then you'll be done, and you can get the hell out of here and forget this town ever existed."

The temptation to say fuck it to the whole plan was almost too strong to ignore. If she wanted, Laila could bolt outside right now, get in her car, go find her mother, and have them both well on their way to Seattle before anyone stopped to consider the possibility.

If it hadn't been for Sam, who had to still be somewhere in the building, Laila was sure she would've left already. The pressure was just too much.

But Laila and Angela owed Sam quite a bit. Which meant she couldn't just walk away from this now. Not yet.

She stopped only to set her purse down on her desk before heading upstairs to Pete's office as requested — or demanded.

When she reached his office, the door was already open, and David was also inside, sitting at one of the two chairs on this side of Pete's enormous executive desk while Pete himself sat behind it, looking smug as hell.

But what else was new?

"Take a seat." Pete nodded toward the other empty chair, and Laila had no choice but to comply. When she sank down onto the uncomfortably firm cushion and glanced at David, the club manager scowled but couldn't quite meet her gaze.

Nor could he hide the huge black eye he certainly hadn't had the last time she'd seen him. That combined with the fact that she wouldn't have expected him back at the clubhouse after she'd warned him about being caught on camera, everything just felt off now.

Not just off. Something was very wrong.

On the infinitesimally small chance that this was about something else, she tried to maintain her composure and act like everything was fine. No point in preemptively proving herself guilty.

Pete stared at her, enjoying her growing discomfort. "Last night, David and I had a little chat back at his place. Cleared up a few things. Put the house back in order, as it were. And I figured it was a good opportunity to talk about the hauntings around here too, seeing as no one has much of an idea what the hell's going on. As it turns out, David doesn't have anything to do with a fucking ghost in my club."

Big Pete narrowed his eyes, swiveling in his office chair and tapping his fingers against the armrests as he fixed Laila with a predatory smile. "I can't see it as anything but a fantastic coincidence that David had a few secrets of his own to keep. But once I looked into them, I realized the source of the problem has been right in front of my nose this whole time. David isn't the one who's been haunting this place. That only leaves one other person with all the necessary access to pull off this kinda thing."

Laila's heart thudded in her chest, and it actually started to hurt. Or maybe that was her imagination running away with her because now the anxiety was turning into terror, and she wasn't sure how much longer she could force herself into normal breathing.

She said nothing.

Pete glanced at David, and the manager pressed his lips tightly together. But *he* wasn't the one on private trial here.

Then Pete turned his glinting eyes back onto Laila. "So, here's what I'm gonna say. I take responsibility for my part in this. I should've done a better job of vetting you before bringing you on, Laila. Should've done my due diligence just like I do with damn near everyone else. But when you walked in six months ago with that pretty little smile and those legs for days and you didn't bat an eye when I mentioned both of 'em... Well, that oversight's on me. Because honestly, who could've known I'd have to vet another shitty hostess? First, I brought on Dina because she had that same something you have. But I suppose it runs in the family, doesn't it?"

Shit.

Somehow, Laila managed to sit back in the chair, cross one leg over the other beneath her pencil skirt and fold her hands on top of her thigh. How she hadn't completely broken down by now, she had no clue. But while her strength and composure still existed, she would take full advantage of them.

"It's not illegal not to divulge my relationship with any of your past employees, Pete," she said, her voice surprisingly level. "I haven't done anything wrong."

"Well now, normally, I'd agree with you there, as much as I don't like it. But see, you did do something wrong. You destroyed my property several times, trying to write the whole thing off as goddamn ghost messages. Worse than that, though, you destroyed my peace of mind. And I just can't have that."

"This is ridiculous. I won't sit here and subject myself to these outrageous accusations." She leapt to her feet with no idea what she was doing or what came next. Her body moved on its own as she spun toward the office's closed door. On the way, she caught the knowing look and curt nod Big Pete sent David's way.

Before Laila had taken more than three steps, David was after her, reaching out to snatch up her wrist.

"What are you doing? Get your hands off me, David. Stop!"

The man only tightened his grip and jerked her backward toward him, painfully twisting both her arms behind her back. All he needed was a set of handcuffs, and this could've been a citizen's arrest. Total bullshit, sure, but she didn't really have a leg to stand on at this point.

"You can't just grab me and throw me around," she spat, struggling against David's surprisingly strong hold.

"Don't fight it," he murmured in her ear. "Things could go a whole lot worse for you if you do, so just don't try to fight him on this."

"What? Are you fucking kidding me?" she shouted, trying to spin back toward Big Pete to glower at him.

Her employer had already risen to his feet to skirt around the side of his desk and head for the door. "I just don't have the time to deal with your shit right now. Got far more important things to get to at the moment, and you're keeping me from all of them. So it'll just have to wait until after Sunday brunch. Once all the festivities are over."

Despite every part of her crying out to just give up, to

accept what was happening, that she had lost and there was no chance of getting away with it now, Laila couldn't back down. She struggled against David's grip, fighting not to cry out at the pain whenever she twisted in the wrong direction.

Laila let herself walk forward across the office under her manager's guidance, sneering at Big Pete the whole time. "Fine, then. Go ahead and call the police. Bring them all out here. There's nothing you can do to pin any of this on me, Pete, because there's no evidence. You have no proof."

"That might be true." He opened the door and nodded for David to exit first, leering after her. "But I don't plan on bringing the brave men and women of the Rush Police Department into this, sweetheart. My plans for you don't involve the law. At least as far as operating within their confines is concerned."

"What?" Laila tried to look over her shoulder at David as he shoved her through the open office door, her eyes wide and her footsteps staggering all over the wooden floor. The three-inch stilettos she wore every day to work wobbled beneath her for the first time in her adult life. "You can't do this. Pete, you can't!"

Words clearly wouldn't be enough.

As soon as Laila realized this, the terror finally set in and took over.

She sucked in a desperate gasp to ready herself for a violent scream that would most certainly have attracted quite a bit of unwanted attention, but David was already prepared for it. His hand clapped painfully across her mouth as he jerked her backward against him and pinned her there.

Laila's scream came out as a muffled yelp of powerlessness. Struggling in David's hold was even more difficult now because he wasn't just yanking her around by the arms anymore. He had full control of her body, and she couldn't even free her mouth to try screaming again.

"Just let it happen," he snarled in her ear.

Which only made her struggle that much more desperately.

This couldn't be happening right now. She had to get out of here.

Pete followed them out of his office, paused only to close the door and lock it behind him, then glared down at her. "Is your phone in your purse with the rest of your things?"

Obviously, she didn't have her phone on her. She was wearing a skin-tight pencil skirt and a formal work blouse without any pockets. Where the hell was she supposed to put a phone?

Pete looked her up and down, then nodded. "I'll take that as a yes."

Laila couldn't have predicted what came next because she wasn't exactly sure what was happening.

All she saw was Big Pete taking one lunging step toward her, his arm swinging back as if he were yanking open a cabinet drawer instead.

The next thing she knew, all the air was knocked painfully out of her lungs, and she couldn't tell which hurt more — the deep, all-encompassing ache bursting through the center of her stomach and radiating into her back, or the searing burn of breathlessness as she gasped and unsuccessfully tried to draw air back into her lungs.

He just killed me. He crushed my lungs, and I can't breathe, and now I'm gonna die.

That was the only coherent thought racing through her mind as her knees buckled and she sagged in David's arms, her mouth gaping open and closed like a landed fish.

At least she wasn't flopping around on the floor. But it might have been too soon to make a call on that one.

"Take the back staircase," Pete grumbled.

As if they were suddenly in a long, echoing tunnel, Laila heard the man's footsteps pounding away from her.

"Make sure no one sees you. I don't wanna have to answer any more questions today, and you don't want another chat with me."

Laila still felt like she couldn't breathe. Like she couldn't draw in any air. But somehow, she retained consciousness.

She wasn't dying. Maybe she could breathe after all, though it was almost impossible to tell through the agony like a bowling ball thrown into her gut and the burning in her lungs.

All her strength had left her, though, which was the only thing that allowed David to unceremoniously drag her along the second-story hallway and down the back staircase as ordered.

Laila tried to move her arms and legs, but that still wasn't happening. Her heels thumped down the stairs as David half-carried, half-dragged her with him. She was vaguely aware of the sharp crack of one of those stilettos snapping apart.

Then her eyes rolled back in her head, and the pain overtook her completely.

FORTY-NINE

Sam

If Big Pete hadn't been there the whole time too, Sam would've jumped David before he ever made it to the basement. She knew she had a decent chance of knocking out a guy like that for two minutes, maybe three at the most. Plenty of time to help Laila escape.

Sam also knew full well how poor her chances were of standing against Big Pete in any kind of physical altercation. It hadn't ended well for her the first and last time she'd tried it, and getting herself laid out by the man's hammy fists again wouldn't help her out of this.

It wouldn't help Laila, either.

So she forced herself to bide her time as she snuck through the back of the clubhouse after Big Pete and David while the manager dragged an unconscious Laila across almost the entire building.

Getting into the basement with them without being seen was impossible, so she ducked into the staff bathroom in the back and kept the door open just a crack to watch the door at the top of the staircase. She waited a few minutes after seeing Big Pete and David both re-emerge without Laila. Then, when she was mostly sure the coast was clear and no one else was coming to the basement, she hurried out of the bathroom and slipped through the basement door without a sound.

Not that anyone would've heard her anyway with all the club members and their plus-ones taking up so much space in the lounge and the social areas surrounding the dining room. It would've been difficult to hear someone clearly in a one-on-one conversation up close and personal, let alone from down the hallway or across the mansion.

Which she figured was exactly why Big Pete had ordered Laila into the basement.

No one would ever know she was there.

When Sam reached the bottom landing, she ran her hands up and down the wall and found the light switch.

Her heart sank down into her gut where failure and shame and hopelessness belonged after only five seconds.

There was no sign of Laila.

In fact, the basement's single room that looked like it had been finished sometime in the 70s and never updated since was almost completely empty. Cardboard moving boxes were stacked in one far corner beside wire shelving that housed an eclectic mix of landscaping tools, maintenance supplies, construction odds and ends, and extra paper goods and office supplies. Beside that was a large metal storage cabinet, both doors shut. Beyond that, though, there was nothing else to indicate anyone had been down here in quite some time.

No chairs, no other doors leading to other rooms, no Laila chained to a support beam with a gag in her mouth.

Wrinkling her nose, Sam turned in a slow circle to further investigate because none of this felt right.

The murmur of so many club members and their guests upstairs was still audible from down here, though significantly muted. Even still, Sam thought she heard something.

A soft rustle followed by something that sounded like both a sigh and a whimper.

Either that, or she was hearing things.

Then the sound repeated, and Sam cocked her head, listening for more.

Oddly enough, it sounded like it came from the large metal storage cabinet on the other side of the basement.

The second she settled her gaze on that cabinet, its locked double doors rattled with a startling thump inside followed by a gasping sob.

"Holy shit."

The rattling and banging stopped. "Who's there?"

"Laila?"

"Sam!" The banging started all over again with renewed fury. "Sam, I'm in here! Let me out! Sam! Open the doors! I'm in here!"

"I'm coming, I'm coming. Just hold on a second." Sam raced toward the doors, cranked down on both handles, and jiggled them as fiercely as she could, but they wouldn't budge. Go figure, they were locked.

The banging continued.

"Laila!" Sam shouted, sticking her face right up toward the crack between the double doors. "Can you hear me?"

"Open the doors!"

"Laila, listen, I need you to take a deep breath and count to twenty, all right? I'm gonna get you out of here. I just need to find the right leverage."

"I can't breathe in here, Sam," Laila whimpered.

"Yeah, I know. You're doing great anyway, all right? Deep breaths. Count to twenty."

Instead of following those directions, Laila burst into sobs inside the cabinet. Sam couldn't blame her for that, but at least she'd stopped pounding on the doors and screaming her head off.

Sam rifled through the items in the basement as quickly as she could. Of course, there weren't any fucking keys down here. Big Pete would've kept those on him. There had to be something else she could use.

Fortunately, on the shelving of metal bars was a toolbox, and no one had bothered to lock that. Sam threw open in the lid and rummaged around before snatching two different types of screwdrivers and taking them with her.

"Back up away from the doors," she told Laila.

"Does it look like I have a whole lot of space in here?"

"Just as much as you can, okay?"

The first screwdriver was too thick to fit into the space between the cabinet doors.

And the second screwdriver, to Sam's complete bafflement, snapped in half after ten seconds of applied pressure.

The metal rod clanged against the floor, and Sam chucked the handle over her shoulder with a hiss. "Fuck."

"Sam!"

"Yeah, yeah, almost there."

It took her another five minutes, but she finally discovered a crowbar buried beneath a pile of old curtains. She pulled it out, looked it over from top to bottom, and entertained herself with a brief moment of disgust for whoever was in charge of organizing supplies down here.

Sam wasn't the neatest and tidiest person, either, but at least she knew how to keep functional items within close reach.

"All right, here we go," she said as she raced back toward the cabinet with the crowbar in hand. "One more time, Laila, okay? Just back away from the doors as much as you can. I'm gonna try this out."

There was no response. Then again, this wasn't exactly a social call.

Sam fit the crowbar's end into the space between the cabinet doors and pushed against her makeshift lever.

It took a hell of a lot more effort than she'd expected. The crowbar screeched against the metal doors, which eventually buckled until one of them finally folded under the pressure and snapped the lock apart.

Sam almost ended up on the floor with the crowbar, but she kept her footing so she could throw both cabinet doors open.

And there was Laila.

She stumbled out, wobbling on one broken heel before she kicked off both her shoes.

"You okay?" Sam asked.

Laila swiped at her tear-streaked cheeks and sniffed. "Fucking bastard locked me in a cabinet."

"I know, but other than that?"

"Other than that, I'm pissed."

"Right. Hold that thought, though. We need to figure out what we're doing from here."

That was as far as she got because footsteps approached the top of the staircase right outside the closed door, and a short conversation in muffled voices through the walls and basement ceiling came from upstairs. Someone was definitely at the top of the staircase, and it sounded a whole lot like they were about to come down.

"Shit." Sam spun toward Laila, then pointed at the staircase and snatched up the crowbar again. "Stay behind me, no matter what. Don't stop for anything. Even if you can't see. Got it?"

"Wait, *what*?"

"Just do it!"

Sam took off running toward the stairs, hoping they had enough time for this desperate escape. She heard the slap of Laila's bare feet behind her, then Sam slapped a hand against the wall to switch off the basement lights.

In complete darkness now, she raced up the stairs as fast as possible, whispering to Laila, "Hurry and stay close."

The element of surprise was literally the only card they had left.

Sam expected David or Big Pete or maybe even some other random club member to appear at the top of the staircase when that door finally opened, spilling wan hallway light down into the basement.

It hadn't even occurred to her that Little Pete Wilder might have been the one to open that door, but he was. Now he was also the one standing there at the top of the stairs in mute shock at the sight of one frazzled-looking Sam Salazar with a crowbar in hand and a barefoot and tear-streaked Laila who most certainly wasn't manning her post as her job duties entailed.

Everyone froze for one eternal second to stare at each other. Then Sam finally regained her wits and carried out the rest of her half-cocked plan.

She swung the crowbar at Pete's legs, which was hard enough in the narrow staircase, but she definitely made contact. He cried out and doubled over. She grabbed him by the back of the shirt collar with both hands and tossed him down the stairs.

Rush's mayor tumbled head over heels — literally — down the stairs with heavy grunts and groans along the way and didn't stop until he lay sprawled out on the bottom. Then Sam chucked the crowbar behind her, smiling at the heavy clang of metal hitting the carpeted floor before it came to a rest beside a groaning Pete.

"Time to go," she whispered harshly, then she and Laila were up and out of the basement.

She made sure to close the door again behind them, though there was no danger of anyone hearing Little Pete scream for help or moan in pain or completely lose it while lying in the dark.

The noise upstairs from the start of the Kalamack's 75th anniversary Sunday brunch celebration overpowered everything else. Fortunately for Sam and Laila, the excitement was on the verge of exploding into the kind of chaos perfect for distracting from and therefore concealing a quick and relatively easy getaway.

Sam had already stuffed the papers from her file down the front of her shirt, and now she led Laila down the back staff hallways by the hand. By the time they'd closed the basement door, Big Pete had apparently decided it was time to unlock the dining room doors for the big reveal of his anniversary-bash setup he'd been so preoccupied with lately.

The guests were so engrossed in watching the opening of those doors, like some grand unveiling, none of them noticed Sam and Laila slipping into the front of the clubhouse and moving behind the gathered crowd.

Both women knew exactly what was on the other side of those doors, because they'd put it there themselves. What they needed now was to get the hell out of the clubhouse before things got way too hairy and their window of escape closed permanently.

The explosive reaction from the members and their guests erupted way faster and with far more vehement outrage than even Sam had expected.

The roar of angry male voices was instantly joined by

shrieks and gasps from their female counterparts, all of whom currently remained unmasked and visible to everyone in attendance simply because the festivities hadn't yet kicked off.

Above it all rose Big Pete's thunderous bellow of rage when he realized all his efforts to preserve the already decomposing integrity of his beloved Sunday brunches had been for nothing.

Even as she dragged Laila by the hand to help them both get out of there as soon as physically possible, faster if they could swing it, the entire gathering of brunch participants devolved into one angry mob of ruthlessly entitled socialites all scrambling for an explanation to such an abominable discovery.

Sam was fairly certain some of them would even be calling for blood after this, Big Pete among them. Whether that was figurative blood or literal was anyone's guess.

The clubhouse's front door banged open when Sam threw her weight against it. Then she and Laila stumbled into the mid-morning sunshine lighting up the parking lot filled with the vehicles of Rush's elite.

They made it all the way across the front porch, down the steps, and into the lot before Sam stopped and turned around to face the oncoming chaos.

"What are you doing?" Laila hissed. "We have to get out of here."

"You can go to the car," Sam said. "I just gotta handle one more thing first."

"Are you kidding me? You were stuck here overnight. And I was thrown in a fucking storage cupboard in the basement. We need to go."

Sam watched the crowd spilling through the front doors. She found a surprising amount of pleasure in the knowledge that every one of these people racing back into the parking lot would place the entirety of the blame for this disaster on Big Pete Wilder's shoulders.

For once, he was getting exactly what he deserved.

She scanned the faces of people swarming outside toward their cars, all of them wanting nothing to do with the Kalamack Club at a time like this. Not now that it had been so disastrously defiled with another crimson-red paint-splatter message from the alleged ghost of a former employee.

Plus countless photocopies of the good Dr. Jones' suicide note.

That didn't exactly put anybody in an orgy kinda mood, did it?

Sam finally caught a glimpse through the open door of Hank Topping moving with the outraged crowd as she ignored Laila's increasingly urgent pleas to just get the hell out of there.

As soon as she had her final word with Mr. Topping, then they could go.

There wasn't enough time to explain her intentions or her reasoning, so Laila would just have to deal with it.

Finally, Hank was outside with the rest of them, stomping down the porch steps where just a few days before his father-in-law had hanged himself.

Hank's scowl settled on Sam and stayed there.

Just before it seemed he might have gotten away from her in the crowd, she caught up to him and matched his pace just a few feet away.

"Hey, Hank," she said, jerking her chin up at him in an exaggerated greeting.

He said nothing.

"I just wanted to check in with you. You know Reginald laid out an entire confession of what you all did that night after Dr. Greg Masterson spoke up against the Good Ol' Boys, right?"

"You think I give a fuck about any of that?" he grumbled. "Reggie's dead."

"Well, that's true," she said, matching his stride. "But I have a feeling you do give a shit, Hank."

He shook his head and kept walking. "You'll say anything to get a reaction out of somebody. But I'm not falling for it. So you might as well give up now. Whatever you're trying to do won't work."

"You sound so sure about that. But what happens to you when the whole truth comes out, huh? It's all marked down and documented in Dr. Jones' full confession, naming everyone involved, of course, and detailing exactly what you all did. Then he made sure that confession was safely delivered into the right hands to be used at the right time."

That finally got Hank to stop, and Sam almost kept walking past him because it was so unexpected. She turned around to meet his gaze and spread her arms. "It's about time a little justice got served, don't you think?"

He studied her a moment longer, then rolled his eyes. "You're so full of shit."

"Maybe. But you know what? You don't have to take my word for it. Why don't you go ask Greg yourself? I heard you two are pretty close. Oh, wait. That's right. You *used* to be pretty close. Beating the shit out of somebody and putting him in the hospital doesn't exactly make it onto the best-friend checklist, does it?"

Hank's scowl deepened, and that was when she knew she'd caught him on the hook. Whatever she said now, Hank Topping was definitely paying attention.

"Why Greg?" he asked. "Why bring him into this?"

Sam spread her arms and walked backward across the parking lot toward the side of the property, removing herself from the chaotic crowd of members and their guests surging toward their vehicles. "You know why, Hank. And once they release him from the hospital and he's cleared to be back on his feet, he's sending that confession straight to the police. They'll have all the details the rest of you tried to keep buried for so long, but you just didn't bury it deep enough. Not everyone who was involved that night is dead, you know?"

His sneer had morphed into a snarl of rage now as he glared at her. If they'd been alone, the man might have tried to attack her and physically shut her up. But Sam had timed this little chat of theirs perfectly, and now there were dozens of witnesses and plenty of people between them. He couldn't do anything without being seen and most likely also implicating himself in a whole hell of a lot.

With no other options, Hank Topping hissed in frustration, muttered something Sam couldn't hear over the noise, then stomped off toward his vehicle.

She stayed where she was and watched him until his car turned onto the frontage road and picked up speed toward town.

"Sam!" Laila jogged toward her with her purse over her shoulder, her eyes wide with fear as she kept looking back at the clubhouse. "Sam, we need to go right now."

Sam turned around to follow Laila's gaze. The only things she registered in that moment were both Petes and David standing on the front porch, all three of them scanning the quickly dispersing crowd.

Big Pete saw Sam almost immediately, then barked some command she couldn't hear and pointed directly at her and Laila.

"Go," she shouted. "Go, go, go! Run!"

Both women spun around and took off across the parking lot.

"Where are we going?"

"Back to the car!" Sam looked over her shoulder.

Little Pete ran after them, his arms pumping at his sides. Big Pete remained on the porch. David was now nowhere to be seen.

Fortunately, Laila had parked in the rear lot for staff when she'd shown up to work this morning, prepared to act like it was just another regular day at work. They didn't have to run far. She struggled to find her keys within the greater mess of her overly large purse, but then she had the car doors unlocked with a click of the key fob and a dainty little chirp from her vehicle. By the time they both leapt into the car and Laila cranked the engine, Little Pete had veered around the corner of the building and now headed straight toward them, his face contorted in a furious snarl.

"Go, go, go!" Sam slapped the dashboard.

"Don't yell at me," Laila snapped before shifting into drive and flooring the gas.

The squeal of tires and the acrid scent of burning rubber drowned out everything else, and her vehicle lurched forward. With a hiss of surprise, Laila jerked the wheel to the side and narrowly avoided running Little Pete down right there in the rear lot. She might've done just that, however accidentally, if he hadn't leapt away at the last second.

Then they barreled through the parking lot, avoiding other vehicles as members left the club's premises. Horns honked at them, and Sam spun around in the front passenger seat to watch Little Pete disappear behind them. "Can't you go any faster?"

"And ram right into all the other cars here?" Laila hissed. "Yeah, sure, no problem."

The vehicle rocked, tipping dangerously, when Laila took a daringly sharp right-hand turn onto the frontage road. The engine roared again before they raced away at top speed, both women breathing heavily while Laila white-knuckled the steering wheel and stared blankly ahead of them as if she'd suddenly switched to autopilot.

"Now I'm just heading straight for the highway, right?" Laila sounded numb.

Sam looked behind them again and grimaced. "Not just yet."

"*What?* Why the hell not?"

"You can drive fast, can't you?"

"Sam, what the hell?"

"Because there's someone coming up on our ass," Sam explained. "Fast. So if I were you, I'd step on it again."

"What?" Laila shrieked and looked urgently up into the rearview mirror. "Oh shit."

"You know who that is?"

"That's David's car."

"David as in the club manager?"

"As in the only David I know! He's the one who held me down while Big Pete socked me in the stomach."

"Son of a bitch," Sam snarled. "Pete sent him after us. Had to. Just drive, Laila. You gotta drive like your life depends on it."

"Are you seriously telling me that's what's happening right now?"

"Will it make you drive faster?"

It was a harsh thing to say in a tense moment, but it was exactly what Laila needed.

She set her jaw and stepped on the gas. The engine revved, they picked up speed, then they flew down the frontage road toward who knew where.

"Jesus, Sam, where am I supposed to go?"

"Anywhere. Just keep driving. We gotta lose him."

Sam kept turning around to look back at David's vehicle. He could drive too, but he didn't have the same desperation fueling him like Laila's.

Sam hadn't missed the shiner he sported today, which could have come from any number of things. Knowing Big Pete had sent his manager to run down one of his own employees gave Sam a clear enough picture of what had happened between them. Most likely, though, David wouldn't push himself to the far extremes of a high-speed car chase just to deliver two women to his boss.

She imagined Laila hadn't gone down easily before they'd thrown her in the basement storage cabinet.

She didn't know David, but she hoped the guy was smart enough to cut his losses while he still could.

Laila managed to lose David's tail when she left the frontage road to turn randomly through the twisting sideroads on the outer edges of town.

After ten minutes of scanning the roads behind them with no sign of David's vehicle or another tail, Sam slumped back in her seat. "Good work. Looks like you lost him."

"Holy shit." Laila puffed out a sigh, shook her head, and wiped sweat off her forehead and cheek with the back of a hand. "I was actually just in a car chase."

Sam barked out a laugh. "And you handled it like a pro. I had no idea you could drive like that."

Laila shot her a quick glance before returning her attention to the road, her hands still tightly gripping the steering wheel, but now she grinned. "Neither did I."

FIFTY

Sam

THEY PARKED Laila's car on the long frontage road leading up to Greg's cottage. No, it wasn't reassuring to leave their getaway vehicle a mile and a half away from where they'd execute this last part of Sam's plan, but it was the best they could do. Any visible cars besides Greg's would give them away, and Sam was convinced that if Hank Topping was smart enough to keep his personal life secret for as long as he had, he was smart enough to recognize a foreign vehicle on his former best friend's property.

Sam stuffed the papers from Big Pete's private file on her into the glovebox of Laila's car before they left it on the frontage road's wide dirt shoulder.

She and Laila trekked through the woods and back down the winding dirt road on foot toward Greg's cabin. Sam wanted to be there first, yes, but she'd already suspected it would take Hank about an hour or two to mull over the pros and cons before deciding to pay Greg's cabin another visit.

They would be there waiting for him.

No one else was there yet when they arrived, which meant they had plenty of time to prepare.

They entered the cabin without difficulty because Sam had the man's keys.

Laila stopped in the middle of the living room and looked around, wrinkling her nose. "Are you sure this is gonna work? What if Hank doesn't take the bait? He might not. He might already be on to you."

"He'll take the bait," Sam said. "He's been hiding this for so long now, he's got too much to lose."

All they had to do now was wait for Hank Topping to show up, catch him in the act of attempting to destroy evidence, and make him talk once he realized he'd been well and truly cornered.

What they'd do after that was anyone's guess, but Sam had a feeling Laila wouldn't press charges or try to make these men pay for what had happened to her sister. They just needed to find out what had happened first, and they could go from there.

Half an hour later, tires crunched across gravel outside the cabin.

"Come on." Sam beckoned Laila to follow her down the short hallway into the back of the cabin and into its single bedroom. She closed the door almost all the way but left it open a crack both to watch whoever entered the cabin and to much more easily spring out at the perfect moment to catch them in the act.

To catch Hank Topping, more specifically.

It was about damn time someone did.

Outside, a car door thumped shut, then footsteps crunched over gravel and up the short flight of stairs onto the front porch. The front door of Greg's cottage swung slowly open.

Sam listened intently, unable to hold back a frown.

For a guy who's this desperate to protect his reputation, he sure is taking his sweet time about it.

Footsteps clicked slowly across the hardwood floors, then Sam finally decided she'd had enough waiting.

She slipped through the bedroom door, ignoring Laila's hesitantly whispered protests, and headed down the hall into the living room.

Surprise, surprise — she found herself staring not at Hank Topping from behind but at the back of a woman Sam didn't recognize.

"Greg's not in right now," she said.

The woman standing beside the bookshelf jumped in surprise and spun around.

Sam folded her arms. "But if you like, I'm happy to take a message and let him know you stopped by."

The woman blinked quickly, looked Sam up and down, then gazed around the living room. "Hi there. I was looking for Greg, actually."

Sam raised an eyebrow. "In the bookcase?"

The other woman's calm, relatively friendly smile disappeared. "Not specifically. Do you know when he'll be back?"

"That depends on when the hospital says he's healed enough to go home. And who the hell are you? Just by the way."

The scanned the room again, then puffed out a sigh and shook her head. "Never mind. I'll come back later to check on him."

She headed for the door.

Then the lightbulb went off in Sam's brain, and she took a chance on her newest hunch. "Hey, you're Hank Topping's wife. Valerie, right?"

The woman froze, looking completely baffled when she turned back toward Sam. "I'm sorry, do I know you?"

"Definitely not. I dropped by your sister-in-law's house the other day. Shell? There's a nice picture sitting on her mantel. Her and Matt and the kids, plus you and your husband and your parents. Everyone looking so happy all together. That's what really stuck in my mind about it."

Valerie's frown deepened as she peered into the corners, as if she expected someone she knew to pop out of hiding any second and declare this as one giant practical joke.

She was sorely disappointed.

"I'll just go, then. Whoever you are."

"The name's Sam. And we don't know each other, but I'm helping a few people look into someone else I think you *do* know, actually. Dina Copely?"

Valerie's flawless face done up with all the best makeup money could buy still paled noticeably at the mention of Laila's sister. Unfortunately for her, she didn't have to provide Sam with an answer or any kind of verbal response. Just one look at Valerie's reaction, and Sam knew.

"You're the one who hurt her, aren't you?"

Valerie scoffed. "Excuse me?"

"Dina. You did something to her, and everyone else who was involved has desperately tried to keep it covered up. I know it was you. You found out about Dina and Hank, right? Then you decided to handle it yourself? So why don't you cut the clueless act and tell me what happened? Who knows? Could be a major relief to finally get it all off your chest."

For a moment, Valerie looked stunned. Cornered. Trapped, even. She reached up with both hands to readjust the strap of her purse over her shoulder, then without warning moved far more quickly than Sam could have anticipated.

The next second, Sam was staring down the barrel of a pistol pulled straight from Valerie's purse.

Neither the gun nor the woman's hand so much as twitched after that.

"Whoa, hey." Sam lifted both hands to show she was unarmed. "Valerie, that's completely unnecessary."

"Is it, though?" the woman snarled. "Personally, I find this kind of thing tends to make people take me seriously."

"I *am* taking you seriously. Even without the handgun. So why don't you put that down, and we won't have to worry about making this any more serious than it already is."

"No." Valerie shook her head, weapon still trained on Sam, muscles taut and her entire body coiled and ready to spring if necessary. Maybe even a little too taut. "No, I let things go far enough. For way longer than I should have. And this is me being deathly serious. I want my father's confession."

Sam raised her eyebrows. "Oh."

So Valerie's *the one doing her husband's dirty work instead, huh? Interesting little twist.*

"It wouldn't happen to mention you by name, would it?" Sam asked. "That doesn't seem like something a loving father would do."

A bitter smile flashed across Valerie's lips before disappearing. "You have no idea what kind of father he was. But *I* do, and I will not let his reputation be smeared like this all over the whole damn town just because he wasn't strong enough to deal with his own decisions."

"Not like *you* are, though, right?" Sam asked. "Is that what this is about?"

"We're not having a conversation here," Valerie hissed. "Where's his confession?"

"I just don't understand why you're the one standing here right now," Sam said.

While she talked, she poured the rest of her focus into actively not looking at the gun in Valerie's hands. That would only remind the woman of her current advantage. Now, Sam had to keep Valerie talking and hope they came to some kind of agreement, where lowering the pistol and avoiding a physical altercation could join hand in hand.

"I don't understand why you're here and not Hank. I mean, what the hell happened that night, huh? That made Greg open his mouth to stand up against something he just didn't agree with, and everybody turned him away. That's what you're so afraid of happening to your father, right?"

"If he wasn't dead," Valerie spat through gritted teeth. "Yes."

The woman's breath quickened, and Sam blinked at yet another private realization when all the other pieces clicked into place.

Hank's wife here instead of Hank. Valerie's involvement. Her father's suicide brought on by his own insufferable guilt. Greg, who was also a doctor, who was also in love with Dina. And Dina, who had still been alive when she'd made it back home to Seattle despite having changed irreparably.

"She was pregnant," Sam murmured.

Valerie said nothing.

"Dina was actually pregnant. Hank was the father, and you found out about it. What happened? Did he try to do the right thing by telling you? And then what? You couldn't let that stand, so you hurt her?"

"I didn't do anything to her," Valerie hissed. "I never even touched the girl."

Sam tilted her head. "No, but you got the ball rolling. You wanted it taken care of. You wanted your picture-perfect life in Rush restored, yeah? A baby would've screwed it all up. And how convenient for you that your daddy was a doctor."

Valerie's lips twitched again, this time with nothing but malice. "Sounds like you read his confession."

No, Sam hadn't, because there was no confession. Just a vague and mysterious suicide note, but her bluffing had clearly paid off. "There's always more than one side to a story. I wonder just how much your memory of that night differs from your father's. So here's my version of things the way I see it. You had to clean up your husband's mess. You went to Daddy. He said he could help you and … what? Commandeered a few buddies of his at the club?"

For the first time since she'd drawn it, the handgun in Valerie's tight grip trembled slightly. She barked out a bitter laugh, looking like she wanted to spin around and run away, but she held her ground. "None of it was supposed to happen like that. Especially not at the Kalamack Club. Jesus Christ. Sunday brunches were supposed to be fun. A chance for us to let loose a little. Shake things up. Add a little spice to our marriage."

"There are plenty of other ways to spice up a marriage," Sam said. "Most of them don't include other people or their unborn children."

"You talk about this like you have any idea what it's actually like." Valerie shook her head and took another step toward Sam, gun still raised. "You have no idea. Sunday brunches are our little secret, and we're all in on it, and everyone has dirt on everyone else. Nobody opens their mouth.

"But Hank had to go and break all the rules, didn't he? He had to fall in love with that little whore who was barely more than a child herself. He got her *pregnant*. That wasn't even the worst part! When he married me, he said he didn't want kids. That wasn't in the cards for him. All he ever wanted was me, and that's why I said yes.

"Then he comes home one night and tells me he and the fucking hostess from the club are leaving because he got her pregnant and he loves her. And I'm just supposed to … what? Stand there and pat him on the back and say good luck, I wish you well? Fuck that. This is *my* life too."

"So that makes it okay to ruin someone else's?" Sam asked.

"It's not like I had her killed," Valerie shouted, her eyes glinting with malicious fire.

Sam was pushing her luck now, but they were on a roll. She couldn't stop before she had the rest of the details. She just didn't know how to do that without getting herself shot in the process.

"She didn't die," Valerie said. "She didn't disappear, either. The girl was fine, and then she went home, and that was the end of it. No harm done."

"Are you sure about that?" Sam asked.

"Of course. Daddy just fixed the situation. After that, we were all free to go back to life as normal. I didn't do anything wrong, and neither did he. So where's that confession?"

The hint of hysteria rising in Valerie faded into a much calmer, much more assured steadiness. Yes, she was still deathly serious about this whole thing, and Sam would have to pull something impressive as hell out of her own ass just to save it.

Now it all made sense.

Hank had told Valerie about him and Dina. He'd done the right thing. And they'd all paid for it. Because Valerie had gone straight to Dr. Jones after that, explained the problem, told him exactly what needed to be fixed, and the man had agreed. Reginald Jones. Big Pete. And

Greg. Maybe even a few other club members. All banded together to help one of their own do what had to be done.

Greg had spoken up about it, which got him kicked out of the club, exiled from Rush, and cut off from everyone and everything.

And Dina never said a word about any of it to anyone.

"Did you hear me?" Valerie shouted, renewing her tight hold on the handgun and shaking it in Sam's direction as an ill-advised warning. "I want that confession. Now!"

Sam had prepared for this, fortunately. Though once Valerie got close enough to receive this alleged confession, she wouldn't have much of a chance to do anything. Sam just needed to get her close.

She pulled Dr. Jones' original suicide note in its original envelope from the back pocket of her black jeans and extended it in Valerie's direction. "This confession?"

"Set it down." Valerie pointed at the kitchen table with the pistol before training it on Sam again. "Right there on the table. Let's go."

Sam was ready and willing to play this all the way out to the very end.

Unfortunately, having a firearm pointed at her face made it all too easy to forget that she and Valerie weren't alone.

"You fucking cunt!" Laila darted down the short hallway, her fists clenched and her face an alarming shade of furious red.

Valerie had never threatened anyone with a loaded firearm before, nor had she fired live rounds from that pistol. That was obvious when she spun toward the hallway, startled by the unexpected insult from an unexpected third party, and the pistol went off.

Sam ducked at the deafening report of a single shot inside the tiny cabin.

Laila dropped halfway to the ground before staggering backward and thumping against one of Greg's full bookcases.

"No!" Valerie screamed, then turned back toward Sam.

At this point, Sam had already moved.

When Valerie saw her charging, she squeezed off another round, this time most definitely not by accident.

Sam weaved her way out of a close call with the second round just before she tackled Valerie from below and sent the woman flying backward to the floor.

Valerie gasped as her back hit the hardwood with a thump, followed instantly by a sharp crack when the back of her head did the same. The pistol flew from her grasp and clattered across the living room, spinning over and over before sliding under the furniture.

Fuck the gun. Sam had to get out of here.

She had to get Laila out of here.

Sam leapt to her feet and ran toward Laila while Valerie struggled to rise to hands and knees before racing toward the couch and the loaded handgun beneath it.

"Come on," Sam said, reaching for Laila's hand. "We gotta go. Right now."

"I… She just…" Laila gasped, then looked down at her side above her left hip where she'd been clutching herself. She grimaced at the sight of her black camisole glistening with thick wetness, and her hand came away smeared with blood.

"Yeah, we gotta get you help. Come on." Sam grabbed Laila's arm and threw it over her own shoulders before rising out of a squat and hauling the woman along with her. Laila cried out again, almost a scream, but she stayed on her feet and let Sam guide her across the cabin in a hobble, blanched and shocked and freely bleeding from the bullet wound in her side.

They hurried out of the cabin, and Sam fought hard not to yell at Laila to hurry the hell up because the crazy woman behind them was about to get her hands on her pistol again and clearly didn't have a problem using it on either of them, but she kept her mouth shut and instead tried to both support and urgently usher Laila down the cabin's few porch steps and across the dirt clearing.

"Oh my god," Laila finally whispered as they half-ran, half-hobbled down the dirt in the direction of her car parked way too far away for comfort. "Oh my god. That bitch *shot* me."

"Pretty sure it just grazed you," Sam muttered, though she wasn't sure. There wasn't any time to take a look first. "You'll be fine. Just keep moving. Whatever you do, keep moving."

Instead of continuing down the winding dirt road leading back to the frontage road, Sam took a sharp left turn to head northwest through the woods. She had no idea if she was on the mark for making it to Laila's car, but she sure as hell would make it a lot harder for Valerie to follow them this way.

Behind them, the echoing bang and clatter of the cabin's front screen door echoed, followed by Valerie's screaming growl of rage and her footsteps stomping after them.

FIFTY-ONE

Dina

FIVE YEARS AGO...

THE SUNDAY after Dina finally had the chance to share her news with Hank, she still couldn't believe how incredibly lucky she was. Everything was going so perfectly. She was happier than she'd ever been. The chances of never having to hide her relationship with Hank ever again increased by the day.

Dina fully believed him when Hank had said he would speak to Valerie about their private relationship and her pregnancy, as well as their plans to leave Rush together and start a new life on their own, just the three of them.

In keeping with her promise to Hank in return, Dina still hadn't told anyone about her pregnancy or their plans. He'd told her to keep moving through her daily life as if nothing had changed, and she followed that directive to the letter, leading up to and including today's Sunday brunch at the club, which Dina worked as the Kalamack's hostess just like every other Sunday since Big Pete had officially invited her to participate.

Dina was all smiles and nods and compliments as she greeted the guests before the event began.

When Hank and Valerie Topping stepped through the front doors, Dina had a particularly special smile reserved for both of them.

"Good morning, Mr. and Mrs. Topping. Please, let me take your jackets. It's wonderful to see you."

"It's wonderful to be here." Valerie shrugged out of her long coat and let Dina take it. "I've been looking forward to this for a while."

Valerie had attended just as many of these Sunday brunches as Hank had, and most of them she spent elsewhere with other masked members without once searching for her husband or stopping by to find out how he was doing or even join him.

Today, though, Valerie kept shooting Dina flirtatious glances and even complimented her little black dress and how pretty her hair looked down and that she should wear it like that more often.

When Valerie settled a hand on the small of Dina's back and leaned in to plant a quick kiss on her cheek — but not too quick — Dina had a feeling Hank's wife planned on spending today's Sunday brunch with them. That was fine by her.

It wouldn't have been the first time, and Dina wasn't necessarily opposed to another woman joining them. Even if the other woman was Hank's wife.

As the morning progressed and more members and their plus-ones arrived for the festivities, Valerie really turned up the dial on her flirting with Dina — biting her lip, tossing her hair, setting a hand on Dina's shoulder or hip or cheek and letting it sit far longer than would have been appropriate if this weren't Sunday brunch.

Hank, though, looked ill.

He stayed close to Dina, and she tried more than once to ask what was wrong, why he looked so upset. Every time, though, he shrugged her off, saying now wasn't the time or that he was fine or that she had other members waiting for her and should go tend to them first.

Dina wondered if he wasn't just nervous about everything, that maybe their relationship had brought up a few reservations in him, that maybe he'd already spoken with Valerie and they'd fought before coming here.

It couldn't have been the latter, though, because Valerie looked more excited and engaged and ready to go than any other time Dina had seen her here on a Sunday.

Maybe Hank just genuinely didn't feel well.

Then Big Pete and Elaine entered to kickstart the festivities, and the entire mood in the Kalamack Club changed.

Every minute, new couples or small groups formed, some of them moving away from the bulk of the event to find private rooms upstairs or uninhabited areas of the clubhouse for more intimate locations. The bulk of participants, however, remained in the dining room.

Wearing a black sequined mask today, Dina quickly found Hank and playfully pulled the mask away from her face to grin at him. "Hey, there."

Hank grimaced and wouldn't look at her.

"Hank…" Frowning, Dina stepped toward him, gazing up at his face. He hadn't even bothered to grab a mask today, which wasn't like him. "What's the matter?"

"I really just don't feel well. Honestly, I'd rather be home right now."

"Are you sick?"

She caught the discomfort and hesitation behind his eyes when his gaze settled on her for the briefest moment.

Then Valerie found them as she completed another circuit of her rounds through the dining room.

"There you are." Smiling from beneath the bright-red mask covering most of her face, Valerie settled both hands on Dina's hips from behind and dipped her head to plant a kiss on the crook of Dina's neck. Then she looked up at her husband, her smile unchanged. "This is for you."

She produced a bottle of wine seemingly from nowhere and handed it to Hank. "Why don't you to go upstairs, find us a room, open up this bottle? I'll join you in just a bit. It won't take too long, I promise."

"Well, as long as you promise…" Dina was already headed toward the stairs.

Dina and Hank passed a number of other couples getting cozy in either the stairwell or the second-floor hall-way. Dina found an available guestroom — she kept her personal room locked every day, especially on Sundays. She'd never brought Hank up to the private room where she'd technically been living for the last several months.

She might have finally invited him into her actual room today now that so many things were changing and improving between them, but Valerie was clearly intent on joining them. Denying the woman what she wanted this morning wouldn't go over very well. This was, after all, a Sunday brunch at the Kalamack Club.

Dina took Hank's free hand and pulled him into the randomly selected bedroom, leaving the door open a crack so Valerie could find them when she was ready. The wine bottle in his hand clinked down onto the standing dresser when she led him past it. Then they were at the bed.

Dina guided Hank onto the mattress. At first, it took far more coaxing than usual to get him to lie down, which she definitely found odd, but if he really was feeling ill, maybe lying down just reminded him of wanting to go home.

At one point, he tried to stop her, catching her hands in his and frowning up at her as he leaned back against the stacked pillows. "Dina, I don't think this—"

"Shh. Just try to relax, okay? We don't have anything to worry about. Not now. Not today. Let's just enjoy this while we can."

He didn't look nearly as excited to have her there on the bed with him as every other moment they were together. He didn't tell her to leave, either. Dina knew he wouldn't.

He'd said he would tell Valerie about their relationship and her pregnancy.

Maybe he hadn't revealed it all to his wife yet, and the anticipation of it made him uncomfortable. Dina fully intended to help ease away most if not all of that discomfort.

She got only as far as unbuttoning Hank's shirt to leave a slow trail of hot kisses down his neck and chest before Hank gently grabbed her wrists and pulled her away.

"I can't," he whispered.

"What do you mean? Of course you can. It's Sunday brunch. Anyone can."

"That's not what I mean, Dina."

Only then did she suspect something was off, and it wasn't just a cold.

"Listen," he said. "You and I, we need to talk."

"Oh, this sounds familiar," she said playfully.

"I'm serious. About our plans ... the two of us. There's something I need to—"

"Found you," Valerie said from the open doorway

before stepping into the bedroom. "What's been going on in here? Hank, you didn't open the wine."

He had no response, but Valerie didn't seem to care. She moved fluidly toward the dresser, quickly rummaged through the top drawer for a bottle opener, and uncorked the wine with a muffled pop. Then she pulled three glasses from the cabinet on the other side of the room. "It's not really a Sunday brunch without a few drinks, right?"

Smiling the whole time, Valerie filled their glasses one by one, then brought all three toward the bed where Dina and Hank still sat. She offered a glass to Hank, then to Dina. "I picked this out especially for us today."

Dina held the woman's gaze. "I'm flattered. But no thanks. I don't want any today."

"Oh, come on. Dina." Valerie extended the glass again, stepping closer. "Have a little fun and a few drinks. Don't say no to me."

"I…" Dina gazed at the glass, then shook her head.

Tilting her head, Valerie pouted. "Oh, come on. You're not pregnant or something, are you?"

Dina instantly flicked her gaze toward the woman's face. Valerie's smile was as flirtatious and hungry as ever. Most likely, her comment had been a joke. It certainly sounded like the kind of thing Valerie said from time to time when she tried to loosen up and break through any pre-existing tension during these brunches.

And if she was joking, that just meant Hank hadn't told her yet, and the irony was only too clear.

"Fine." Dina gingerly took the glass, then raised it toward Valerie in a silent toast. "But just one."

"You can have as many as you like," Valerie replied. "If you don't want to stop at one, don't stop."

Dina downed the entire glass in two breaths, partially because she just wanted to get it over with and partially because being in this room with Hank and Valerie at the same time, knowing Hank hadn't yet said a thing to his wife about their plans, suddenly felt far more uncomfortable than all three of them in the same room together with the proverbial cat already out of the bag.

Hank sighed heavily when she finished the wine, and Valerie chuckled. "Now let's have some fun, hmm?"

Setting her glass down on the dresser, Valerie climbed languidly onto the mattress with Dina and Hank. She ignored her husband for the time being and instead focused all her attention on Dina.

Dina really didn't mind. In fact, she'd even enjoyed it on the occasions Valerie had joined her and Hank during Sunday brunches. Dina got most of the attention from Valerie in the beginning, which she supposed was just all part of warming up, so she didn't think anything of it when the other woman cupped her face in both hands and pulled her closer for a long, slow, deep kiss that had Dina's heart racing a million miles per second.

Making out with Valerie was nothing like making out with Hank. That didn't mean it wasn't still amazing.

Especially amazing today, apparently, because when Valerie finally released her, Dina's pulse still raced, her head swimming. It had to be from all Valerie's attention, because one glass of wine certainly wasn't enough to make her feel like this.

Valerie stroked Dina's cheek with the back of a finger and studied her face. "How do you feel?"

Dina blinked quickly, trying to clear her now warped and blurring vision. "A little dizzy, actually. That must've been some really good wine."

"It's definitely special." Valerie kept grinning. "Just relax, sweetheart. It'll all be over soon."

"What?" Frowning, Dina tried to push herself up off

the bed and would have hit the ground face first if Hank hadn't been there to grab her under the arms from behind and help lower her back down onto the mattress.

"What … w-what's going on?" Her lips felt like pillows, and her voice sounded so far away while the entire world spun around her. Within it all, she just kept seeing Valerie's face.

"Oh yeah." Valerie smiled down at her, taking up Dina's entire field of vision. "It was definitely enough."

Oh my god, the wine… It's the wine. Did she just drug me?

The thought was terrifying, but Dina couldn't move. She couldn't say anything. She could barely even see, and what she could make out from where Valerie and Hank had laid her down on the bed still didn't make sense.

There was a knock on the door, and Valerie answered it, her mask abandoned now.

The door creaked open, and Dina thought she recognized the other man's voice, but she couldn't tell for sure. She couldn't even remember her own name right now, let alone anyone else's.

"Is she ready?"

"She's not going anywhere, that's for sure," Valerie said.

"All right, then we have to move quickly."

There was a flurry of footsteps and movement all around her, but Dina still couldn't move. She tried to turn her head, searching what little of the room she could see for Hank. Instead, she only saw a tall man in a business suit with a black leather bag in hand. She thought there were other people in the room too, beyond Valerie and Hank. Men moving quickly back and forth. While cases were opened and supplies and random materials were set out, items clinked down onto the dresser beside the opened and only partially consumed bottle of wine. Murmuring voices filtered in all around her, and Dina didn't understand any of it.

Nor did she understand why she lay there, awake and watching the bustle of activity but couldn't speak or control the movement of her head or even her own fingers. She tried to call out for Hank, to ask where he was, but only a low moan escaped her.

"Damnit, can't we just put her out now?"

"Hank?" Dina asked, or at least she tried to. She wasn't sure if his name actually emerged from her lips, no matter how badly she'd wanted it to.

"I know that seems like the best way to start, son," another man replied, "but the sedative only lasts so long, and we don't want her waking up too soon."

"Jesus Christ."

"So then the rest of you better hurry the hell up," Valerie said. "You heard him."

Whoever else was in the room just kept moving. Dina couldn't follow.

At one point, she thought she was being lifted off the bed, though she couldn't have said where she went instead. But she caught sight of the sheets being stripped and something that looked like plastic stretched across the mattress instead.

An incredibly bright light switched on from the other side of the room. Dina's eyes were already drooping heavily anyway, but that didn't mean she didn't notice the difference. None of the private rooms in the Kalamack Club had lights like that.

"All right, put her back on the bed."

Then Dina was moving again. She couldn't feel the hands beneath her and had no idea who they belonged to. Another moan escaped her when she settled back down on the bed. Then those unfamiliar hands tugged at her clothes, pulling her dress up over her thighs. She could do nothing to stop them.

"The other sedative's in my bag. It's already measured out in the syringe and ready to go."

"This one, Daddy?"

"That's it."

Dina couldn't comprehend the sharp pinch in the crook of her arm or why the rest of the bedroom just kept spinning before everything went fuzzy and warm and darker than she'd ever known.

Her last thought before she completely lost consciousness broke her heart.

Where was Hank?

~

THE NEXT THING Dina knew was a deep, throbbing pain worse than any stomach cramp. Her insides felt like they'd been yanked out by a hook and stuffed back in again without rhyme or reason. Her head pounded. Her throat was dry and raw, and that damn bright light still shone directly down on her as if she'd just stepped under the spotlight on a brilliantly lit stage.

She tried to move, which brought an instant flare of pain from deep in her belly and between her legs. The sensation instantly made her freeze, and she lay there on the mattress, panting beneath a sheen of sweat breaking out across her forehead, cheeks, and neck.

Her tongue stuck to the roof of her mouth, and her own breath sounded incredibly loud in her ears.

Where was she? Why did she feel like this? What had happened?

A different sound interrupted her groggy thoughts,

which she didn't immediately recognize because she had honestly never heard it before.

The sound of a grown man openly sobbing somewhere in the room.

Who was that? What had happened to *him*?

Dina wanted to push herself off her back and find this man, whoever he was, to at least ask if he was okay, but she couldn't get her limbs to move the way she wanted.

She'd had no idea there was anyone else here besides her and the sobbing man until a woman's voice cut through the heartbreaking sound.

"Jesus, Hank. Will you just grow a pair already? You need to pull yourself together. This is ridiculous."

The man just kept sobbing.

Then Dina blinked heavily, hoping to clear her blurred vision. Instead of clearing, though, it was instantly filled with the face of a woman she thought she recognized. It took her longer than it should have to put a name to that face.

It was Valerie.

"You're waking up." The woman no longer smiled. "At least the timing was on point."

A hurried knock rose from the door, then Valerie disappeared from Dina's view. Sharp, clicking footsteps crossed the room, and the door squeaked open. "Took you long enough."

"I came as quickly as I could, okay? What's going on?"

Dina recognized that voice too. A voice that should have made her feel better. Relieved, maybe, or safe, or at the very least content. A voice she'd associated with fun and happiness at one point. She knew that much, but the rest of it she just couldn't put together. Her brain was still too full of mush. It hurt too much. Everything hurt way too much.

"Doesn't matter what happened," Valerie hissed. "What matters is that this is over and we never have to deal with it again."

"What do you want me to do?"

"I want you to get rid of her," Valerie snapped. "So that's what you're gonna do. Get to it."

More footsteps across the room. The sobbing in a man's voice continued, and Dina finally turned her head on the mattress toward the door.

"Oh my god. Oh my *god*…"

"Saying that over and over won't change anything," Val snapped. "Get her out of here."

The newcomer hurried toward the bed, her bright-blue eyes wide with shock and her thick, intensely curly mane of blonde hair framing her face like a halo.

There was nothing angelic about any of this.

"Dina, can you hear me?"

Dina stared at the face she knew she should recognize, then it finally hit her. It took two tries before she managed to squeeze out one word. "Shell?"

"Yeah, hi." Shell's smile was tight and fake and lacked reassurance. "I'm here, D. Come on. Let's get you out of here, okay? I got you. Can you sit up for me? Come on."

Dina somehow managed to move with Shell's help. Her body felt like it was on fire now. Her head pounded and swam all at once, and her insides felt both strangled and loose, like they'd been caught in a trap and were about to fall out of her to spill all over the polished hardwood floors.

"Come on, hon," Shell said. "That's it. Just one step at a time. Let's get you home. Get you some rest and a bath, maybe. Does that sound good?"

Dina moaned again, though she hadn't tried to say

anything. Her gaze flickered all over the room, blurry and spinning, everything lacking color and life.

She thought she saw Hank sitting in a chair in the corner.

When she tried to call out to him, only another groan escaped her. The last thing she saw before Shell led her from the room was Valerie standing there in the middle of it all, her hands on her hips, smirking as if she'd just proven some incredibly important point that made her better than everyone else.

THE NEXT FEW days moved like boiling molasses, each of them blurring into the next like a quickly forgotten dream.

Or a waking nightmare from which Dina could never escape.

She knew she'd been brought back to Rip's farm, where she was provided a private room in the main lodge, away from the last of the trimmers sticking around at the end of the season. Rip let her stay there in secret, with Shell as her only visitor, so she could rest and recover.

Dina was aware of Shell coming to visit her twice a day. The blonde brought her meals and water. And while Dina knew full well that her body needed to eat and drink as well as rest, she couldn't bring herself to ingest more than a few sips at a time before lying back down on a mattress she hardly felt and disappearing again into the void of something not quite catatonia and not quite despair.

More than this meager awareness of her surroundings, Dina was acutely aware of what had been done to her.

It hadn't taken her very long to figure it out. The last of the sedative and whatever drugs Valerie had given her had all worn off by the time she and Shell were halfway out of town on their way to Rip's.

She'd refused to see a doctor. Not that there were any other available doctors in Rush who either weren't the bastard who'd done this to her or didn't know who he was. But she didn't need a doctor to confirm what she already knew, what she already felt deep in her bones and every fiber of her being.

Her baby had been taken from her. This unborn child, this life she had created with a man she thought she'd loved, was gone. Now all Dina felt was a hollow, aching emptiness where once she had nurtured so much joy and hope for the future.

No matter how hard she tried, Shell couldn't get her friend to say anything during those days at Rip's farm. Finally, however, when it seemed Dina was strong enough to stand on her own two feet while also recognizing where and who she was, Shell decided the best thing for her friend was to go home, to be with her family, to get the kind of support she needed because, though Shell cared about her, she had no idea how else to help the girl.

So she packed Dina's bags herself, drove her to Rush's bus station, and handed her the ticket back to Seattle she'd bought in the hopes it might help somehow.

Even when Shell repeated again that she fully intended to stay in touch, Dina didn't say a word. She had nothing left to say. When she stepped onto that bus heading from Rush, California back to Seattle, Washington, she didn't look back once.

There was nothing left for her in this town anymore anyway, and there never would be.

FIFTY-TWO

Sam

BY THE TIME Sam and Laila got back up to running speeds through the woods, Valerie had already caught up to them by a dangerous amount. The desperate woman behind them was easy to keep tabs on as she stumbled through the woods, crashing and bumbling about and cursing whenever her clothes snagged on branches or the wrong footing that sent her stumbling off balance.

The whole time, Sam tried to impart to Laila the importance of being as quiet as possible to not give away their position. Then again, Laila was the one with a bullet wound in her side, but if she didn't stay quiet, one or both of them was more likely to get another bullet from Valerie's gun.

Then Sam caught a glimpse of Laila's car up ahead through the trees, and she changed tactics to hopefully buy them a little more time.

She doubled back, still supporting Laila, and they went the long way around toward Laila's car before Sam got to work.

She opened the passenger-side door and ushered Laila

into it as gently as she could. Then she stripped off her own black long-sleeve shirt to lift its collar to her mouth.

Trying to rip through the seams with her teeth, though, didn't work.

"Keys," she grumbled.

"What?" Laila panted.

Sam snapped her fingers. "Keys, give me your keys."

When they were handed over, Sam used them like an incredibly dull saw to rip up her shirt and tore the rest of it apart with her hands.

It was moments like these that made her wish she'd just stuck with her own vehicle and all the available tools she kept in the Jeep. That would've kept her from having to improvise like this and only waste even more time.

"What are you doing?" Laila asked.

"Helping you first." Sam tore her shirt into as many strips of fabric as she could, then tied three of them together so they'd be long enough.

Laila made too much noise when Sam leaned her forward in the seat to wrap her up in this makeshift tourniquet bandage. At this point, any noise wasn't nearly as dangerous as not wrapping the wound and putting some pressure on it. Then Sam let the woman lean back against the passenger seat. She grabbed Laila's hand, pressed it over the woman's side, and got a snarl of pain for her effort.

"You need to keep pressure on it," she said. "You can do that, right? Just keep the pressure on it like this and leave the bandage where I put it."

Laila nodded.

"Okay. Here." Sam pulled out her own phone, handed it over, and nodded. "Call 911. Get them up here as quickly as possible. Tell them where you are first, then you can tell them about everything else. Right now, you need real medical attention, and I'm pretty sure my shirt won't cut it."

"What about you?"

Sam glanced into the woods, then spun back toward the car and spread her arms. "I'm gonna go make sure the crazy lady with a gun doesn't do anything else stupid. At least not before the cops arrive. Don't worry about me. Just do what I said, and you'll be all right."

With a final nod, Sam left Laila's car, having now gone from the hunted to the hunter.

Not that she had much in the way of hunting weapons right now. Part of her mentally kicked herself for not having fought for Valerie's gun under the couch instead of going straight for Laila. The other part of her, however — the part with more than sufficient military training and field experience — knew full well that with a woman like Valerie Topping, it was far less about who had the gun and more about figuring out how to distract from the weapon's existence in the first place.

Sam needed to find Valerie, disarm her, and then any danger the woman's out-of-control emotions might have posed to either Sam or Laila would be over.

Just like anything else, it was all just a matter of timing.

A little bit of acting and showmanship, more or less.

The instant Sam left Laila's car, she made as much noise as possible moving through the forest. Valerie was out there somewhere with a loaded handgun, searching for two women and expecting them to either hide or run or both. There was a good chance that if Valerie heard too much noise coming from the woods, she'd chase after it in her haste.

That was what Sam was counting on, anyway.

She hoped to hell Valerie Topping hadn't been some

kind of amateur hunting prodigy in these woods as a kid, or Sam and Laila were both fucked.

What were the chances of that, though, really?

Then again, what were the chances of Valerie having shown up at Greg's cabin instead of Hank, and with a handgun in her purse?

After quickly getting her bearings again and directionally orienting herself in the forest, Sam crashed about, making plenty of noise to hopefully draw Valerie away from Laila.

It worked.

She heard Valerie gaining on her, though visual sign of the other woman was still lacking.

As soon as she did catch sight of her unknowing assailant, however, Sam took off running southeast, away from Laila's car and toward Rip's farm. It was the only other property she knew of up here, and by now, Rip, his security men, and Jordan all knew her by name. They'd recognize her when she showed up.

Hopefully, they could offer a lot more help this time. If she hadn't been so busy running through thick underbrush and ducking beneath and around low-hanging branches, Sam would have laughed at herself. What was it with high-speed pursuits on foot through the woods up here, anyway?

Maybe this part of the mountains just had that come-chase-me vibe.

Valerie's lack of self-awareness or knowledge of moving stealthily through this type of terrain grew clearer by the minute. Sam kept up a decent pace, but she let the other woman gain on her bit by bit. Mostly so Sam could keep track of exactly where Valerie was at any given time. To make sure the woman didn't suddenly give up the chase and double back to try her luck with a much easier target.

Like Laila.

When she thought she was close enough to Rip's farm to risk it, Sam looked back over her shoulder. She hurried through the woods and caught a brief glimpse of movement through the trees. The heavy crash of bumbling, staggering footsteps through ferns and bushes and branches was punctured by the crack and echoing splinter of another shot fired from the woman's handgun.

Sam ducked again at the sound, vaguely aware of bits of bark flying off the side of a tree five yards in front of her and to the right. But she kept going.

Valerie had to have commandeered this handgun from someone else. Her husband or her father, maybe. Because no way in hell did a woman who shot like that while running through the woods have a gun license or carrying permit or any experience on a range.

Sam's heart fluttered with relief when the wail of sirens in the distance joined the deafening crack and splinter Valorie's clomping footsteps behind her.

Good. Laila got ahold of the police.

If Sam played her cards right, she could stall for time and ensure no one else was physically harmed. She just had to keep her wits about her. Keep paying attention. Because if Valerie managed to catch her off guard again, there was a good chance Sam would miss her shot to finally finish this and put an end to the whole damn thing.

When Sam finally stumbled unexpectedly out of the tree line without knowing what waited for her, she was stunned to find the terrain opening in front of her into rolling hillside fields.

There was the main lodge, right there. And down the tree line about a quarter of a mile was Rip's temp-building office.

She'd made it.

Sam also found herself staring at Rip and half a dozen

security men as she staggered out of the trees and her shoes kept tripping over each other to propel her forward.

She had just enough time to see Rip raise his eyebrows, then came the telltale crunch of someone else moving through the thick underbrush behind her.

A second later, Valeria crashed through in much the same fashion, though not nearly as gracefully as Sam had made it look in comparison. Probably.

The woman stumbled forward, surprised by lurching out of the woods, and raised the pistol in her hand, swinging it about as she searched the open ground for Sam.

She found her target a split second before she noticed they were no longer alone.

Sam had made it almost all the way to Rip and his guys. Then she slowly turned around and lifted both hands again.

"It's over, Valerie," she said, shaking her head in warning. "Let this go."

Valeria glanced back and forth between the woman she'd been chasing and the men who were clearly on Sam's side. "Let it go? I can't just *let it go!*"

"If you ask me," Sam replied with a shrug, "that's all just a matter of perspective."

"You have no idea what you're talking about!"

"I'm pretty sure I do. We've got the full story. You admitted to your part in what happened to Dina. So did your dad, though, unfortunately, he's not around anymore to bear the consequences of what you all did that night. It's too late to do anything about it now, Valerie. Put the gun down. It's over. And if you keep going like this, it's only gonna make things worse for you."

That clearly wasn't enough.

The pistol was still trained on Sam, but this time,

despite her two-handed grip on the weapon, Valerie's hands now shook. "I can't let you ruin us like this!"

Sam kept her hands raised. "Hey, you and your family already did a bang-up job of that all on your own."

"All right, now," Rip cut in, stepping forward with his hands also lifted in front of him. "Why don't you just lower your weapon, ma'am? Or better yet, toss it out in front of you and put your hands in the air. Then we can all be on the same page."

Valerie scowled at him, then the rest of her reserve broke. Hissing in frustration, she took one more step forward, pivoting to spin with her pistol and aim it not at Sam anymore but directly at Rip this time. "Don't take another step!"

"Oh, come on now," he said. "Are you out of your damn mind?"

Rip's security guys, to their credit, did not take the threat on their boss's physical wellbeing very lightly. Two of them surged forward before pausing, forcing Valerie to remove her aim from Rip's head so she could swivel it back and forth between the two men now standing much closer.

Then the air was punctured by the terrifying one-two clunk of a single-action shotgun being pumped into firing readiness. Valerie's eyes widened even more when she saw that shotgun, which he'd aimed directly at her gut. *His* hands, however, held perfectly steady.

"You heard the man," he growled.

Sam backed up a few steps. Getting one or two of Rip's security guys between them would be a massive help, given the circumstances.

But the second Sam took her first step backward, Valerie noticed and swung her pistol back toward Sam again, shaking it as she screamed, "I can't let this happen! I can't let you tell anyone what we did. My family's whole reputation is at stake!"

"What reputation?" Sam called back. "Seriously, Valerie, there's nothing left. Your father and your husband have been sitting on this for five years. I can't imagine there will be any love lost there. Laila made it back to her car, and she's already called the police. They're on the way up here as we speak."

Sam sincerely hoped she hadn't misinterpreted the timing here, which would only mean more time for a whole bunch of shit to go wrong.

"I can't keep your father's confession in the dark," Sam added. "Neither can you. The truth has to come out, and it will. It'll come out in a very public way, as will every decision you make from this moment forward, Valerie. So if I were you, I'd seriously consider exactly what it is you wanna add to the story while you still have some control over the way this turns out."

The other woman's chest heaved as she considered her options. With her teeth bared, those breaths huffed out of her in short, hissing bursts, spit flying from her lips. Then Valeria glanced from Sam to Rip's security guy with the shotgun trained on her, and her eyes widened.

In that split second, Sam already knew what the woman planned to do, but it was too late to stop her.

Sam tried anyway.

"No, no — wait!" She lurched forward, reaching out toward the woman in a desperate swipe at nothing but air. It wouldn't have been enough to stop anyone in Valerie's position from doing what she did now that she'd clearly made up her mind.

Valerie had already acted on it.

She took another lunging step forward and swung the pistol directly at the security guy with the shotgun.

Two shots fired in quick succession, one right after the other. The first was an almighty roar of a single, booming shot cutting through the field. And the next shot, milliseconds later, was small and fragile-sounding in comparison, like an afterthought squeezed from the barrel of a handgun by a woman who realized too late that she was simply too slow.

Valerie dropped the pistol before clamping both hands down around the center of her stomach and the immediate well of dark-red blood springing from the burst of buckshot that had peppered her with enough force to make it look like she'd just about been cut in half. She half-staggered backward, half-flew under the force of the shot, her eyes wide with terror and instant regret. Then she fell face first into the grass and didn't move.

Sam grimaced.

That was one way for the woman to control the narrative. But now Valerie Topping wouldn't be around to see for herself how it all played out.

FIFTY-THREE

Sam

THE KNOCKING on the door that woke Sam the next morning didn't sound like it normally did. The firmness of the mattress beneath her didn't quite match, either. Then Sam opened her eyes to find herself startlingly much lower to the ground in the exact middle of the trailer instead of at the very end where she put her bed.

A small part of her lizard brain panicked at the unexpected change in her environment. Then a low canine whine rose from the floor beside her, followed by Dog's warm, slimy wet tongue lapping at her hand and arm hanging over the side of the couch cushions.

That's right… The couch.

Syc's couch in Syc's trailer with Syc's dog, because they'd changed things up a little.

The knocking on the trailer's door continued — a mixture of gentle politeness and hesitant urgency.

"All right, all right," Sam muttered as she swiped a mess of thick dark hair out of her eyes and sat up on the couch. "I'm coming."

Dog leapt to his feet, tail wagging furiously as he whined again in excitement.

"Guess it doesn't matter where I sleep, huh?" she said with a chuckle. "Everybody needs Sam for something."

He trotted along at her side as she headed across Syc's trailer, which from the inside felt at least twice as large as her old Airstream had been, and opened the door. Dog shoved the door open with his nose and bolted into the grass for his morning constitutional.

A yelp of surprise quickly followed by laughter greeted them.

"Did we wake you?" Angela asked.

Sam thought she smiled, though she was still too groggy to be sure. "Yeah, but that's fine. Everything all right? The Deville work out for you guys? I'm sorry it's a little small."

"Don't even go there, Sam," Laila said with a growing smile. "There was plenty of space, and we were perfectly comfortable. Thanks so much for giving up your home to let us hang out for a while."

"Anytime." Sam glanced over her shoulder toward the end of the hallway where Syc's bedroom door remained closed. Then she stepped out of the trailer to avoid waking the man up.

The door cracked shut behind her, and she settled her bare feet in the grass, folding her arms against a brisk chill in the morning air. "What's up?"

"We're leaving town, Sam," Angela said. "We're going home."

"Hired a moving company to clear out my apartment," Laila added. "They'll be a day or two behind us, but we thought it was best we get back to Seattle as soon as possible. Back into my mom's house. It's better that I'm with her for a little bit."

"I'm guessing you didn't bother with giving your two weeks at work, right?" Sam joked.

Laila huffed out a laugh and didn't even dignify that with a response.

"We just wanted to say goodbye to you officially," Angela said, "and in person. And thank you for everything, Sam. You really made such a huge difference, and we can't fully express how much it means to us."

Sam accepted the other woman's hug when Angela stepped forward to embrace her, and she didn't squirm or try to quickly worm her way out of it, either. When they broke apart, she held Angela away at arm's length, her hands on the woman's shoulders, and added, "If you ever feel like sending me more flowers, I guess I'd be okay with it next time around."

That made Angela laugh despite the tears in her eyes.

Then Laila stepped forward to hug Sam too, wincing and favoring her side where she'd been grazed by a mad woman's stray bullet two days ago. Sam took care not to bump up against her when they released each other.

"So what's waiting for you two at home in Seattle, then?" she asked.

"We hadn't decided what we were going to do with all the money Dina brought home with her," Laila said. "She'd made more than enough to cover her first semester of med school and then quite a bit left over after that, to be honest. We were actually just talking about this last night."

She and Angela exchanged a knowing look between mother and daughter, which Sam found herself envying for a fraction of a second before she ripped herself back into reality.

"We're gonna use the rest of what Dina earned to create a scholarship fund for incoming pre-med students.

It's not an astronomical amount by any means, but I know a really good financial advisor might even be able to help us set something up to make this a yearly thing if we can swing it. But at the very least, we'll be able to help two, maybe three young people cover the costs of their schooling for a little while."

"That's a hell of a lot better than anything I could've come up with," Sam replied.

"Don't sell yourself short, Sam," Angela told her. "You came up with far more than your fair share of brilliant ideas for us in the last few weeks."

"Yeah, and I've had my fair share of really fucking terrible ideas too."

"That doesn't mean they cancel each other out." Angela winked, patted Sam's shoulder one more time, then turned and headed across the grass toward her daughter's car.

Laila stayed behind a moment longer until she was sure her mother was out of earshot. Then she turned toward Sam and grinned. "I have a present for you."

Sam barked out a laugh. "Obviously not more flowers."

"Trust me, this is way better than flowers." Laila reached into her purse and pulled out a small sleek black thumb drive, which she handed to Sam with a smirk. "I pulled these files off Big Pete's computer in his office while I was haunting the clubhouse. Wasn't quite sure what to do with it, though I guess I never really needed to use it after all. But now I think this is even better."

Sam took the thumb drive and raised an eyebrow. "Does it come with instructions?"

"Definitely not. I'm leaving that entirely up to you, because I know it's in good hands."

"Sounds good to me."

After saying their goodbyes, Laila and Angela piled into Angela's Honda and left both Songbird Park and the town of Rush for good.

Sam stood outside in the grass beside the firepit and watched them leave until the last glimpse of the vehicle's rear fender flashing in the morning sunlight disappeared around the corner of the frontage road. Then she considered the flash drive in her hand and returned to her own trailer.

Stepping into the Deville again after two days of sleeping on Syc's couch was like stepping into a completely different world. Sam barked out a laugh when she saw what her two recent houseguests had done to the place.

The kitchen counters had been scrubbed, cleaned, all the dishes washed, dried, and put away. Every small knick-knack had been given a home up and away from cluttered surfaces. The trashcan was empty with a brand-new bag in it. They'd even made the bed, which Sam didn't think she'd done once since moving in. And because she had a strong hunch that just wouldn't leave her alone, she couldn't help but run her fingers along the narrow windowsills and over the tops of the cheap, paper-thin blinds covering the windows.

"And they fucking dusted," she muttered, then laughed again.

Angela hadn't been entirely honest with her but she and Laila had found a fairly decent way to show Sam their gratitude for all she'd done.

Sam went straight to her tiny one-person kitchen table where her guests had left her laptop after cleaning above and below and all around it. She sat, opened it up, plugged in the thumb drive, and took a look.

The provided folder contained a hefty number of video

files, several of which Sam perused because their file names had stoked her curiosity even more:

Watch Me First.

This One Too.

You Won't Be Disappointed.

It wasn't exactly viewing worthy of bringing out the popcorn, but Sam watched those files beginning to end, with a significant amount of fast forwarding in between, and nodded. "Hell of a present, Laila. Thank you very much."

Dog started barking like a fiend outside, joined by the steady crunch and rumble of tires slipping and sliding across the gravel drive into the trailer park. Dog kept barking when the car stopped with the engine still running and a door opened and slammed shut again. Footsteps crunched after that, then cut off as their owner moved through the grass until another knock announced someone else's arrival.

Curious beyond belief, Sam stood from the table with an expectant smile and headed for the door.

Little Pete stood in the grass outside the Deville, snarling and kicking out like a frightened child at Dog, who'd followed him to Sam's front door and now crouched beside the man, teeth bared in a much fiercer, much more threatening snarl and his hackles raised.

"Pete," Sam said. "What a surprise."

"Get this damn mutt away from me," he snarled without looking at her. Then he tried to shoo Dog away with a wave of his hand. Dog jumped once on all fours, his tail sticking straight up in the air, and just kept growling.

"Nah, he's good," Sam said. "Dog's actually got a pretty accurate asshole radar, so it makes me feel a lot better to know he's already got you figured out. Wish I'd had him around the first time you and I met, though."

That made Pete look up at her with overwhelming hatred in his eyes before he straightened and tried to act like he wasn't afraid of getting bitten by a trailer park dog. "Fuck you, Sam."

She shook her head. "No, I learned my lesson on that one, trust me. Something else I can help you with, though?"

"There's no way you can escape this now. So if you try to run, you're still screwed either way."

She leaned sideways against the open doorway, propping the door open with her hip, and folded her arms. "Is that so?"

"And I'm gonna make you pay for throwing me down that staircase." He thrust a finger toward her just like his dad. "You could've crushed my head in with my crowbar, too. I'm pressing charges. Chief Colton will be here to arrest you for breaking and entering, for trespassing, and then for assault."

Then he ran out of things to say and stood there, fuming and breathing heavily and occasionally shooting a quick glance toward Dog, who still hadn't stopped growling at him.

Sam frowned. "Well, this is a fun conversation. And you came all the way out here to my front door just to give me a heads up about your plans?"

"I wanted you to hear it straight from me," he told her. "And I wanted to see the look on your face when you realized you can't get away with anything. Because now you've been caught."

"I'm not sure what you're talking about, Pete. I don't remember you or a set of stairs."

"Bullshit. I've got security footage of you running your grimy hands all over everything at the Kalamack Club the night before the 75th-Anniversary celebration. You were there. It's your face. You're screwed."

After pursing her lips in thought for a moment, Sam nodded. "Sure enough."

A leering grin broke out on Little Pete's face, and she wondered how the hell she'd ever thought this worm in rich-boy's clothing was ever attractive in the slightest.

"But hey, while we're sharing fun facts," she added, "I've got something to show you too, actually. Wanna come inside and check it out?"

He looked her up and down, his leering grin twisting into confusion and greed, which wasn't a good look on anyone. Then he glanced over his shoulder as if wanting to make sure there wouldn't be any witnesses. "Two minutes."

Sam snorted. "Yeah, I'm not even going to need that long. Come on."

It was awkward as hell trying to make enough room for him to enter the Deville with her, but she made it work. Then Sam gestured toward the tiny table with her laptop sitting open on it. "It's right over here."

Pete scanned the inside of her trailer with a haughty grimace and followed her directions anyway.

"What's this?" he asked.

"A little present. For me, anyway. But I'll give you a hint. Someone dug up some really fantastic footage of Sunday brunch at the Kalamack Club. Multiple Sundays, in fact. And there's some genuinely creative shit on here, if you ask me. Not that I'm into that kinda thing."

Pete had almost reached the table, but then he stopped and took a step back. All the leering and greedy excitement dissipated when he realized what Sam was trying to do. "You've gotta be fucking kidding me."

"I promise I'm not," Sam said, fighting back a victory

grin of her own. "I've got all this footage, and here's what I'm gonna do with it. I'm thinking I might try my hand at a public movie screening, you know? Blast this out to the *Gazette* and the *Daily Rush*. Maybe send it on over to the local news station. Could be interesting. What do you think?"

"I think you have no idea who you're dealing with," he growled.

"Maybe. Maybe not. That's one option. The other option is that you stop going after Birdsong Park and Syc and everyone who calls this park home. You drop the zoning issue, call the whole thing off, and this footage stays hidden. Won't make it into anyone else's hands. I won't go to the press. I won't even make it public at the Redwood Rings, yeah? And we both know how much the guys down there love to talk. But no one ever has to know."

Pete stared at her, then glanced at her laptop. "Go ahead. Send it to whoever you want. I know for a fact you can't confirm it's me on any of those videos. I never take my mask off. On purpose. So, by all means, spread it around. At best, you'll get a few comments on amateur moviemaking. You'll make a complete idiot of yourself, and even worse, enemies of everyone in this town who means anything at all."

"You know what, Pete? You're absolutely right."

The look of startled bafflement on his face was well worth having dragged this out as long as she had. Hell, it was worth having invited him into her trailer in the first place, and she hadn't even gotten to the best part yet.

"*If* I were talking about footage of *you*," Sam added. "But what I've got here, Pete? This is something really special. You haven't even taken a look yet, so here. Let me help."

She approached the table and centered the mouse on the video's play button before clicking. Then she stepped back, folded her arms, and watched Little Pete watching the pilfered security footage.

As the figures on the screen moved together — and thank god she'd turned off the audio — Sam cleared her throat and nodded toward her laptop. "It'll be *this* footage. Of your beautiful, loving, faithful wife during Sunday brunch with … oh, wait. Who's that? Pete Wilder, right? Your *dad*."

Pete's face flushed a dark, raging shade of scarlet, and his entire body trembled as he clenched his hands into fists. Even then, he kept staring at Sam's laptop until she finally leaned forward to press the pause button.

That snapped him out of it, and he looked quickly up at her with a snarl that said he couldn't wait to wrap his hands around her throat and squeeze for everything he was worth.

Sam spread her arms and smiled. "It's up to you, Pete. Really. I just wanted to give you a little heads up so you had a choice in how this plays out. But of course, no one can control your actions. You'll do what you're gonna do. I completely understand."

He said nothing before spinning away from her with a furious growl and stalking toward the front door. It banged open beneath his hand and slapped back against the door-jamb. Dog continued his fervent barking and growling and snarling as he followed Pete all the way back to the man's car parked just inside the entrance to the trailer park.

Sam didn't bother to call Dog off. She figured it was a good chance for the mutt to get it out of his system one way or the other.

"Have a nice day," she called after the mayor.

Pete finally released a warbling bellow of frustration that echoed across the grass and between trailers and off into the trees. He lashed out with a kick, not at Dog still trotting behind him and growling, but at the town barricades. They no longer blocked the entrance to the park but instead sat there now like a reminder of Sam's threat that was really more of a promise.

Pete slammed his car door shut behind him, stepped on the gas like a lunatic, and spun half a donut on the gravel drive before racing back off the park's premises and onto the frontage road.

Then the door to Syc's trailer creaked open and swung shut before Syc emerged, frowning deeply and rubbing his forehead. "What the hell did you say to him this time?"

She spread her arms and shrugged. "Have a nice day?"

He snorted, stuck a freshly rolled joint between his lips, and headed for his regular morning spot in his lawn chair beside the firepit.

Sam paused only to grab the thumb drive from her laptop before she left the Deville to join Syc by the fire for a bit.

He frowned up her with more apathy than curiosity when she handed over the drive. "What's this?"

"A gift. Or you can call it insurance, if that feels better. But if I were you, I'd get in touch with that attorney of yours and tell him you might've jumped the gun a little on this zoning fight. Something tells me you won't have to worry about it from here on out."

"Huh. Is that so?" Syc didn't need an answer but took the flash drive from her just the same, which he pocketed before lighting up his joint.

Smiling to herself, Sam returned to the Deville. She felt like she hadn't slept in years, and today was one of the few days lately where she had absolutely nothing on her schedule. Meaning she fully intended to catch up on lost sleep.

The thought of that sleep — and in her own bed, no less — grew more and more enticing by the second. Back inside her trailer, though, she paused when her gaze fell on the repurposed coffee-grounds tin sitting on her laughably small kitchen counter.

Sleep was important, sure. Right now, though, it felt pretty damn important that before Sam did anything else, she took at least a little time to stop and smell the roses.

The End

What To Read Next:

In the heart of the forest, a killer lurks...

Sam Salazar finds herself out of a job and an old Army buddy turns up a problem: his daughter is missing. Sam investigates the girl's disappearance and finds rumors of a serial killer who's been preying on women for decades. Sam must face her demons and find a serial killer before he claims another victim.

Get your copy of The Girl Who Couldn't Be Found today.

About The Author

Lauren Street has always loved a mystery. As a kid growing up in bible belt country she devoured every whodunit book she could get her sticky little hands on and secretly investigated all of her (seemingly) normal boring neighbors. Sometimes their pets and farm animals too. All grown up now and living in the UK with her thoroughly unsuspicious (and often unsuspecting) husband, she writes domestic psychological thrillers about families torn apart by secrets and lies. And she sometimes still peers over garden walls to check up on the neighbors.

Also By Lauren Street

The Bishop Smoky Mountain Thrillers

Hide Me Away

Fuel To The Flame

Closer By The Hour

A Gamble Either Way

Calling My Children Home

Too Far Gone

Here You Come Again

Replaced with Nolon King

Replaced

In Her Place

Irreplaceable

The Salzar Redwood Forest Thrillers

The Girl Who Couldn't Stop Dying

The Girl Who Couldn't Get Out

The Girl Who Couldn't Be Found